Obsession

(Cordova Empire, #2)

By Ann Mayburn

The unauthorized reproduction or distribution of this copyrighted work is illegal. Criminal copyright infringement (including infringement without monetary gain) is investigated by the FBI and is punishable by up to 5 years in federal prison and a fine of $250,000.

Please purchase only authorized electronic editions and do not participate in, or encourage, the electronic piracy of copyrighted materials. Your support of the author's rights is appreciated.

This book is a work of fiction. Names, characters, places, and incidents are the products of the author's imagination or used fictitiously. Any resemblance to actual events, locales or persons, living or dead, is entirely coincidental.

Sweetest Obsession
Copyright © 2017 by Ann Mayburn
Published by Honey Mountain Publishing

All rights reserved. Except for use in any review, the reproduction or utilization of this work, in whole or in part, in any form by any electronic, mechanical or other means now known or hereafter invented, is forbidden without the written permission of the publisher.

DISCLAIMER: Please do not try any new sexual practice, BDSM or otherwise, without the guidance of an experienced practitioner. Ann Mayburn will not be responsible for any loss, harm, injury or death resulting from use of the information contained in this book.

Dear Beloved Reader,

Welcome to the wonderful, scary, and sometimes horrific world of the Cordova Empire. This isn't a place for the faint of heart, but for the women brave enough to love one of the Cordova men there is beauty among the pain, redemption among the sorrow, and a chance at happiness that few ever get to experience. So buckle up, my little buttercups, and get ready for a bumpy ride to Ramón and Joy's HEA.

Ann

Prologue

Joy

The leathery-skinned guard manning the little white booth behind the elaborate black iron gates looked from me, to my license, and back again with far more scrutiny than I think the situation warranted. His bushy grey and black brows furrowed as he spoke softly into the microphone strapped to the shoulder of his uniform. I couldn't make out what he was saying, but it was in Spanish, and he was kind of creeping me out. Usually, the booths at gated communities were manned by lazy rent-a-cops, but this guy reminded me more of someone you'd see guarding a military base. He was one hundred percent no-bullshit and obviously regarded me as someone unworthy to pass through the flowering desert cactus lined gates.

"I look different with my hair down," I smiled at the guard holding up my license and comparing it to me, trying to appear harmless.

Ignoring me, he looked down at something inside the booth and spoke into his mic while shooting me a quick glance. I forced what I hoped was a sweet smile, and he grimaced in return. Okay, maybe trying to look sweet when I was inwardly fuming wasn't the best idea. I'd had a couple hours to stew over the injustice of this situation during the drive from Phoenix to Sedona, and my already hot temper was at a slow boil.

If there was one thing I hated, it was being taken advantage of.

He slid the window between us shut while still holding my license. I was tempted to bang on the glass and yell at him to let me through, but that probably wasn't the best way to handle this situation. My twenty-year-old silver Honda Civic—one year younger than me—gave a hard rattle and my gaze darted to the dashboard. I wondered, again, if taking a car with over two-hundred thousand miles for a drive through the desert was such a great idea. Without looking away from the guard shack and the guy still examining my ID, I gave the sun-bleached dash a little pat, mentally encouraging my ride to keep on chugging.

Normally I didn't drive outside the greater Phoenix area, other than to go back home to Tucson, but desperate times called for desperate measures.

Finally, the window slid open again. The uniformed guard leaned out, handing me my ID back with an impassive expression. "Thank you for your patience, Ms. Holtz. If you'll follow the drive up to the main house, Mrs. Roja is expecting you. Just park out front."

I gave him a toothy smile with no warmth. "Thanks."

As the mammoth wrought iron gates smoothly slid open, I put my car into gear and eased up the long, winding asphalt drive that led to a massive Mediterranean style home perched on the edge of a big hill, dominating the red stone landscape. The entire property was gorgeous and well maintained, like celebrity homes you'd see on TV.

I knew Jacob's family had money, but not *this* kind of money.

Growing up in wealth like this would certainly explain his 'entitled little shit' behavior.

The nervous clench of my stomach increased. I was sure that, if I touched my abs, I'd find them rock hard with tension, something they never were. Nope, I was a curvy girl, about thirty pounds over my 'ideal weight' as my doctor liked to put it, and soft all over. It wasn't that I was lazy and sat around eating crap all day. I was pretty active and tried not to pig out too much, but my body held onto those extra thirty pounds like my life depended on it. No amount of dieting seemed to make a difference. Thankfully, most of that weight was distributed between my breasts and ass. But my belly always had a pooch, no matter how many salads I ate, and the last time my thighs didn't touch when I walked was when I was ten.

The landscaping was beautiful, all done to compliment the desert surrounding the driveway, with big cactuses and flowering succulents brightening the red rock boulders surrounding the house. Overhead, the clear sky burned an impossibly bright blue and I was thankful the weather seemed to be at lease twenty degrees cooler here. Back home in Phoenix, I

Sweetest Obsession

baked anytime I was outside and longed for the days when I had nothing better to do than hang out in my parent's backyard and swim in our small, aboveground pool.

What I wouldn't give for a dip right now—but, no, my moral compass demanded I address injustice immediately. Instead of sleeping in on Saturday morning, like any sane person with my busy schedule would, I decided to get up at the butt crack of dawn and drive my ass north. I had to be crazy if I was willing to sacrifice the one day I had to myself *and* waste thirty dollars in gas for the trip, all because some punk ass little spoiled rich kid *lied* to me.

Repeatedly.
To my face.
Mother fucker.

My palms were sweaty as all hell beneath the bright morning sun. I felt completely out of place surrounded by such luxury, but I put some steel into my spine as I parked behind a black Range Rover with sweet matte black rims and tinted windows.

Money, something I desperately needed and this family had in abundance.

Money that they owed me or, more specifically, what that little fucktard Jacob owed me for tutoring services.

Doubt tried to worm its way into my head, telling me that maybe driving up here unannounced wasn't the best idea, but I was out of options. Jacob had skipped our last three sessions. If he didn't show up, I only got paid twenty percent of what I would have earned. I knew he was trouble as soon as I was assigned to him—another spoiled pretty boy who didn't give a damn about academics, because Mommy and Daddy paid for everything. He drove a BMW, wore fancy clothes, and I'm sure his designer sunglasses were worth more than my car, but that didn't mean he got to blow me off.

Repeatedly.

Worse yet, he played me. I have a kind nature—it's who I am, and I try to give people the benefit of the doubt. I like helping people and taking care of them. I pride myself on trying to give everyone a chance and trying not to stereotype. Who knows? Jacob could have been going through some serious shit, like a death in the family or something. So I gave him the benefit of the doubt, and he played me but good.

When Jacob first gave me a sob story about being sick, I believed him and emailed him a study guide then coached him through it. The second time, he allegedly got food poisoning, and once again I took time I didn't have to spare to try and help him pass his class. Stupid me, he probably didn't even glance at the study guides I spent so much time putting together. His shitty grades certainly didn't reflect a person who'd reviewed the material I carefully compiled for him.

This last time, he swore up and down that he'd be there, that I didn't have to worry, that I had his word. Yet, at 7 pm on a Thursday night, I sat in Arizona State's library waiting…and waiting, and waiting for his ass. Finally, at nine, I gave up and went home, but I was pissed. Really pissed. When I get pissed, I do something about it. But this morning, when I arrived at his frat house, ready to ream him a new one, they told me Jacob went home to Sedona for the weekend. Instead of waiting until he came back on Monday—like any normal and well-balanced person—I pulled up his personal file, got his home address, then hopped on the freeway and drove, fuming the whole time.

If Jacob didn't give a shit about failing out of college, maybe his parents would make him care.

My door creaked as I opened it, the hot breeze instantly drying the nervous sweat that had beaded my nose as I tried to look poised and professional, not the easiest thing to do when you're built like a chubby porn star.

I hit puberty early at eleven, grew quickly into a full double D cup, and since then, my breasts had been the bane of my existence. First, they drew the attention of any tit man who happened to be in my immediate area—and the vast majority of them saw nothing wrong with staring at some strange woman's chest, even if she was just a teenager. Second, it was hard to dress with an hourglass figure in a world that seemed to cater to women without curves. Shirts never fit right, because my breast to waist ratio was on the extreme side. They were either fitted on top and super loose around my waist, or fitted around my waist with my bewbs about to bust out. Third, some people looked at my body and instantly assumed I was a slut or a bimbo. Having naturally curly dark blonde hair, blue eyes, and dimples didn't help people take me seriously, nor did the fact that I was only 5'3". People liked to judge, so when they looked at me, their first impression was rarely flattering.

The world isn't kind to people who didn't fit society's narrow stereotypes about how a person should look. Fortunately, I had a strong mother who equipped me well for dealing with a world full of assholes. And my evil bitch older sister had flayed my soul alive with her foul words when we were teenagers, so it took a lot to piss me off. Going through the hell my sister had put me through, and coming out the other side alive, gave me the strength to pull myself together and not chicken out.

I'm a big girl. I can be professional, and I can do this.

I smoothed the black blazer I wore over the coffee brown silk shirt, resisting the need to check my hair. As usual, when I was trying to look like a grown up, I had my mass of hair pulled back into a tight, high bun and wore more makeup than usual. For a moment, I considered grabbing my briefcase. It was like a safety blanket for me, a visible icon that said I was a serious businesswoman, but thought it might be overkill for this situation. I was simply going to ask Mr. and Mrs. Roja to please make sure their offspring showed up to his tutoring sessions…otherwise, I wouldn't be able to afford my books next semester.

Well, I probably shouldn't mention my tale of financial woe to people with a three-story mansion, but I was out of options.

Wide, grey and white marble steps led up to the dark maroon painted front door of the house. Beautiful cut glass inserts flanked the entrance on either side, and potted flowers added a touch of color.

I pressed the button for the doorbell, mentally berating myself for the crappy condition of my nails with half the pink polish worn off.

When no one answered, I rang again, wondering if anyone was home, or if it just took twenty minutes to walk from one end of the massive place to the other.

I was just getting ready to ring a third time when the door opened with a rush. My breath caught as I took in the man standing before me. Probably in his late twenties, I swear he was the sexiest and most dangerous man I'd ever seen, but the sneer curving his beautiful, full lips wasn't exactly welcoming.

When I glanced up, I caught a glimpse of his eyes—gorgeous dark brown, flecked with amber and green, highlighted by his cinnamon brown skin. He studied me with a cold detachment that made me want to shrink into myself, those intense eyes framed by wide cheekbones and well-arched brows. His dark black hair, long enough that it swept over his forehead, almost covered his eyes as he cocked his head to examine me. I allowed myself a quick darting look down his body, taking in the wide shoulders hidden behind his black, button up shirt, the thick chest, and powerful arms all tapering down to a trim waist. His black dress slacks fit him perfectly and, as he leaned against the doorframe with a bored expression, his gold watch flashed in the sunlight. A hint of a tattoo on the side of his neck peeked through, and I could see the shadowy suggestion of more ink on his wrists that trailed down to the back of his left hand in the form of a stylized climbing rose vine.

Across his square jaw, he had a thick, dark shadow that only grown men got when they haven't shaved in a few days.

Damn, he was sexy, dangerous catnip to any woman with a single working hormone in her body.

Then he totally ruined my pervy fantasy by opening his mouth. "What do you want?"

His lightly accented, harsh tone and arrogant, disgusted expression snapped me out of my admiration. "I need to speak with Jacob, please."

"He's busy. You can talk to me."

I gritted my teeth but forced my hands to remain relaxed at my sides. "Fine then, Mr....?"

"My name is none of your fucking business."

I jerked back. "Excuse me?"

He gestured to the drive behind me, his gold watch reflecting the light. "Look, bitch, whatever you're selling out of your piece of shit car, we ain't buying."

"What? No, I'm here about Jacob. I'm not selling anything. He owes me money."

His pretty upper lip curled in obvious distaste as he scanned me up and down, his eyes lingering on my breasts for a little too long before he sneered. "Let me guess, he knocked you up? You need money for an abortion?"

"I—pardon me?"

His Latin accent thickened as he crossed his muscled forearms over his broad chest, the gold and diamond watch on his wrist catching my attention again with its sparkles. "Whatever bullshit you had in mind coming here, you can forget it now. He's never gonna be your baby daddy, so I don't know what strip club or escort service—"

"Escort service! Did you just call me a whore?"

"I see how you're eyeing my watch, trying to figure out how much money you can get from it. But you can forget that shit, because I would never touch a *puta* like you."

My hands clenched down painfully into fists and I took a step forward, crowding him in the doorway and catching a hint of alcohol on his breath. Great, I get to deal with a drunk asshole. *Why me? Seriously, what did I do to piss off karma to deserve this?*

Gathering myself, I hissed out, "I'm not a stripper, you arrogant fuck. I'm short and I wear heels to come even close to looking people in the eye. I'm Jacob's tutor! Not his 'baby mama' or a whore, thank you very much."

His snort of derision made me see red. "Right, tutor? With those tits? Get back in your car, trailer park Barbie, and drive away, before I *make* you leave. You're not the first gold digging stripper to show up claiming he's the baby's daddy."

"I am not a stripper!"

He took out his wallet with a sigh, pulled out a few one hundred dollar bills, then tossed them at me. They fluttered to the ground between our feet. "There, that should cover his lap dances. Now, get the fuck out."

As I stared at the money laying on the glowing wood floor between our shoes, something inside of me snapped.

I don't think I've been so mad in my entire life. He actually took a step back when I moved into his personal space then grabbed the front of his shirt to keep him from backing up further as I stared up—way up—at him. "I don't know what kind of messed up, misogynistic world you live in, but a woman's breast size has *nothing* to do with the size of her brain. I am *not* a fucking stripper! I am Jacob's *tutor* at ASU, an honor student working on eventually getting my PHD in education. Jacob hasn't been showing up to his appointments for the last three weeks! He promised me he would be there, and he broke his word. Now, I need to speak to Jacob, and I need to do it right fucking now, or so help me…" I trailed off for a moment, not sure what his name was, then went with my initial pet name, "You arrogant dick, I will make you regret the day you were born."

"Too late," he said in a bitter voice, but something in his eyes sparked to life. The sneer curving his rather nice lips softened. Hell, his entire face warmed in a way that made me distinctly uncomfortable. "Do I know you?"

I wanted to look around to see if I was on one of those prank shows with the hidden cameras.

"What?"

His pupils widened as he slowly examined my face, that disconcerting warmth turning to full on heat. "Do I know you? You seem...familiar."

"Are you high?"

"Excuse me." A woman's husky voice came from my left. "I'm Mrs. Roja, and who might you be? And why are you roughing up my nephew?"

I turned to see an older Hispanic woman with long black and grey streaked hair standing at the base of the stairs. Her cheeks were nicely rounded, which should have given her a kind old woman look, but her gaze was pure ice. A flush burned my cheeks as I realized I was still holding onto the arrogant asshole's shirt, which I quickly released and then smoothed into place. As I did that, I realized the man's heart was thundering beneath my palm, and that his skin was warm, so warm. Mrs. Roja cleared her throat, and I snatched my hand away from his chest, feeling guilty like I was caught groping him instead of trying to fix the damage I'd done to his pristine look.

"Ah...uh, I'm sorry. My name is Joy Holtz, and I'm Jacob's math tutor at ASU." I cleared my throat then licked my lips, trying to gather myself after my temper tantrum. "He hasn't shown up to his tutoring appointments for the last two weeks, despite his promises to do so. Normally I wouldn't bother you with this, but I don't get paid if he doesn't show up and...well, I need the money for tuition next semester. He's missed three sessions. I could have used that time to tutor other clients, but each time Jacob swears he'll be there, then he isn't. I've tried to hold him accountable for this, but he's avoided me at every turn, which left me no alternative but to come here. I'm so sorry for interrupting your day, but this is important. Not just for me, but for Jacob. He's going to fail out of school, and I'd hate to see that happen to anyone, but he's going to leave me no choice but to report him to the school."

Her lips thinned, and I swallowed hard at the anger filling her deep brown eyes. "No, I completely understand. I'm so embarrassed you've had to take time from your no doubt busy schedule to come here. I know who you are, Ms. Holtz. You were highly recommended by the Dean of the Education Department. I was hoping you could perform a miracle with Jacob and get his academic affairs in order."

I couldn't help but glow a bit about the words of praise from my usually prickly boss. "Thank you, but I'm afraid it's going to take a miracle for Jacob to pass at this point, unless he really applies himself."

"Oh," Mrs. Roja said in an ominous voice that made me faintly alarmed for Jacob, "that won't be an issue. I'll be having a talk with my son about responsibility, and I assure you he will be most eager to do whatever you wish. You have my word."

I let out a mental sigh of relief. "Thank you."

"Ramón," she snapped. I darted a glance at the handsome, brooding man now staring at me in a rather disconcerting manner. "Pick up that money. This poor young woman is going to think all the men in this family are ill-mannered animals. *Dios*, wait until I tell your mother about this."

I gave Ramón a good glare as he picked up the money he'd thrown at me, then mouthed the word 'asshole' at him.

Instead of looking pissed or embarrassed, he smiled at me suddenly in weird way that made the hair on the back of my neck want to stand up. His entire face softened, and I swear his dark eyes were near dancing with laughter. When his gaze dropped to my lips, my stomach filled with a thousand tingling, bursting bubbles. Something…powerful passed between us as he stood and gave me a long, slow look. Before I could protest, he crossed the room and took my hand gently in his own.

The moment our skin touched, a riot of pleasant tingles raced through me. I found my breath picking up. This close, I could smell his sinfully spicy cologne, could admire the perfectly sculpted bow of his upper lip. He had a great mouth, almost pouty, the kind that reminded me of stars from the silent movie era. I bet those lips would feel like velvet against my own. Soft as pillows.

"Please, Joy," he said in a low voice that seemed to flick my clit. "Accept my apologies. I—well, there is no excuse for the way I treated you. I was an ass. You can smack me if you want. I know if my mother was here, she'd be whacking the back of my head right now for being such a—what did you call me? Ah, yes, an arrogant dick, wasn't it?"

"No biggie. I mean you aren't the first guy who looked at me and assumed I was a whore." My voice came out sounding like I gargled with glass as he continued to hold my hand, my brain short circuiting as I tried to do something other than think about how hot he was, how sparks seemed to flare across my skin at the simple caress of his thumb.

He flinched like I'd hit him in the gut, then gently squeezed my hand before dropping it. "I normally have much better manners than this. Life has been…not good, and I haven't been sleeping much, but that's no excuse for the way I treated you."

"Really, it's okay."

"Ramón," Mrs. Roja interrupted him. "Why don't you join us after you find Jacob? You can give Ms. Holtz a tour of the grounds to make up for your earlier behavior. Or maybe you could take her out for dinner before she has to drive back."

Just like that, he went cold, as if someone had thrown a bucket of ice water on his emotions. "Nah, I gotta run."

Mrs. Roja looked between myself and her nephew, her hands clasping together as concern tightened her brow. "Are you sure?"

He replied in Spanish, obviously assuming because of the blonde hair and blue eyes I had no idea what he was saying. "Don't push me. You know I can't go there, especially with someone like her."

Stung, I tried to pretend I didn't comprehend his hurtful words as Mrs. Roja replied, "But she's sweet, Ramón, and—"

"I said no," he snapped, but I swear he looked at me for a moment with a longing so intense it made my breath catch. "No."

I pretended to be confused by their exchange as Ramón strode away and Mrs. Roja forced a smile. "I'm so sorry about that. We suffered a loss in the family. My great-nephew passed away, and Ramón loved him very much. He's very protective of his family and tends to assume the worst in people."

"It's okay," I fibbed, my pride and feelings still stung by Ramón's harsh words. "I'm very sorry for your loss. Maybe that's why Jacob's having some issues in school. If you want, I can check around for a good therapist at school, if he wants."

"You are very kind," Mrs. Roja said with a thoughtful look. "Come with me, Ms. Holtz and have some coffee. I'd like to talk with you more about your work at ASU while we wait for Jacob to arrive."

Chapter 1

Joy

Nine Months Later

I was pissed, so pissed I don't think my butt cheeks had unclenched since I read the notice taped to our front door. I couldn't believe that Kayla, my third roommate and an all-around selfish bitch, hadn't paid our rent on our apartment in four *months*. We were going to be evicted.

Yeah, our small three-bedroom place wasn't anything special. There were water stains on some of the ceiling tiles in the kitchen, and our furniture—with the exception of Kayla's pricy stuff—was secondhand, but it was our home. We lived close to school, within walking distance on a good day, and that saved me much needed wear and tear on my car.

Unlike Kayla, I didn't grow up with money. Four kids in the house meant things were always tight and both my parents had to work. We struggled, even with help from my maternal grandma watching us after school, and there was no way they could afford college for us. My *abuela* had offered to put a mortgage on her house to pay for our schooling, but none of us had taken her up on her offer. Like my mom often said, we might not be rolling in money, but we had our pride. We all paid for our own schooling in one way or another. While it did give me the gift of feeling independent, some days I really, really wished I had a family that could help me out financially.

Especially when I realized with growing horror that we would be expected to come up with three months back rent and the next three months paid in advance.

Even if I drained my bank account, it wouldn't be enough.

A tremor went through me and the threat of overwhelmed tears burned my nose.

Hannah, my best friend in the world and second roommate, stared at me with shock as I paced. She was dressed to the nines in a cute pink and white shorts and tank top set that no doubt cost bank, and she looked like a million bucks, while I was sweaty and stressed in my polyester clearance rack pants that didn't fit right and fake silk shell top. While Hannah had smooth, dark hair that flowed like silk, my crazy ass curls had decided to frizz out. I'd given up on taming them and had thrown my hair into a sloppy bun.

Hannah's very, very rich and very, very devoted boyfriend had given her those clothes, and I had no doubt he'd help us out with rent, if we asked. After all, Leo Brass worked for one of the biggest business conglomerates in the western United States as a security expert, and he was rolling in dough. A pang of worry went through me as I wondered if Leo would use us getting evicted as an excuse for Hannah to move in with him. I was woman enough to admit that I was jealous of their relationship. Not only did it take away my best friend since kindergarten for increasingly long amounts of time, I also had to watch them fall deeply in love. The epic kind of love that they wrote fairytales about, while my dating history was craptastic.

The door to our apartment opened, and Kayla stumbled through wearing a sexy little glittery emerald green dress and nude high heels. While the dress and heels were nice, Kayla was a hot mess. Her normally razor sharp black bob was totally fucked up in the back and pieces stuck to her sweat soaked forehead. She'd lost so much weight that the thigh gap between her legs had become the Grand Canyon and, when her bleary eyes swept through the living room to us, I noticed her pupils were all blown out. As if her stumbling home high as a kite wasn't bad enough, three men followed her inside and they were dangerous. The hair on my arms stood up, and I suddenly found myself struggling to catch my breath. The men were all in their late thirties and looked like they'd lived hard lives. It showed in the lines of their face, permanent frowns marring their skin as they stared at us.

The one in the middle smiled, and gold winked from a false tooth as he smirked. His grey peppered brown hair was swept back with a ton of gel, and he just reeked of sleaziness. More gold adorned his thick neck, and he wore rings on every one of his fingers—big, diamond encrusted, gaudy ones that sparkled in the light. I'd never seen a man who wore so much jewelry before—outside of a movie, that is—and the guys in the movies who wore rings like that were always big, big trouble. I felt a sharp, paralyzing fear like nothing I'd experienced before. Some primitive fight or flight instinct kicked in, telling me danger was near.

For a long, scary moment there was complete silence. Well, other than our neighbor above us playing screaming heavy metal loud enough that I could easily make out the words. They studied us with the focused intent of a true predator, and I tried to keep from freaking out.

These guys were trouble, dangerous. I've always been proud of the way I could stand up for myself, keeping my head in tense situations, but these men terrified me into silence. I froze, hoping to avoid drawing their attention as they tried to get Hannah and myself to do drugs with them. The more we put them off, the more insistent they became, and my heart raced with fear as they closed in on us.

Then I made an epic mistake.

Manny, the guy who seemed to be in charge, was manhandling Hannah. He had a gold tooth that kept on flashing when he smiled wide like a shark, and his huge, overweight frame dwarfed my fragile friend. His two friends—Doug, a tall guy with pale brown hair and a serial killer's smile, and Ray, a short and thick man with dark hair and small, dead brown eyes—watched with matching smirks.

The mood instantly turned deadly as Manny, pissed that Hannah wouldn't confirm that she was dating Leo, smacked her hard. "I asked you a fucking question, bitch. Use your fucking words, or I swear to God, you're going to regret it."

He hit her again, drawing blood from her lips with the power of his blow, and I broke.

"Yes," I blurted out, trying to spare my friend another slap. "She's dating Leo Brass. Big guy, long blond hair, scary. Rides around in a Rolls. Please, don't hurt her. They've only been together for a few weeks. She hasn't done anything."

Ray, the guy with the dead eyes, grabbed me by my hair. To my complete shock, he began to slap me around, hard. This was the first time anyone other than my brother or sisters had smacked me, and they'd never done it with their full strength. Pain exploded in my face and I cried out, clawing at the hand holding my hair as Kayla's scream cut through my own high pitched sobs. Ray ignored my pathetic attempts to get away and hauled me, along with Kayla, down the hallway to my bedroom.

He threw both of us to the floor, where we landed in a tangle of limbs. Kayla tried to get up, but before she could do more than get to her knees, Ray had a gun out and pistol whipped her with it until she collapsed with a terrifying gurgle.

Screams were pouring out of me at this point. I tried to scramble to Kayla's side to protect her somehow, but I was so terrified I was clumsy, getting caught up in my own feet as I struggled to pull myself up on my bed. I was going to grab something, anything, to defend myself, but Ray was on me before I got further than my pillows. He grabbed me by the hair again and threw me to the ground, kicking me in the stomach and back until all I could do was curl up in a ball and try to shield myself.

It hurt to cry, and I struggled to draw in a breath, my gasps choking for air.

Ray hauled me up by my hair and grinned as I heaved with sobs. "That's right, cunt. That's what you fuckin' get for scratchin' up my hand. Think I'm gonna keep you so I can fuck you to death. Yeah, you're gonna make me some money. Gonna make you famous for dyin' with my cock stuffed in your heart. Watching your heart stop beatin' while I fuck it through the hole in your chest'll make me cum hard. In fact, I think I'll jizz on your heart as it beats its final pump. My fans'll love that."

The vile picture his words painted made my stomach heave. I tried to use my feet to push away from him, but he merely laughed and hauled me back, clearly enjoying my useless struggling.

He leaned down, and I wanted to wretch as he pulled my hair out of my face, studying me. "Gonna keep you pretty before the fun starts. Cute girl like you? My fans'll love it when I fuck your face up. Cut your eyebrows off, then your eyelids so you have to watch, so you have to look me in the eyes while I fuck your wounds. I'm gonna cut you from pussy to asshole and, then I'm gonna let my dog either eat you alive or fuck you, his choice."

Bile, hot and bitter, filled my mouth. My brain short circuited, overwhelmed by fear and revulsion, and it seemed to stop working. I'd read about being struck dumb by terror, had seen videos on the nature channel of it happening to animals, but I'd never grasped how horrible of a thing it was until it happened to me. My flight or fight instincts didn't even kick in. Instead, I just lay there in shock when Ray gave me one final smile before smashing his gun against my temple and dissolved my world into bright white and black sparks.

~Ramón~

My older brother, Fernando, thrashed against the padded leather cuffs we'd had to restrain him with, his agony pouring off him in waves. Sweat beaded his exhausted face, and his black hair was plastered to his skin. He'd fought us so hard, every tendon on his body seemed to stand out with sharp relief. His lips pulled back from his teeth in a snarl of anger as we secured him. The man who'd once been my kind, compassionate older brother—the best out of all of us, to be sure—was reduced to an animal, crazed by grief. Nina, his late wife and mother of his only child, had betrayed us all in the worse way, her attempt to extort money from the family resulting in her child's death at the hands of a rival cartel.

It had been close to a year since we lost Jason, my bright eyed and loving nephew who'd been one of the few sources of real happiness in my life. To say he'd been adored was an understatement. From the moment I first held his tiny form in my arms and looked into his baby blue eyes, I'd lost my heart to the kid. And I wasn't alone.

While Leo had extracted his pound of flesh from Nina before my mother tortured her to death, there was a list of people a mile long who wished Nina was still alive so they could make her suffer. Even in the fucked up criminal world I lived in, a mother getting her kid killed for money was shocking, and they all agreed that my mother's slow dismemberment and slaughter of Nina, with me and my cousin's physical help, was a fitting end to a ruthless bitch. Some may say we went too far, but I promise you, if your child was tortured to death, your outlook on justice would swiftly change.

While her end was fitting and swift, the destruction Nina wrought while she was alive continued to hurt us, day after day, with her evil actions. My nephew's death changed me, hardened me in a way I knew could be dangerous if I didn't find some way to bring some light into my life. In many ways, I'd never experienced unconditional love until I met my nephew, never really knew what it was like to love someone like I loved him.

But no matter how tormented I was about Jason's passing, for my brother Fernando...well, his life was living hell.

Sorrow filled me as I sank to my knees next to the bed of my older brother. He continued to fight weakly against his bonds while my mother's personal physician, an elderly Asian man who worked miracles, sank a needle into Fernando's arm. The doctor's expression was tight with sadness and anger as he gave Fernando's shoulder a soothing pat. Like most of the people that worked directly for my parents, he'd known us since birth and, also like the rest of us, it hurt him to see my brother reduced to this.

My heart ached as I looked at Fernando's gaunt cheeks, his full lips pulled into thin pale slashes as he sobbed and cursed us. "Please, Dad, I'm begging you. Let me die."

"I will not," my father spat out. He struggled to hold himself together and remain calm despite his visible tremble. "I'm tired of this shit, Fernando. You have to stop trying to hurt yourself."

The drugs must have hit my brother's system, because he slowly relaxed. He looked over at Leo, the Cordova cartel's torture master and one of my best friends, then slowly shook his head. "Leo, you have to let Hannah go."

"Never," Leo replied in a cold voice, his dark eyes menacing as he glared at Fernando. "You're lucky as fuck you're insane, or I'd be beating the shit out of you right now for what you said to Hannah tonight. This was supposed to be a nice dinner, to introduce you all to her, and instead we have to deal with yet another fucking suicide attempt, another drunken rage where you hurt everyone around you. Hannah didn't deserve all that bullshit you flung at her. Enough, already."

Fernando flinched, but continued to hold Leo's gaze. "You brainwashed her into loving you, brainwashed her to be loyal to the cartel, and you expect me to just be okay with it? To be all right with the fact that you and my mother messed with her mind? You turned her into a fucking sheep. If she's smart, she'll run as far away from you as she can and never look back."

"You know that's not fucking true," Leo roared. "You can't brainwash someone into loving you. It doesn't work. My

Hannah loves *me* because I worship the ground she walks on, and she knows it. I give her what she needs, I take care of her in every way, and I love her more than anyone in this world. So, watch your fucking mouth, you pathetic piece of shit, and man the fuck up."

Clearly glassy eyed with drugs, Fernando snorted, then said, "Baaaa."

I leapt up to restrain Leo as he lunged for Fernando, my moron brother cackling in the background like a lunatic.

"Easy, my friend."

"Enough," my father growled as he straightened the cuffs of his shirt, his bald head gleaming with perspiration.

It had taken all three of us to wrestle Fernando into the restraint bed, my drunk and high brother insisting we let him kill himself so he can join his dead son in heaven.

Stupid fuck was too drunk to realize that, when he died, he was going right to hell with the rest of us.

"Hey," I said while tapping Fernando's cheek, forcing him to open his eyes. "You can't keep doing this, man. You can't keep trying to destroy yourself. Every time you do it, you tear me up inside."

With a weary sigh, Fernando nodded slowly, his eyelids drooping. "It hurts so much. I miss Jason every second of every day. Sometimes, I dream about him. It feels so real, so amazingly good to hold him again, to tell him how sorry I was and how much I love him. I can feel him, Ramón, feel his warmth and the softness of his hair against my chin. Then I wake up, and I'm so alone. We failed him…all of us…"

With that, he mercifully went to sleep and Diego, Fernando's twin, pushed himself up from the chair he was sitting in across the room, his long hair mussed from being pulled on while we fought to get Fernando into bed.

As he got closer, I noticed a nice bruise coloring the side of his face and wondered if I bore a similar mark. Even wasted, Fernando was a fierce fighter, and we'd had a fuck of a time getting him down without beating him to death. My back ached as I stood, moving to my dad's side so I could rest my hand on his shoulder. He was a quiet man, patient and even kind in his own way, but he was a man of action and it bothered him down deep that he couldn't heal his son. None of us could, no matter how many shrinks he saw or what kind of drugs he was on, or not on.

"We need to get him a different nurse," Diego said as he removed one black leather cuff from Fernando's wrist. "I think he's palming his meds again, and the bitch you have with him now thinks she's in love with him."

Rubbing my face, I pushed my hair back and thought again about getting it cut. Before all this tragedy happened, I wore my hair long because the ladies loved it, and I loved the ladies. After Nina's betrayal, I couldn't stand the thought of touching one and hadn't been laid in eleven months, a record for me. The only way I'd been able to relax enough to get hard was when I had the woman tied down and a bodyguard watching me—literally watching me—fuck her. The tying down part was completely normal. I take charge during sex; I run the show, and binding women is part of what I like to do. But I don't share my women and I sure as shit wouldn't let a bodyguard watch me fuck my submissive, but times had changed.

I had changed and not for the better.

With Fernando basically losing his mind with grief, I had to step up in my role in the Cordova cartel, taking on some of my brother's duties, even though I kept my main role as assassin. As far as the public was concerned, I was the heir apparent, being groomed to someday take over my father's role as President of the Cordova Group, a multi-national conglomeration of pretty much every profession under the sun, all encompassed in one corporation. The legitimate money we made wasn't anything to be sneezed at, but our real income came from drugs. Lots and lots of drugs. Not just ones that get you high, but also drugs that the FDA has yet to approve, or ones that'll never be approved but nonetheless have a huge market.

Real medical miracle treatments that could save lives...for the right price, of course.

Cracking his neck, Leo frowned at his phone then said in a preoccupied voice, "Judith said Hannah went home, but she's not answering."

I absently fingered one of the sore spots on my face where Fernando's elbow had caught me. "She's probably busy talking with Joy. What's today...Thursday? Isn't this around the time Joy gets home from tutoring? She usually grabs some food on the way, so they're probably hanging out. You know how much she misses Hannah, so she's probably talking her ear off."

Everyone in the room stared at me, and I fought to keep my expression blank. They all knew I was slightly...possessive of the blonde, brilliant, super curvy, and mouthy as hell woman who happened to be Hannah's roommate. And they all knew I watched Joy via the cameras hidden in the apartment she shared with Hannah and their bitch roommate, Kayla. They were also no doubt aware of the cameras I'd set up in Joy's bedroom, cameras I'd forbidden anyone else from watching.

While I admit I violated Joy's privacy on every level by recording her while she was in her bedroom, I didn't analyze every minute of her day. Mainly I watched her at night, when she was either sleeping or getting ready for bed. I wasn't spying on her, I just found a peace I'd yet to encounter anywhere else when I looked at her. Due to her lack of dating lately, I'd also gotten the occasional treat of watching her masturbate, a torturous affair for us both. Me because I'd give anything to be the one to satisfy her, and Joy because it took her forever to orgasm.

That wouldn't be an issue with me. She flat out had the worst luck in finding a competent sexual partner. From what I've learned while watching her, she would always choose needy, lazy men who wanted her to do all the work and rarely reciprocated her efforts—guys who took advantage of her giving nature. They'd let her do all the work, cum, and that'd be it. *Selfish fucks.* Once I got her in bed, she'd finally learn that there wasn't anything wrong with her, that the fault lay in her partner's lack of giving a shit if she climaxed or not. That wouldn't be the case with me.

I fucking loved watching her cum, and just the memory of her sultry moan as she came with her vibrator has my cock twitching.

Leo gave me a wry smile, then returned to his phone. "Yeah, they're probably watching some zombie movie and eating Chinese. What is it Joy always gets?"

"Almond chicken and fried dumplings," I replied instantly and ignored the chuckles around me.

My obsession with Joy was the worst kept secret around, but I wanted my family to stay the fuck out of it, so I pretended I didn't know everything about her in the way only a true stalker could.

My mind turned to the suit Joy had been wearing before she left for her tutoring job, the professional armor she put on to try and minimize her mouthwatering curves, to make people look past the fact that she was built for sex. Not that it worked. In a way, she resembled a really young Dolly Parton, who was, oddly enough, one of my mother's favorite singers. My first hint of a sexual awakening was looking at the covers of one of my mother's country albums and staring at Dolly's magnificent rack as I got wood. When I was fourteen, I watched *The Best Little Whorehouse in Texas* and my dick fell in love. From that moment on, I've been fascinated by dimpled natural blondes with large breasts. Joy's tits were magnificent, and her dimples drove me crazy. While her tan and black suit had been built to minimize her sex appeal, nothing could hide her perfect, exaggerated hourglass figure.

My dick started to fill, and I quickly shifted my thoughts back to the present, ignoring my base urges to possess, to own Joy.

An odd noise came from across the room, and I turned to find Leo sagging to his knees. He'd paled so much, he'd turned yellow—a pallid, cheesy yellow that made my stomach sink. I'd only seen Leo go pale with emotion once, and that was when we'd found Jason. My heart raced as sour, rancid fear filled my mouth.

"Son?" my father said as he took a step closer to Leo. "What is it?"

Leo let out a roaring scream of anger that raced up my spine like ice and stilled even Fernando. "Hannah!"

Less than forty minutes later, even though it felt like forever, I was shoving my way to one of the guest rooms in my parent's palatial mansion, cursing my mother's need to have a house that resembled a hotel with its amount of guest rooms.

Hannah and Joy had been attacked by a snuff porn producer named Manny Santiago, a relatively high-ranking member the Santiago cartel. Those evil motherfuckers specialized in human trafficking and sex slavery. Thanks to the power of the Dark Net, they profited from sick fucks around the world willing to pay huge sums of money to watch women fucked and killed. They were lower than low, in my family's opinion. We'd gotten into battles and skirmishes with them in the past, but they'd never fucked with us directly—that we could prove—so we couldn't retaliate without starting a war.

Kayla—Joy and Hannah's drug addict roommate—brought Manny and his bodyguards home with her. They'd hit on the girls and had learned of Hannah's involvement with Leo. Unfortunately, one of Manny's bodyguards had a brother who Leo had tortured to death for kidnapping and killing one of the escorts under the Cordova Cartel's protection. My stomach lurched as I tried to keep my overactive imagination from running through different scenarios in which Joy had been hurt much, much worse than the beating she'd received.

Thankfully Leo's second-in-command, Mark, had arrived in time to rescue the girls and bring them back to my parent's house, but they'd been hurt and my gut churned with anger at the thought of anyone touching Joy.

When I burst into the room, I fought back a growl at the sight of my mother's personal plastic surgeon, Dr. Gato, stitching up a gash on Joy's temple.

"Ramón," my mother snapped from behind me. "Control."

The word, drilled into my head since birth by my rather fearsome mother, had me freezing in place and trying to force down the primal urge to maim, to shred and destroy everything and everyone that had hurt my girl.

Unable to keep myself from her any longer, I went to the side of her bed and sank to my knees, my chest seizing as I studied her bruised face.

She appeared incredibly pale beneath the bright light streaming from the physician's lantern on the brass and glass table next to the bed. Even against the warm backdrop of the rose silk headboard and blanket, she appeared nearly colorless. The tan freckles on her nose and cheeks stood out against her parlor, adorable spots Joy usually hid beneath makeup. Part of the shield she used to protect herself from a harsh world driven by men greedy for a taste of her beauty. While I may be slightly enamored with her, there wasn't a heterosexual male who saw Joy and didn't take note on some level. I wondered if the doctor had taken liberties with Joy while he examined her, then cursed myself for being an insane dick. Dr. Gato was seventy-five years old and happily married for the past fifty years—of course Joy was safe with him. He was an honorable man who'd saved my life over and over again.

Shit, I've never had to deal with feelings of jealousy like this for a woman, and it was screwing with me.

Mom had Joy put in the guest room next to my bedroom at my parent's house, something I decided not to comment on at the moment. Part of me wanted to protest, to play off any feelings I had for Joy, but dried blood matted her curly, dark blonde hair and there was bruising around her throat and upper arms from where someone had manhandled her. Her full, Cupid's bow lips parted as she began to stir, and the doctor quickly finished stitching her up.

"There," he said in Spanish to my mother, "Mrs. Cordova, good as new. There will be very little scaring, nothing that will detract from her beauty. The accelerated healing cream will have most of the bruising gone in a few days."

"Get your hands off her," I growled while my mother sighed with exasperation.

The rise and fall of Joy's chest calmed me as my mother said, "Thank you, Dr. Gato, for your time. I appreciate you coming all this way."

She gave me a censoring look, the silver streaks in her black hair shifting as she tilted her head, but I ignored her and tried to get control of my guilt. I should have realized that no one was watching Joy, that she was vulnerable, but I'd been too caught up in Fernando's bullshit. I briefly wondered if someone was with him as he slept off his latest episode, but then decided I didn't give a fuck. He was a grown man who needed to deal with his shit.

Joy stirred again and made a sleepy, unhappy sound.

"Did you give her a painkiller?" my mother asked.

Dr. Gato nodded as he turned the bright light off, leaving the room softly illuminated by a cream porcelain lamp near the door. "Yes, just a mild one. She will sleep deeply for at least the next four hours. She'll be sore, but nothing permanent."

My mother's voice came out tight with anger as she said, "Jose will see you out. Goodnight, Dr. Gato, and thank you again."

"Goodnight, Mrs. Cordova."

After he left, I spared my mother a glance. Her soft, rounded face appeared heavy with grief and guilt as she gazed at Joy. "I'm so sorry, Ramón."

Part of me wanted to rage at her, to yell and scream that it was all her fault that Joy had gotten hurt, but those would be the words of a cowardly child, not the man she'd raised me to be. "It's okay. You had no way of knowing that their roommate would bring filth like Manny Santiago into their home."

She touched her bloodstained fingertips to her forehead as her shoulders sagged further. "Poor Hannah. She's…they hurt her."

I liked Hannah. I had the ability to trust her because of her brainwashing, so she was fast becoming a true friend. "How is she?"

"As good as can be expected. She hasn't woken up yet, and Leo is beside himself. I understand your desire to stay with Joy, but I will need your help dealing with the animals who did this to my girls. I can't ask Leo to leave Hannah's side, and I'm afraid I don't have the strength to give those men what they deserve."

"Absolutely. Are we gonna face blowback from the Santiago Cartel?"

"I *hope* they're foolish enough to try and take us on. I've been waiting years for an excuse to go after the Santiago cartel." She turned her anger filled eyes to Joy's bed and tears trailed down her cheeks as her breath hitched. "It tears my heart apart to see these sweet girls hurt by that filth. I want you to make them bleed. I need you to make them hurt. Make them scream for me, Ramón."

The suppressed fury in her voice had me turning away from a battered Joy to find my mother looking at the girl with what I can only describe as maternal affection.

Fuck.

That was bad for Joy, very bad.

If my mother liked her, Joy's chances of ever returning to a normal life were reduced to zero.

"Mom, don't get attached."

"You mean like you already are?"

"I don't know what you're talking about."

My mother's dark gaze sparked, and I wanted to groan, but

managed to keep my face blank as she said, "Ramón, don't lie to me. You care about her, deeply, and I can see why. She's a good woman, strong and protective, but also very sweet. Someday, Joy will make an exceptional mother and wife. I understand your need to take things slow, to be sure, but you're running out of time. By your age, I was married. I already had Fernando and Diego. You need a wife, Ramón, someone to love. I worry about you, worry about you only feeding the darkness in your soul, not the light."

"I'm not interested in her like that."

The lines around my mom's mouth deepened as she frowned, and I bit my tongue before I got myself in real trouble. If there was one thing my mother hated, it was being lied to. This was something she'd taught me over and over again when I was growing up, but I must be a slow learner 'cause the lesson never managed to take.

The warning in her tone was clear as she toyed with the large diamond pendant adorning the hollow of her throat. "I suggest you think very carefully before you say anything else. I'm not a fool, Ramón. Don't start treating me like one now."

Straining to control my temper, the back of my neck prickling, I muttered, "I'd rather not discuss this."

For a moment, I thought she was going to push it, to try to force the jumbled, dark mess of my tangled emotions to the surface, and I resented her prodding. I was at war with myself. One part of me wanted to keep Joy, to make her mine forever, and to bind her to me in every way known to both man and God. I wanted to get her pregnant, to watch her already rounded belly grow bigger as she nurtured our baby inside of her. She was going to be an excellent mother and wife.

There was the other part of me, like my conscience, that occasionally spoke up on matters of right and wrong. I'm not amoral; I just don't usually give a fuck. When I want something, I take it. But Joy was different. I cared about her, deeply, and wanted what was best for her. The ugly truth was that loving me was dangerous. Being associated with my family was clearly hazardous, and the thought of Joy's bright, warm light being extinguished from the world drove me to madness.

But I'd almost lost her anyway, despite the constant ache in my chest that came from denying the need to touch her. Hold her. Love her.

The woman I was hopelessly obsessed with had almost been taken from my world before I'd had a chance to kiss her, to taste her, to feel the hot clasp of her body around my cock as I fucked her. I looked away from my mother and took in Joy's still form. The chance for those moments to happen had almost been taken from me, and I felt something inside of me start to shift, a new purpose being born somewhere deep in my psyche.

I had to protect her, from everyone.

Including my mother.

With a sigh, my mother began to walk away after she made sure Joy was tucked in tight. "Fine, fine. I'll need you downstairs in twenty minutes to help Leo in any way he needs dealing with the men who did this."

My blood sparked at her words, the need for revenge trumping all other emotion. While I wasn't as savage as my mother and Leo about torturing someone, I did have a highly-refined sense of justice, of honor, and both demanded a blood price from those that had hurt the beautiful girl who tried to save the world. Images from the surveillance video of Hannah getting beat up while Joy was dragged out of the room by her hair, her face stark with terror, sent a tremble through me, and my heart pounded with the need for action.

"Calm," my mother urged as she gently cupped my cheek, her dark eyes filled with love and worry. "You'll have your chance, but you're in a sick room and there is no place for anger here. Stay with her, but make sure your thoughts, your heart, is gentle. It will sooth her to have you close."

Rolling up the sleeves of my shirt, trying to find the self-control to let go of my anger, I nodded. "I'll meet you downstairs in a little bit."

With a soft sigh, my mom paused, her hand on the door and a rare flash of guilt tightening her face. "All I want is for you to be happy, my heart. That is all I want for all of my boys—all I've ever wanted."

Knowing that it really tore her up that my brothers and I had pretty much sworn off relationships because of Nina's betrayal, I fought the urge to try and reassure her I was fine, knowing she'd see through my lie. "I know."

I could tell she wanted to say more, but held back, satisfying

Sweetest Obsession

herself with a brief hug before releasing me. "I love you."

"Love you too, Mom."

As soon as she left, my phone rang. I growled with irritation before answering it, turning my gaze back to Joy's still form. "This had better be good news."

Terrance, one of my enforcers, replied in a tight voice, "Got another girl beat to shit tonight. Guy matches the description of one of the Salvatore cartel's pimps that's been trying to lure our girls away. What do you want me to do?"

My brother Fernando used to deal with our high-end escort business, but when he'd lost his son due to his bitch wife's treachery, he'd also lost his mind.

Now, in addition to being in charge of the nightclub branch of my parent's empire, and in charge of head hunting for new talent and doing the occasional assassination, I also helped out some with keeping the high-end escorts that worked for us safe.

From what Terrance said, I'd failed at that as well.

With a heavy heart, I watched Joy sleep. "I have some things I have to deal with here. Have David take care of it and tell him to make a statement. How bad was our girl hurt?"

"Not too bad. The training we gave her when she signed with us kicked in, and she managed to mace the guy before he did much more than slap her around. She has some bruises, but nothing big."

"She got kids?"

"Not that I know of."

"Send her to our spa out in Laguna Beach for two weeks. Give her one of the bungalows and let her rest and heal up. If she has someone she wants to bring with her for support, that's fine. Either way, make sure she has a nurse and a therapist available to her."

"Will do."

"Call me if you have any problems."

After I hung up, I took in the silence of the room and the soft sigh of Joy breathing in her sleep. The reality of the situation sank in and a tremor shook my hands as I tossed my phone on the couch. My girl was hurt, and I fucking hated myself for not claiming her earlier like I'd wanted. Instead, I'd let my fear of trusting a woman almost rob me of my chance at happiness.

Looking down at her, I tried to resist the lure of touching Joy, knowing I should let her get her rest, but I couldn't.

For months I'd watched her, studied her, observed her life with a single-minded focus that baffled even me. I'd fantasized about what it would be like to just happen to run into her on the street, wondering if she'd recognize me, if she'd find me attractive. If she'd even speak to me. Our first meeting at my Aunt's house had not gone well, so I kind of hoped she didn't remember the fact that I'd assumed she was an exotic dancer or a gold digging whore.

I'm ashamed to say I judged her solely on her body and looks, two things she'd been born with and couldn't help. Unfortunately for her, in many ways I am a sexist pig, and when I see a woman built for sin, I assume she's aware of that gift and uses it to her benefit. Beauty makes men dumb; it's a proven fact. I know some women who use their good looks to manipulate and scam their way through life.

Joy, however, secretly hated the way she looked. I saw it when I watched her, alone in her bedroom, standing naked before her mirror and sighing with dissatisfaction as she tried to suck in her adorable round belly or jiggle her ass with a scowl. If only she knew how fucking beautiful she was; if only she could accept that she was literally a goddess. I'd never imagined a body as perfect as hers, extra curves and all, existed. Those big, heavy, brown tipped breasts of hers were constant stars in my jerk-off fantasies, and I've imagined a thousand and one ways I'd defile her tits.

My gaze had wandered to the rise of her chest, covered by clean sheets, before I forced my attention back to her swollen face.

No, she was out, as in O-U-T out and I wasn't the kind of guy to take advantage of any woman, especially Joy.

But I had to touch her.

I moved to the side of the queen-sized bed and sat down next to Joy, the depression of the mattress making her lean against me.

Just the contact of her soft, warm hip against mine sent my blood boiling, and I fought myself, wrestled with this roaring need to hold her close and never let her go.

Instead, I allowed myself the pleasure of stroking her curly golden hair away from her sleeping face, the ringlets still holding traces of dried blood. A tremor went through me as I gently ghosted my fingers over the clean bandage covering her temple, an ugly bruise rising around it. My heart thundered in my ears as I continued to gently stroke her face, dusting over her freckles, rounding down to her pouty little lips. They weren't large, but they were perfectly shaped and begged for a man's kiss. As usual, she wore very little makeup. I leaned closer, running my nose along the curve of her jaw, drawing her scent in.

Fucking peaches and strawberries. She smelled like a goddamn pie, and I wanted to eat her so bad, my mouth filled with saliva at the thought of tasting her. Just one small taste, one lick, one kiss against those softly parted lips.

With a growl, I tore myself away from the bed, running my hands through my long hair and clutching it so hard my scalp stung. What the fuck was I doing? I was about to kiss her while she was passed out, after she'd been attacked, without her consent. Jesus, the sweet temptation of her drove me insane. Sweat prickled over my skin as I swore I could still smell her. When I lifted my hand that I'd touched her with to my nose, the faint hint of strawberries and peaches lingered. My already hard dick pressed painfully against my pants and I turned around, unable to resist the lure of looking at Joy from up close.

In an almost trance-like state, I approached her again. This time, I sank to my knees beside her bed and took her small hand in my own. I began to gently stroke her exposed arm with the tips of my fingers, marveling at the light golden hair, soft as rabbit's fur, on her forearms that only added to the silky feel of her body.

I knew from watching her, Joy slept naked. She had hair a few shades darker between her legs, the curls trimmed into a neat v with her vaginal lips waxed bare. She had such a pretty, tender little pussy. Joy stirred a bit and I stopped, freezing when she opened her eyes, confusion and sleep still filling their beautiful green depths. With a slow blink she studied me, and I stared back, unable to do anything but dumbly gape at her like a fool.

A little line formed between her brows as she frowned at me. "Who're you?"

"A friend."

"Friend?"

"Friend."

Her voice came out slightly slurred as she said, "Don't stop touching me, friend. It's nice."

A real smile warmed me from the inside out, and I nodded. "Go back to sleep, *mi amor*."

She blinked twice, her eyelids getting heavier as I caressed her arm, marveling at the sparks that seemed to tingle across my fingertips with each stroke.

"Why did you call me your love?"

I didn't want to admit the real reason—that I'd been watching her, learning about her, and falling in love. And I sure as shit didn't want to admit that when I looked at her, I saw a woman with so much potential, locked behind emotional shields that had turned from something that protected her to something that inhibited her growth. Joy needed a strong man in her life, someone she could trust, someone to protect her. Someone like me. I would take the time needed to nurture her, adore her, and give her the life she always wanted and the love she's always craved.

She was almost asleep when her body jolted and her eyes opened up wide. Panic flooded her face, sending an ache through my chest as everything inside of me focused on her, on the unacceptable fear darkening her jade green eyes. "Hannah!"

"Shhhh, it's okay. You're safe."

Her frown would have been adorable, if she hadn't flinched in pain then touched her head. "I'm hurt."

"Go back to sleep, sweetheart."

"You're nice." Her lips pursed and she reached out, holding my hand in hers. "You're also very big and scary, but you seem nice. And you're hot. You'll protect me if I go to sleep? Won't let them hurt me?"

Unable to resist, I raised her hand to my lips and softly kissed her knuckles, satisfaction filling me as she relaxed, as the fear left her face. "I swear it. Nothing will harm you when I'm by your side."

"I believe you."

My heart filled with pride as she visibly relaxed.

The edges of her pink lips tilted slightly and her hand began to go limp in mine. I have no idea how long I knelt next to her, just watching her sleep as she continued to hold my hand. Every once in a while, I'd try to pull away, but she'd grumble in her sleep and not settle until I returned to touching her, returned to the feeling of her warmth flowing into me. I've been with women, lots of them, and I've never denied any of my carnal desires, but Joy stirred something in me I've never felt, never imagined. A bone deep feeling that was an odd mixture of pleasure and satisfaction, like I had the ultimate prize in my grasp.

My phone buzzed, and I reluctantly let go of Joy's hand, darkness filling me at the words on the screen. It was time to deal with the motherfuckers that did this to Hannah and Joy. Kayla, their third roommate, was still high out of her fucking mind on heroine and being dealt with by Leo's men. That stupid bitch hadn't just brought a drug dealer and his friends home, she'd brought home a snuff porn producer, the real kind that thrived on the evil side of the Internet and was a blood family member of the Santiago cartel.

With the utmost care, I ghosted a kiss over Joy's round cheek right over her dimple, and forced myself to leave her.

Justice had to be served, and I was just the man to do it.

Chapter 2

Joy

My dry mouth tasted like it had been coated with the contents of an ashtray. I stared at myself in the massive mirror that stood over two black marble sinks before looking away and trying to distract myself from my battered state by examining the bathroom. Slate tiles adorned the floor, bordered by a complex mosaic of brass, coral, and turquoise glass tiles. The place reeked of wealth and elegance, a lovely space that I would normally have admired, but I was just trying to resist freaking the hell out.

I looked like I'd been in a car crash.

Felt like it, too.

When I pulled the bandage covering the wound on my head off with a wince, I gasped when I saw the damage. Nausea filled my mouth with spit as I examined the wound running from my temple into my shaved hairline, the tiny black stitches making my skin crawl. They'd had to shave a small section in order to stitch the cut, nine in all, and I was thankful my crazy blonde hair was fluffy enough to hide the damage.

One time, when I was fifteen and bored with Hannah during a sleepover, we'd brushed my hair out until it stood up in this crazy blonde afro, reminding me of the fluff on a dandelion.

The memory of my friend, of that night, helped to ground me, and I managed to shake off my growing panic. Crap, how long had I been in here, staring at the mirror? When I'd awoken, a very nice old Hispanic lady named Juanita helped me to the bathroom after making sure I was okay on my own. At first, I'd been confused, utterly unable to remember how I'd gotten into this luxurious place. Once I'd relieved myself, I finally gathered the courage to look into the mirror so I could figure out why my head hurt so bad. The fragmented memories had come rushing back as I remembered the terror that filled me as that man, Ray, hurt me.

An unwanted flash of memory seared through me like a bullet—the blinding blast of light and pain that had accompanied being struck across the head twice with the butt of a gun left me whimpering. Pain flared along my ribs as I gasped, and my hands went to my sore sides, the agony of being helpless to defend myself as I was kicked repeatedly fresh in my mind.

The pathetic sounds escaping me echoed through the bedroom as I braced my shaking hands on the edge of the sink and looked down into the drain, away from my shattered expression.

Okay, wherever I was, I was safe. And if I was safe, Hannah was probably safe as well. *God, please let her be safe.*

Fucking Kayla. My idiotic roommate had brought home her drug dealer and his friends. And not just any drug dealer. No, Kayla had to bring a drug dealer who was evidently mortal enemies with Leo Brass, Hannah's boyfriend, into our home. I'd told them she was his girlfriend. As soon as I said those words, trying to scare Manny off because Leo was a scary dude, I knew I'd made a mistake. The moment of silence as they all looked at me still made me shake and my throat fill with acid. There was no life in their eyes, only evil.

The knowledge that people as evil as they were truly existed fucked with my sense of reality. Never in my life would I have imagined anyone would beat me up. While I fought with my siblings, I've never been really hurt before. I mean, I've broken bones and had the usual childhood injuries…but being beaten was different. Those blows didn't just hurt my body, they destroyed the naive belief that the world was a good, safe place.

The things Ray said he were going to do to me…to film while he tortured me? God, hadn't he said something about cutting me open and fucking my heart? I rushed over to the toilet just in time to throw up the bitter bile from my heaving stomach.

"Oh, *mija*." An older woman's voice came from behind me as I lay over the rim of the toilet and wanted to just die. "Come on, let's get you cleaned up. You have a mild concussion and may feel out of sorts for a bit. You're on pain medication, but you're due for another dose soon, so please let me know if you feel like you need it now."

When I opened my eyes, I found a very elegant, older Hispanic woman watching me with heavy-lidded brown eyes. Dressed in a cranberry watered silk pantsuit, there wasn't a hair on her silver and black head that was out of place, and her makeup was impeccable. When she reached to help me up, I was surprised at how strong she was. For a woman in probably her late fifties or early sixties, she had some muscle on her.

"N-no pain medication. I'm good." The need to never show weakness had me smiling as much as I could with my bruised cheek.

The older woman's Latin accent became heavier as she said, "Come now, let's get you into the shower. It has a bench, so you can sit, but we need to get the blood out of your lovely hair as much as we can without getting your wound wet."

I could only stare at her as she helped me undress, totally thrown for a loop before I managed to stutter out, "Hannah, is she okay?"

"Yes, she's fine. Well, she's suffered some injuries, but nothing permanent."

"And Kayla?"

"That one is being sent back to her parents, so they can deal with her."

"Where am I? Who are you?" She reached for my bra, and I smacked her hand away. "Hey now!"

The woman cocked her head and gave me a stern look that had me wanting to apologize for hitting her when she'd been trying to take off my underwear. "Can you manage it yourself?"

"I'm not doing anything until you tell me what's going on with Hannah."

I realized that I must look a little silly, with my hands on my hips, in my not matching black bra and grey panties, glaring at her. But I had enough, and I wasn't backing down until I knew what was going on my best friend.

"Hannah is going to be okay. She's resting. My name is Judith Cordova, Leo—Hannah's boyfriend—is my son in everything but blood. You're at my house, recovering in safety and comfort, after the terrible ordeal you endured." I must have swayed, because she reached out and put her hand on my shoulder, steadying me as she tilted her head down to look me in the eyes. "The men that hurt you have been dealt with. They will never bother you again."

For some strange reason, I believed her. "What happened to them?"

"They didn't survive the gun battle at your apartment."

"Gun battle?"

She turned on the shower for me. "We'll talk about it after you've cleaned up. The dried blood must be making your skin itch."

Now that she mentioned it, my whole body suddenly felt itchy and yucky. "What about the police? Do I need to give a statement or something?"

"When you're better. You had quite a knock to your head, but my physician assures me you will be just fine." She paused for a moment and her gaze went soft in a way that changed her whole, intimidating façade into maternal warmth and concern. "Did those men...touch you in any way?"

"You mean besides pistol whipping me and kicking me around like a soccer ball?" I rubbed my suddenly chilled arms. "Other than that, I'm okay."

The wrinkles around her mouth deepened as she frowned, that ice queen look she wore so well taking over. "Please, *mija*, take a shower. I find the sight of the blood in your hair quite distressing."

Lifting my hands to where my curls were crusted with my dried blood, I took in a deep, shivery breath. "Yuck."

"Do you need help washing? You must keep the bandage dry."

No doubt blushing my ass off, I shook my head. "No, I'll be careful, and I can take it from here. I was a rough and tumble kid. This isn't the first cut on my head I've ever had."

She nodded. "I'll be waiting for you in your bedroom. There are clothes for you on the vanity. I'm going to leave the door cracked, so if you feel dizzy and need me, I can get to you before you break your stubborn head open again on the tile. And let me tell you, a second knock to your head at this point would be very detrimental. If done in the right area, you could lose precious memories or the use of your limbs. With a hard enough crack, you could spend the rest of your days as a vegetable or suffer from daily seizures. But, since you appear to be a smart young woman, I'm sure you won't push yourself too far. Correct?"

Man, she was scary. "Yes, ma'am."

"Judith will do." She gave me a small smile that warmed her mercurial brown eyes as she left, keeping the door opened about two inches, as promised.

After soaking my sore body in the deliciously hot water, and carefully washing my hair as much as I could, I dressed in a very pretty, feminine ruffled peach skirt and off-white peasant blouse with small flowers stitched around the edging.

There was also a hair dryer with a diffuser on it and a can of high end styling mouse for curly hair. Whoever Judith Cordova was, she sure knew how to make a girl feel welcome. Top of the line cosmetics and girly stuff occupied half the cabinets, all sealed in small, sample sizes. If I wasn't so eager to find out why my world had suddenly turned into an episode of the *Twilight Zone*, I would have had fun playing with all the high brand girly stuff. There was even lotion in my favorite strawberry and peach pie scent.

After drying my mass of curls and brushing it as best I could, I sighed and stopped avoiding leaving the bathroom. When I fully opened the door to the bedroom, Judith and Leo were waiting for me. While Judith was as cool as a glass of ice water, Leo was a hot mess. His eyes were even more sunken in than normal, and blood stained his white dress shirt in irregular, drying patches. At the sight of all that red, my stomach lurched and I had to look away, breathing deep.

"Joy?" Mrs. Cordova asked, "Are you all right?"

"His shirt, the blood."

"Oh...oh, of course. Yes, you would find that distressing. Leo, go clean up before you join us, please."

He murmured something and the door clicked before I dared to raise my eyes again, a sickly sweat breaking out on my skin and erasing the temporarily clean feeling the shower had left behind.

"Was that Hannah's blood?"

"It was."

My pulse thundered hard enough that I could barely hear my voice over it. "How badly was she hurt?"

"They beat her rather severely."

My knees wanted to buckle, but I made myself stay strong, my worry for Hannah so immense it cut me. "Did...did they rape her?"

"No, thank the blessed mother, they did not. Mark arrived in time to stop them from doing her any permanent damage."

A shudder worked through me. "Who were they? They...the

guy named Ray, he said he was going to slit me open from m-my vagina to my bottom and have sex with me in the cut while filming it. He said...he said he was going to make me a star."

Judith stood so swiftly, the chair behind her toppled to the floor before she began to pace. "He said that to you?"

I nodded, shivering and totally freaked out by the intense vibe Judith was giving off.

"That animal. If he wasn't already dead, I'd kill him myself."

"What?"

"Those men were smut peddlers of the worst kind, evil men who pandered to the dregs of humanity on the Dark Net."

"The Dark Net? You mean the hidden internet? That's not real, it's just in movies. And what do you mean, they're *dead*?"

Abruptly stopping, Judith nailed me with a shadowy stare that was more than a little bit crazy. "Every myth is based on a kernel of truth. In this case, the Dark Net is very real, and the men who assaulted you catered to snuff film enthusiasts. Trust me when I say that, across the world, families are rejoicing that the killers of their sons and daughters have been brought to justice."

"How did they die?"

"In your old apartment," Leo said from the doorway in a broken voice. "They opened fire on Mark, and he had no choice but to shoot back in order to save Hannah."

I turned to look at him, freshly washed. His long dark blond hair was tied back and he'd dressed in a new, clean black suit. While it was obvious he loved Hannah with every bone in his body, he seemed to look at the majority of the rest of the world with disdain. I think he liked me, in his own way, but he would never be what I could think of as affectionate with anyone but Hannah. Between him and Judith, the dangerous, intense vibe in the room rose up by like a thousand percent. I tried to put some distance between myself and them, wandering over to the window with the pretense of looking out into the gorgeous desert garden illuminated by the early morning sunlight.

"How did you know we were in trouble?"

"There was some miscommunication and Mark, my bodyguard, was unaware Hannah had left. As soon as he found out, he went to your apartment to check on Hannah and instead found Manny Santiago and his men...."

His whole body shuddered and there was so much pain in his gaze that I couldn't stop myself from going to him and taking his hand in my own, trying to ignore the traces of dried blood still trapped in the crevices of his knuckles.

"But she's okay, right?"

"Yes." He squeezed my hand briefly, then let go. "She's okay."

Leo didn't like people in his personal space, so I quickly gave him room by taking a seat on the edge of the bed. The bruises I'd seen on my side where Ray must have kicked me throbbed. "Do I need to speak with the police? Like, give them a statement or anything? I don't want Mark getting in trouble."

"Yes, some officers will come to my home to question you," Judith said in a kind voice. She fiddled with a large rose quartz paperweight on the table next to the bed which sparkled in the light coming through the windows. "I'm afraid you can't go back to your apartment right now, Joy. It's a crime scene."

"A crime scene? Right…I didn't think about that."

My lower lip trembled as I fought back tears. Crap, our home was probably covered with blood and bullet holes. I mean, our apartment wasn't luxurious by any means, and our stuff had seen better days, but it had been my first place of my own. Well, kind of my own. I mean Hannah and Kayla were my roommates, but it was *our* home. Only now, it wasn't. And the thought of setting foot in what had been my refuge from the world, but was now a murder scene, made me queasy.

Leo's deep voice pulled me from my thoughts. "Hannah wants you to stay with us while she recovers. Mark, my second in command, has a house on my property. Its good sized, five bedrooms, and he lives there alone. Because he works insane hours, he's never home. Even when he is, all he does is play video games. You'd have your own room with an attached bathroom, as well as a room we can convert into a study for you to do your schoolwork."

Overwhelmed with his generosity, but not wanting to take advantage of it, I babbled out, "Thank you so much. I promise I won't be there long, Mr. Brass, and—"

"Call me Leo."

It seemed stupid that something as small as him asking me to call him by his first name would make me feel better, but it did.

Leo was a very closed off man, but I knew he loved Hannah to death, and I was so happy she had him in her life. He was good for her, really good, and she'd blossomed beneath his attention in the short time they'd been together. Yeah, their relationship was kind of kinky and unconventional, but for Hannah, he was just right. I wanted us to be friends, and the whole *you can only call me Mr. Brass* thing had irritated me.

"About damn time."

Judith chuckled while Leo shook his head. "I take it back."

I started to laugh, but it hurt my head and I winced. "Shit."

Judith was suddenly all business as she helped me back into bed. "The doctor said for you to rest, and take it easy. Are you hungry? I can have some brunch sent up. I believe the chef made some *Sopa de Pollo con Fideos*."

Hunger roared through me as I sat up quick enough to make my sore body flinch. "Really? I love that soup. It's my favorite. My *abuela* Rosie made it for me all the time growing up."

"Did you spend a lot of time with your *abuela*?"

"Yeah. My mom's a nurse, and she worked full time. So did my dad. My *abuelo* died before I was born, so my *abuela* moved into a house nearby and watched us until my dad or mom got home from work. Sometimes also on the weekends. I loved spending the night at her house. It was always so comfortable, so peaceful. You'd walk into her home and leave your troubles at the door, you know what I mean? She knew how to make you feel like you were always welcome and loved."

The combination of stress, my aching body, and hunger had me raising a shaky hand to my face as I brushed away tears, overwhelmed by memories and emotions.

"I do understand," Leo surprised me by saying. "My mom was the same way. Our apartments were pieces of shit, but she'd work some kind of magic so that, once that door closed, the rest of the world disappeared and you were home."

Blinking my watery gaze at him, I forced a smile. "So, yeah, long answer short, I spent a lot of time at her house growing up."

Leo raised his hand briefly in a silent goodbye as he left the room. Judith checked her phone then took a seat in the chair next to my bed. "If you don't mind, I'll keep you company while you eat."

"No, please, join me. I really…well, I don't want to be alone right now."

"Understandable. Tell me about your tutoring. Do you have a favorite subject?"

We talked all through the meal and long afterward. By the time we were done with our visit, I was just about ready to pass out. From what I learned, in addition to being a very successful businesswoman, Judith was a philanthropist who donated a great deal to the public school system and was involved in over a dozen scholarship foundations. I was also surprised to learn that we'd both lived in Tucson at one point, but on different ends of the city. Her boys had gone to my high school, but the youngest was nine years older than me. There was no chance I would have known them, since they'd moved to Phoenix while I was still in junior high.

When my belly was full, and I'd eaten my body weight in fresh baked bread layered with sweet butter, I sighed and watched Judith shake some pills out of a prescription bottle. "What are those?"

"Mild painkillers my physician left to help you relax and heal."

I held out my hand, eager to find some relief from the building ache, and washed them down with a swallow of water from the glass on the mahogany table next to the bed. I'd felt something similar to this pain when I was thirteen and I'd been in a car accident with my mom. We'd been rear-ended, and even though I'd only had bruises from it, my body had ached for days afterward. It was close how I felt now, but magnified by these weird, brief flashes of panic. I'd be fine, then suddenly my muscles would tense, and I'd find myself watching the door of the room, waiting for someone to burst through it. Judith must have noticed, because she casually mentioned that the doors, which appeared to be pale wood, were solid steel on special hinges that prevented them from being kicked in.

Evidently the Cordova's were big on security, and I wasn't complaining.

It felt like I'd had my rose-colored glasses ripped off, and the true world behind the illusion of safety and peace was a dirty, evil place full of predators.

A chill raced up my spine, and I pulled the covers closer to me.

"Joy?" Judith leaned forward and put her hand on the edge of the bed, her accent a little more noticeable. "Are you all right?"

Not wanting to admit my weakness, I forced a smile. "I'm fine."

I frowned as Judith rolled her eyes at me. "Mother Mary, give me strength."

"What?"

"I'm fine, you're fine, we're all fine—until we're not. There is no shame in admitting it. I remember the first time something terrible happened to me." Her gaze went distant as she sat back in her chair and laced her fingers together, her perfectly polished nails gleaming in the sunlight. "Things can mark you, change you."

Curious and eager to indulge in my favorite coping mechanism—ignoring my own problems so I can take care of someone else's—I lay back into the royal purple pillows and tipped my head so I could still watch her. "What happened?"

She hesitated, examining me closely. "That, I think, is a story for another day. Would you like to hear about how my mother and father met, instead?"

I nodded, growing drowsy. "I would, thank you."

"My mother, Victoria Hernandez, was a very beautiful woman. She was the popular mayor of a small tourist town on the west coast of El Salvador. Through her careful supervision, strength, and brilliance, she managed to turn the town into a thriving tropical resort. You see, the area of El Salvador I lived in as a young child was wild, lush, and oh-so beautiful. I grew up in a small town, sheltered from the massive Pacific Ocean storms by cliffs with soft, sandy beaches perfect for watching the sunset. My family was fortunate enough to build a hotel in one of the most beautiful spots in the world. As world travel increased, so did their profits. After all, they owned a piece of heaven. The sunsets over the ocean, the dark sand beaches...truly paradise on earth." She sighed and it was obvious she was deeply caught up in memories of the past. "Unfortunately, the more profit the town made, the more it attracted the attention of the local cartels. People started to move into her territory, bringing their money with them. Money the cartels felt belonged to them. Even back in the 1940s, the crime lords were as powerful as the official government...and twice as deadly. A few of the smaller cartels tried to move on her territory, to horn in on my mother's business and basically take over her town."

I snuggled deeper into comfortable bed. Judith stood and pulled the curtains closed as she talked, shrouding the room enough to dim the light to a soft glow. She took a seat again, toying absently with the large diamond pendant on her necklace as her gaze went unfocused with memories.

"My mother put them off as long as she could, pretending to consider which cartel she wanted to affiliate the town with, but eventually they grew tired of her delays and kidnapped her. They took her to a meeting where they demanded she pick one of them for a partner. To everyone's surprise, she went with a powerful young cartel lord from the northern part of the country. A man still making a name for himself. And she didn't just become business partners with him, she married him."

"Why? Did she love him?"

"Oh, very much. People used to joke that Victoria and Pablo's love was one of the great romances of the age. There were even some local folk songs written about their courtship." A twinkle of warmth entered her dark eyes as she smiled at me. "My mother was instantly drawn to my father, but she said the moment she kissed my father for the first time, she knew he was the love of her life."

"So, like, real love at first sight?"

"Real love at first sight. Or should I say, first kiss?" Judith confirmed with an odd look on her face. "It seems to be the way it works with my family. Nothing as obvious as Cupid's Arrow, at least for me. I *can* tell you, the moment I met my husband, I knew he would be someone special in my life. Our first kiss sealed the deal. My children, of course, think I'm foolish, but they'll learn."

The drugs were getting to me, and my mind was hazy as I fought off sleep. "Don't leave."

She patted my hand with a mysterious smile. "I won't, *mija*. Now, go to sleep."

"Promise?"

"I swear you are safe, Joy. I won't let anything hurt you anymore."

Reassured, my thoughts slowed and the world around me

faded to black.

Chapter 3
Ramón

    Spent adrenaline still pinged around my system, my muscles twitching from the effort involved in literally beating the life out of a man. I won't lie or bother to cover up the truth. I enjoyed killing those mother fuckers that hurt Joy. Normally I felt a sense of pride and peace at a job well done, but not now. The only thing I felt was anxious to get back to her side, to see if she'd woken up yet. The doctor said her concussion wasn't bad, but I knew how easily a good knock to the head could scramble a person's brain forever.
    My dad wordlessly handed me a glass of tequila, my family's poison of choice, and I gave him a small salute before downing it. With his bald head gleaming, he raised his glass as well before sharply tipping it back with me. The sharp burn of alcohol cleared my tired thoughts, and I sucked in a breath of air, tasting the delicious undertones of the drink. I'd spent time as a teenager at my grandparent's hotel in El Salvador, tending bar when I was seventeen. My grandfather Pablo had been at my side for the first two weeks, giving me a crash course on the different types of high quality spirits they served. Considering some of the shots cost thousands of dollars, my grandfather didn't want anyone, even his beloved grandson, literally pouring money down the drain.
    My dad ran one thick finger around the rim of his empty glass slowly, his prominent features drawn tight with anger. Both he and my mother usually appeared far younger than their actual age, but tonight he wore every year, every torment and sadness he'd experienced, on his tanned face. He'd assisted with the torture of Manny while I focused on Ray—the fucker who'd hurt Joy.
    A sound caught my attention, and I turned to find a shaken Leo sagged against the doorway leading to my father's library, his normally tan face a waxy, yellow color. "Hannah hates me."

My dad and I exchanged a look. I could see his worry as clear as my own. Leo was a shattered man, and it disturbed the fuck out of me to see my normally stoic friend in such a disheveled state. His long hair hung around his face, and his dark eyes were haunted with pain. Seeing him so obviously hurting made me wish I could make Hannah forgive him, although I knew it wasn't my place to butt into their relationship. The whole thing was a huge mess, and I had no idea how he'd win Hannah's heart back. She was pissed we all deceived her, hiding the fact that the Cordova Group was also a cartel, and I'd been on the receiving end of her silent treatment when I'd gone to visit her. It wasn't fun, and I'd felt an unusual sense of guilt as she'd silently judged me.

"Hannah will come around," my father replied in a soothing voice. He handed Leo a crystal glass filled almost to the brim with liquor. "You just need to let her adjust, give her time to heal."

Downing the glass, Leo sucked in a ragged breath as he stared at the floor. "She can't stand the sight of me. She hates me."

I bit my tongue, knowing Leo was right. Hannah did hate him and with good reason. Before Manny and his thugs had beat the fuck out of her, she'd discovered that Leo was part of the Cordova cartel, and that his job was as our torture master. For a young, sweet girl with no criminal background, it was quite a shock. I wasn't sure if her love for Leo was going to be strong enough for her to forgive him.

The venom in Hannah's voice when she was screaming at Leo to go away struck even a cold bastard like myself.

While my father guided Leo into a chair near the grass green marble fireplace, filled with white pillar candles instead of wood, I moved to the one across from my friend, unsure how to comfort him. What the fuck did you say to a guy whose world had just imploded? An uncomfortable feeling pinched my chest. I almost sighed with relief when my dad spoke up, knowing, as always, the right thing to say.

Giving Leo his space, my dad sat in the chair next to mine. "It will be all right, my son. I promise. Just give it time. Judith has been mad enough to try to shoot me more than once, and yet here we are, over thirty years later still happily married."

"I can't live without Hannah," Leo said in a rough, broken voice. "She's my everything."

Fuck, it really bothered me to see him so despondent. I lamely echoed my dad, "Give her time."

Diego entered the room, still weaving his damp long, black hair into his customary braid.

Rubbing his face hard, Leo leaned back in the leather chair then stared at the cold fireplace before his dead eyes flickered to Diego. "Did you learn anything else from Manny or Doug?"

Of the three men that had attacked Hannah, Joy, and their fucking useless drug addict roommate Kayla, only one was still alive. I'd accidentally killed Ray during my questioning. Usually, I wasn't so sloppy with my torture, but the hatred I felt for a man who'd hurt Joy was so intense, it reduced me to an animalistic rage. I'd beat him to death with a baseball bat. By the time I was done with him, he was a useless flesh bag of broken bones and organs. As satisfying as it had been to release my rage on that evil fuck, I'd screwed up. We'd suspected the Santiago cartel had something to do with the working girls that the Cordova cartel protected, and I should have questioned Ray more. Hopefully, my dad wasn't as stupid with Manny and Doug, and managed to get some information.

When the Santiago cartel found out about the deaths of Manny, Doug, and Ray, they would retaliate. For years, we've been almost enemies—not openly combative, but constantly fucking with each other. The Santiago's were criminal scum. Yeah, the Cordova cartel ran guns, drugs, and worked in the sex trade, but we didn't kill innocent women and carve them up for sick fucks on the internet to jerk off to. When I thought of all the ways they could have hurt Joy, abused and degraded her before killing her, I wished I could beat Ray to death all over again.

Shaking his head, Diego sighed. "Manny lost too much blood because Mark shot him. He died before I could learn much. Wouldn't admit to taking our girls, but he did let it slip that there's a warehouse outside Sedona where they film some of their fucked up shit. Doug gave us a little more before he died, but he was a low man on the totem pole and didn't know much."

My father's nostrils flared with anger. "I'll contact your Aunt Doris and see if her men can find anything."

"Good idea." Diego's gaze shot to me, and he smiled a shit

eating grin. "Thought you might be interested to know there's a pretty little *mami* having lunch with Mom. I'm on my way to join them. She sure is a sweet little handful. Those blonde curls and big, round—" He dodged me as I lunged at him. "Eyes."

"Fucker. Stay away from her."

His shit eating grin had the muscles along my upper back twitching. My brother was a pain in the fucking ass and loved to irritate me. He knew Joy was my weak spot, and in typical brotherly fashion, went right for it. "Why? You going to join them for lunch? If you're not, I am. Mom really seems to like Joy. She says she's going to make some man very, very happy one day. Wouldn't mind coming home to a woman like that. I mean, I don't usually go for blondes, but in her case, I'd make an exception."

I grabbed for him again, but the asshole always managed to be quicker. He easily moved out of reach. "Yeah, that's what I thought. Better hurry up. I wouldn't want to leave her alone with Mom too long, if I were you. She may decide to speed things up between you and Joy on her own."

Ignoring him and my smirking father, I stalked off in the direction of the kitchen, once again cursing my mother for building a home the size of a shopping mall. When I was a kid, I'd ride my skateboard through the hallways, much to my mother's irritation. It was either that or run from one side of the house to the other. Knowing Joy was somewhere close enough to touch, to smell, blocked out everything else as I became focused on getting to her side as quickly as possible.

I didn't deserve her, wasn't good for her, but fuck it.

She was mine and, even though she didn't know it yet, I was hers.

For months, I'd been in denial. Even when I was trying to convince myself I was acting like a crazy man, I couldn't stop thinking of her, fantasizing about her. I always dreamed of Joy touching me, stroking me, drowning me in her overabundant affection. Some men would feel smothered by her need to nurture of those she loved, but I craved it. I wanted a traditional, old-fashioned marriage, where the man takes care of the woman, protects her, takes care of all the problems so she could be happy and love her family without stress or worry. I knew Joy wanted that, too.

I'd secretly watched her on hidden cameras in her apartment as Joy had drunkenly confessed to Hannah one night that she wished she could be a housewife, like her *abuela*, but that her mom had been appalled at the idea. Evidently, Joy's mom and older sister were somewhat militant feminists, and they'd found the idea of a ten-year-old Joy telling them she wanted to be a stay-at-home mom like grandma Rosie when she grew up horrifying. While I didn't have the details, it sounded like they'd shamed Joy for not wanting to go to college, for having the desire to stay home and raise a family instead of having her career first.

I had to pause as I neared the kitchen, the voices faint enough that I was sure my mother was having a late lunch with Joy out on the patio. A longing to join them filled me, but I stayed inside instead, inching over so I could see through the large window and try and catch a glimpse of Joy. I wasn't ready to face her yet. I needed a moment to gather my thoughts and get control of my dick. It was like my cock could sense she was near as he tried to get hard.

Taking a deep breath, I controlled my body and forced myself to relax.

The warm breeze from the outdoors filtered into the kitchen, and I swore I could smell a hint of strawberries and peaches in the air.

My Joy.

My skin prickling with anticipation, I scanned the yard for her. When I saw her laughing in the sun, my chest constricted in a weird way. My heart began to thunder, and my dick got hard and aching, despite my best efforts to remain unaffected. I swear, even the fucking hair on my arms stood up. I braced my hands on the counter, but the need to go to her, to touch her, urged my body to move. Some primitive part of me demanded that I claim her as soon as possible, that I get a taste of her sweet lips.

Fuck, I was like a goddamn animal in rut around her.

One sniff of her on the breeze, and I was ready to stake my claim.

"Look at her, all those curves." Diego's low voice came from behind me. "She's a natural beauty, inside and out."

I ignored him, instead grabbing a green and black plate from the tall walnut cabinets then heaping it with a rice and eggs mixture simmering on the massive stove. "Your point?"

"My point is, if you don't go after her, I will."

"The fuck you will."

He took a step away from me, a teasing grin on his face, but his dark eyes were cold and hard. "Then why are you standing here looking out a window instead of talking to her? I would have thought that you'd be sick of just staring at her from a distance. What? The only way you can look at her is on a screen? Too scared to see her in person? Stalker."

Gritting my teeth, I tried to keep my temper in check. "I haven't been stalking her. I was watching over Hannah for Leo."

Diego snorted. "Please. You're obsessed with Joy, and everyone knows it."

The need to knock the arrogant smirk off his face tore at my self-control, making my hands twitch. "Why the fuck do you care?"

"Because..." Amber flashed in his eyes as he stepped into a pool of sunlight pouring in through the open doors. "I want to see if the experiment will work on someone as spirited as Joy. Not that Hannah's spineless, but Joy has steel in her. I don't think she'll be as easily manipulated. I have to see if the programming will work on a stubborn woman."

"She's not some fucking lab animal for you to poke and stare at." My stomach clenched at the knowledge that I would have subject Joy to Leo and my mother's brainwashing if I wanted to keep her. "I don't want anyone fucking with her head."

"You lie."

I was about a second away from punching him. "What?"

"Deep down inside, you want what Leo has. A woman who can never betray him. We all do. At least I'm honest enough to admit it."

I didn't bother to deny it. "What if she gets hurt?"

"Look, Ramón, she already knows too much. Yeah, Mom had some of the cops on our payroll come out and take a bullshit statement from Joy to cover up the fact that we never contacted the police, but Joy has seen too much. Eventually, she'll figure things out for herself. You'll want her bound to you as tight as possible before that happens. If Leo is going to have any chance in hell with Hannah, he better hope all his worship paid off, and she loves him as much as he loves her. Face it, you're gone for her, and she's going to be part of this family sooner or later, one way or another. You need to get out there and get your time in with her before Mom loses patience and takes things into her own hands. You know that *loco* woman would do it."

I knew he was right, and I knew the moment Joy crossed the threshold of my childhood home that she would never be allowed to leave, but I was strangely conflicted about the whole thing. After watching Joy for so long, I felt like I knew her…like I could trust her. Something in my heart relaxed as I realized it was true. I trusted Joy, even without the brainwashing.

Diego shook his head then stared out the window, the bright sunlight making him squint. "If you don't claim her, Mom will set Joy up with someone in our cartel. She likes her a lot. Mom said Joy is one of those women born to be a wife to a strong man, to stand at his side with love. Gotta say, even beat up, she's easy on the eyes. That smile…you want to spend the rest of your life watching someone else win that smile? Watch her run around with some other guy's kid in her belly?"

Without thought, I threw a punch at Diego. It was quick and unexpected enough that, for once, I caught him square on the jaw, sending him flying back into the granite island where he knocked over a stack of plates that shattered to the floor. My legendary temper had hold of me now, and like the berserkers of old, all I wanted to do was fight, maim, and kill. I launched myself after Diego, and we wrestled to the ground, each of us grunting and cursing as we fought.

"Ramón! Get off your brother," my mother cried out. I paused in the act of trying to choke the shit out of a snarling Diego, turning to see my mom standing at the patio by the open kitchen doors, looking shocked.

Swaying next to her was a pale faced Joy who appeared to be on the verge of tears. The pale jade green sundress she wore shimmered with her trembling. Her fear hit me like a bullet to the gut, and I instantly found the will to swallow my instinctive anger back. I wasn't mad at her, I was mad at myself for scaring her.

This was not how I wanted my first—well, second—meeting with Joy to go.

Diego, ever the peacemaker and diplomat of the family,

cleared his throat as he pushed me off. We both stood, and I quickly straightened my clothes. "It's okay, we're fine. Just a friendly disagreement. Are you okay, sweetheart?"

He moved a step closer to a pale as cream Joy, but I beat him there, catching her as her knees gave out. She gave a sharp, terrified scream, but I swept her into my arms, holding her tight, the thought of her being frightened by me, by my raging anger, completely unacceptable. Her whole body shook, and I sank to my knees, cradling her while I made soft, soothing noises.

"Shhhh, please don't be afraid. I'm sorry. I promise, you have nothing to worry about. I've got you, beautiful. I'll never scare you like that again. You're safe with me, okay? I know I'm a big guy, but I promise you, Joy, you're safe with me. Just take in a deep breath for me, okay?"

A little sob left her as she tried to push away, then she burst into tears and buried her face against the front of my button-down shirt. Her tears darkened the navy fabric to black as she cried.

I hated that she was crying, but damned if my entire body wasn't lit up like a fucking bonfire as I finally held her in my arms. Despite all my fantasizing about this moment, I realized I'd underestimated how small she was as I cradled her against me. If I wanted to, I could almost totally envelop her body in my own. I liked that, liked knowing that I could shield her against the world and keep her safe. She seemed to have a presence bigger than she was, but curled up in my lap, she was a sweet little armful. The sugary, edible peach and strawberry scent of her shampoo filled me as I held her close, trying to give her the comfort she so obviously needed. A sense of pride and satisfaction thundered through my veins as she clung to me, taking my strength without reservation, gripping me and allowing me to cuddle her close.

I never cuddled women, it just wasn't something I had any desire to do. That's not to say I never held a woman I was dating, I'm not that big of a dick, but it wasn't a big deal to me. With Joy's warmth seeping into me, I realized how amazing it could be to hold someone you loved close, to immerse yourself in their presence. She somehow managed to shut out the world around us, leaving me in the blessedly silent dark with her bright, gentle light.

My whole body seemed to vibrate with electricity but it was the feelings, the emotions unfurling inside of me that had me closing my eyes and resting my cheek on top of her curly little head. Warmth, euphoria, and desire all barreled through me with a strength that made my heart thunder as energy surged through me. It reminded me, strangely enough, of the one time I'd tried cocaine—a drug I liked way too much, so I never touched it again.

People were talking around us, but I ignored them. I hummed softly to Joy as I rocked her in my arms, trying to keep an erection from forming as she wiggled her plump little body against mine. Fuck, I was a right bastard to be thinking about anything sexual at a time like this, but Joy affected me like no woman ever has before. Her small hands wrapped around me, hugging me back, and I tried to stifle the groan that wanted to escape from somewhere in the pit of my chest. Her big, soft tits pressed against my body, and I was sure I could feel her hard nipples poking me.

Finally, her hold on me eased. Her sobs petered off into hiccups before she said in a husky voice, "I'm so sorry. I'm not usually like this. I'm getting you all snotty."

I attempted to smooth her wild dark blonde curls back, but they had a mind of their own and wrapped around my fingers instead, tempting me to touch the soft, fluffy mass of her hair. The white bandage on her temple brought me back to reality. She was crying because I scared her with my temper—that was the slap in the face I needed to regain control of myself, something very important to me. With my rage, when I lost control, people died.

Moving slowly, I stood then set her on her feet, holding her steady in case she needed it. "Better?"

She blinked at me, then frowned and said in an empty voice, "Better...do I know you? You seem familiar."

Clearing my throat, I had to bite back a grin as I wondered what her reaction would be when she placed me.

I didn't have to wonder long, because suddenly those pretty bowed lips of hers turned down in a frown. Her icy green eyes narrowed in anger as she spat out, "*You.*"

"Yep, *me.*"

"What are *you* doing here?"

I don't know what it is about her, or what it says about me, but I loved it when she got angry at me. On some deep, fucked up level, her attitude made my need to dominate her, to drown in her submission, roar to life. It was like she was begging me to stand up to her, to take control, to prove I was strong enough for her.

I couldn't help but grin. "Visiting, something I do quite often considering this is my childhood home and my parents still live here."

A lovely flush filled her tanned cheeks as she turned to face my mother.

Clearing her throat, and shooting me a look that promised I'd be getting a lecture later, my mom gave a strained smile. "Joy, this is Ramón, my youngest son."

"Hello, Joy. Nice to see you again."

Joy's gaze narrowed in on me as my mother arched her brows then smiled. "Oh, you know each other?"

"I wouldn't say we *know* each other," Joy said in a tight voice, obviously trying to hold her temper as she smoothed down the edges of her short green skirt, drawing my attention to her tanned legs. Fuck, even though she was short, she had great legs with plump, curvy thighs I wanted wrapped around me. "We've met once before. It was…memorable."

Turning her attention to me, my mother tilted her head. "Ramón, why didn't you tell me you knew Joy?"

"Like she said, we don't really know each other. A couple months ago, we briefly met when I thought she was a gold digging whore trying to get money out of Jacob."

"Jacob? Your cousin?" my mother echoed as she blinked at me in shock. "What does he have to do with any of this? And why in the world would you ever insult such a sweet young woman in such a foul manner? Really, Ramón, I raised you better than that. You should be ashamed of yourself."

"I didn't know she was a good woman. I mean look at her." Inwardly, I rolled my eyes as Joy gave me a little evil glare that only made it harder not to have an unwanted erection. "I said I was sorry."

"He threw money at me," Joy added. The clouds parted, and sunlight turned her curls into gold as her little nostrils flared. Boy, she was pissed. And sexy.

And mine.

My mother gasped in genuine dismay. "You didn't."

"He sure did," Joy said through gritted teeth.

Diego slowly shook his head while rubbing his jaw. "You threw money at her?"

"Look at her," I said in frustration. Joy appeared just about ready to slit my throat. "She's walking, talking, breathing sex."

"Not helping," Diego said in a low voice, filled with suppressed laughter.

"I didn't want her to bother Aunt Doris. I was trying to be a nice guy and take care of the problem. How was I to know she was Jacob's tutor? No tutors of mine were ever as hot as she is." I sucked in a breath through my teeth as I drank Joy in. "Lord have mercy."

"Right." Joy marched up to me, the top of her head barely reaching my chin as we stood almost toe to toe. Energy arched between us like erotic, painful lighting. "You, being the misogynistic asshole that you are, looked at me and assumed I was a whore. Why? I was dressed in a conservative suit, I wasn't wearing anything beyond a tasteful amount of makeup, and I wasn't acting in a flirtatious manner. Where in that scenario do you get the idea that I was a prostitute?"

"I—"

She didn't give me a chance to get another word in, instead shocking the shit out of me as she grasped her breasts, holding them up like an offering. My dick twitched as they jiggled slightly. "Is it these? Is it the fact I was born with large breasts? Something I have utterly no control over, something God decided to give me? Is it the fact that you're so narrow-minded that you can't see past my body to even consider that I have a brain? That I might have a legitimate reason for being there?"

The world around me seemed to hold its breath as I stared down at this defiant little creature that consumed me. I lowered my voice, saying, "No, it was because the second I saw you, I would have given everything I own for the privilege of calling you mine."

Her lovely eyes went wide a second before I grasped the back of her neck and looped my other arm around her tiny waist, pulling her up so I could slam my mouth down onto hers.

Finally.

For one long moment, I savored the feeling of her pillowy lips against mine, gently rubbing against my own. I gripped her full hip tight in my greedy hand, squeezing gently then growling at the lush feel of her. The moment our mouths connected, I knew I'd been right. She was the one. The woman I'd been waiting for. Guess my mom wasn't full of shit about the 'love at first kiss' family legend. An immense sense of relief blended with the warmth and lust churning inside of me. Something settled in my mind, in my heart, as everything seemed to click into place.

The feeling of contentment swept through me, washing away the world until it was just me and my Joy. She was the reason I'd held all other women at arms distance, knowing they weren't right for me, keeping my emotional distance from them by using BDSM as a buffer. I'd been their Master, but never their man. I wanted to be Joy's man. I'd been waiting for her—searching without knowing—and now that I had her, I was never giving her up.

Joy tried to fight me at first, her teeth flashing as she snarled, but the pull between us was too strong. Our bodies fused together. My blood burned as my dick throbbed with want, the feeling of euphoria searing my senses. The animal inside of me urged me to take, to own, to mark her, but the man I strived so hard to be held my base instincts in check, tempering my fierce arousal into a gentle brush of our lips. My tenderness seemed to disarm her, and her hands went from pushing me away to pulling me closer.

Her low, desperate moan vibrated from her body and into mine.

For twenty-four rapid beats of my heart, she softened against me, her mouth tasting me in a way that had a deep growl ripping from chest. Her scent of strawberries and peaches, and the hot-lush warmth of her round body against me, drove me wild. With another soft moan, she grasped my shoulders and parted her lips, the fire from kissing her burning my system like a shot of the best tequila I'd ever had. She ruined me in an instant, made it impossible to ever go back to touching any other woman after I'd had the pleasure of her lips. An electric shudder ripped down my spine and into my balls, making me harder than I'd ever been in my life.

Unfortunately, my feelings appeared to be one-sided.

Just as I was about to turn and carry Joy into the house to break my celibacy against the nearest hard surface, my mother wacked me on the shoulder.

"Ramón! You put her down this instant!"

Moms—the ultimate cock block.

Joy must have agreed with my mother, because she abruptly twisted in my arms, almost kneeing me in the junk and forcing me to drop her. A second later she slapped me, hard, across the face. The animal inside of me pushed me to retaliate, to tie her sassy little ass up and fuck her until she was weeping my name, bending to my will. A soft snarl escaped before I could stop it, but she simply lifted her cute little nose in the air in silent defiance.

Our eyes met, held, and my dick *throbbed* with the need to feel her body clasped tight around mine.

"Do that again, and I'll kick your balls down your throat," Joy snarled at me, fire and passion sparking in her jade green eyes.

Fuck, she was magnificent.

My mother cleared her throat. Before she could speak, I said, "Mom, Diego. Give us a moment alone, please."

"Ramón, I don't know if that's the best—"

I turned and gave her a look that let her know I was done fucking around. "Please. I need a moment alone with Joy. I promise, she'll be safe with me."

I didn't miss the way satisfaction flared in my mother's gaze, or the little smile that tried to lift the corners of her mouth, but I'd deal with her meddling later.

"Joy?" she asked. My suspicions about my mother's infamous matchmaking skills raised my hackles at her sweet tone. "Is that all right with you?"

Joy was going to object, but I stopped her by saying, "Unless you're afraid of me."

Just like I knew it would, any mention of weakness had Joy's back going up. My girl had a lot of pride, and it was easy to tweak. She'd rather face me alone, something she clearly didn't want to do, than admit I intimidated her.

She sucked on her lower lip before saying, "Do I have anything to be afraid of?"

Sweetest Obsession

An echo of real fear haunted her gaze for a moment, and I slowly shook my head. "No, beautiful, never from me."

"Fine. But make it quick. I want to see Hannah."

Closing the distance between us once again, and ignoring my mother's unflattering mutters about my appalling lack of manners as she left, I grinned at the way Joy's eyes went wide. What I was about to say to this little spitfire wasn't for my family's ears. Joy tried to step away from me with a startled squeak, but I backed her into one of the large cedar beams holding up the small Spanish tile roof over the patio area. Before her head could hit it, I had my hand there, cushioning her delicate skull. Amazing, even when she'd pushed all my buttons, drove me right into my red zone, my first instinct was to protect her from any harm.

She didn't see it that way, and her cheeks darkened as she tried to knee me in the junk. "Get off me!"

I cupped her skull and easily pinned her against the fragrant wood, the softness of her curls distracting me for a moment. "You have the most beautiful hair."

"What?" She stared up at me like I'd lost my mind, and maybe I had. "Get off me. If this is your form of an apology, it really sucks."

I lowered my face toward hers, holding her still so I could rub my nose along hers. The sparks igniting between us as the air grew heavy with pressure reminded me of the feeling before a storm hit. A small tremble went through her, and her breathing picked up, crushing her big tits to my chest and making me inwardly groan.

"You're right. Let me make it up to you."

The breathy tone of her voice drove me crazy. "By what, mauling me?"

"Mmmm, I'd love to maul you, but you're not ready for that yet."

More useless struggles on her part, along with a huff of annoyance as I squeezed her gently. "You have lost your damn mind."

"Oh, sweet baby, that's where you're so wrong. I've never been more present, sane, and sure of anything in my life as I am of you."

I went in to steal a kiss, but she snapped at me with her sharp little teeth. If my reflexes hadn't been so good, if I hadn't known somehow on a gut level she'd try to fight me, I'd be on the way to the ER right now to reattach my lip. Instead, I pressed my hands to her jaw and held her still, her pissed off snarl only arousing me further. I liked having to tame her, to immerse myself in her reaction and try to win her compliance. She was stubborn, but as I gently kissed her lips she eventually went from fighting to a reluctant hum of desire as she began to kiss me back. Her small hands trailed up my body, rubbing and caressing me, playing with the indentations of my shoulder muscles.

    I was a slave to her caress, to her will, and I finally got to experience the mind-numbing pleasure of kissing a woman I actually cared about. Deeply. Euphoria suffused me, and I reveled in the endorphin high I got from feeling her body pressed against mine. I'd missed this, the touch of a woman, but I'd kept my last few bed partners tied up most of the time.

    Oddly enough, the constant burn of temper just waiting to flare to life had been banked to ashes. I was calm in a way I'd never experienced before. Content, like I finally held the proverbial brass ring in my hands, the prize I'd been working for without even knowing it. Shit, holding Joy in my arms was like capturing sunshine, warmth, and everything good about the world. I'd never felt any emotions like this profound connection that I couldn't explain to a woman who barely knew me. I didn't know if it was love that I felt for Joy, but whatever it was, it felt so damn good, so perfect, that I didn't want it to end.

    In the past, I would have taken Joy right into my bed, but she deserved better. I needed to show her how serious I was about her, seduce her, and take my time. Show her how special she was, how I could treat her right. We were going to be together forever, so there was no need to rush her, but I wanted to make it clear she was mine now. I admit, in the past I'd been a dick to some women. The last few submissives I'd been with, I didn't even fuck, preferring to only empty myself in their mouths or asses.

    The thought of fathering a child with any of my sex partners made me shudder.

    But Joy…she was different. The thought of getting her pregnant had me so hard, I was going to cum in my pants if I didn't slow this down. Her pussy was so warm, and I knew sinking into her tight little body would be bliss. I'd have to stretch her out, work into her, but I couldn't wait to fill her up with my seed and wait for it to take root. She was currently on birth control—thanks to my observation, I knew she was protected—but I hoped I could talk her into ditching her birth control after we were properly married.

Pressed as close to her as I was, I could feel the thunder of her heart against mine, our pulses racing as our breathing picked up. Though her lips were curled in disdain, her small hands were clutched to my sides, holding me in a death grip. I'm not even sure if she was aware of how she was now slowly rubbing against me, her every breath betraying the desire flowing through her. I'd bet, if I slipped my fingers between her legs and gave that big clit of hers a pinch, she'd gush for me.

I knew from watching her masturbate that Joy got wet, very wet, and I couldn't wait to feel that slick fluid easing my cock into her body as I fucked her sweet brown and pink pussy.

I've been fantasizing about this moment, dreaming about all the ways I'd take her after I made her mine. I'd planned just how to seduce her, just how to bend her to my will. I want her to love me before I had to program her. After Nina's betrayal, it couldn't be any other way. There is no way my mother would ever, ever allow Joy to walk away at this point. The best way I could protect Joy was to do it myself before my mother decided it was time to take matters into her own hands. While I love my mom, there is no way in hell she's getting her hands on Joy. Who knows what kind of messed up shit she'd do to my girl's beautiful head?

I would do it myself, have Leo train me on what I needed to say, have him guide me through the process until I could do it in my sleep. When the moment was right, I would bind Joy to me forever, make her mine in a way that not even God could take her from me. I will never tire of her, never want anyone else. She's the sweetest thing I've ever touched, and I would devote my life to bringing her nothing but pleasure.

My already hard dick throbbed and a hard burst of pre-cum wet the pierced tip of my shaft. Part of the programming process involved the use of an illegal, ultra-rare drug called D128 that would send Joy into real, physical heat. It was one of our labs greatest inventions, a true aphrodisiac that sent women into a mating frenzy. The drug was extremely expensive, each batch had to be custom made for one particular woman, but the results were worth it. D128 couldn't force a woman to become aroused—too much of turning a woman on was a mental rather than physical process—but when a woman did naturally become aroused, the D128 would multiply both her passion and pleasure to the point of unbearable ecstasy. Once I finally got my dick in her, she'd come until she passed out, using me until she'd drained me dry. I'd fucked women on D128 before—obnoxiously rich women who could afford the exorbitant cost of the miracle drug and were desperate for the pleasure it could bring them.

Hell, I'd seen women cry after their first experience using the drug, so fucking blitzed out of their mind on orgasms that they broke in the most beautiful way.

My new goal in life was to watch Joy shatter while I fucked her, to lick the tears from her face as her intense release destroyed her, ripped her open and laid her bare for me to take.

But I didn't need a drug to make her respond to me. The proof was in the desire clouding her gorgeous green eyes, to the flush on her pretty round cheeks, down to her nipples stabbing at me through her shirt. Unable to help myself, I thrust my thigh between her legs, the heat of her core burning me through our clothes.

"Stop that," she whispered while rocking herself against me and panting lightly.

"Here's what's going to happen." I easily subdued her as she halfheartedly struggled against me, her pupils wide with desire. "You're going to go home with Mark and get comfortable. Take a bath, eat something, relax. I want you to do whatever makes you happy. I'll take care of retrieving your things and having them delivered to his house. The only thing you have to do is heal, sweetheart. Let me do this for you."

Red blossomed in her cheeks, but I didn't miss the faint yearning in her voice as she said, "I'm not a child. I don't need anyone to take care of me. And you can't tell me what to do."

"I just did." Before she could protest further, and tempt me into fucking her too soon, I released her then quickly stepped away after making sure she was steady on her feet. "Now be a good girl and go let my mom know you're ready to leave for

Mark's place."

When she narrowed her eyes at me, then licked her lower lip, I ached to be inside of her. The head of my cock was slippery with pre-cum, and I'd never wanted a woman more than I wanted Joy. While I'd hoped we'd have chemistry, the attraction between us had proven to be stronger and more explosive than I'd even imagined. This feisty, little blonde with big tits and ass for days was going to be exclusively mine to worship.

When the time was right.

My cock, however, disagreed and jerked against my pants in protest at the thought of leaving her without at least one more kiss, but I'd reached my limit. My determination to give her time to accept my place in her life was waning as she took a deep breath, her breasts straining against the sundress she wore. I'm not sure what she said, I'm sure it wasn't complimentary, because I was moving fast as I forced myself to leave. Her nipples, her fucking dark chocolate drop nipples, were so fucking stiff, they practically begged for my mouth to suck on them. My control almost slipped, but I managed to force myself to walk away after giving her a wink, then I practically sprinted up the stairs to my room.

The minute the door was closed behind me, I freed my aching, throbbing cock and grasped it tight, the heavy gold ring piercing the tip doing nothing to drag my rampant erection down as it strained for my belly button. Fuck, I don't think I'd ever been this hard. All the blood in my body seemed to rush to the head of my shaft as I circled the base, and I groaned with need as my balls drew up tight. Licking my lips, tasting the echo of Joy's flavor, I lifted my free hand to my face and inhaled the peaches and strawberry perfume that she wore, now branding me.

I loved that, loved her smell on me. I pumped my cock while fantasies flew through my mind, dirty snapshots of all the things I wanted to do to Joy, of all the pleasure I wanted to give her, of all the ways I would violate her.

It didn't take long for the climax to blast from me in strong waves, each rush of release making me choke back my cries.

Panting, I slumped back against the door, grimacing as I looked at my cum covered hand. In a perfect world, Joy would be on her knees before me, a vibrator strapped to her clit as she sucked me dry. Longing filled me, and I promised the possessive animal that lived deep in my soul that Joy was ours now.

Chapter 4
Joy

Turning my head to the side, I took in the gigantic, all white, extravagant bouquet of flowers. They graced the pale blue, shabby chic side table next to my brass bed and added a sense of elegance to the room. I'll say one thing for Mark's house, I never imagined one of his guest rooms would look like this. The large bed had a soft teal and pink quilt that was totally girly, which complimented the ultra-feminine decor of this room—or should I say, my new temporary bedroom. While I would never decorate a room with such a heavy floral theme, it had a designer flare and looked super expensive. I had to admit I'd never pegged Mark, the guy who owned this house and my new roomie, as the kind of person to spend the time picking out the distressed wood armoire or perfect antique mirror hanging over the matching dresser.

Mark kind of reminded me of a G.I. Joe doll, with his buzzed haircut and classically chiseled face. The kind of guy that would have either a bachelor pad or a place decorated with mahogany and dark leather. Certainly not the kind of guy what would have framed, pressed floral arrangements hanging as art in his guest room.

He was something of an enigma to me. Quiet, but not unfriendly. Just one of those people that liked to listen, to take in the world around him. To my surprise, he'd been the one that took me from the Cordova's mansion to Leo's massive place. We'd spent the ride to his two-story mission style home chatting about ourselves, and my anxiety eased as I realized he was a genuinely nice guy beneath all his gruffness. I found that despite his intimidating persona, he reminded me of Daniel Craig in one of his action movies—all stoic and strong, but he was funny and kept our conversation light. Mark was Leo's right-hand man. They both worked for the same company together, so he was a part of Hannah's daily life here at Leo's compound.

Yes, compound. Leo owned twenty acres of prime real estate in one of the most exclusive areas outside of Phoenix. His home was an amazing twelve-thousand square foot monstrosity that, according to Hannah, completely kicked ass. I know the glimpse I'd gotten of Leo's pad had left me staring through the window of Mark's Land Rover with my nose pressed to the glass like a tourist. Who could blame me? There was an honest to goodness red rock water sculpture out front that looked like something out of a museum. I knew Leo had money, but I didn't realize he had *money*.

I'd done a little research on Leo after he started dating Hannah, and didn't find much other than he worked for the Cordova Group in security, and had been in different news articles from time to time about this business deal or that.

Hannah had invited me to come over and visit with her while she stayed with Leo, but out of stupid jealousy, I hadn't gone. Hannah and I have always been inseparable, and I'd really missed spending time with her. My older sister Brittney was a flat out raving bitch, and my younger sister Winter was just a baby, so growing up Hannah was my sister by another mister. I loved her like she was my twin. After constantly having her around, watching her fall in love and starting to drift out of my life had been painful.

Logically, I knew I was being stupid and clingy—something I always accused Hannah of being, so I'd sucked up my negative feelings around her and tried to be as positive as I could. It wasn't her fault I didn't have much luck in the relationship department. But I hadn't been able to put aside my petty feelings and force myself to come visit her at Leo's place, something I now deeply regretted. Life was too short for that bullshit, and when I saw Hannah again, I'd be nothing but supportive about her and Leo's relationship. Lord knows, he saved our lives last night.

My temple throbbed with my increasing heartbeat, bringing me out of my dark thoughts and back to the present and my lovely new bedroom. The bruises on my torso ached and I tried to distract myself, reaching out to grab the card hidden among the white blooms. Once again, I held it to my nose, inhaling the light scent of the jasmine flowers it had been touching, then opened it. The paper was pale cream, and the scrawled note inside done in pure black ink. Reading it at once infuriated and calmed me, a strange reaction to a man I was pretty sure I despised, but wanted to fuck with an intense need that scared me.

Joy,

I'm sorry I couldn't be there to give these to you myself, but there was an emergency at work that I had to attend to. I've taken the liberty of having my personal shopper supplement your wardrobe, and had your old clothes placed in a storage locker along with your furniture. I'm sorry I couldn't be there with you tonight, but I promise I'll make it up to you. Sleep tight, sweetheart, and make sure you dream about me.

Ramón

I should shred the card, flush it down the toilet and toss the flowers in the garbage, but so far I couldn't even bring myself to stop looking at them. That man drove me crazy. If I had a polar opposite, it would be Ramón. He was a sexist dick who seemed to get off on ordering me around, and kissing me without permission, and being an assuming asshole. Arrogant man, with his shoulder length black as night hair, his glowing tanned skin, his dangerous hazel brown eyes, and his firm, sinful mouth. Not to mention his body. He wasn't super ripped, but his muscles were huge. I'd loved the feeling of them beneath my hands. My heart sped up as I relived the possessive kiss he'd given me, the way he'd cushioned my body so I didn't get hurt when he manhandled me against the beam in the backyard.

Heat flickered from the pit of my stomach and flowed outwards, dampening my already wet panties.

The man was unfairly potent and hot.

My lips tingled, and I rubbed the card against them. There had to be something wrong with me that I found his domineering attitude arousing. Strong women didn't allow a man to sweep them off their feet and kiss them senseless. Yeah, it was fun to read about, but that was fantasy. I've had more than enough experience with pushy assholes in the real world. Finding a man, who'd at one point assumed I was a whore, arousing was plain humiliating. Yet, the attraction was undeniable. I once again cursed chemistry. It was just hormones, an unconscious reaction to someone my body knew would be a good mate. I bet that man could pound me through the mattress. And, God, his lips…his taste. I've never been so thoroughly kissed in my life.

My pussy started to pulse softly and I groaned, gently putting the card next to the bed before pulling the pillow next to me over my face.

All my life I've had to work for my arousal, struggle to have an orgasm with my chosen bed partners, but with that d-bag Ramón, I'd gone up like a nuclear bomb of lust had exploded in my panties.

Maybe the attack had something to do with it. Ramón was just so...big. When he wasn't talking, he could be really nice. I hadn't forgotten the way he'd held me as I cried, being internally wrung apart by what had to be a panic attack. The metallic taste of adrenaline filling my mouth, the shaking, the racing heart and sweating palms...all of those symptoms were classic signs of a panic attack.

Along with the unrelenting fear.

The sound of Ramón and his brother Diego fighting had triggered some crazy fight or flight response in me, but the moment he wrapped me in his arms, I no longer felt afraid.

Me, the girl who always had to stand on her own two feet, be her own champion in a messed-up world that sexualized women who looked like me, swooned because some big, bad ass guy cradled me like a child.

All around me, dead silence reined and I tried in vain to get to sleep. I was exhausted, my body beyond strung out, and my mind just wouldn't shut the fuck up. I've had this problem all my life, overthinking everything. I dwell, ponder, and dissect situations and people until I drive myself crazy. Right now, I had a lot of negative things to dwell and ponder on. Shifting on the bed, I flipped over for a third time, secretly loving the feeling of the real silk nightgown Ramón had bought for me.

While I would have liked to scoff at the feminine, icy blue gown with its thigh high split, it was so beautiful, I couldn't help but stroke the soft fabric over the curve of my belly. This gown was something a princess would wear to bed. I traced the slightly raised bumps of the intricate cherry blossoms embroidered around the scoop necked bodice. Held in place by spaghetti straps, it should have been uncomfortable, but instead it felt like a dream. I flipped yet again, sighing as I stared at the ceiling. It would probably help if I turned off the low bedside lamp, with its frilly lemon chiffon shade, but I didn't want to be in the dark.

The gown, along with a dozen outfits, had been left for me in boxes piled high on the bed from exclusive stores, all thanks to Ramón. I didn't plan on keeping any of them, and had only looked through a few boxes before finding the nightgown along with its matching silk and lace panties. I knew they were from him because he'd left me another note on top of a box containing a pair of Chanel nutmeg suede boots. They were divine, and I'd felt a pang of longing but I knew I had to reject his gifts. I couldn't let him buy me things. My mom always taught me a smart woman bought her own gifts, and she didn't rely on a man to supply her with anything.

Hell, she basically taught me men weren't worth much at all for a woman to have in her life. Don't get me wrong, she loved my father, but her mother—my beloved *abuela*—had been very old school Puerto Rican in her beliefs about a woman staying home and raising a family versus working. When my mother went back to work, my *abuela* had not approved and let my mom know it.

What my grandma didn't understand was that my mom was happier when she was working and having a family. She needed that balance in her life. My dad had a good job as an accountant, but he made just enough for us to get by. With my mom working, we had enough to cover emergencies and put clothes on the backs of four growing teenagers. I'll admit, I sometimes wished I had a mom who stayed home like some of my friends, but my *abuela* more than made up for it. Those years she'd watched over us before she passed away had been some of the best of my life. I loved listening to tales of her life as a young bride to a handsome and ambitious young man in Puerto Rico. My grandfather was the love of her life, her hero, a man's man who'd brought her to Arizona and made her gloriously happy.

As a child, I'd wanted that life, wanted to be able to do what my *abuela* did—love and take care of people. Nothing had seemed more right to my young self than finding a man like grandpa and marrying him. My mother had been horrified, convinced my grandma had brainwashed me into wanting to be a housewife. Just like her mother couldn't understand my mom's desire to work, my mom couldn't understand that I had no desire to have a career. My oldest sister had teased me mercilessly about being a loser, and I'd stopped talking about wanting to be a mom when I grew up. Instead, I talked about college, having a profession, and being the best at whatever it was I was going to be.

Rolling onto my back, I stretched out, my body exhausted but my mind hyper clear. I was having one of those moments when I just seemed...aware of everything in an almost omnipotent way, and I had a moment of lucidity as I examined my life. Was I going to school, busting my ass, and doing it all on my own because it was something I wanted, or was I chasing my mother's dream?

Did I push men away because of her influence?

My mom encouraged me to play the field, not to settle down like she had. She'd given birth to my sister when she was only nineteen and newly married, so she'd never really had a chance to party and be young. When I'd go home to visit, she wanted to hear all about my love life, like I was some episode of *Sex and the City* for her. I think it made her feel young to gossip with me and Hannah about life at college, and I'm sad to admit I often embellished my dates so she wouldn't be disappointed I wasn't out living it up. Between work and school, I really had no time and I wanted more than just sex.

I wanted love.

My heart sped up as I realized the truth I'd hidden from myself, buried deep long ago. My childhood dreams, ones that used to make me fall asleep with a smile on my face as I thought about my future. I need someone to love, someone to have a family with, someone who would protect me and keep me safe. I wanted someone like my grandfather, a strong and honorable man who fought to bring his family to America, to start his own furniture store and give my grandmother everything she ever wanted. From her stories, it was obvious he'd loved her with everything he had. I used to daydream about what it would be like to have that kind of devotion.

All my life, I've avoided men who put off an arrogant alpha male vibe, but after being at the mercy of a monster, I craved the safety of being in a powerful man's arms. I wanted the kind of man who would keep me safe, no matter what, because I was his. The bitter truth was, I wasn't strong enough to take care of myself.

I was weak, small, and alone.

Before I could drive myself out of my mind with useless

worry, there came a soft knock from my door.

Thinking it was Mark, I pulled up the covers to my chin to hide my scantily clad body and said, "Come in."

Only it wasn't my new roomie who entered my new bedroom, but a very tired looking Ramón.

"What the hell are *you* doing here?" I hissed even as my greedy eyes drank him in.

Dressed in a very nice dark brown suit that must have been tailored to his large frame, he gave off an elegant air, despite the way he'd loosened his tie and opened a button on his collar. He'd also taken his hair down, and it momentarily swayed forward to cover one side of his face as he bent to remove his gleaming black leather shoes. The breadth of his shoulders made me internally swoon, and I admired how big his hands were as he pulled off his black dress socks.

Looking up at me through the fringe of his hair he grinned. "I told you I'd be here for breakfast."

I blinked at him, stunned by his presumption. "People normally eat breakfast in the kitchen, after sunrise."

He winked roguishly at me, like some dirty pirate out of the bodice rippers I read as a teenager. My belly clenched. "Most people do, but if you'd like, I can make an exception and eat you for breakfast in bed."

Oh shit, my pussy clenched so hard I had to bite back a moan at the thought of that big, hulking man kneeling between my thighs.

"Get the hell out of my room!"

"Nope."

I threw a pillow at his head, and he merely laughed as he batted it away. "Calm down, *mami*. I know you're not ready for that…yet."

Shrugging off his jacket, he reached for his belt. I yelled, "You keep those pants on!"

"I am." He waggled his eyebrows at me, his expression suddenly playful. "I was just taking my belt off because it's uncomfortable as fuck to sleep with one on."

"Sleep? What in the ever-loving fuck are you talking about? You put your clothes back on right now, mister."

"Why do I like it when you yell at me? Normally, I wouldn't take that kind of disrespect from anyone, but with you? It turns me on."

"You're insane."

"Only for you."

His eyes never left me as he unbuttoned his shirt before shrugging it off and revealing the tight, white tank he wore beneath. I'd felt his body intimately, but seeing all that muscle and power up close wasn't helping me keep my wits about me. He was so built, but not lean enough to make the veins on his arms stand out. He had a huge barrel chest with a deep dip between his solid pectorals that I wanted to lick. A smattering of dark hair covered his chest, dusting over a large chest tattoo. It was a skull surrounded by roses and tribal art, with the name Cordova beneath it. *Sexy.* I wondered how silky his chest hair would feel beneath my fingers. Against the ultra-floral backdrop of the room, he seemed out of place, a dangerous shadow on a sunny day.

Tossing his phone on the little blue table next to the bed, his nostrils flared as he took a deep breath. "Sorry, sweetheart, but I'm not leaving. I need to sleep with you tonight."

Whatever tongue lashing I was about to give him was ripped from my lips as he clambered into bed with me then pulled me close, his body curving around mine as he spooned me.

"Listen," he whispered in my ear as I tried to squirm away. "When I saw you at my mom's house, hurt and unconscious, it fucked with me."

I shoved at him. "What the hell does that have to do with the fact that you think it's okay to be in my bed right now?"

"I need to protect you, can't sleep without you at my side."

"You're insane."

"I know you don't know me, but I swear to you I have nothing but the best intentions for you in mind."

I no longer struggled to get away from him, but my voice was dry as I said, "You being half-naked in my bed is hardly in my best intentions."

"Absolutely." Damn, his grin was even better up close. "You'll see. You deserve nothing but the best, and I'm gonna make sure that you get whatever you need to make you happy from now on."

I was so, so tired, and his body warmed mine as he continued to cuddle me like a champ. "I don't understand why you're saying that. You barely know me."

"That's not true. Hannah talks about you all the time. From what she says, you're an amazing woman. Kind, smart, and funny. Fuck, you're so smart. You have no idea how sexy that is. I've been wanting to meet you for a while."

I made another halfhearted effort to put some distance between us, but it was more like rubbing myself against him and purring than an actual effort to leave the drugging warmth of his body. "Just because you hang out with Leo and Hannah, it doesn't give you the right to invite yourself into my bed."

Rubbing his nose along my neck, he took a deep inhalation and let it out with an extremely pleased sigh that burned my sensitive skin. "I'm not going to violate you, but I am going to sleep with you. I have to make sure you're safe, and the best way to do that is to have you with me."

"If you're sleeping, how are you going to keep me safe?"

"Trust me, Joy. They'll have to shoot through me to get to you."

"Has anyone ever told you that you're for real crazy?"

"All the time." He chuckled, the vibration traveling from his body pressed tight and into mine. "Anyone ever tell you that you can argue about just about anything?"

"All the time." My nipples pebbled, and I tried to ignore the fact that he was getting erect behind me. "For someone who said he wasn't going to touch me, you're touching me an awful lot."

"Nah, this is just cuddles. Relax. You mind if I put on some background noise? This place is so fuckin' quiet."

"Uh-no, because you aren't staying here."

"Give it up, beautiful. I'm staying, and I'm too tired to argue anymore."

I didn't fight him as he leaned over to grab his phone, because deep down I was glad he was here, and happy that I was no longer alone in a strange place after what I'd been through. Even though he could be a class A asshole, Ramón Cordova was also disarmingly sweet when he wanted to be.

A second later, the soft sound of the sea with its crashing waves mixed with soft piano music filled the air. I turned my head to look at him as he reached over and turned off the light, the muscles of his thick biceps flexing in a most interesting manner. I didn't want to admit it, but the soft roar did help my racing mind slow down. There was something about the rhythmic ebb and flow of the waves that settled me. It was one of my favorite settings on my white noise machine at home.

After listening to the sea for a minute I halfheartedly whispered, "I can't sleep with you here."

"Yes, you can."

Jesus, how do you argue with an irrational person?

Wiggling into an even more comfortable position, my whole body relaxed after a big sigh. "Are you on medication?"

"Give me your hand."

"What?"

Tucked up against my back once again, he took one of my hands in his massive paw and began to massage my palm with his thumb. I instantly slumped against him, the response automatic. I lo-o-o-oved being massaged. Anywhere, any time. I'd often beg, whine, and plead with Hannah to give me a hand massage after typing up long papers for work or doing a ton of homework for school. But Hannah's slender hands had never felt like this.

"Oh, my God," I sighed in delight as his big thumb pressed into my muscles.

"Like that," Ramón growled against my ear, sending hot and cold shivers through me.

Trying to rally my wits, my voice came out extra husky as I said, "No, not at all."

"Liar," I could hear the smile in his voice as the heat of his breath warmed my neck, and his large body curled around mine. "I told you, you're safe with me, Joy. Just relax, let me take care of you."

"Can take care of myself," I grumbled in a totally petulant way, my muscles going limp as the tension slowly left my body. "You smell good."

I couldn't stop the sleepy smile from curving my lips as he laughed behind me. "Glad you approve."

"Makes me want to lick you."

His hips pressed against my ass, and his thick erection nestled between my silk covered butt cheeks. "Let's save that for later. Just relax."

He rolled us over so we lay chest to chest with him on the bottom. Startled out of my sleepy contentment, I started to wiggle away, but he kept me pinned to him. His chest was so wide that when he began to massage my back, I simply collapsed on him and used his broad form like a muscled and warm mattress. I was tired, so tired, and he was so cozy and comfortable. His touch was magic. I'd feel bad about it in the morning, I decided, as he expertly rubbed out some of the tension from the muscles around my spine, his hands sliding over the silk of my nightgown.

In this position, his large erection was even more obvious, but he didn't grind it into me or anything like that. I momentarily debated yelling at him for being aroused, then decided that was just hypocritical considering my clit was pulsing with the slow beat of my heart. The smell of his cool and woodsy cologne came from the skin of his chest, and I gave up the fight, sinking into him.

His voice blended into the crash of the waves from his phone as he said, "I know you can take care of yourself, but I like taking care of you. It makes me feel good—proud that I can make you happy. I've never wanted to do this for anyone before. Let me do this for you, Joy, please."

That was usually my line, my security blanket. If I was busy taking care of other people it fulfilled me in a way nothing else did. I liked making people happy, liked being the one they turned to for comfort and love. It fed my soul to look after other people, especially those that really needed it.

Oddly enough, I often felt guilty if someone showed me that same kind of care, like I was wasting his or her time. I don't know why I'm this way. God knows, I've tried to analyze myself enough over the years to figure it out, I just know it's one of my personality quirks. This eccentricity of mine had me trying to return the favor to Ramón, stroking his shoulder softly as he continued to give me a world-class massage while sprawled out over his big frame.

"Kay," I mumbled, my lips not wanting to move enough to form the word.

He let out a happy, rumbling sigh. The way he kind of growled the sound out reminded me of the sound our Irish Wolfhound would make when we rubbed his belly. That thought had a soft giggle bubbling out of me, my mind already drifting toward sleep. I cuddled deeper into him, scooting up so I could rub my nose against his neck as my hand went limp.

"Night, Ramón."

My words slurred slightly, and he laughed before rolling my now limp body to the side and arranging me so I was comfy with my head resting where his shoulder and chest met, my leg slung over one of his thick, firm thighs. It was a very intimate position, but I couldn't bring myself to care. The ever-present babble of my mind was absent and I sank into a grateful sleep, safe in his arms.

Seven hours later, my stomach growled, reminding me I'd skipped breakfast and it was time for lunch. Too bad I was dressed in an oversized men's robe that belonged to Mark, arguing with Ramón as he pointed to three outfits on the bed that he'd put together for me to choose from. *Seriously.* This motherfucker seemed to think I was some brainless doll he could dress and order around.

"I gave you a choice," Ramón growled with an aggrieved look. "Three of them."

"You can't tell me what to wear!"

Sighing, he ran a hand through his damp hair. While I used my shower, which had come pre-stocked with all my favorite stuff in brand new bottles, he'd washed up elsewhere and reappeared wearing a pair of black shorts that showed off his muscular, hairy calves and a faded maroon t-shirt with the name of a local boutique Tequila distillery. To my dismay, he looked sexy as fuck this morning. The soft cotton hugged his big frame and showed off that delicious V of a man's frame, the wide shoulders tapering to his trim waist. Last night, he'd been all business and totally fuckable, but today he was totally casual, yet dangerous. He wore his usual small, thick, gold gauge earrings and had just shaved, making me wonder what his smooth, sensitive skin would feel like against my own when we kissed.

I looked into his oh-so-soft, beautiful, light brown eyes and tingled from head to toe.

Gripping the edges of my robe harder, pissed at myself for being attracted to him, I snarled, "I'm not some trophy for you to dress up and parade around."

"Jesus, woman, can I pay you any compliment that you don't find offensive? You're not a trophy, you're a beautiful woman. I thought these outfits would look good on you." Frustration rolled off him in waves before he took a deep breath and let it out slowly through his nose. "I thought you would like them. I'm sorry I was wrong."

My gaze was drawn once again to the gorgeous, designer dresses and outfits that were absolutely stunning and exactly to my taste. It was almost eerie how well Ramón's personal shopper had bought for me, how well they'd guessed my style. Shit, I don't even know if I have a style. Most of my clothing was chosen to conceal, to hide my curves, to 'support.' These lovely creations spread out on the bed were made to flatter, to highlight, to gracefully define. None of them were slutty, but they certainly weren't conservative either.

Knowing I was being an ungrateful, and irrational bitch—one of the outfits was head to toe Coco Chanel, for God's sake—I tried to calm myself. "I appreciate you going to all this effort for me, really I do, but I have my own clothes. I just need to go...crap, I'll have to take a taxi to get my car then I can go to whatever storage unit has my things. Is Mark still here? Maybe he'll give me a ride."

To my surprise, Ramón pinched the bridge of his nose and squeezed his eyes shut before murmuring out a prayer in Spanish for the blessed mother to give him strength. "First off, I will take you anywhere you want to go. Second...I'm guessing no one has informed you of the damage your apartment sustained?"

Blinking at him, I cocked my head to the side, my wet curls momentarily blinding me before I flipped them back. "Yeah, there was some damage, but it's not like my clothes got destroyed, right?"

"Yeah, they kind of did. The walls at your apartment were as thin as fuckin' paper. I'm shocked none of your neighbors got hurt. Your bedroom was right behind where Manny and his fucktards were standing when Mark opened fire on them. Your stuff didn't fare too well."

"They shot up my bedroom?" My knees went a little weak as I thought about his words. "Holy shit, if I hadn't been unconscious on the floor—I'd be dead."

He closed the distance between us, sweeping me up into his arms before relaxing on the low loveseat that sat at the end of the massive bed. "Easy, *mami*."

I wrapped my arms around him, resting my head on his chest, the steady thrum of his heart giving me something to focus on other than my growing panic, a distraction I desperately needed. "I'm sorry. I'm not usually clingy like this."

"I know."

"What?"

"Hannah's talked a lot about you. Especially how strong you are, how you basically rescued her from the abusive fucks she calls parents. You were a little girl, and still you recognized she needed help *and* you made sure she got it."

Blushing, I fingered the soft material of his t-shirt. "Anyone would have done that."

"No, sweetheart. I wish that was true, 'cause the world could use more people like you, but it's not. Reality is, most of us are selfish fucks and assholes."

"Which one are you?"

He grinned. "Both. You know it's true. Think about how I was when we first met. So wrapped up in my own bullshit, I was just lashing out at anyone that came near me. Don't tell me you weren't pissed at me over my shit attitude."

Leaning back in his arms, I didn't fight him when he took the lapel of my robe and dried my tears with a gentle touch that melted me. "You were *such* an asshole."

"I was, and I'm sorry. Like I said before, I was going through some shit at the time and feeling angry at the world."

A tiny ball of hurt that I'd still carried around somewhere buried deep inside of me dissolved and I reached up, cupping his cheek and enjoying his smooth, warm skin. He'd shaved for me, and his dark skin was like rough velvet beneath my fingertips. For a moment, I simply enjoyed touching him, and Ramón seemed to revel in the attention. His full lips parted and a look of peace came over his face that nearly broke my heart.

Clearing my throat, I said, "I forgive you. But if you ever pull shit like that with me again, I'll kidney punch you. Normally, I'd say I'd knock you out, but you're so big I'll have to stick with your kidney."

"I appreciate that," he said with a wry smile, the pine green flecks in his eyes fascinating me as he leaned closer.

Shifting on his lap so I straddled him, I tried to keep from wincing when he grabbed my hip to help steady me. He was a big man and I was stretched wide over his pelvis. It made my sore muscles ache. I had a rather spectacular deep purple and green bruise going from my hip to my ribs from where I'd been kicked repeatedly, and the area was super tender. Ramón's grin faded and he ran his fingers down my cheek until they rested lightly on my pulse. "Are you okay?"

"Yeah, just a little uncomfortable there."

To my shock, he yanked my robe up to reveal my naked, bruised side.

He sucked in a hiss of air and started to speak, but before he could, I smacked him across the face, hard, then yanked my robe closed. "How dare you!"

Instead of getting pissed, Ramón grinned as he rubbed his jaw, and I wondered if he was seeing a therapist regularly. "Sorry, got carried away."

I tried to get out of his arms, but he merely tightened his grip. "Get your hands off me you—you super douche."

Our struggles made the shoulder of the overly large robe slip down, almost revealing my entire breast.

Ramón froze and let out a low, feral groan. "Fuck, you're so pretty. You have no idea how much I want to suck on those big, chocolate nipples of yours, Joy. Will you let me do that? Let me draw as much of your luscious tit into my mouth as I can? Let me bite you, suck you, tease you?"

My mouth hung open, words failing me as he easily held both my wrists with one hand, then gently—almost reverently—lowered the robe until my breast was fully revealed. We both looked down at my exposed flesh, my already tight nipple growing even stiffer beneath our combined gaze. Another one of those sexy as hell, animalistic growls escaped Ramón, and I quivered in response.

Slowly, ever so slowly, he lowered his mouth to my breast, then paused with his lips almost brushing the tip. "Give me permission, Joy."

My pussy pulsed to the beat of my heart, and my inner thighs were wet with my desire. If he didn't touch me soon, I was going to go up in flames. The moist, hot air from his mouth felt better than anything I've ever experienced, and I wanted more of this amazing sensation. "Please."

His tongue burned me as it brushed over the aching tip of my breast, the thundering of my heart surely audible to him. My whole body was flushed with desire, and I felt so very alive as he drew my breast into his mouth, sucking much harder than most guys usually do at first. The almost painful pressure was bliss for me, enough stimulation to actually get me off. His rhythmic sucking had my hips rocking against his jeans-covered erection. Shivers of pleasure ran through me as my clit ground down on the fly of his jeans. The thickness of his cock had me so hungry for him that I was close to orgasm just from grinding on him.

Releasing my nipple with an audible pop, he groaned. "Are you wet for me? Gonna come for me?"

I could only nod as my eyes closed fully, my body preparing for my release.

Before I could get there, Ramón flipped me onto the bed on my back, once again treating me like his little sex doll to throw around. "First time I make you cum, it's gonna be on my face."

I couldn't even take a moment to become self-conscious before he spread my robe open and shoved his broad shoulders between my thighs. It was during moments like this that I was reminded of how much bigger he was than me, how I must look like a curvy version of Tinkerbell in his presence. My legs had to stretch wide to accommodate him, and the muscles along his neck flexed as he snarled at me.

Seriously, he fucking snarled, and it was the sexiest thing I'd ever seen.

Grasping healthy handfuls of my generous ass with a firm grip, he lifted my pussy to his mouth and gave my slit a nice, long lick. Then another. Tingles raced up and down my spine, sending sparkles of pleasure through me. Gasping, I gave into temptation and plunged my hands into his long hair, loving the way it felt between my fingers as I fisted it.

Tugging slightly against my grip, he leaned up enough to meet my gaze over the generous curves of my body.

More tingles this time, bigger sparkles that threatened to turn into all out flames.

After giving the well-trimmed dark blonde hair on my mound a kiss, he said, "Love how big your clit is, how it's sticking out and begging for me to give it a nice suck."

I couldn't respond, struck dumb by the sound of his deep, accented voice telling me such deliciously dirty things. His breath warmed my already hot flesh and the very tip of his tongue brushed lightly over my nub. Normally, oral sex wasn't all that exciting for me. It was rare that I was able to get off from having my pussy eaten, something I'd always felt weird about. I mean, what woman said 'meh' to being kissed between her legs? My friends would talk about how many times their guys had made them come, and I'd just smile and pretend I knew exactly what they were talking about. I often found myself too worried about how I looked, smelled, and tasted to get into a guy slobbering around down there.

With Ramón's gifted mouth between my legs, I got it.

As he suckled my clit, stars burst behind my eyes, and I let out a choked sound of pleasure.

He was amazing. A master at working me up quicker than anyone ever had before. But he wasn't rushing me. Oh no, he was being exquisitely gentle, making me focus on every nuance of his touch, making me ache for him. He licked around the entrance of my body, penetrating it just enough with his tongue to tease me. Evidently, I loved being teased. It wasn't something any other lover of mine had done before. At least not successfully. Teasing took time, it took paying attention to your partner, and it took skill. Ramón had all three in spades, and I think I might have told him I loved his tongue as he began to slowly fuck me with it.

Never had I been with a man who was so focused on me, and I found the attention utterly blissful.

His nose brushed my clit with each thrust. I began to make grunting noises that I would have found embarrassing in normal circumstances. With Ramón's massive shoulders stretching me wide, his big hands massaging my ass as he fucked my body on his face, I couldn't find a single fuck to give about how crazy I sounded.

My gasps and the wet sound of Ramón licking between the folds of my labia filled my world as my eyes closed and my head rolled on my neck like I was drunk. He took the swollen bud of my clitoris into his mouth before ever so gently flicking his tongue over the tip.

I cried out then sat up enough to bury my hands deeper in his hair, holding him to me as my body flushed with heat and the tension built inside of me. Thankfully, Ramón didn't pull away, instead increasing his suction until my whole body tensed, harder, harder still, then everything inside of me shattered. Waves of euphoric bliss washed through me and I knew I was babbling something that sounded like *thank you* to Ramón's spectacular lips, but I didn't care what the hell I was saying. This orgasm was better than anything I'd ever experienced, his erotic teasing making the release exceptionally strong, and I rode his face hard as he held me tight.

Hypersensitive now, I tried to push his head away but he kept licking me, toying with me as I begged him to stop, that it was too much. Oversensitive pain mixed with pleasure confused my mind, and I gave up tugging at his head, instead falling back on the bed fully and grasping handfuls of the bunched up comforter. Ramón made a pleased sound and threw my shaking legs over his shoulders as he opened me further to his mouth. He was a man on a mission. As he began to fuck me with his tongue again, that wonderful heat coiled tighter in my pelvis, letting me know I might get my first chance at have a multiple orgasm with a man. My body twisted in his hard grasp, driven higher by the sounds of him licking and sucking at my sopping wet pussy. I'm naturally a well-lubed girl, and men in the past had been put off by it, but Ramón seemed to love literally licking me clean.

He licked up every drop of pleasure my body had to offer with an enthusiasm that bordered on animalistic. Stretching my legs wider, I relaxed and sighed as his soft, fluttering tongue strummed my clit. It was so nice to have full confidence that he was enjoying himself, that he wasn't just doing this to make me happy. The way he rubbed his pelvis against the bed, as if fucking it, sent tingles of pleasure down my spine.

"Show me your clit," he whispered against my wet labia, "Pull those pretty butterfly lips of yours apart."

While some women had a nice, neat pussy with everything tucked up inside, my inner lips extended past my outer labia, and I had some body issues in the past with the way my inner labia was longer than what seemed to be normal. Some of the guys in my school in Junior High, during sex ed, had made fun of the drawing of a vagina in our sex ed text book, talking to each other in hushed whispers about meaty flaps and other offensive shit like that. Intellectually, I know all women's bodies are beautiful, but part of me will be forever scared by those guy's careless words.

Except with Ramón. I wanted to show myself to him. To watch him enjoy my body.

Slipping my fingers between his mouth and my sex, I held both my outer and inner labia open, showing him how my pussy went from soft brown on the outside, to bright pink within. He smiled down at me, then began to lap at my exposed clit before grasping it between his teeth by the base, hard. I gasped, the pain strong enough that I let my pussy go and grabbed his hair instead.

"Ow!"

He began to gently nibble on my clit and I cried out his name as my hips bucked, feeling incredibly empty.

"Please, Ramón, more."

"Beg me."

"What?"

"You want more, you tell me what you want and beg me for it." He returned to tormenting me, holding me still and forcing me to endure his sharp bites and blissfully gentle kisses. "Tell me what you need, Joy, and I'll give it to you—always. But in my own time. You won't rush my enjoyment of you. I know it's hard for you to understand, but I need to do this for you. I need to know I'm makin' you happy. Tell me what you want, and I'll do it."

"I need your fingers inside of me."

"Ask nicely."

"What?" I groaned out as he rimmed the entrance to my body with one thick finger.

"Ask me nicely."

I wanted to strangle him, but I was so horny I wasn't above pleading for release. The idea actually turned me on—asking him for pleasure knowing he'll give it to me. Plus, I think he liked it when I gave in to his sensual demands.

"Please, Ramón, will you put two of your fingers inside my pussy and fuck me with them?"

My request lit a fire in his eyes that made my pussy clench. Oh yeah, he liked it when I did what he wanted. I wanted him to be as crazy with lust as I was, to know I wasn't alone in this bizarre, overwhelming attraction. He consumed me and the strength of my attraction to him was like nothing I'd ever experienced. Electric, amazing, and totally addictive.

Being shy in bed has never been one of my issues. I admit, it's hard to make me orgasm on the first, second, or even third date. If I didn't tell men right out the gate what I liked, we'd play a guessing game that usually ended with me sexually frustrated and them sweating like they'd just run a marathon. That also meant I appreciated it when a man was upfront with me with what he liked. I got off on making whoever I was with feel good. I loved my partner having an orgasm almost as much as I liked them myself. I wanted to blow their mind. To be the best they'd ever had.

Things didn't always work out that way, but I needed Ramón to want me as much as I wanted him. This pull between was far too strong to resist, and I shuddered as he kissed my inner thigh while whispering something appreciative against my skin. He was saying something about a kind of softness that made him hard. I think he was talking about my more than ample, dimpled thighs, but the man was totally enthralled by my body. That in itself wasn't unusual. See, a lot of guys have a secret—or not so secret—desire for very curvy girls. If the way he was worshiping my body was any indication, Ramón was one of those men, for sure. He squeezed my thigh with his hard grip, and the heat, the lust coming off him overwhelmed me.

I waited until he looked up at me, his skin so dark against my golden tan, and my hips lifted to his mouth involuntarily as I took in the pure need in his gaze. We were on fire together, and I loved the fact that I could make him burn. I wanted more, wanted to see him lose control, but I had a feeling he never allowed that to happen. Knowing this only made me want to tease him more.

"Ramón..." I made sure to roll the r in his name, turning it into a purr. "I need two of your big fingers inside my pussy, please. I feel so empty, so tight. I need you to stretch me open while you lick my clit and make up to it for being so rough."

His dark eyebrows rose, and I had about a second to read the shock in his expression before it turned to fierce pleasure. "Anything for my woman."

Once again, Ramón was perfect.

The slow, scissoring thrust of his fingers, the feeling of his thumb rubbing against my clit with unhurried strokes, tore a

Sweetest Obsession

moan from me that was shockingly loud.

Ramón laughed, the jerk, but his voice was strained as he said, "You make being good so very, very difficult."

"I...never understand you."

My words came out in breathy pants, and I could feel the flush of heat moving from my chest and up my neck. The need to cum quickly became a physical ache, and I sobbed his name as he replaced his thumb with his lips on my distended clit. I had no shame as I rode his face and fingers, screaming when he began to rub my g-spot. I've had super wet orgasms because of g-spot play before, and I knew some guys were freaked out by it, so I tried to warn him.

"Wait, Ramón, I'm going—"

"To squirt in my mouth? I know."

I could only moan in reply.

Dirty, he is so wonderfully dirty.

Shivers ran from the pit of my belly all the way to my scalp as I felt both frozen and burning alive. I was so sensitive, so aware and in the moment, wrapped up in his open adoration of my body. Remembering he was a sexist asshole was impossible when he began to curl his fingers inside my pussy while he flicked his tongue over my clit.

"You sure?"

His gaze lifted to mine and my breath caught in my throat at the pure dominance shining deep within his hazel eyes. This was the man that lay beneath the civilized surface he projected to the world. This was the animal that really ruled his spirit. It was a crazy thought, but didn't seem any less true as I felt my body submit to him. The strength left my limbs, and I felt strangely relaxed, yet so incredibly turned on. He smiled at me with genuine happiness as I let my hands fall back to the soft, cool sheets.

"I'm a man of my word, Joy. When I say something, I mean it. This is all new to you, I get it, but you'll learn that when I give you my word, I keep it. Now, I promise you, I'd fucking love to have you soak my face in your cum. Give it to me."

"Okay."

"No, say 'Yes, Ramón.'"

That tingle like glitter in my blood raced through me again. "Yes, Ramón."

"Fuck, sweetheart, you have no idea the terrible, nasty things I want to do to you." He gave my pussy a soft kiss then whispered, "I'm thirsty, give me your sweet cum to drink down."

He didn't give me a chance to catch my breath before he was devouring my pussy like a starving man, one of his hands tugging at my nipple while that wonderful tongue of his swirled through my folds. Two of his fingers stretched me, then a third, and I gasped at the feeling of being filled. When he curled his fingers, I sank my hands back into his hair, needing to hold onto him, needing him to anchor me before I blew apart into little pieces. I'd never felt anything near as good as Ramón's tongue and the way he suckled on my clit had me grinding into his face.

With a low growl, he pulled his mouth back, his eyes locked on my pussy as he began to finger fuck me. I spread my legs wide as my orgasm hovered just out of reach, the power of his thrusts shaking my body. Heat pooled in my pelvis and his fingers pressed and rubbed my g-spot, sending stars and bursts of pleasure through me. I sucked in a deep breath, then pushed out slightly when I could feel the beginnings of my deep, internal orgasm. I loved to squirt, it just felt so good, even if it was messy.

More burning tingles filled me and I closed my eyes, bright lights bursting behind my lids as Ramón sucked my clit hard and removed his fingers from my pussy. The instant release of the first burst of clear fluid leaving my body had my neck arching as my I turned my head back and forth in the pillows, my gasps and groans guttural and coming from somewhere deep in my throat.

Ramón, true to his word, began to lap at my pussy as he coaxed more cum out of me, my breasts shaking with the strength of his thrusts as he slid his fingers back inside me. When he latched onto my clit, flicking it as he continued to play with my oversensitive body, I screamed loud and long. The second orgasm ripped through me on the heels of the first. My legs shook hard enough that I felt like my fucking pussy was quivering. I begged Ramón to stop, that it was too much. Making a soothing hum, he lapped gently at me, easing my shaking body until only an occasional tremor flitted through my limbs.

I was sweaty, totally wrung out, and so high on endorphins my brain was in the clouds.

Ramón crawled up next to me, his face and shirt wet from my release. "You okay?"

The smile on my face must have been as dreamy as I felt, because I nodded, then stretched as he began to stroke my belly in a soothing motion that had me all but purring. "Mmmm-hmmm."

"Fuck, you're so beautiful."

"And you're amazing at eating pussy."

"Thank you. It's not something I do often. In fact, it's been years since I did that with a woman."

"Uh—what? You haven't gone down on a girl in years?"

"Nope. I told you I was an asshole, and I wasn't kidding."

I sputtered as I glared at him. "Why not? You seemed—well, you seemed to enjoy it."

"No, with you I fucking *loved* having you in my mouth, drowning in your juice." His gaze went heavy. He stroked my cheek gently with his rough fingertips, his touch as delicate as a butterfly's wings against my heated skin. "You taste delicious, better than any other pussy I've ever had. Perfect."

I tried to look away from him, but he held me chin and forced me to look at him when I spoke. "So, you're trying to tell me that I'm the first girl you've given oral sex to in *years*?"

Giving me an uneasy look, he nodded. "Yeah."

Taking a deep breath, I tried to give him the benefit of the doubt, to hear him out. "Why?"

"To me, that act is something special, something that I'll only give my woman."

"Your woman?"

"Yeah, baby. You're my woman." He kissed my nose, and I tried not to melt inside like a candle in warm sunlight.

"When did this happen?"

"Oh, we were always meant to happen. Should'a happened sooner, but I kinda fucked it up with my big mouth." He placed gentle kisses on my face, cuddling me close and making me feel amazingly safe and happy. "I want to kick myself in the ass for waiting so long to come claim you, but I had some shit to work out in my head."

"What do you mean?"

"We'll talk about it later, I promise. Right now, I want to just soak in the fact that you're in my arms, making my chest hurt with your beauty. And my dick feels like it's about to explode."

The soft brush of his lips felt wonderful against my neck as he kissed me while making these husky, deep noises in his chest that sent chills through me.

"What about you?"

I went to reach for his dick, more than eager to show him the pleasure that I could give him, but he grabbed my hand with a frown. "No."

"No?" The clouds began to lift from my thoughts, and I suddenly became aware that the bed beneath me was damp from my orgasms. "Why?"

Ramón sat up and took his damp shirt off, revealing all that delicious bronze skin of his I wanted to lick. "I'm not going to be one of your quick fucks."

"How dare you." I was tempted to smack him, but he seemed immune to my slaps. "Get the fuck out of my room."

The left side of his lips quirked up into a smirking smile, and I had to restrain myself from scratching that smile off his face. "I will, because I need to change clothes before we eat. Mark is my friend, but he doesn't need to know that you soaked me, and your bed, with your cum."

Embarrassment cleared my head further as I wondered if I'd just ruined Mark's beautiful comforter, and how I could smuggle it out and get it dry cleaned without him noticing. My debauched state began to register as well and I snatched at my clothes while glaring at Ramón. He merely watched me, that smirk of his still in place. "I'm not eating lunch with you."

"After lunch," he continued as if I hadn't said anything. "You need to Facetime with your mom. I talked to her earlier and let her know what was going on."

I struggled to regain control of my temper long enough to say, "You talked to my *mother*?"

"Yes, I talked to Paula. I didn't want her worrying about you when she wasn't able to get ahold of you." Guilt that I hadn't called my mom assailed me even as I tried to ignore Ramón when he caged me in his arms. "I didn't tell her everything about the attack. There are some things she's better off not knowing. It keeps her safe. She knows you're staying with Mark. I made sure she talked to him as well, then I did a walkthrough of Mark's place with my phone so she could see it. Oh, and she's talked with my Mom. I told her that the men Kayla brought home were drug addicts, and that they slapped you around a little, but then Mark arrived and saved the day. Thought that was better than telling her that you almost ended up as the star of a snuff film."

My stomach cramped up, and I allowed myself to lean back into Ramón. "Yeah, wouldn't want that."

"I told her who I am—"

Letting out a somewhat hysterical laugh I said, "It just occurred to me that I have no idea who you are."

Shuffling us over to the mirror above the dresser, he looked at me while he stood behind me, dwarfing me with his presence. Not only was he physically intimidating, he was older, probably late twenties maybe early thirties. A grown man for sure. I looked like a little doll next to his dark menace. He was all tattoos, dark tanned skin, and scars—someone that I should be scared of, but wasn't. It was hard to be frightened of a man whose entire being melted into something softer, warmer, when he looked at you. I've never had a man so focused on me like this before. It was disconcerting and somehow sweet.

"My name is Ramón Cordova. I'm thirty years old, never been married, no kids, and I'm CEO of the Investment arm of the Cordova Group."

I frowned up at him. "You're a CEO?"

A small smile cracked his face as he fingered his heavy gold ear gauge. "You find that hard to believe. What? You look at me and only see a criminal because I have a few prison tattoos? Kinda judgmental if you ask me, considering how offended you get when someone looks at you and only sees your body, not the beautiful soul within."

Okay, this guy totally threw me for a loop. On one hand, he was super sweet. On the other, he was a jerk. Also, unfortunately, he was right. I was judging him. "I guess you just don't seem like a nine to five kind of guy."

"I'm not. My mom was smart enough to recognize that when she put me in charge of Investments. Instead of spending all my time behind a desk, I get to travel the world, looking for the best people to support, finding the next must-have product. Since I took over four years ago, I've been all over, meeting some of the most brilliant, and flat-out crazy, people in the world."

"Wow," I whispered, slightly stunned as my idea of who this man was shifted. "That sounds amazing. I would love a job like that."

"Hannah said you're going to school to be a teacher, right?"

A feeling of melancholy hit me as I thought about my old life. Funny how that works, how your life becomes divided between terrible events. For me, it would forever be the day I discovered monsters were real and they roamed the earth. All my old dreams, my old life, seemed like a bunch of superficial bullshit. Suddenly depressed at how anchorless I felt, I sighed.

"Yeah."

He squeezed me a little tighter, making me look back into the mirror. "That wasn't a very enthusiastic *yeah*. Teaching not your thing?"

I sighed, wondering how honest I could be with this man, this intimate stranger—whether he'd understand. "It's not what I thought it would be."

He made a motion with his hands for me to go on.

"It's depressing." I blurted out. "These kids that I see? They're so bright, they have so much potential, and they're forced to fight and scrape just to get enough to survive, let alone thrive. Broken families, poverty, drug addiction—you name something awful, and these kids have had to live with it. It hurts my heart." Tears burned in my eyes, and I rubbed the back of my hand over my cheeks, not really seeing Ramón anymore. I stared at the far wall of my room, at the lovely floral watercolor framed between the two windows. "I mean, we struggled when I was growing up. Four kids were a lot for two working, middle-class parents to raise, but I've never had to deal with the reality of my mother being a prostitute, or my father being in prison for dealing drugs. Yeah, most of the kids I tutor are on the road to a bleak future, full speed ahead, but there are some really, really good kids out there that are fighting with everything they have to get out of the life they were born into. It's not fair."

I waited for him to tell me life wasn't fair or some other well-meaning nonsense. Instead, he took my hand in his. I gratefully linked my fingers with his, needing his warmth to steady me. "You're right, the world isn't fair. I know I come from money, but I've spent a lot of time in South America in some savagely poor countries. Places I wouldn't send my worst enemy. I've seen how bad poverty can get, and I know exactly what you're talking about. Those kids, none of 'em asked to be born into that filth. Shitty hand that life dealt them. All that potential, wasted. It's a fucking shame, which is why my parents, through the Cordova Group's philanthropic foundation, donate hundreds of thousands of dollars in scholarships every year to low income students. It's called the Maria's Hope Scholarship, named after my maternal grandmother. Have you heard of it?"

I gave him a watery smile, that feeling of living in a surreal bubble surfacing again. "I have heard of it. In fact, I've helped a couple of the students I tutor in AP classes fill out applications."

"Who are they? I'll make sure they get extra consideration."

I hesitated and tried to weigh my words carefully. "I don't know if I should tell you, if it would be fair."

"Are they good students?"

I thought of Javier, the son of an ex-prostitute dying of AIDS who worked two jobs part-time to help feed his family. And the sweet junior, Marci, with her sunny smile and kind heart, who lost her brother last year to a gang dispute. Each of them worked so hard to get where they were and stay out of trouble, sacrificed so much for a chance at something a lot of my friends take for granted, the opportunity to go to college. The Maria's Hope scholarship was highly coveted, because not only did it cover school, it also covered living expenses both for the student and their family. They wouldn't be living a baller lifestyle, but to a kid like Javier, not having to worry about paying rent would be a huge burden off his shoulders. And Marci could escape from the endless cycle of crime and violence that had swallowed her family whole.

Looking up at Ramón, I said without any hesitation, "They're amazing students."

"Then give me their names and let me help them." His dark brown eyes warmed to liquid toffee flecked with green as he smiled, making me melt into a puddle of happy hormones. "Think of how happy they'll be next time you see them, how much of a burden you'll be taking off their shoulders. You'll change their lives and help me get the money to where it will do the most good."

After I gave him the info, a little sparkle of happiness filled me and I impulsively hugged him tight. "Thank you."

"No, *mami*, thank you." He leaned down and kissed the tip of my nose. "Thank you. It's people like you who make a difference. You're a very special woman."

Flushing, I ducked my head, but continued to hold his hand. "No, I'm not.

"Yes, you are. You're making the world a better place by sharing your time with those kids. Hannah said you do tutoring in Phoenix, right? In some of the worst school districts, you go and bring hope to those kids who sometimes have no one looking out for them at home. Do you have any idea how hard it is to find hope in places like that? How much a good you do just by giving a shit?"

I swear my heart skipped a beat, and I blinked back tears. "It's nothing. People—"

"No, it's not nothing. It's everything." His thumb brushed over my lips as he cupped my jaw and looked me right in the eyes. "It fucking kills me that you can't see your own worth, but I see you, *mi corazón*, and I'll make sure you know every day how special you are."

Trying to rally some resistance, I protested, "We're strangers, Ramón. Strangers. You may know about me from Hannah, but I don't know anything about you other than the fact that you were a *massive* asshole when we first met."

"I wasn't at my best that day." He leaned down to rub his chin against the side of my messy bun. "That's why we're going to spend some time together. So we can get to know each other. Please, Joy? Spend the day with me. I promise we'll take care of everything that needs to be done, and I'll be a perfect gentleman."

I snorted but didn't step out of his arms. They felt so good, so strong and safe. Touching him soothed me, and my sex clenched as I allowed myself to grope his various hard, thick muscles. Despite his bulk, he moved with an almost feline grace. I had to resist the urge to rub my cheek against him like a kitten claiming a lion as her property.

"A perfect gentleman?" I rolled my eyes then yelped when he smacked my ass. "Hey, now!"

"I admit, I've been a little…intense with you." He ignored my snort and gently caressed the upper swell of my well-rounded butt. "But in my defense, I've been interested in meeting you for a while. The moment you walked away with my aunt, I realized what a dick I'd been. I wanted to run after you, but I was pretty sure my aunt would have shot me in the ass with buckshot."

I giggled, remembering his cool and poised Aunt Doris. She'd been intimidating. She had the same powerful aura that her sister Judith possessed, but her strength was different. Quieter, if that made any sense. She didn't freak out when I told her about Jacob's screwing up, but I had no doubt by the time we were done meeting that Jacob would be taken care of. Whatever she said to him must have worked, because he was doing great academically—even if he seemed to avoid me after our tutoring was done.

"Would have served you right, but your aunt didn't strike me as the kind of woman who carried around a shotgun."

An odd look came over his face before he smiled. "You'd be surprised."

I rolled my eyes. "But *why* do you want to spend time with me? Don't you have better things to do? Like your job? Certainly there's some great gadget awaiting your approval."

Running his hand through his shoulder length black hair, he smirked. "I'm sure there is, but you're more important."

"You confuse me." I released a soft sigh, unable to resist the urge to stroke his heavily muscled forearm, my fingers trailing over the light dusting of soft black hair. "I don't understand you, and I feel like I'm never on firm ground when I'm around you."

"Good, 'cause I can't sweep you off your feet if they're still on the ground." He gave me a wink as I groaned, then one more squeeze before releasing me. "Get cleaned up, and I'll meet you downstairs."

He walked across the room, all that delicious muscle flexing with each stride. That ass of his...it was perfect, and I regretted not giving it a good squeeze while I could. He grabbed his shirt, then grinned at me as my face heated. My sex still pulsed with the aftereffects of all those amazing orgasms, and I crossed the room, meeting him at the door.

"Wait." I leaned up on my tippy toes, placing a kiss on his firm lips before pulling back with a small smile. "Thank you for the orgasms."

His eyes sparkled, and he threw back his head as he laughed.

"Anytime, *mami*. I mean that. If we're out in public, and you tell me you need to cum, I'll find a way to make it happen."

I blinked up at him, taken aback by Ramón openly talking about one of my favorite fantasies. I have no idea why, but I find the idea of secretly having sex in public to be exciting. I've never done anything like that—making out in the back of a car doesn't count—but, oh, how I love the idea of doing something so naughty where I could get caught. And punished.

"What are you thinking about?" Ramón asked with a soft growl. "It has your nipples hard as bullets."

I crossed my arms with a nervous laugh. "Uh, nothing. I have to get cleaned up, again, so I'll see you downstairs!"

His laughter receded behind me as I practically ran to the bathroom. "Someday, I'll find out what you were thinking about, and I'll make it happen."

Chapter 5
Ramón

After throwing on a new pair of jean shorts and a black t-shirt, I wasn't surprised in the least to find Mark sitting in his kitchen with his gun pointed in my direction.

In his early thirties with flecks of grey in his short light brown hair, Mark could be one scary son of a bitch when he wanted, but even if he had a gun pointed at my head, I wasn't worried.

His mouth barely moved as he muttered, "I should shoot you right in your dumb ass."

Normally, I'd be pissed that he was pulling a gun on me, but he had good reason to be angry. I'd broken into his home and violated his trust in me. While I may not give one flying monkey fuck for most of society's rules, I did follow my own personal moral code. My code clearly stated that you did not break into a friend's house.

Lifting my hands in the air in mock surrender, I made my way over to the stainless-steel coffee pot sitting on the deep chocolate and gold-flecked granite counter tops. "I'm sorry, I'm sorry. I couldn't be without her last night."

With a sigh, Mark holstered his gun then leaned back in his white leather chair in the ultra-modern white and brown kitchen. He looked like shit, dark circles beneath his bloodshot silver eyes and lines of strain around his mouth. I took in his worn jeans and the stain on his t-shirt along with the harsh slope of his shoulders. No doubt, he was hurting after the fight he'd had while rescuing Joy and Hannah from Manny and his dirty fucks. My fingers tightened on the edge of the counter, my knuckles white as I reined my irritation in as the fact that I'd almost lost Joy put me instantly on edge.

It wasn't easy, but the knowledge that Joy would be joining us soon made it easier to put a leash on my hair-trigger temper than usual.

"I knew you wouldn't be able to stay away from her."

Rubbing his face, Mark shook his head. "I find one camera in my house, and you will regret it. If I find any in my bedroom or bathroom, I'll shoot you in the head myself, you sick fuck."

Shaking my head and fighting my grin, I grabbed a coffee cup from the cupboard. "Trust me, I have no desire to watch you take your morning shit. Besides, I wouldn't do that to you."

He arched a brow at me. "Just like you wouldn't break into my house?"

"Only reason I was able to sneak in was because you were playing that game you're addicted to. Besides, I didn't really break in. You gave me a set of keys when you moved in."

He rolled his eyes, but some of the tension left his jaw. "So you could take care of shit for me while I was out of the country on a job, not show up in the middle of the night for a booty call."

I froze, then made sure I had his gaze. "Watch your mouth. That's my future wife you're talking about, not a booty call."

"You," he pointed his finger at me with a grimace, "are completely screwed in the head."

I couldn't deny it, so instead I changed the subject. "Admit it, the only reason I was able to get in here without you noticing was you were playing that fucking game all night again. Did you and the Hobbits go to the Candy Cane Forest and slay the Jabberwocky for its magic skin flute?"

He gave me two middle fingers, and I laughed.

Mark played games online like it was his second job. He had a whole group of people he regularly gamed with, but had never met, and they would play for hours on end. Leo and I gave him shit about it, mainly because, when you looked at the man, you'd think his hobby was bashing skulls in real life, not going on raids with a group of elves.

"Piss off." His gaze went to the stairs. "How's Joy doing?"

"Okay, I think. All things considered."

Mark's mouth hardened as he leaned forward. "What the hell are you doing here, Ramón?"

"You really have to ask me that?"

Lowering his voice, he kept his gaze directed at the stairs. "She's a very sweet, young girl."

"Yes, she is."

"You sure now is the right time to… pursue this? She's been through a lot in the last few days and may not be ready for…everything. Maybe you should back off, give her some room to get over the trauma."

I shot him a look that let him know he was treading on thin ground by suggesting I stay away from Joy. "You're wrong about that. She's mine; she belongs to me, and there's no way I'm letting her handle this alone. You understand how fucking fast the world can take people away. You, better than anyone, should know that time, and how you spend it, is the most precious commodity there is."

He visibly flinched, and I felt like a dick for bringing up his late wife. "I get it."

"Look, nobody is going to protect her, watch over her, take care of her like I can. No one. She was born to be mine. I will do whatever it takes to keep her and make her happy."

Mark must have picked up on my tone, because his gaze hardened further. "Do I need to worry about being around her alone?"

For a second, I wondered what the hell he was implying, then realized he was asking in a roundabout way if I'd started her dose of D128. "No. She's not ready for that yet."

"Has Leo been alone with her?"

"No."

His posture eased, and he gave me a small smile. "Decided to try things the old-fashioned way?"

Mark wasn't a fan of my mother's insistence that Joy would have to be brainwashed into the same loyalty that Hannah had. I might have objected to it, if I hadn't seen firsthand the difference Leo's mental tricks had made in his girlfriend's life. Hannah had gone from an insecure doormat to a blossoming young woman who practically glowed with happiness. I never thought Leo would have it in him to be able to connect with a woman on such a deep level, but he surprised me. In their own fucked up way, they were perfect for each other.

I flipped Mark off before grabbing a *SpongeBob SquarePants* mug from the sleek white cabinet. "Look, she deserves to be treated like a lady."

"Yes, she does. She's a keeper, but you need to go slow. Delicate touch."

I cut a look at him, but by the bland expression on his face, he didn't appear interested in Joy in the least. Not that I'd expected him to be. Other than one night stands here and there, Mark led a very solitary life. The death of his wife had damaged him in such a way, I wondered if he'd ever be in a relationship again. Well, a relationship with a woman outside of his video games. I'd occasionally played with him before, and there was this chick on his team who had the sexiest fucking voice I'd ever heard, but talking to some unknown female while you hacked up trolls online wasn't the same as having a real woman in your life and on your lap.

"Trust me, *amigo*, I'm more than aware of all the shit she's been through. Right now, I'm handling her with kid gloves." I poured myself a cup of coffee and added a dash of cream to it.

Mark slowly arched one eyebrow. "Breaking into my home isn't a delicate touch."

"Fine, delicate for me." I grinned and took a sip of the perfectly bitter brew.

Joy's voice, raised in a happy chirp of, "Aren't you beautiful! What a sweet girl. You must be Honey," came from the stairs followed by the sound of dog nails clicking on the hardwood floor above.

My heart thumped, and I got this weird, tight sensation in my middle that I couldn't identify. The anticipation of seeing her heated my blood, and my cock tried to harden. Shit, my whole body tensed. It took everything in me to resist crossing the room and following the sound of her voice. I needed to give her some space, let her have some downtime with the dog. God knows, she'd had enough chaos in her life, and there was something healing about spending time with a good dog.

From Joy's delighted chatter, she adored Honey. The baby talk she used with the dog had me laughing quietly. She called the pit bull *sweetie cakes yummy yummys* and *my little gummy wummy tummy bear*. While it was funny, she'd also lowered her voice into this sexy croon that made me think about the feeling of her body against mine, all that soft warmth beneath me, at my mercy. I wondered how I was going to keep my hands off her, because I craved the feeling of her in my arms again, bringing me peace.

Mark smiled as Joy made a fuss over Honey. Technically, the white and tan pit bull was Hannah and Leo's dog, but she usually spent as much time with Mark as she did Leo and

Hannah. In his previous life, before his faith in humanity was lost, Mark was a world-renowned police dog trainer, as was his wife. After her passing, he said he couldn't bear to train without her, so seeing him so bonded with Honey gave me hope that he'd start living life again instead of just enduring it.

When Joy entered the room with Honey at her side, I sucked in a quick breath. Fuck, she was so beautiful it made my dick and my heart hurt. She'd changed into a pair of dark navy capris pants and a red silk blouse with a neckline that exposed a good two inches of her more than generous cleavage. There was something almost retro about the look, reinforcing her hourglass shape and tiny waist with a metallic gold belt. I wondered what bra she was wearing that lifted her tits like that and held them so close together, creating that deep valley that I wanted to fuck at some point in the future. My balls tightened as I imagined her wearing one of the lacy bits of lingerie that would show the dark shadows of her large nipples. The sun hit her golden curls, piled high on her head and made them glow as she stopped at the kitchen table and smiled shyly at Mark, a hot blush staining her face.

"Um, morning."

To his credit, Mark didn't say anything to Joy that might embarrass her. He gave her a small smile then lifted his chin toward the stove. "There's pancakes and hash browns in there, if you're hungry."

"Famished." She smiled then avoided even looking at me as she grabbed a plate from next to the stove and went to open the oven.

"Just to let you know..." Mark continued. Joy got her breakfast together while totally pretending I wasn't there. "You can change that room however you want. My sister decorated it, so you won't be hurting my feelings if you don't want to live in a florist shop. I was overseas on business when she did it, so I came back to find that Laura Ashley nightmare."

Laughing, Joy shook her head and gave Mark a wide smile that sent a prick of jealousy through me. "No, it's fine. It's very pretty...and pink. Besides, I'll only be here for a few weeks until I can find a new place, so changing anything would be silly."

"Stay as long as you want," Mark said while ignoring the sharp look I sent him. "Seriously, I'm never home. When I am, there's only Honey to talk to, so it gets lonely. I have to go hang out with Hannah and Leo if I want conversation that isn't in dog."

Joy grinned. "I'm a good roommate, I swear. Ask Hannah. I always clean up after myself, and if you have female company over and want your privacy, I know how to make myself scarce. I work weird hours, in addition to going to school, so we'll be like two ships passing in the night."

"Well, I don't have any female company coming over that I'd need that kind of private time with." He gave her an easy grin, but his eyes shifted to me, letting me know he was about to fuck with me. "What about you? Any boyfriend in the picture?"

"Nope, I'm single."

I gritted my teeth before growling out, "You are *not* single. You're with me."

That defiant look that I was becoming very familiar with flared to life in her eyes. "No, I'm not."

"Yes, you are."

Turning her nose up at me—*the little brat*—she forked some food into her mouth and chewed before pointing in my direction. "Just because you say it doesn't make it true."

Licking my lips slowly, I grinned at her. "I can still taste you. Like sweet, tart peaches."

"Ramón." Mark groaned.

Ignoring my friend, I narrowed my eyes and let little Miss Joy see just how serious I was about the situation. Never before had I felt the need to publicly claim a woman like this. But with Joy, I wanted my name tattooed on her body, maybe over the curve of her ass so I could grab it and stare at my mark while I fucked her doggy style. My dick started to ache, something that was becoming the norm for when I was around Joy, and I let every bit of my lust for her show in my eyes.

"Make no mistake, Joy, you're taken in every way a woman possibly can be. I'm your man now, and you belong to me."

She was adorable as her face went red. She stuttered out, "You're such a misogynistic asshole!"

"Don't worry, I'll make up for it with multiple orgasms."

Joy gasped in outrage, her cheeks darkening with a pretty pink blush. Mark shoved his chair away from the table. "And, on that note, I'm out. Oh, and please don't fuck in my kitchen. It's not hygienic."

Watching Joy turn almost crimson with embarrassment, I fought back a grin. "Eat your breakfast. We've got places to go."

I've never seen a woman sputter before, but Joy was so mad, she couldn't even speak in full sentences, only managing a steady stream of swear words in an increasingly loud voice that ended with, "I wasn't born with enough middle fingers to properly express to you how I feel about you! You are such a sexist dick!"

Calmly finishing my coffee, I rose and went to the sink to wash it out. "If I can interrupt your hissy fit, we really do need to get going."

She sucked in a breath, and I tensed, waiting for something to come flying at my back. "How dare you!"

After drying my hands, I decided it was time for a little lesson. I couldn't do much physically—she was no doubt sore, and I hadn't forgotten the sight of her bruised torso and ribs—but I needed her to know that I'd only put up with so much. Being a brat was one thing, but being a bitch was something else entirely. I studied her closely, noting the sheen of tears in her eyes and the way her lower lip was trembling, then internally sighed.

Time for a little tenderness with my beautiful girl.

Lowering my voice, I made sure I held her gaze as I said, "I understand you're overwhelmed, and normally I wouldn't ask this of you. Trust me when I say I'd rather spend the day in bed with you, but Leo needs my help, and Hannah needs yours." Grasping her chin in my hand, I absently noted the way her pupil's dilated as I brushed my lips over hers. "We're going to see the dean of the University of Arizona, so we can arrange for Hannah to take her class online while she heals. I need you there with me because you probably know her schedule better than anyone. You'll have to help me make sure they're treating her fairly."

Tears shimmered in her eyes, and I stroked one away as it trailed down her soft cheek.

"We're going to help Hannah?"

"Yes."

However pissed she might be at me, I knew her need to take care of Hannah would override her anger. "Okay."

I brushed my lips over hers. "Okay."

Two hours later, I held Joy's hand as we walked out of the Dean's office, her head held high even though she gripped my fingers tight enough to hurt. The Dean had positively fawned over her, while simultaneously shitting himself every time he looked in my direction. I'd dressed down on purpose, foregoing my usual suit in favor of something that would blend in with the ASU college crowd a bit more. Not that it had worked. People stared and I felt a deep sense of pride at how many men cast my woman a brief, longing gaze before quickly looking away.

Joy was, without a doubt, the absolute shit.

The bright Arizona sunlight hit the red silk of her blouse and made it glow, highlighting her exaggerated curves and feminine figure.

They might not know who I was, but they knew better than to eye fuck Joy, even if she was so sexy it made me fight getting hard. Her breasts jiggled with her every step. Because the neckline of her shirt was lower than what she normally wore, the tops of her breasts bounced every time her gold platform wedge sandals hit the concrete. The shoes were tall enough to bring the top of her head up to just under my chin, and I liked the way they made her hips sway when she moved. Damn, her tiny waist flared out into a pair of heavenly, thick hips, and I had to look away before I got a noticeable bulge. I'd worn a tight pair of boxer briefs to try and minimize the visible signs of an erection, but they'd only do so much.

Late afternoon sun beat down on us, and I glanced over at Joy, who was doing her best to ignore everyone staring at us.

"You hungry?"

She slipped on a pair of designer sunglasses and gave me an angry look then said in a low voice, "Why was the dean afraid of you?"

"He's afraid of me," I smiled and lied to her face, feeling like an asshole but unable to trust her with the truth, "because my family donates a great deal of money to the University directly, even more money in the form of research grants, and through the various scholarships we fund. Like the ones we gave your students. He knows that if he pisses me off, we'll take our money elsewhere."

"Right," she muttered, once again lifting her chin minutely as she ignored everyone watching us walk by. "Must be nice to have that kind of power."

"Considering I was able to use it to help right an injustice that both you and Hannah suffered, and provide a chance at a life those kids deserve, it is nice to have that kind of power."

The mention of the scholarships distracted her, and I let out a mental sigh of relief. She didn't need to know that the Dean at one time had owed my family a great deal of money for smuggling in a cancer drug for his wife from our lab in El Salvador. A cancer drug that was still going through testing with the FDA, wasting time he didn't have. Another thing he didn't have was money, because her repeated treatments for stomach cancer had drained them to the point of bankruptcy. Lacking the funds to get what he so desperately needed, he approached my mother and pleaded his case. She, being the master manipulator that she was, bought his loyalty that day by saving his wife's life. A loyalty that had been tested many times over.

I bet he regretted not taking out a third mortgage on his house to pay for the pills, because my mother's price was much higher.

Allowing the girls to take classes online was probably the easiest thing we'd ever asked of him, and my treatment of Joy seemed to puzzle him. At first, he'd appeared angry as he stared at Joy—angry at me in a way I hadn't seen before. It was probably from the huge bruise on Joy's temple that inched down the side of her face to her cheekbone. Despite her attempts to disguise it with makeup, the dark mark still drew the eye.

During our talk, it no doubt became obvious that I was wrapped firmly around Joy's pretty little finger. I've never been an affectionate man in public with anyone but my family, so I'm sure it threw the Dean to see me hanging on her every word. Still, I wonder how close he'd been to calling the police before he figured out I would never hurt Joy. I hated the bruises covering her pretty golden skin, but the experimental healing cream we'd used on her was doing its job and healing her much quicker than normal. Dealing in illegal drugs made by the best mad scientists in the world had its benefits.

I vowed that the only marks she'd wear in the future would be ones made while I fucked her until all her worries went away. Her mind was always moving in hyper drive, thinking ten things at once, and I often wondered how she didn't drive herself crazy. She had to be busy, had to be doing something, and she collapsed exhausted into bed each night. It had both surprised and gratified me this morning when she'd slept for so long in my arms, barely stirring as I got up to use the bathroom. She'd been so soft, squishy, but in the best way. Women hear that word and they freak the fuck out, thinking it's something negative, when that couldn't be further from the truth. Curvy women felt so fuckin' good to hold tight, and Joy was just about as sweet of an armful as any man could ever hope to have.

And she was smart, so smart.

While we were with the Dean, I let her do most of the talking and just sat back, enjoying the show as my strong, determined woman made sure her best friend was taken care of. She emphasized Hannah's good grades, how she worked to support herself, and how Hannah was a good person. I could tell Joy was nervous, because she didn't seem to notice that the Dean had already agreed to give Hannah the time. In fact, he gave Joy a month off to recover from her injuries as well, telling her that she could do her assignments online, and someone would take over her tutoring.

I couldn't help but smile as she surprised the Dean by arguing that she still had to make her tutoring sessions, explaining that she was the only one who was giving them solid college advice. The school guidance counselors were already overwhelmed with kids in real danger of dropping out of school who needed their help, so Joy spent two hours every other Thursday after school doing college prep classes for the kids who had the grades to go. I enjoyed watching the Dean's eyes go wide as he realized that, yes, even though Joy was as cute as a fucking Playboy Bunny, she also had a big brain in her pretty head and a big heart to match.

Giving her a small smile as we walked beneath a row of trees, I said in a low voice, "By the way, you did great back there. You were very impassioned in your friend's defense."

She turned away as I held her hand, then rubbed the back of my hand with her thumb as we walked past a gawking trio of girls in short shorts. "I think I spewed verbal diarrhea all over him."

Laughter burst from me, and she shot me a quick grin. "No,

you were fine."

"When I feel strongly about something I tend to get very…excited about it."

We turned around the corner of the building, and I spotted my red Maserati GranTurismo being guarded by one of my men, keeping the college students at bay.

"Well, you got Hannah all the time off she needs, and yourself, as well."

"It was nice of the Dean to offer to send a bunch of people from the register's office in my place at the high school. They'll be able to give those kids so much valuable advice. Really, thank you for all your help. You have no idea how much what you're doing is going to change people's lives."

"I know you don't believe me when I say this, 'cause you don't know me well enough yet, but there isn't anything I wouldn't do to make you happy."

A soft pink blush stole over her cheeks, and she lightly swatted my arm. "Shut up."

A big smile curved her lips, and I couldn't stop myself from lifting her up for a brief, soft kiss before setting her back down on her feet.

Wobbling a bit on her heels for a second, she blushed as we resumed walking. "What was that for?"

"You're adorable."

She slugged me lightly on the arm. "Stop."

"You don't like compliments, do you?"

"Not really."

"Why?"

"They make me uncomfortable."

"Someone saying something nice about you makes you uncomfortable?"

Her shoulders drew up a bit as she tensed. "I know it sounds weird, but yeah."

"Why?"

"I don't know."

Her tone and body language were evasive, so I slowed our walk as we approached my car, heat from the pavement baking us beneath the bright desert sun. "What don't you like about it?"

"Why is this such a big deal to you?"

"Because I'm going to compliment you a lot, and I don't

want it to make you uneasy. I want it to make you feel good. That's why I point out the things I like about you, the ones I appreciate, because I want you to feel good, not bad."

Sighing, she scanned the crowd standing about twelve feet back from my car, taking pictures with their cell phones. I have to admit, my ride was sexy and built to attract attention. Kind of like my girl. Watching the boy's eyes light up when they got an eyeful of my woman never failed to send a spark of pride through my chest. Sexist, misogynistic, whatever—I was proud that my woman was beautiful inside and out. Even as she aged, as time wore on and our bodies changed, I would always find her stunning. I knew this deep in my gut, and it only deepened my resolve to win her over.

"Can we talk about this later?" Her voice was tight as she pretended to not see the people watching us like we were some live reality show for their viewing pleasure.

She was clearly uncomfortable being the center of attention, but she had to learn she belonged to me, that she was my queen now, and she deserved to be treated and worshiped like one. People would look at her everywhere she went, and not just because she was with me. They'd look because my woman was so hot, it was hard to believe she was real. And she was all mine, but I had to treat her right.

Instead of letting her get her own door, I escorted her around to her side of the car then blocked her body with my own as she slid in, a habit ingrained in me by my mother. Some people might think that just because I enjoy beating the fuck out of people for a living, I'm a savage, but I'm not—thanks to my mother. Say what you will about Judith Cordova, but she tried her best to civilize me and my brothers. It wasn't easy, because all three of us inherited both her brains and her crazy streak, but between her and my father, I knew how to treat a lady.

I'd just never bothered to do this for any woman but Joy.

While I may rile her up, yanking her chain just so I could kiss the anger off her pouty little lips, I would never disrespect her in public.

I wanted to lean forward and steal a kiss. Instead, I gently brushed my lips over the delicate hinge of her jaw then her bruised cheek, and wished I could kill the motherfuckers who'd hurt her all over again.

Sweetest Obsession

As I slid into the driver's seat, two black, highly modified street bikes slowly rolled up behind us. I wanted for the hand sign from each of them that would confirm they were my men before turning my car on. The deep, rumbling purr of the engine vibrated the cream leather seats slightly as I pulled out of our spot.

Looking behind us, Joy absently took off her sunglasses, "So, you have at least two guards following you at all times?"

Actually, I had four guards following us at all times. Two for me and two for her, but she wasn't ready for that truth yet. I held her hand in my own and reveled in softness of her skin. So smooth and lightly tanned, with her golden hair and skin, she radiated light that was strong enough to banish even my darkness. I was so fucking lucky to have her in my life, and I couldn't imagine living in a world where I didn't own every inch of her beautiful mind and body.

She turned back around and sighed before rubbing her temples. "I don't know how you can live like this, with everyone watching you all the time. It's so weird."

"Weird for you, but normal for me. I've always had bodyguards. Hell, my nanny was a former highly decorated Russian soldier and a complete badass. When I was seven, someone tried to kidnap me, and she took a bullet in the leg protecting me."

"Holy shit. Was she okay?"

I nodded. "Yes, and she works for my family to this day. She's in her seventies now, but she helps run our charitable organizations. You should meet her. I know she'd be interested to hear your views on the different programs we sponsor. You're wicked smart, and I know Ula, my former nanny, would enjoy the help. We can even call it an internship."

"I'm not working for you," she said in a cold voice.

While I loved her temper, she did tend to jump to the wrong conclusions a lot. "No, you're not. You'd be working beneath my mother's branch of the company, not mine. She doesn't play favorites when it comes to the welfare of the family dynasty."

"Dynasty, huh?"

I shrugged. "Fine, my parent's empire."

Giggling, she leaned her head back against the seat and closed her eyes, entrancing me with her half smile. "I'm not sure if that's any better than dynasty."

The big engine hummed as I passed a slow moving car, my attention once again on the road. "Whatever you want to call it, I know you'd be an asset to the company. We'd be lucky to have you."

I darted a glance at her as we came to a stop sign, more people watching us from the sidewalks as we rolled past.

She slipped her glasses down so I could see those lovely green eyes of hers, and the hesitate hope filling them hurt my heart. "Really?"

"Absolutely. You're very smart, Joy, and compassionate as well as being honest. That's a hard combination to find, a once in a lifetime type of thing. I'm known for my ability to recognize talent and you, sweetheart, are about as talented as they come."

It bothered me that her first reaction was to deflect the praise. "Ramón, I'm not that special."

I reached over and gave her hip a little pinch, hard enough to make her squeak. "Stop it."

Smacking my arm, she growled at me. "What the hell?"

"Every time you put yourself down, I'm going to pinch somewhere on that curvy body of yours."

I didn't miss the way her nipples hardened as we merged into slow moving traffic, my guards easily keeping up with us. "I wasn't putting myself down."

"Joy, you just said you weren't anything special. That's bullshit."

With a sigh, she looked out the window. "Where are we going now?"

"We can either go home, or we can go through your stuff in storage."

Her shoulders slumped. "I'm sorry, but can we just go home? I'm not up for all that right now."

"Home it is. Are you okay?"

"Yeah, just tired. I need to decompress a little bit."

"No problem, *mami*. Put on something you like, and we'll chill and listen to music, okay?"

"Okay."

After placing a soft kiss on my cheek, she turned on the radio. I allowed a comfortable silence to fall between us, already planning the next step in my seduction.

Sweetest Obsession

By the time we pulled up to the construction zone that was the site of my future house, Joy had fallen asleep in the deep leather bucket seat. I already had the builders sent home for the day, and I smiled at the progress they'd made. All the exterior walls were up, and they'd finished installing the windows and doors. Inside, the drywall was almost completed, and the tubs installed. Some rooms had even been painted and decorated. It was a modest house by my parent's standards, only eight bedrooms and ten baths, but it was the perfect home for Joy.

It should be, because I'd built it to her dream house tastes.

Hannah loved to talk about Joy, and it hadn't been hard to steer her into a conversation about what Joy's dream house would be like. I'd been surprised at first by her preference, but the more I thought about it, the more sense it made. Joy's love of 80's John Hughes movies had given her a taste in homes that was more Midwestern than Southwest. Getting it right had required no small amount of effort on my part, but it had to be perfect for her. Even when I was lying to myself and pretending I was finally building my own place near Leo, I customized every inch of it to her tastes.

God bless Pintrest inspiration boards. They made it a hell of a lot easier to know what a woman likes and wants. Leo clued me into them after I started to get serious about Joy, and I'd spent many hours poring through her dreams, picking out her fantasies and making them real. That's not to say I hadn't thrown my own personal tastes into the design, but I wanted a place she'd feel instantly at home. Somewhere she'd never want to leave.

You didn't usually see Tudor-style places in Phoenix, but that's exactly what I'd built for her. Three stories tall, with cream stucco and black wooden beams; it was surrounded with the old growth trees I'd bought this lot for. Joy was always complaining that everything was so brown, so I'd spent a fucking fortune on genetically engineered grass in the backyard surrounding the pool. Emerald green and soft, vegetation which thrived in the desert conditions—while not technically legal in the US, it gave my girl the green she craved.

I tried to keep from waking her as I scooped her up in my arms, but she came to with a gasp and tried to scramble away from me, knocking her sunglasses off in her haste.

"Whoa, easy, sweetheart."

"Jesus Christ, Ramón," she gasped as I slowly slid her down my body, relishing the drag of her large breasts. "You scared the shit out of me."

"Sorry, I was trying to keep from waking you."

"It's okay." She frowned as she scanned the construction site. "Where are we?"

"My home."

"Wait, I thought you were taking me to *my* home—or Mark's home. Whatever."

"Nope."

She huffed with annoyance, but I didn't miss the excited gleam in her eyes as she turned and took in what I hoped would be the place where we would raise our family. "This is yours?"

"Yeah."

"Wow, I mean…wow." Her arms dropped to her sides as a smile began to curve her lips and round her cheeks. "This is your house? You live here?"

"Not yet. As you can see, it's still under construction. I'm staying at my parents place until it's done." Giving her a wink, I took her hand. "I hope you don't think I'm a loser for still crashing on my mom's couch."

She grinned up at me, and my chest felt tight and funny. "Nah, we're good."

Her stomach audibly growled, and I tugged her after me. "Come on, lunch is waiting for us out back."

I was eager to show her the backyard I'd designed with our future family in mind. Lots of grass to soften the blow if my future kids fell while playing, good size wrought iron safety fences around the edges of the hill the house was situated on. I'd bought up twenty acres adjacent to Leo's place. All the mansions around us were on large plots of land, so there was a lot of uninterrupted wilderness from our view. Plus, Thomas was checking out some land adjacent to mine and thinking of building as well.

The wind seemed softer as it blew through the filter of mature, healthy vegetation surrounding the house. In addition to the grass, I'd also had some genetically modified honeysuckle and ivy planted against the house—drought, disease, and pest resistant enough to survive the harsh climate. I had to admit, I never thought I'd enjoy this small oasis as much as I do. Something about all the greenery and nature calms me.

A bright blue pool shaped like a long oval took up the center part of the big yard, with retractable iron gates that went underground and became flush with the travertine stones surrounding the pool. When we had kids we'd use the railings to keep our little ones safe, but for right now I wanted Joy to have the full effect of the view and gardens. I knew she liked it when she froze behind me, then let out a soft sigh.

"Oh, Ramón, this is amazing. A little bit of heaven in the desert. I always dreamed of growing up in a home like this, one of those places you'd see on TV with the big family and lots of land. You don't find a lot of trees this big in Phoenix."

"This used to be a giant orchard that stretched for miles back when water wasn't a big deal. This whole area was green with peach, plum, and apple trees. These are all that are left, the rest destroyed long ago by water restrictions. We use a special cistern system here that traps run off water into huge tanks below us that we use to water the gardens. That water then gets filtered back into the cisterns through yet more drains. It's a new desert friendly watering systems, one that doesn't use a single drop of city water."

She gazed up at me with a small, amused smile. "Wow, you're really into this stuff."

"Of course I am. Using land effectively is a big deal. If we can harvest the rain and use it to water public gardens in an effective manner, we could feed hundreds of thousands of people. Food, especially fresh and healthy food, will become increasingly scarce as we pollute the fuck out of our planet and poison our oceans."

"That's a cheerful thought. So there's no hope?"

"There's always hope, as long as you're alive." I brushed my hand slowly down her soft cheek, loving the way her blush seemed to follow my touch. "You're someone worth fighting for."

Clearly uncomfortable and fighting a smile, she moved away from me on the pretense of admiring a rose bush leftover from when this place was the site of a farm house.

We were standing on the brick stairs that went down the side of the house, following the curve of the land until it leveled out in the backyard again. Brass lanterns had been set up at various points around the property, and at night they gave everything a golden glow. She was a few steps ahead of me, and the almost innocent pleasure shining from her eyes made me feel ten feet tall. I'd managed to make her happy, to please her, and my heart filled with an unfamiliar, addictive pleasure unlike anything I've ever experienced.

"Ramón," her soft, sweet voice killed me. "It's so…everything. It's just—it's perfect. You have the perfect home."

Fighting the urge to strut like a proud rooster, I gave her a small nod. "I'm glad you like it. Come on, there's more to see."

I pulled her past the pool pausing only a few seconds as she ohhed and ahhed over different aspects of the yard and home. Having her see all the things I'd bought for her, had built in her honor, and watching her love every one had me just about ready to burst with pride. Happiness radiated from her. I struggled to process an odd inner euphoria as I pointed out a small sculpture of a garden fairy, which made her clap her hands and smile over how cute it was. Every time she grinned, it was a pleasant shock to my heart. I absently rubbed my chest while she giggled. Her sassy mouth and smart mind were some of the things I enjoyed most about her, but I also liked it when she let her guard down. Let herself relax around me. Let me see the real Joy, who was far more complex than the image she projected to the world.

By the time we made it to the blue and white gingham blanket spread on the grass beneath a mature ash tree, she was beaming. I'd never seen a woman so happy that she glowed, but fuck if looking at Joy wasn't like bathing in the warmth of the sun. My reaction to this girl was insane, and I knew the kind of chemistry we had was a once in a lifetime thing. The shade dappled in Joy's brilliant curls, making a halo of bronze and gold around her angelic face. All the green around us somehow softened the desert air, and I drank in the priceless sensation of peace as it settled over me, deepening my devotion to the woman who gave me purpose.

I'd slay armies, give her the world, all for the pleasure of her smile.

"You had a picnic made for us?"

Her excited squeal and little hop made both my heart and my

dick happy. "Thought you might enjoy some downtime."

Kicking off her shoes, she took a seat on the massive blanket and lifted the silver dome off her serving tray. "Wow, this looks amazing."

I'd had the chef make us club sandwiches and fresh potato chips. "Glad you like it."

She grabbed a sandwich then took a big bite, her eyes rolling back with pleasure. "Oh my god, this is so good. Totally one of my favorite meals. How did you know?"

"Lucky guess," I lied, not wanting her to know the depth of my obsession yet.

We spent the remainder of the meal talking about the house and my plans for it. By the time we were done, I'd shoved the remains of our meal off the blanket and laid back with my hand on my full stomach. Instead of feeling sleepy, I was energized and awake while Joy looked like she was about to pass out in the shade beneath the big tree.

"It's so quiet here," she murmured with half-closed eyes. "I'd gotten so used to the city, I forgot what quiet was like. Not silence, but quiet. The sound of the wind and trees instead of traffic. When I was really young, my *abuela* used to live on the outskirts of town, and at her house after school I always liked to take a moment to go outside and enjoy the quiet of the desert. Well, as quiet as it could be with my brother and sisters running around."

"Tell me about your family."

"I love them," she said in a sleepy murmur. "But they drive me crazy."

"How so?"

She turned her head a little then reached out and cupped my face with her small hand, rubbing at my whiskers with her thumb. "You know, just family stuff."

I wanted her to open up to me, to tell me more, but I didn't force the issue. She obviously didn't want to talk about it, and I already had a file on Joy that contained enough info on her childhood for me to piece shit together. I knew she got along with her brother Matt and her younger sister Winter, but that Joy's oldest sister Brittney was a complete bitch who poisoned everything she touched. According to Hannah, Brittney would endlessly torment Joy. Because Joy didn't want to sound like a tattletale, she just sucked it up and didn't tell anyone about Brittney's endless cutting remarks.

I ached to fix the damage her older sister had done, but it wasn't the right time yet. I gave myself the mental deadline of having our home ready to move into before I proposed to her. But once that happened, I knew my mother wouldn't allow me to put off programming Joy any longer. I wasn't ready to take that step with her anytime soon. The longer I stretched out our courtship, the more time I bought myself to make her fall in love with me. Leo said over and over again that I couldn't make Joy love me, and I didn't want to. I wanted to win her heart all on my own, not with the aid of hypnosis and aphrodisiacs. For a moment, the craziness of my life crashed over me as I allowed my gaze to roam over her generous curves while I contemplated the best way to brainwash her without taking away her free will and inner strength.

I didn't want to harm Joy; I wanted to heal her.

She gently ran her thumb over my cheek to my lips, then she traced the bow of my mouth.

"You're so handsome," she said in a soft, gentle voice. "I hated that about you."

"What?"

"When we first met, you were such an asshole, but you were so hot. I hated that I found you attractive."

With a groan, I placed my forearm over my eyes so I wouldn't have to face her. "I was a dick, I'm sorry. Forgive me?"

"Maybe." Ever so slowly, she began to run her fingers down my chin and over my neck, sending chills of lust down my spine. "Depends."

"On what?"

"On how nice you are to me now."

Her playful grin lightened my heart, and I enjoyed the way she snuggled into me. Everything about her invited me to squeeze, to hug, and I gave into the temptation and stroked her until she was purring. The hot, heavy look in her eyes punched me straight in the gut, and I pressed my hard dick against the softness of her belly.

"Sweetheart, I can be *very* nice."

"Mmm hmmm." She traced her fingers along my collar,

scrolling over the edge of a colorful phoenix I had tattooed around my neck and upper shoulders. "You have been very nice to me. In fact, I think you've been nicer to me than I have to you."

The way she licked her lips as she stared up at me had me mesmerized beneath the shifting shadows of sunlight.

My voice came out rough as I grabbed a handful of her ass and squeezed. "How's that?"

"Well, I've had far more orgasms than you've had. That's rather bad manners, don't you think?"

"No, because seeing you get off is the best fuckin' thing in the world."

Her blushing smile was a tease of the best sort, and I longed to fuck her until she was raw. I managed to restrain myself. Denying myself what I wanted most only deepened my craving for her, and I could feel my psyche shift, changing in a way I hadn't anticipated as my priorities realigned themselves around this girl. Her lush body pressed against mine as I pulled her down so her magnificent tits were pillowed against my chest. She was small enough to use me like a mattress, and my cock jerked as I thought about what it would look like when I rutted into her and stretched her wide open.

A shiver raced through her when I began to run my thumb along the crack of her ass.

"Gonna lick you here," I whispered against her lips, the faint scent of the fruit she ate for dessert clinging to her breath. "Gonna fuck that little asshole of yours with my fingers, stretching you out, while you cream on my chin."

Her breath came out in a harsh stutter, and her hips jerked. "Promise?"

"Would you like that?"

Her flush was lovely, but she whispered, "Yes, please."

If my dick got any harder, I might rupture something, so I reached between us and fisted myself for some relief. "Now, about that apology…"

She glanced around then bit her lower lip. "Do you think anyone can see us?"

"You want anyone to see us?"

Her pupils dilated, but she shook her head. "No."

Lies, but now wasn't the time to push any boundaries with

sweet Joy. When I first started watching her last year, she'd fucked a guy in a park late at night and had managed to quickly orgasm during sex, the first and only time that happened with that particular boyfriend. However, knowing she got off on the thrill of having sex in public didn't mean I wanted to share her beauty with my guards.

My phone rang, and I grimaced as the tone I'd programed in for my father filled the air.

I pulled out my phone and apologized to Joy before standing up and taking the call.

"The Santiago Cartel has retaliated," my father said without preamble.

Joy watched me closely, and I turned my back, not wanting her to see the monster that lived inside of me starting to surface. "What happened?"

"They hit one of our gambling operations. Went in with AK-47s and took our men, along with a few patrons, out."

"Mother fucker," I whispered. "Which one?"

"Small operation outside of Mesa in the desert."

Mentally going through the hundreds of men and women that worked for the Cordova Cartel, I settled on a name to go with the location. "Diego Marto ran it, right?"

"Yeah. He didn't make it."

I cursed and strode further away from Joy, not wanting to taint her with my growing rage. "How many men did we lose?"

"Four, and two women. Shot execution style. They let a waitress live with a message for us, so we knew it was the Santiagos who did it."

A soft touch on my arm had me whipping around and grabbing Joy by the throat before I could stop myself. She paled and let out a startled scream as I quickly released her, shame and regret filling my gut as she stumbled away from me. My father was asking what was going on, but I hung up on him, the need to take away Joy's fear a compulsion.

"Sweetheart, I'm so sorry. You startled me."

Sweat shone on her nose and forehead, her breath hitching. "Do you always try to choke the shit out of people that startle you?"

Holding out my hands, I approached her slowly, my steps light and easy as I tried to make myself as unintimidating as possible. "Did I hurt you?"

She brushed her throat with her fingertips, and I could see a slight redness, but nothing that would leave a mark. That didn't help the shame that was clawing at my stomach. I gently grasped her trembling hand in my own, gently pulling her into my arms. Resting my lips atop her head, I wished I could tell her what was going on, that I could share the burden of my grief, but she clearly wasn't ready for anymore shocks. When her small arms wrapped around my waist, returning my hug, I felt like the luckiest man in the world.

"Joy, answer me. Did I hurt you?"

"No," her voice was muffled as she buried her face in my chest. "You-you moved so fast. I've never seen anyone as fast as you are."

"I spent many, many years training to be that fast."

"Do you do MMA?"

Laughing, I shook my head. "Nah, that's not my thing. My parents are wealthy, really wealthy, and there are people who will do anything and hurt anyone to take that wealth from them. They taught me from an early age how to defend myself."

"Wish my parents had taught me that." She let out a forced, watery laugh. "And I guess taking one woman's self-defense class didn't really help, either. He...that man and his friends? I couldn't do anything to stop them. They were so strong, I-I didn't realize they'd be so strong. I couldn't stop them from hurting...from hurting my friends."

Fuck, my heart ached at the obvious mixture of fear and guilt in her voice. "You're safe, *mi amore*. They will never harm you again."

When she rubbed her nose against my shirt, I pretended not to notice the wetness of her tears against my skin. "I know. It's just...I don't recognize the world I live in anymore. It's like I was wearing blinders to the truth about how ugly and unsafe it really is. Bad things happen constantly, and no one is really safe."

"You're safe, Joy. I swear it."

"When I'm with you, I feel safe, but I can't be with you all the time."

A hot wind blew in off the hillside, whipping her curls around my face as I cupped her chin. "As much as I want you with me every second of the day, you're right. But you need to know that even if I'm not physically with you, you're still protected. And Leo's compound is a fucking fortress."

She relaxed a little bit then looked up at me. "He used to freak me out a little bit, but he really loves Hannah."

"Leo freaks everyone out a little bit, and yeah, he really loves Hannah."

That earned me a smile. I wiped away the traces of her tears off her cheeks, keeping my touch as gentle as I could. Like a kitten, Joy responded to my touch, rubbing herself against me and letting out a little coo that made me wish I didn't have to leave. I struggled between drowning myself in Joy's response and remembering my duty.

"I hate to say this, but I have to go."

Right away, she pulled back, nervously tugging at the edges of her red silk blouse. "Why?"

"That was my father. There's an important meeting I have to attend for work."

I thought she was going to protest, but she took a deep breath and nodded with a distracted look. "Okay."

Not liking how quickly she withdrew from me, I pulled her close for a quick brush of my lips against her own. "As soon as I'm done, I'm in your bed."

Looping her hands around my neck, she gave me a faint smile. "What makes you think I want you in my bed?"

I cupped her pussy, the heat of her sex searing my hand. She let out a small, strangled gasp as I squeezed. "I'm not gonna give you a chance to say no."

Her eyes closed as I rubbed the flat of my palm against her clit, a pink flush racing up from her neck to her tanned cheeks. "Okay."

Releasing her, I stepped back and adjusted myself. "My bodyguard, Nick, will drive you home. And don't touch your pussy. You're orgasms belong to me. Understood?"

Looking all too fuckable and disheveled, she brushed her hair from her flushed face as she panted. "You can't tell me what to do."

"I just did."

"What if I do it anyway?"

"Then I'll have to punish you with orgasms."

She blinked, once, twice, then squeaked out, "Is that a thing?"

Laughing, I began to walk backward. "Yeah, that's a thing. You wanna find out first hand?"

"Um, no? I don't think I'm brave enough for that right now."

"Didn't think so. Wear something sexy to bed for me. I'll make it worth your while."

With a final wave in her direction, I turned away from her light and embraced the darkness.

Nine hours later, my whole body ached as I dragged myself up the stairs at Mark's place, water still dripping from the ends of my hair after my hasty shower. I had scrubbed myself just enough to get the sweat and blood off me, determined to sleep next to Joy. After a long night of hunting down the fuckers who'd killed our men, and the resulting fight once we'd found them, I was both physically and mentally exhausted. Normally, this was a dark time for me where I relived the terrible shit I'd seen and done, a restless time where my mind roamed in darkness.

But not tonight.

Tonight, I had heaven waiting for me.

Even when I'd been slicing into the man who'd killed Diego, I wasn't completely gone into my usual berserker state. Instead, I held myself back just enough to keep aware of my surroundings, to monitor my personal safety in a way I hadn't done since my nephew was murdered. Since I gave up women until I could have Joy, killing had become my drug of choice, and I chased the oblivion it offered.

As good as that high was, it didn't even come close to the pleasure of knowing Joy was waiting for me in bed a few steps away. The house was quiet. Mark was still dealing with shit on Leo's behalf so he could stay with Hannah while she recovered from the attack, and I drank in the silence. At the top of the stairs, Joy's bedroom door was shut, but when I turned the handle, it opened easily and revealed a goddess waiting for me.

She'd left the bathroom light on and had cracked the door just enough to allow me to see her spread out in her sleep.

Every beautiful inch of her exposed by the sheets around her hips showed lightly tanned skin. My dick jerked in my pants when I noticed a golden chain glimmering around her waist, and on both of her wrists. Her hands were over her head in a relaxed pose, and her head was turned to the side, her mouth slightly open as she slept. The temptation of her breasts called to me and I wanted to go over and worship those glorious mounds, but I had to take a pain pill to make it this far and I was in no shape to give her the proper attention her outfit deserved.

My cock didn't like that idea, and urged me to slide myself between her legs and wake her up with him buried inside her soft heat.

Sparks of energy slid over my body as I stripped to my boxers, keeping that last barrier between myself and Joy in place.

When I pulled her against me, she made sounds like a grumpy kitten. I laughed softly into her hair as I curved my body over hers in an instinctive and protective gesture.

The soft stroke of her hand as she drew my arm over her chest had me sighing with pleasure.

"Go back to sleep, sweetheart."

She made some noise that sounded like agreement, and I smiled as I pulled her close into me. Joy was a sound sleeper—like, once she was out, she was out—so I wouldn't have to worry about disturbing her when I inevitably came home late. For the first time, I considered scaling back a bit in my work for the cartel, to go on that vacation my mom was always begging me to take. We had a mammoth home on an island off the coast of El Salvador that sat empty most of the year. I could take Joy down there and spend some alone time with her, treat her right and focus only on her happiness and pleasure.

As she curved trustingly into me, an idea began to form of how I wanted to take the final step of bringing Joy into my world—forever.

Chapter 6
Joy

Someone was sucking on my finger. My pointer finger, to be exact. His soft, skillful lips and tongue played over my skin and drew me from my sleep in a most pleasant manner. My sleepy, warm body had never been roused like this before, and the novelty of having someone devote so much attention to me was absolutely lovely. He then licked my palm, turning even that odd sensation into erotic tingles that settled between my legs, making my pussy start to pulse with need. Warmth pooled deep in my core, and I sucked in a sharp breath when he lightly nipped my skin with sharp teeth.

Keeping my eyes closed, I stretched out, the sensation of the soft sheets against my bare skin a direct contrast to the rough scrape of a big, hairy, muscular man's frame curving over my body. I wasn't cuddling with a fumbling boy, I was being owned and worshiped by a grown man who knew what he was doing—and I loved it. His stubble scraped my skin, and I shivered then smiled. While I've dated my fair share of men, I've never been with a guy who was as…hairy as Ramón. Not that he was extra furry, but I've grown used to metrosexual guys who wax almost every inch of their bodies. While his back and ass were fur free, he had hair just about everywhere else, and I absolutely loved how it seemed to stroke my skin with each breath I took.

Especially his chest hair as it rubbed against my tingling nipples, offering a small amount of relief from the seemingly never-ending ache.

His heat left me, then he drew my hands up over my head.

"Keep them there, *mami*, and let me take care of you."

I nodded and the cool air of the room made my nipples harden even more as he drew the sheet down my almost completely bare body. When I'd gone to bed, I'd made sure to wear something I knew would get me laid. I wanted Ramón, badly, and I intended to have him.

In an effort to up my seduction efforts, I was completely

nude, except for a thick gold chain at my waist and matching gold chain bracelets and anklets. They were part of a jewelry set he'd left me, and while I don't think they were meant to be worn like this, I did enjoy the effect on my curvy body. I loved playing dress up in sexy lingerie, and chains like these had always made me feel like some sultan's harem girl. Evidently Ramón liked the look as well, because his pleased murmur drew me full awake.

"The things I'm going to do to you, my little slave girl. Need a collar for that pretty neck. Ring on that finger. My name tattooed on that fantastic fucking big ass of yours, *mami*."

He growled the last part while gripping my ass hard enough that I was glad I didn't bruise easily.

"Too rough," I complained in a thick, sleepy whine.

"Sorry, sweetheart." He released me right away, then soothingly stroked me. "I get carried away with you. I'll get better, I promise. It's just that right now, having you here with me is a fucking dream come true. I keep feeling like any second I could wake up. I don't want that to happen—think I might have a heart attack, if I did."

Forcing my heavy lids open, I reached for him as my gaze adjusted to the dark room. He was a shadow, large and intimidating, but the smell of his cologne filled me and I relaxed into his touch. He lowered his head to my nipple and sucked it between his lips with a long, strong pull that went right to my clit. Unable to resist, I buried my hands in his hair and held his head to my breast, my fingers tightening in the thick strands as he added some teeth to his sensual onslaught.

"Ramón," I sighed as he gently laved my nipple with his soft tongue.

"Love the chains. Makes me wish I'd brought some toys with me."

In the dark, with the remnants of sleep softening my mind, I smiled. "What kind of toys?"

"Why, you curious? Want to get dirty with me?"

As he said this, he began to run his thumb up and down the soaked slit of my sex. "Yes, please."

"Yes, please. You're too fucking sweet. How can you be so sweet and so kinky?" He circled my clit with his thumb and I moaned, my legs falling wide open. "You gonna be a freak for me? Let me fuck you how I want, when I want? Gonna let me dress you up like a maid, so I can force you to suck my cock in order to keep your 'job'? Gonna let me paddle you on the ass for being a bad girl for coming all over my dick?"

"Yes—all of it. I want to do everything with you." A low moan seemed to come from the pit of my belly, but I forced myself to speak. "Are you going to let me tie you up? Ride you and make you cum inside of me?"

His hips flexed into the bed and he pressed down hard on my clit, his voice nothing but a rough growl as he said, "For you, anything."

"I need to come," I lifted my hips, chasing a harder touch, but he merely smiled and lifted his hand away altogether.

"Ramón," the word was half whine, half angry shout. "Please!"

I was so turned on, my clit was throbbing. When he began to gently rub my swollen pussy, I was so close to orgasm it hurt. "I love how sensitive you are, how quickly I can make you cum. You like it when I touch you? When I make your little cunt all slick and creamy?"

His low, accented voice was going to drive me crazy. "Please, Ramón, stop teasing me and fuck me."

"Not yet."

I was ready to cry as I said, "Why?"

"Because you're worth waiting for."

I spun in his arms and attempted to shove him back and straddle him, but he was so strong it was like pushing at a wall. "I'm tired of waiting."

Laughing, he gripped my waist chain and jerked me forward so I fell, my breasts pressing against his wide chest, the feel of his rough hands smoothing down my back a sensory delight. "Trust me, Joy. Let me make this special for you."

Frustrated, I ground my hips against his cock covered by the thinnest layer of cotton. I was already wet, so wet he no doubt felt it as my pussy lips spread over his length with each roll of my pelvis. A strangled sound left him as I reached between us and slipped the head of his cock through the nifty little flap at the front of his boxers.

"Just the tip," I whispered against his mouth with a small smile.

We were pressed so close that when he laughed it rumbled through my body like thunder, adding happiness and warmth to the lust swirling through me.

"No."

"Please," I whispered as I rubbed my clit over his hard length. "I feel so empty."

In response he easily maneuvered me so I was straddling his face, my thighs clenching his head as I steadied myself on the headboard with an undignified squeak.

Ramón took in an audible inhalation of my sex then let out a throaty groan that burned through me. "You smell good, like sex and dessert."

He then stole my breath away by pulling me down onto his mouth and licking me from my ass all the way to my clit where he lingered. The soft stroke of his tongue against my folds, rubbing up one side of my clit then down the other, sent almost painful streaks of pleasure through me, my whole body tensing when he began to suck. I swear I was so sensitive, even the brush of his cheeks against my thighs was almost too much and not enough. His grip on me was firm, secure, and knowing I was at his mercy only made me hotter.

"Fuck yes," I hissed out as he licked lower until he was at the entrance to my sheath, then he began to fuck me with his tongue.

The headboard shook as I arched back, helpless against his knowing mouth. Right when I was about to climax, he pulled back, leaving me gasping for air and trying to figure out why he'd stopped. I got my answer when he flipped us around so I was once again straddling his mouth, but this time I was facing his erection tenting his underwear.

A needy moan escaped me when he teased my clit, keeping me on the edge of orgasm while I reached for his cock. I was so hot, so turned on. I grasped the thick stalk of his erection in one hand, unable to get my fingers all the way around it to grip him properly. Shit, he had a porn star dick. The way he tensed beneath me sent a thrill through me, and I began to gently pull his boxers enough to free his engorged length and firm balls. The skin of his cock was darker than his body, and the pink tip was covered in a thin layer of pre-cum.

Best of all, a big gold ring with a large ball pierced the head and I nearly came just at the thought of having him inside of me.

I tried to climb off his face, intent on seeing if I could even handle a man his size stretching me open, but Ramón wouldn't let me move.

"I want to fuck you," I said in moaning whisper as he used one of his thumbs to rub over the entrance to my ass. "Please."

He pulled away from my pussy only long enough to say, "No."

Determined to get my way, I began to tease his cock like he was teasing my body, licking it slowly while barely tightening my grasp on the hot base. He growled beneath me, trying to thrust up into my mouth, to make me suck him harder. That only had me licking the head of his dick, toying with the thick gold ring piercing him, while I rubbed his balls with my free hand. My toes curled as he nibbled my clit, and I rubbed my pussy shamelessly against his face, wanting more. Needing more.

"Please," I begged. "Please, Ramón, I need you inside of me. *Please.*"

Two of his big fingers pushed into me and right away my pussy clamped down on him, a ragged cry leaving me when he began to rub my g-spot. This time when he thrust up my mouth was there to meet him, and I let him fuck my face while I fucked his. And what we were doing was fucking. This wasn't sex, this wasn't making love, this was rough and nasty, dirty just the way I liked it. The way I needed it.

My pleas were turned to moans as he increased the pace, a slippery sweat building between us as I rubbed my curves all over the hard, delicious planes of his frame. Reaching forward, I grasped his thickly muscled upper thighs, digging my fingernails into the rock-hard flesh and bobbed down further, taking as much of him as I could. The big ring had me gagging, so he eased the depth of his thrusts, responding wordlessly to my distress as he gently rubbed my ass. It was screwed up, I know, but that little act of caring did something to me. I've been with men before who could have given a shit if I choked to death on their cock, as long as they got off. Sad, but true. Despite his dangerous vibe and clearly aggressive nature, Ramón took care of me in a way I'd never experienced.

Even now, when he was so close to coming, his dick swollen and stiff between my lips, he paid attention to my body, to my needs, to make sure I was right there with him. Warmth exploded from my core as he flicked my clit rapidly with his tongue while adding a third finger, stretching my pussy out until I detonated on his face. My scream was lost as he arched beneath me, his salty hot cum covering my tongue and throat as I tried to remember how to swallow when I was having the best orgasm of my life.

Sizzling hot waves of erotic energy seared through me and I pulled off his cock with a gasp while Ramón drew my orgasm out further. By the time the last shock had burned through me I was done. D.O.N.E done. Every inch of my body quivered, and my clit pulsed with the racing beat of my heart. I managed to crawl off Ramón, but he didn't let me go far, pulling me back to his side so I could rest my cheek on his chest.

I managed to sling one arm over him, and basically petted the hair on his chest while I lay there in what amounted to sexual shock. The endorphins roaring through my body were stronger than anything I'd ever experienced, and I could tell by Ramón's occasional full body twitch that he was still feeling the effects of his release as well. The scent of sex and passion hung heavy in the air and as I gently drifted down from my high, I snuggled close into Ramón's side.

"Wow," he said in a rough croak, then cleared his throat again. "Damn, woman."

Laughing softly, I sat up on my elbow to look down at him in the weak morning light coming in around the curtains. While we'd been busy frolicking, the sun had risen enough to allow me to see him. When I examined him, I noticed dark shadows on his skin. A closer inspection revealed bruises on his torso that rivaled mine, as well as a mark on his jaw and some swelling on his cheek.

Alarm filled me as I sat up, my hands fluttering over his injuries as I was torn between the need to soothe him, and not accidentally hurt him more. "What happened?"

His formerly warm gaze hardened, and he clenched his jaw. "Don't worry about it. I put some medicine on the worst of it, and I'll be good as new in a few days."

"Don't worry about it?" A shiver went through me, but this time it wasn't a good one. "What do you mean don't worry about it? Ramón, you've been hurt!"

"Sweetheart, I'm really tired. Can we fight about this later?"

He went to grab my hand, but I pulled away, not liking his patronizing tone one bit. "Why won't you tell me what happened?"

"Because it's none of your business, Joy. Now drop it."

The coldness of his words iced through me, and I scrambled off the bed, suddenly feeling very vulnerable and naked. "Fine. Consider it dropped."

"Joy…" He ran both of his hands through his hair like *I* was the unreasonable one. "Not now. I'm too exhausted for this shit."

"Fine."

He watched me throw on a loose cream silk dress, his arms behind his head, his expression one of exasperation. "Come back to bed."

"No."

"Baby…"

I ignored him, shoving my feet into a pair of cork wedge sandals before striding across the room to grab my purse.

"Where are you going?"

"Away from you."

"Joy…" This time there was a clear warning rumble in his voice. "Enough. Come here."

"Tell me what happened to you and I will."

"Can't you just give it a rest? I'm fucking tired, and I don't need you bitching at me."

"Bitching at you? Ramón, you've been hurt, refuse to tell me what happened, and you think I'm just throwing around drama? Fuck you." I glared at him as he sat up, a band of sunlight illuminating his jaw. I was right, a big bruise was forming there like someone had hit him hard. Memories of what it felt like to be beaten filled me, and I had to fight back tears, my emotions a whirlwind that I barely had a grasp on.

A harsh sweat broke out over me as I touched the aching bruises on my ribs, then whispered, "I expect you not to be here when I get back."

A stricken look crossed his face, but I didn't let myself stay to see what his reaction was. Instead, I practically ran through the house with Ramón's voice following me as he yelled my name. After darting through the kitchen, I went to the rack of keys on the wall next to the door leading to the garage. Mark had pointed them out yesterday and told me to feel free to take his

SUV if I needed to run any errands. Clutching my purse in my hand, I grabbed the set and quickly unlocked the doors to a deep red Land Rover. Ramón still yelled for me from somewhere in the house, but his voice became muffled as I slammed the door behind me.

Thankfully, the garage doors were already open. While Mark's sleek green Mercedes's convertible was there, his motorcycle was missing. I said a silent prayer of thanks he wasn't here to witness me fighting with Ramón.

I pulled out of the garage as fast as I dared. By the time I had the SUV turned around in the driveway, a shirtless Ramón was barreling out of the house. Fear mixed with anger lumped in my throat as I put the SUV into drive and gave him the middle finger without looking at him as I drove past. While I drove away, I allowed myself one glance back and took in the big, super pissed off man standing at the entrance of the garage, clearly furious. His dark hair streamed around his shoulders in the hot breeze and the muscles of his chest flexed as I swear he snarled at me.

Wow, he was mad.

With my heart pounding, I drove away as tears began to fall down my cheeks. Was I overreacting? Yes, on some level I knew I was being irrational, and I didn't feel in control of myself right now. My emotions were all over the place, and I didn't know which side was up. It was only when I reached the guarded gates leading out of Leo's compound that I realized I had no idea where I was going. Putting on my best smile after brushing away my tears, I waved to the guard as I pulled through, ignoring the way he stared at me while he talked into his phone.

When I hit the main road, I let out a deep sigh of both relief and regret. Now that I was away from Ramón, I missed him and wished I was back in bed, safe in his arms, but I couldn't be with a man who acted like such an asshole. I don't care how nice to me he's been, he dismissed my concern like it was no big deal, like I was being a nosy bitch.

I forced myself to calm down a little and took some deep breaths, trying desperately to get ahold of myself.

Okay, maybe what happened to him wasn't my business, but he'd made me feel like it was, like we had the beginnings of a real relationship. All the nice things he said, all the nice things he'd done for me…had it all been bullshit? This was the second time he'd been a dick to me, and I was beginning to think his true personality was that of an asshole. Maybe he was just charming enough to get away with treating people like shit. I've run into guys like that before, even dated a few, and I knew the warning signs. I had to be smart about this, had to protect myself.

My phone rang a couple times, and I ignored it until I pulled into the back of a shopping center beneath the shade of a small tree. With my fingers trembling, I scrolled through my phone and saw that Ramón had called nine times and left ten text messages, but I deleted them all without reading or listening. I needed to be away from him right now, away from his overwhelming presence and personality. The world and all its problems seemed to disappear around him, but they never really went away. He just seemed to somehow blind me to reality. Was I so desperate for comfort that I clung to the first person who'd offered me any form of solace? Or was I overreacting to everything like a psycho girlfriend?

I took a deep breath and my aching ribs brought back unwanted memories of the feeling of Ray's foot connecting to my back, the harsh fear that he'd break my spine and leave me crippled, unable to defend myself.

This recollection led to more crying, and I bitterly wished I could go home, but my home was now a crime scene.

Hannah.

As soon as I thought of my friend I snapped upright and took a deep breath, wiping at my face with some tissue I had in my purse.

I couldn't believe that in my self-absorption, I'd forgotten about Hannah and everything she must be going through.

Looking through my phone, I found the number for Mrs. Cordova and called.

She picked up on the third ring, "Hello?"

Clearing my throat, I said, "Hi, Mrs. Cordova, it's Joy. I was wondering if I could come see Hannah?"

There was a pause before she said in a gentle voice, "I'm sorry, Joy, but she doesn't want to see anyone right now."

My throat tightened, and I had to calm myself before I said, "Maybe, if you like asked her, maybe she'd want to see me?"

Please? I really need to see her. I promise I won't stay long or disturb her rest."

Her tone changed as she carefully asked, "Are you all right?"

"Yeah, just fine." That probably would have sounded better if my voice didn't break.

"I see." There was a moment of silence before she said in a softer voice, "You should come over. You're always welcome in my home, and I'll speak to Hannah and see how she's feeling. I don't want to get your hopes up, because she's heavily medicated right now, but I'll try. Will you stay for lunch afterward? I'd enjoy the company."

"Yes, thank you," I managed to whisper, undone by her kindness. "Can you text me the address please, so I can put it into the GPS?"

"Just have Ramón bring you over."

"Um, Ramón's not with me."

"Oh, I thought he mentioned that he'd be having breakfast with you."

I flushed hot, remembering that Ramón did have me for breakfast. "Uh, no."

"I'm surprised. He seems quite taken with you. I was sure he wouldn't let you out of his sight."

I didn't want to ask why she would think that, or even talk about him at all with his mother. The whole situation was awkward as hell, and I bit my lower lip in discomfort as my already nervous stomach clenched further. I felt guilty for the way I flew off the handle and let my emotions get away from me. I should have given him a chance to explain or something, instead of running away.

Fleeing was a bad habit of mine, one I'd developed thanks to my older sister Brittney. After my *abuela* passed away, my older sister was responsible for us after school, and she could be such a bitch. While she loved to make everyone miserable, she seemed to have a special hatred for me. I have no idea why. I mean, yeah, I was a bratty younger sister, but Brittney liked to eviscerate me until I was crying. The only way I could escape was to leave, and I'd begun to associate fleeing with safety.

For a moment, I wondered if I should have given Ramón a chance to explain, but then I remembered what a giant asshole he'd been.

I needed help.

I needed someone I could talk to about this mess who would understand.

I needed my best friend.

Ignoring Mrs. Cordova's question, I replied in a chirpy voice, "If you could please text me your address, I'd really appreciate it."

"Of course."

After we said our goodbyes, I rested my head against the back of the seat, then womaned up and read my increasingly frantic messages from Ramón, begging me to let him know I was okay.

My phone rang with Ramón's number. I debated not answering it then chided myself for being a chicken. "Hello?"

"Joy," Ramón said with evident relief. "Are you okay? Where are you going?"

Trying to keep my voice normal, I said, "I'm fine, and I'm on my way to your mom's house."

"Why?"

"I need to talk with Hannah." I could hear people faintly speaking in the background wherever he was in Spanish. "Where are you?"

"I was grabbing a few of my guys and heading out after you. I was afraid you were going to your old apartment, and I didn't want you there alone."

I swallowed past the sudden lump of fear in my throat. "No, I wasn't going there."

"Why did you leave? I was trying to talk to you."

"Why did I leave? Really, you have to ask me that?" A small spark of my earlier anger rekindled. "Well, the reason I left is the guy I'm—well, I have no idea what we're doing, but we're doing something, or at least I thought we were. Anyway, that guy came home hurt, like someone beat him up, and when I understandably freaked out and asked him what had happened, he told me it was none of my business. I thought that, considering the fact that I'd recently been beaten black and blue, he'd be a little more understanding with why I was worried about him. Instead, he acted like an asshole and made me feel like shit. I hope you can see why that's a little fucked up."

His tired sigh put my back up. "I can't tell you about it

because it's work related, but I am truly sorry I made you feel bad, *mi amor*."

"Seriously? You can't tell me because it's *work related*? What kind of lame excuse is that?" I scoffed as I waved my arm over my head in the empty SUV, probably looking like a crazy woman. "What are you, a boxer? An MMA fighter? Who gets beat up as part of their job? That doesn't make any sense."

For a long moment, silence stretched between us, and I wondered if the call had dropped.

"Joy." His voice was so serious, it cut through my temper. "There are things I cannot tell you for your own safety. Things that you'd have to sign a NDA six miles long before I could even whisper them in your presence. I'm not trying to be an asshole when I tell you I can't talk about it, because I really can't talk about it. This isn't just about my job, it's about my family's empire, and my vow to protect the ones I love. It isn't that I don't want to tell you, it's that I cannot."

"Oh...I-I didn't consider anything like that." Feeling like a moron, I whispered, "I'm sorry."

"No, I'm sorry. I should have explained myself better. Thing is, I feel like I've known you forever, and I forget that all of this shit is new to you. That I'm new to you. We were raised to see the world differently, and things that are normal for me are totally alien to you."

My shoulders relaxed, and I pushed my wild curls out of my face before digging through my purse with one hand while looking for a rubber band. "Nothing in my life is normal right now."

"I know, sweetheart, and I'm sorry about that. Why don't you pull out of that Starbucks parking lot and head to my parents place? I'll meet you there later today, after you spend some time with Hannah. Just be aware that my mom is fond of you, so she may talk your ear off."

"Okay." I stopped digging in my purse and froze. "How did you know I was in a Starbucks parking lot?"

"Mark's car has a tracker on it, so if anyone steals it we can find it quickly." He said something away from the phone then returned a second later. "Take a look out your rear passenger window."

I turned my head and let out a little startled shriek as a man dressed in a black and silver motorcycle suit roared up on a sleek, black racing bike next to the SUV. He lifted two fingers to his helmet in what looked like a salute and gave his engine a little rev. Startled, I gave him a weak wave and then turned back around to face the parking lot while gripping the wheel with one hand, tight.

"Who the hell is that?"

"Your escort. He's also your chief bodyguard, Tino. Good guy, has a sweet wife who thinks he walks on water and two little girls that have him wrapped around their finger. He'll make sure you're safe."

"Wait, hold up a second here, what do you mean my *bodyguard*?"

"Remember that thing I said about different worlds? Well, bodyguards are part of my world. I've been surrounded by them all my life. It's my normal."

"I'm not sure how I feel about some guy spying on me for you."

He gave a strained laugh. "Don't worry, sweetheart, he's only there to protect you. He'll just follow behind you to make sure you arrive at my parents' house without any hassle"

My heartbeat picked up, and I shifted in my seat, scanning the area around me. "Do you think someone is going to bother me?"

"Nah, I'm just a little protective of you. Want to make sure that you're taken care of at all times."

That made me feel better, and my tension eased as I looked into the rearview mirror and found Tino on his bike nearby. "Should I drive slow so he can keep up?"

He chuckled, "*Mami*, you couldn't lose him if you tried. Tino grew up riding a dirt bike through the mountains of El Salvador as an errand boy for a local d-uh, politician. That man can do things on a motorcycle you wouldn't believe, and all of our bikes are updated with the latest technology. Fuck, they've got some shit on them that people don't even know we've invented yet."

"I feel like I'm dating James Bond."

He laughed again, and I couldn't help but smile in return. "Everything okay with us now?"

"Yeah, we're good."

"Next time I'm an asshole, smack me in the back of my head,

yell at me, but please don't run away."

"Next time?"

"I'm only human, sweetheart."

"Yeah, yeah. Fine." I gave him an exaggerated sigh, but I didn't bother to hide my smile.

"I've gotta go, but I'll see you soon, okay?"

"I'll see you soon, Ramón."

"Mmmm," his rumble sent a little shiver of pleasure through me. "Love it when you say my name."

"Bye, Ramón." I put a little teasing purr in my voice then giggled at his pained sound. I hung up after he said goodbye.

Now that my anger had passed, my empty stomach rumbled, and I grabbed my purse then left the SUV. Scanning the parking lot, I found Tino and motioned him over. He zipped to my side and easily supported the bike with his long legs. A giant of a man, probably nearing six-foot eight, he dwarfed me in size, and I had to swallow back my nerves.

Trying to give him a bright smile, I yelled, "Want anything from Starbucks?"

He pulled into the empty spot next to the SUV and turned off his bike then took his helmet off.

I don't know what I'd been expecting him to look like, but a guy in his early thirties with chubby cheeks and big dimples did not fit the profile I'd built in my head. He may have the body of Paul Bunyan, but he had the face of an aging cherub. His skin tone was a dark, deep brown and his eyes were almost black, but they sparkled with friendliness. It was an odd combination, and I found myself returning his kind smile.

His accent was heavy as he said, "I'm good, Ms. Holtz, but I'd be more than happy to escort you inside."

Shaking my head at the weirdness of the situation, I looked both ways before crossing the parking lot. "So, tell me about yourself, Tino. Are you a cupcake or a brownie kind of man?"

Chapter 7
Joy

As I pulled up the circular drive that graced the entrance of the Cordova's mission style mansion, I spotted Ramón's brother Diego waiting for me at the black wrought iron and weathered oak front doors. Dressed in a pair of pale khaki pants, shiny and no doubt expensive black shoes, and a tailored heather gray cotton button up shirt, he looked like he belonged in a men's magazine ad selling expensive watches. While Ramón had more of a rugged quality to his good looks, Diego's face was more sculpted, his lips thinner and his nose more hawkish.

After I got out of the car, Diego quickly made his way over to me then stopped with a small half-bow, his long black braid falling over his shoulder. "Madam."

"Hi, Diego."

Clutching my hand in his, he gave me a teasing grin, then sighed. "You know my name."

I couldn't help but laugh while tugging my hand back. "Of course I do."

"My life is complete." His phone rang and he gave me an exasperated look. "Excuse me for a moment," he murmured before pulling out his phone. He told someone on the other end that I was there, with him, and I was fine.

When he hung up, I arched a brow and asked, "Ramón?"

Diego nodded then opened the front door of the house. Cool air from inside rushed over us. "Good guess."

A little shiver ran over me as we left the heat of the day behind and entered the silent coolness of the mansion. The foyer was large, two story, and a variety of hallways branched off it. Bright and bold art hung from the walls, while a huge red and black Navajo rug muffled our footsteps as we crossed the circular space to one of the hallways. Family pictures adorned the walls. I had to keep myself focused on Diego when all I wanted to do was check out pictures of Ramón when he was a kid.

Giving Diego a distracted smile, I fiddled with my purse. "I'm sorry, he's a little overprotective."

"I've never seen him like this with a woman before," Diego grinned at me again and this time his face held a trace of real warmth. "It's been fun watching him drive himself crazy over you. Never thought I'd see Ramón this obsessed with anyone."

"He's not obsessed with me."

"He's totally obsessed. Never seen him like this with a girl before. Joy and Ramón, sitting in a tree, K-I-S-S-I-N-G. First—"

I gave him a hard shove with my shoulder. "Shut it."

Diego started to hum the wedding march while I sighed.

I secretly liked the idea that Ramón didn't have a habit of sweeping women off their feet. "We've only known each other a few days. I'm sure as soon as he gets to know me, he'll be running for the hills."

"Yeah, I don't see that happening. Welcome to the family."

His words caused me to stumble on the edge of a carpet. He grabbed my elbow, helping me steady myself as I glared at him. "You're all crazy."

The smug smile that he gave me was just like Ramón's. "Ask my mom about the legend of the first kiss."

Rolling my eyes, I spotted Mrs. Cordova approaching us with a tight smile. Dressed today in a retro bronze dress that would have been perfect on Jacki-O, she looked like a million bucks. But...something about her seemed off. Her dark eyes were as emotionless glass doll eyes. Like a switch flipping, she smiled and the ominous air left her like mist burning off in the sun. The change was so quick I wondered if I'd imagined it as she pulled me into a warm hug.

"Joy, it's so good to see you."

Pulling back, I brushed aside my worries into my increasingly full mental box labeled 'shit to deal with later.'

"It's nice to see you as well, Mrs. Cordova."

"Please, call me Judith." She slowly scanned me then frowned, her large ruby ring flashing as she gestured to my face. "You've been crying."

"I—"

Before I could say anything, Diego quickly spoke up. "Ramón was his usual charming self. No big deal, right, Joy?"

Put on the spot, I tried to find my backbone as they both

stared at me, each seemingly trying to read my thoughts through sheer will alone. "Uh, yeah."

Her peach-frosted lips thinned. "What did my son do?"

Diego started to speak again, but she held up her hand in an imperious gesture that silenced him. "I was speaking with Joy."

"Really, it's no big deal." Her creepy vibe was back, and I quickly tried to defuse the situation. "There was a misunderstanding on my part, and I talked with Ramón and cleared it up. Look, I'm really here to see Hannah. I don't care if she's sleeping. I won't disturb her, but I have to see her. She's...well, she's pretty much my sister, and I'm worried about her."

Diego and Judith exchanged a glance before she turned back to me, her expression serious, but somehow kind.

Jesus, this woman was giving me emotional whiplash with how quickly her moods changed.

"Come with me, *mija*. Let's sit down and talk about this."

I followed her into a large living area with cathedral ceilings. The walls of the room were a beautiful sky blue with a border of shimmering copper leaf that matched the blown glass table lamps. Two enormous distressed brown leather couches sat in the center of the room, and to my right, a carved black marble fireplace dominated the wall. Judith sat on the couch, then patted the space next to her.

"Please, have a seat."

I did as she asked, as far away from her as I could without being offensive.

Her shark stare was making the hair on the back of my neck prickle.

"What's up?"

Diego sat across from us and absently moved his braid from behind his back so it lay over his shoulder. I couldn't read his face, but I did notice the way one of his fingers tapped out a nervous rhythm on the cushion next to him. His tapping finger stilled and I looked away, refocusing my attention on Judith.

Sliding down the couch, Judith took my stiff hand in her own. "Hannah sustained some serious injuries from the attack."

My stomach bottomed out, and I felt dizzy. "What? You said she was all right."

"She is," Diego interrupted. "But she looks bad, really bad, and she knows it."

"And," Judith added in a tense voice, "She isn't handling things very well."

"For fucks sake," I snapped, my temper sparking as fear for my friend made my heart race. "Stop pussyfooting around and tell me what's wrong with her."

"She's suffering from PTSD," Judith said and squeezed my hand tight. "Her mental state is very fragile. If I can convince her to see you, I must have your word that you won't do or say anything to upset her—and understand, I can't force her to see you. She needs time to heal, to deal with things on her own, and I promised her she'd have it."

I wanted to cry, but I smoothed the shimmering cream silk skirt of my dress then nodded. "Okay. But she's all right?"

She relaxed a little bit, and her grip on my hand lessened. "She will be fine, she just needs some time to heal."

Worried she was all alone with virtual strangers, knowing her parents wouldn't give a shit, I asked, "Is Leo with her?"

"Yes." Judith let out a soft huff. "He won't leave her side unless we drag him away."

I may have been stupidly jealous of him in the past, but I was grateful he was with Hannah. I know he loved her just like I did and would keep her safe.

Judith stood and Diego followed suit. "Let me go check on Hannah and see how she's doing. I may be gone for a bit, so feel free to entertain yourself."

I reached into my purse and pulled out my phone. "No problem, I've got a ton of books to read on my phone. Please, take your time."

After they left, I sent off a series of text messages to my family, letting them know my new address and sending my mom pictures of Mark's house. She worried about me staying with a strange man, even if his intentions were honorable. I'm hoping the pictures will help her relax once she realizes how nice Mark's place is, and how big. My dad had evidently had a long talk with Mark at some point, not that anyone had told me about it, and seemed to think I was in good hands.

Licking my lips, I hesitated while texting with Winter, my younger sister, who was a senior in high school. Usually, I was pretty honest and open with her. We'd giggle about sex and the guys I was dating, but talking with my bubbly seventeen year old sister about Ramón wasn't going to happen. I didn't even know how to describe what was going on between us. He seemed so...into me, but we were strangers.

Shit, I wondered if he was a stage-five clinger like Hannah.

As soon as I had the thought, I dismissed it with a soft laugh. Of all the things Ramón appeared to be, needy wasn't one of them. Then again, he did like to micro-manage my life, but that was more a control issue than a dependency one. I'm not the kind of girl that usually likes any guy thinking he can tell me what to do, but I hadn't put up much of a fight when he'd assigned me a bodyguard without my knowledge, had me followed, and showed up uninvited into my bed every night. Arguing with a man about buying me fabulous clothes, making sure all my needs were taken care of, and basically spoiling me seemed kind of petty and stupid when I thought about it. He made me feel amazing inside and out with his seemingly endless affection.

The memory of being held in his arms, the warmth of his embrace as he slowly kissed me, spread through my limbs in a rush of pleasant tingles.

A pungent, but familiar scent made my nose twitch and I looked up from catching up on social media to find a man that looked like a strung-out version of Diego staring at me. He was disheveled, his soft blue dress shirt sloppily buttoned and stained, and instead of long hair, his was cut almost painfully short. A thick and scraggly beard covered his square jaw, and his dark eyes were ringed with the black circles of exhaustion as he squinted then stared at me. A half full bottle of tequila was gripped in his right hand, and a burning joint in his left.

Fernando. My heart gave a hard thump as I realized this was the brother who'd lost both his son and wife in a horrible car accident. Ramón had said something about how Fernando was staying with his parents while he grieved. Empathy filled me and it took all my willpower to hold myself in check. He didn't need my tears, even if my whole chest ached for him.

"I know you," he slurred.

Trying to act as normal as possible, I stood and gave a small wave. "Hi, I'm Joy. Hannah's friend. You must be Fernando."

When I said Hannah's name, he winced then took a hit off the joint. As he blew the smoke out, he said, "No, I *know* you. You're Ramón's girl."

"Something like that."

"No." He stabbed the joint in my direction, his arm shaking. "You're *his*. He watches you. You belong to him now. God fucking help you."

"What are you talking about?"

"Gonna be a sheep." His voice wavered, and I stared at him, stunned when tears filled his eyes. "Hannah's a sheep, and her shepherd did a piss poor job protecting her."

When I called Ramón and Diego crazy, I was half-kidding.

When I called Fernando crazy, I meant it one hundred percent. The death of his family had broken him, it was as clear as day to me. When I was younger, my favorite cousin killed herself after she was viciously bullied by some girls at her school. I'd known she was going through some stuff with them, but I was dealing with my older sister at the time—like most kids, I was more worried about myself. I've wished a billion times I could somehow turn back the clock and do things differently, but that isn't how the world works. The only thing I could do was make sure that if I ever saw someone that looked the way my cousin had in the last few days before she took her life, this time I would step in. Not just for her, but for the scared kid I'd been who was praying someone would help her.

That promise gave me the strength to close the distance between myself and Fernando. He stumbled back, but before he could fight me off, I took the bottle from his limp fingers and grabbed the joint. Unsure what to do with it, I spied a vase of fresh tulips and shoved it down inside, putting the ember out with the water. Fernando was making some kind of protesting mumble behind me, but I ignored him.

I set the bottle down on the table next to the vase, then faced Fernando.

Whoa boy, was he mad I'd taken his toys away.

Lean, wiry muscle flexed in his arms as he fought to focus on me. He took a step in my direction, a low growl spilling out of his throat. I might have been scared, if he didn't trip over his own feet and fall face first into the rug.

Thankfully, some primitive part of his brain made him put his arms out so he didn't smash his face, but he still fell with an undignified grunt.

Making sure I didn't flash him, I tucked my skirt beneath my legs and crouched down next to him. "Wow, nice landing. You okay?"

"Shut up, Queen of the Sheeple," he muttered then rolled over, throwing his arm over his eyes with a dramatic groan. "I'm gonna puke."

I moved back quickly, trying not to laugh at his pathetic groans. "Dude, I wouldn't. I have a feeling your mom would be pissed if you did."

"Cut my nuts off," he muttered. "S'okay. Don't need 'em anyways."

"Right. I bet when you're sober, you might feel a little differently." I sighed as I stared at him lying there, then began to take off my shoes. "You're a pain in the ass."

"Fuck you, sheep girl. Too stupid to see that you're wandering into the slaughterhouse."

"What?"

He muttered something in Spanish, then growled, "Run, stupid sheep, before my brother leads you to the slaughter."

Wondering what his obsession with sheep was, I grabbed his hand then tugged with a grunt. "Get up."

"Fuck off."

Despite his gaunt appearance, he weighed a ton. "I'm trying to help you get to the bathroom."

"Just let me die."

"No."

"Why is it always no?" he suddenly roared, his bloodshot eyes wide and glassy. "Why? Just let me fucking die already."

The sheer desperation in his voice took the strength from my legs, and I sank down to my knees beside him. "Because they love you."

"If they loved me, they would let me be with Jason. I miss him...fuck, every second of every minute of every day, I ache to hold him just one more time."

I reached out and gripped his hand with my own, tears pouring down my face as my nose burned. Sometimes, you can't say anything to make it better. Sometimes the only thing you can do is let them know they aren't alone. At first, he tried to pull away, but after a moment, he turned his hand so our fingers laced together. His breath came out in choking sobs as he curled in on himself, and I wiped the back of my arm across my face, wishing I could do something to make it better.

"I'm sure you'll see your wife and son in heaven."

He let out a mad cackle then, one that had goosebumps breaking out on my arms. "That *puta* is burning in hell."

What the heck did I say to that?

He glared at me through swollen eyes, the flicker of madness now a full out roar of flames. "I hope she spends every minute in unending pain. I hope she's spends eternity burning for her sins. You should hate her, too. She's the reason you're a sheep."

"I-I don't understand," I took a step back, my mouth dry as I stared at him.

"They only told you lies," he hissed. He grabbed my hand and squeezed it so hard it hurt. "The truth is he died because of *her*."

I blinked a couple times, my brain officially shorting out from a combination of fear and confusion. With a yelp of pain, I jerked my hand away and clutched it to my chest as tears burned my nose. Fernando had pushed himself up by this point, his handsome features stretched tight with anger. I was suddenly aware of what a vulnerable position I was in, how much bigger he was than me, and fear soured my stomach as I gracelessly scrambled away from him like a crab until I got to my feet. Putting the couch between us, I held my hands out.

"Please, don't hurt me."

I didn't mean to say that, but panic was eroding my usual self-control. I hated how I could feel my body gearing up to freak out. Normally, I'm good in situations like this, could defuse tension and regain control, but my faith in myself had been broken by my attacker's fists. Now, I feared a broken man too drunk to even stand straight. Frowning, he held out his hand and took an unsteady step in my direction.

"I would never hurt a woman." His grin turned malicious, and I shuddered. "Wait, I'd kill my fucking dead wife over and over again, if I could. Wish my mom had waited. Would have loved to slit her throat myself."

"Leave me alone," I screamed, terrified by his drunk and stoned homicidal ramblings.

He staggered back like I'd slapped him, banging into a lovely table and sending the lamp on it crashing to the ground with an angry crash, the blown glass base shattering against the stone floors in a spray of bronze and turquoise shards.

"Fuck," he sank down to his knees and started trying to gather the pieces of glass while his head bobbed and weaved.

The thought 'he could hurt himself' cut through the fear devouring my mind, severing it so cleanly that my only thought was helping Fernando before he accidentally cut himself.

I was too late. By the time I reached him, he'd sliced his finger good.

Blood dripped onto the carpet in steady drops, making my stomach churn.

Fernando didn't seem to notice the wound, and kept trying to clean the glass up.

"Stop," I shouted, then grabbed his hand. "Shit, Fernando, you really hurt yourself. Shit, shit, shit. It's bleeding pretty bad. I think you need stitches."

He turned melancholy eyes to me, and I saw that once again I was dealing with the gentle, broken Mr. Hyde side of his split personality instead of the insane and raging Dr. Jekyll. "Let me die."

"Oh, for fucks sake, we're back to this again?" I huffed as I pulled him away from the mess, elevating his hand while drag walking him over to a nearby chair. "Look, let's save another tedious round of *woe is me* and keep you from bleeding all over your mom's stuff."

He grunted then slurred, "She hates that."

"I don't blame her. And you got blood on this crazy expensive dress that Ramón got me. Do you know how hard it is to get blood out of this kind of fabric? Might as well turn it into an eight-hundred-dollar cleaning rag now, because I look like I played the part of 'Carrie' in my high school's musical."

"Not that hard to get blood out of silk."

Rolling my eyes, I held his bleeding hand up. "Seriously? Trust me, buddy, it is."

He hissed as I tried to look at his cut. "You scrub a lot of blood, sheep?"

"I'm not a sheep. I'm a girl, and we bleed once a month and often it just comes out of nowhere. I'm not going to throw away my favorite underwear because Aunt Flow decided to show up in the middle of a class. You learn to keep those little stain remover wipes in your purse at all times. Never know when you'll need to clean up a crime scene in your panties."

He visibly paled. "I did not need to hear that shit."

"Oh, grow up."

From across the room, a woman suddenly screamed, "*Madre Dios!*"

I turned to find Juanita, an older Hispanic woman with steel grey hair pulled back in a braid, standing at the entrance to the room with her hands over her mouth in obvious shock. We'd met last time I was here, and she seemed really sweet and nice. When she'd found out I spoke Spanish, she'd been overjoyed and nearly talked my ear off while making lunch for myself and Mrs. Cordova. I gave her a weak smile as she stared at us in horrified shock.

Glancing at Fernando's hand, which continued to drip blood like a leaky faucet, I realized my hand and arm were covered in his blood as well, making it look like a scene out of a horror movie.

"He's okay!" I yelled first in English, then in Spanish. "He accidentally broke the lamp then cut himself trying to clean it up. I think he's going to need stitches."

Diego, looking chagrined, tried to pull his hand away from mine, scowling when I tightened my grip and lifted his arm higher. "I don't need stitches. Leave me alone, sheep."

Juanita leapt into action, saying something into a small black phone before rushing over to our side. She grabbed a navy and white throw blanket from the back of the couch, then took Diego's hand from me, blotting at it while hissing threats in Spanish. Diego, the little shit, actually rolled his eyes at me as the old woman fussed over his hand.

"Shit, Juanita, calm down. I'm fine. This is nothing."

With obvious worry in her voice, Juanita scolded him like he was a little boy, "I swear to you, Mr. Cordova, if you don't start taking care of yourself I'm going to...well, I don't know what I'm going to do, but it will be bad. You hear me? Bad."

The door swung open again and Diego strode in with Judith close on his heels. They both stopped when they caught sight of me and Juanita trying to take care of Fernando, and I waited for Judith to freak out. Instead, she frowned at me and a chill raced down my spine.

"What happened?"

The words dried up in my mouth, but thankfully Juanita spoke up. "Mrs. Cordova, Mr. Diego accidentally knocked over a lamp, then cut himself trying to clean it up."

"Joy," Mrs. Cordova snapped, making me jump. "Are you hurt?"

"No," I stammered while trying to find my backbone around this super intimidating woman.

Diego crossed the room in our direction, his expression dark and grief-filled as he knelt next to his twin. His sleek black braid fell over his shoulder as he tried to catch his brother's eye, but Fernando ignored him. With them together, the resemblance was uncanny except Fernando looked like someone dying of some exotic tropical disease, and Diego radiated good health.

Mrs. Cordova nailed me to the carpet with her cold, shark gaze. "Then why are you covered in blood?"

"I was trying to elevate Fernando's hand. I thought I remembered from my CPR training class that you were supposed to do that. I also remember my mom, she's a nurse, did it with my sister when she fell off her bike and onto a piece of glass hidden in the dirt. It was really gross." I looked down at my hands, solid red as if I'd dipped them into paint. "Actually, now that I think about it, this is really gross. I don't…feel so good."

The metallic coppery scent of his blood seemed to saturate the air around me, and I started to become dizzy and nauseous.

My stomach pitched, and a harsh sweat broke out over me as revulsion made my skin itch. Blood, there was so much blood covering my hands. It reminded me of all the blood I'd shed during the beating, of the blood welling from Hannah's cut lip. I could almost taste it and little black dots danced on the edges of my vision. Just like that my heart started to race and sweat prickled down my back as my vision began to dim.

"Catch her," Judith yelled before someone cradled me in their arms and eased me down to the sofa.

My heart was racing, and I closed my eyes, willing myself to keep the contents of my stomach under control. For some reason, the idea of puking all over myself or this room because of the sight of blood was beyond embarrassing. Normally, I had no problem with bodily fluids, my mom called me her junior nurse, but that red liquid now represented something different than the stuff that flowed through our veins. It seemed to trigger unwanted memories of that night. The smell of the coppery blood hit me again and again with each breath, but I forced myself to stop panting.

Someone elevated my feet, but I kept my eyes closed as slight tremors started in my hands and worked up my arms.

Vaguely, I was aware of Judith berating Fernando, but I didn't really pay them any attention.

At the moment, every bit of everything I had was dedicated to staying conscious.

It wasn't until something cold and wet enveloped my hands that I opened my eyes, and found Diego cleaning my fingers off with a wet handkerchief. A look of concern furrowed his brow. "You okay?"

"I'm sorry, I'm not usually like this. It's just the smell of the blood…it reminds me of that night. I get flashbacks." The shaking got worse, and I loathed the fact that tears were filling my eyes, exposing my weakness. "Really, I'm okay. I'm fine."

Diego stopped cleaning my hands, and instead held them in his own. "Of course, you are. You're here now, with me, and I'd take a bullet for you, kid. Want me to get you a drink?"

Taking an unsteady breath, I shook, hating having to depend on anyone. "I'm fine. Really. I just needed a second."

Mrs. Cordova said something in a hissing whisper and Fernando groaned, "Jesus, Mom, take it easy."

I felt well enough to gently tug my hands from Diego and sit up so I could look over at Fernando.

He was trying to pull his hand away from Mrs. Cordova, who was making little hissing noises through her teeth. "You're lucky you didn't cut a tendon, idiot son of mine. And you're bleeding so much because your blood is more tequila than plasma. You're lucky Joy was here."

He lifted his bloodshot eyes to mine, and I tried to see if I was dealing with sad but nice Fernando or asshole Fernando.

He snorted, "Yeah, real fucking lucky Ramón's pet whore was here fo—"

Before he could finish his sentence, the crack of flesh meeting flesh rang through the room as Mrs. Cordova slapped him across the face.

"You will not talk about your future sis—" Her gaze cut to me then back to Fernando, who was rubbing his cheek with a scowl with his good hand. "You will not talk to a young lady that way in my home, Diego. No matter how much you're hurting inside, you have no right to lash out at her. She's a good girl, and she doesn't deserve such abuse."

"You're right; she is a good girl." He sat up and met my gaze, ignoring Juanita while she treated his hand with stuff from a First Aid kit at her feet. "Which is why you need to run, Joy. Run as fast and as hard away from here as you can and never look back, before it's too late. Ramón, this whole family, is going to chew you up and spit you out. We bring death to the innocent, hurt those we love. Just ask Leo. He broke his little doll, and now she hates him, but there's no escape for her."

"Diego," Judith snapped. "Take Joy to the bathroom so she can wash up. Now."

Diego did as she commanded, hustling me out of the room so fast, I almost fell twice. I looked over my shoulder as Juanita stared at Judith as she said something to Fernando too low for me to hear, her face filled with grief. I tugged at my hand, trying to slow Diego down, but he pulled me after him like I was some reticent child.

Looking like death warmed over, Fernando lurched to his feet then yelled as Diego hurried me away, "Run, little sheep, run!"

Chapter 8
Ramón

I was beat, beyond exhausted, and my whole body ached as I took the stairs up to my parents' house just after sunset. It had been a long, long fucking night. My wet hair clung to the back of my fresh t-shirt, and I looked down at my hands as I neared the front door, checking for traces of blood from my torn up knuckles. Earlier today, after the bullshit with Joy had gone down, I'd had to dispense old-fashioned justice on one of the Santiago cartel's men who'd attempted to kidnap the sixteen-year-old daughter of one of our madams. He claimed that they weren't going to do anything with her, that he was only going to keep her for a little bit as a warning, but the big duffle bag full of torture tools and his video camera told a different story.

Thankfully, the girl had been taught by both her mother and stepfather, one of our lieutenants, how to defend herself, and they had drilled it into her head well enough that she was able to rescue herself. She'd managed to not only escape, but used the military grade Taser her mother made her carry with her everywhere on her captor.

The door opened and a frowning Juanita gestured for me to come inside, her wrinkled face tense with worry.

"Welcome home, Mr. Ramón. Your mother wishes to speak with you on the patio."

"Where's Joy?"

"Please, Mr. Ramón. Your mother wishes to speak with you first."

The look on her sympathetic face let me know the news wasn't good.

I wondered if it had something to do with Joy ignoring my calls and text messages. Maybe she was still pissed at me. I thought I'd smoothed things over with her, but she had a temper to match my own. The thought of kissing her anger away soothed me, but I still worried what my meddling mother wished to discuss. It was no secret she fancied herself a matchmaker, but she was insane with boundary issues, so we never knew what the fuck she'd been up to.

The thought of her trying to manipulate Joy didn't sit well with me, at all.

I considered making a pit stop at the nearest bar in my parent's house, but went straight through to the outdoor sitting area. At this time of night, I knew she'd be by the fountain. Sure enough, she sat in a comfortable chair near the edge of the big water sculpture, but not alone. Leo sat next to her, and his grim expression didn't bode well.

"Where's Joy?"

Her gaze flicked up to me, and the lines around her mouth deepened as she adjusted the light blue shawl covering her shoulders. "Sit down, Ramón."

Fuck, I knew that voice. That was her 'I'm done playing' voice.

I sat a few chairs away from her place on the giant U-shaped outdoor couch, a move that had her glaring at me.

"Where is Joy?"

It was more of a demand than a request, and my mother held up her hand, the large ruby ring she favored throwing off bursts of light from the dozens of candles illuminating the patio. This place had been designed to mimic an old world El Salvadorian outdoor sitting area, giving it a somehow aged feel, even if it was almost new. Lush desert greenery created a privacy screen all around us, and the soft sounds of a Spanish guitar came from hidden speakers. Faint hints of vanilla from the candles scented the air. It should be a relaxing environment, but right now it was about as soothing as a lion cage. Tension crackled in the air, and I had a sinking feeling in my gut that my already shit night was about to get a lot worse.

I wasn't staring at the kind, sweet mother who'd been just about the best mom any kid could ever ask for. I was looking at the daughter of a drug lord, a woman who built an empire with her husband through blood and terror, then held it with willpower and determination. When I was a kid, she'd hidden this side of herself from me, sheltered us all from cartel, but as soon as I entered the family business at the tender age of fourteen, she'd let me see the coldness that she'd kept from me.

To say I'd been a little shocked that my devoted mother was a criminal lord was the understatement of the century.

The coldness that allowed her to rule with an iron first burned in her dark brown eyes now as she said, "It's time to bring Joy into the family."

I knew what she meant, and it wasn't her way of saying I should marry Joy. No, she was telling me that it was time for Joy's programming, something I was increasingly opposed to. She wasn't ready, the trauma of her beating still fresh on her body and in her mind. She needed time to heal, time to be normal. With a start, I realized I no longer felt like she *needed* to be programed in order for me to trust her.

She was Joy, my Joy, and I knew to the depths of my soul she would never betray those she loved.

Something clicked into place in my heart, and confusion flickered across my mother's face. "Ramón, are you all right?"

I realized I was rubbing my chest, and smiling in a way that was creeping my hardened mother out. "I'm fine, but Joy isn't ready."

"Ramón, it is time."

"Why? Why now? What happened?" I drummed my fingers on the arm of the chair, my gaze going between my mother and a haggard Leo. "You were fine with my courting her without interference yesterday. What's changed?"

Her nostrils flared and a minor tremor went through her, breaking the ice and showing the anguish she hid beneath. "Fernando...he hurt himself on a piece of glass. The sight of his blood sent Joy into a panic. An absolute panic. From what Leo tells me, that is as out of character as I thought it was."

"Why the hell was she with Fernando?"

"Joy wanted to see Hannah, badly," Leo spoke up, his voice thick with grief. "Unfortunately, Hannah isn't...handling things well."

"She'll get better," my mother soothed as she leaned over and rubbed Leo's big shoulder. "Just give her time."

Shaking his head, Leo rubbed his face then sat up and stared at me with haunted eyes. "We think Fernando told Joy some things, things she shouldn't know."

"What did he tell her?" My gut clenched as I considered the millions of different things he could have said that would damn me forever in her eyes.

Fuck, I should have bound her to me when I still had a chance.

The wind rustled through the palm trees as my mother adjusted her silk shawl. "He said enough about Jason to let her know the public car crash story was a lie. And he said some other things that upset her as well. When we wouldn't let her see Hannah, she broke down and we had to sedate her." My mother took a quick breath, closing her eyes for a moment before opening them and continuing. "Joy is all right, safe and sleeping in your room, but I am worried about her. Now would be the perfect time to ease her burden."

It took everything inside of me not to choke the shit out of my mother. "Ease her burden? Are you fucked in the head?"

Wrong thing to say.

She was up like a flash, slapping me hard enough that it stung, but didn't hurt.

Between her and Joy, I'd never have not sore cheeks again.

"I am trying to save her. You don't understand. I fear for her, Ramón, and I don't want her to end up like Hannah."

Though some may find it strange, my mother was hurt at Hannah's rejection of her efforts to help her. It was as if my mom didn't understand why Hannah would be upset when she found out her boyfriend was a criminal. My own worry over Joy's reaction had my reply coming out sharper than I intended.

"What the fuck did you think would happen? She got beat to fuck because she couldn't say Leo's name, couldn't save herself from harm because of your programming."

Leo let out a pained sound while a single tear rolled down my mother's cheek, and I felt like a right bastard.

I shook my head and clasped my hands together. "I mean seriously, Mom. You and Leo played God. Did you think it was going to turn out okay? And now you want to do the same to Joy? Maybe you don't give a fuck about her, but I do, and I'm not letting you experiment on her."

Instead of arguing with me, she closed her eyes and nodded. "No, you're right. We made a mistake with Hannah, despite our best intentions. It was a mistake that won't happen with Joy."

For a moment, I considered telling her that Joy was off limits, that I didn't want her programmed, but I knew my mother would do it anyway. It was her nature to be as ruthless as she deemed necessary in order to protect her family, and I could tell she truly thought she wasn't harming anyone with her programming. The best I could do to help Joy in this situation was mitigate the damage, and control this clusterfuck as much as I could.

"You're damn right it won't, because no one does Joy's programming but me. Understood?" Her lips tightened, and I inwardly sighed at the sight of her getting ready to say no. "Mom, she is going to be my wife, the mother to my children. I understand your need to protect me, to protect the family, but I'm the only one that will do this. Agree now, or I'll take off with Joy and you will never see us again without a fight."

To my surprise, she rolled her eyes. "So dramatic. You must get it from your father."

"Promise me." Like all kids, I knew how to play my mother and pulled out all the stops. "Consider it an early wedding present. Please."

I could see she hated it, but she spat out, "I promise."

Relaxation filled me and I tipped my head back, taking in the clear night sky above. "Thank you."

"But please, Ramón, don't wait too long."

"I won't. When she's ready I'll do it, but not until then." Leo watched us with a hard to read expression, but I had a feeling he had my back on this. "Promise me you'll leave her alone."

"You know I can't do that. I care about her as well, Ramón, and if she needs someone to talk to, I'll be there for her."

"Fine, but don't take up all her time, and don't manipulate her into seeing you. Give her space."

She clenched her jaw, but nodded. "I won't rush a relationship, but I will let her know that she is welcome in our family."

"Mom, that's rushing." My mom was wise enough not to argue with me and merely shrugged. "I mean it. Leave my relationship with Joy alone. If I find out you've done anything to meddle in it, did something to manipulate her, I'll be furious."

Instead of responding, she fiddled with her ring, her tell that she was keeping something from me.

Something I wouldn't like.

Praying for patience, I gritted out, "What did you do?"

She lifted her chin at me, the picture of defiance. "Nothing that will harm her."

"Mother...."

Leo leaned forward and narrowed his eyes at my mom as she looked defiantly at me. "Just a small dose of D128, only enough to...distract her. Don't worry, I was very precise."

"What? You drugged her without my permission? Have you lost your mind?" I stood up from my chair and began to pace. "Fuck! God fucking damnit!"

My roar was loud enough to bring my father racing out onto the patio, dressed in a pair of black lounge pants and a clean white t-shirt that stretched over his still solid frame. "Ramón, what the hell is going on?"

"Mother," I spat the word out. "Gave Joy D128 without my permission."

My father's eyebrows climbed up his forehead, then he turned on my suddenly meek mother as Leo stood and joined us.

"Judith," my dad snapped. "Tell me you didn't."

My mom must be crazy. Even I knew that was my dad's 'super pissed' tone of voice, yet she was indignant as she said, "It wasn't much. Just a drop. Enough to make sure it works. Besides, she was sedated, so she'll sleep most of it off."

"You don't know that for sure." My dad said, running his hands through his mostly silver hair, frustration deepening his wrinkles. "You have no idea how it will affect her."

Giving my dad an imperious look, my mom said, "I'm sure she'll be fine."

Leo spoke up from next to me, "Security just alerted me that Joy called a cab from her phone, and is trying to find a way out of the house."

My dad laid a hand on my shoulder. "Go, find Joy. I'll deal with your mother. I promise this will not happen again."

They started fighting as I left, my mother sounding more petulant than apologetic, but I didn't give a shit.

Joy was on D128, awake, and no doubt pissed.

Sure enough, my suspicions were confirmed when I found her tugging at one of the locked doors. As soon as I saw her, I made the motion to the security camera to go black. What I was about to do to this feisty little girl wasn't for anyone's eyes but my own. Wearing a pair of black yoga pants and what looked like one of my old t-shirts that reached almost to her shins, Joy gave the solid wood door leading to the garage a kick, then cursed as she hurt her toe.

I dropped to my knees beside her, drawing a startled scream from her as I grabbed her foot. She almost lost her balance, wind-milling with both arms before I caught her. Looking down at her, I could tell she'd been crying, a lot, and I felt like such a bastard. I should have been with her today, but I couldn't put off my responsibilities. Not with both Fernando and Leo out of commission. I was relying heavily on Mark and a few of my lieutenants to cover for my absent brothers, and we were stretched dangerously thin. Once things calmed down, I'd have to look into advancing men through the ranks that deserved more responsibility.

I had this sweet beauty in my life now, and I wanted to be able to spend as much time with her as I could, which meant cutting back at work.

Instead of feeling guilty, like I was letting my parents down, I felt a sense of relief settle through me as let out a slow breath.

Her face was bare of any makeup, and her cheeks when red before she yelled, "Put me down!"

"No."

She started to struggle, so I flipped her round ass over my shoulder in a fireman's hold. Her shrill screams and foul name calling echoed through the house. To my shock she took a good bite of my butt through my pants, so I gave hers a couple hard slaps in return. That turned her into a thrashing little wildcat. I told her if she didn't settle down, I was going to paddle her ass but good.

By the time we got to my room, Joy was nearly incoherent with fury, a side effect of her body trying to process the D128 without a sexual outlet.

There would be no talking with her, no reasoning, until I gave her what her body so desperately needed.

My cock.

And let me tell you, my dick was more than ready to fuck this mouthy little girl into submission.

I won't lie, I enjoyed fighting her as I used my ties to bind her, spread eagle, to my bed. She resisted the whole time, hurling insults at me that barely made any sense, and often had me hiding a grin. I have no idea who or where this girl learned to swear, but she had a vocabulary that would make a trucker blush. She called me names I'd never even considered using as an insult.

After I finished knotting the last burgundy tie around her wrist, I let out a sigh of appreciation as I leaned back and examined Joy, spread out before me at last.

I couldn't help that my mother had drugged her without my permission, but I could make it up to Joy by giving her everything she needed.

Craved.

I widened my legs, the evidence of my engorged cock straining against my black dress slacks. All pink cheeked and disheveled, she presented a decadent treat. I ran my hands along her legs, marveling at the way the fabric hugged her every lush curve. With her legs spread like this, the fabric was stretched tight over her pussy and I had a craving to place my mouth there and see if she'd soaked through her pants yet with her sweet honey.

With anger still burning in her gaze, she panted out, "Untie me, you mother fucking dick sandwich."

Pondering what a dick sandwich could be, I tested her responses by stroking my hand along the inside of one of her bound arms, the golden skin shimmering beneath my touch like it had been gilded.

She continued to rant at rave, but at a lesser volume, and a light pink blush spread from her chest and up her neck, eventually turning the apples of her round cheeks a dusky rose.

With a slow, slow touch I ran my hand beneath her shirt, letting it rest against her soft skin, feeling the gentle give of her slightly rounded belly.

Unable to help myself, I gave her a good squeeze, making her squeal in protest as I groaned.

"Stop that! Get your hands off me right now and untie me."

Forcing myself to ease up my grip on all her delicious softness, I gentled my touch to a slow stroke, silently apologizing for being so rough with her. "I'm sorry you had a bad day, baby. I should have been her with you."

"Ramón," she obviously strained for patience as I leaned back then took off my shirt, her gaze hungry on my flesh. "You and me need to have a serious talk. Untie me."

"Nope."

I swear I heard her teeth grind before she lifted her head from the bed and glared at me. "What do you mean? Nope."

"I'm going to fuck you until you remember who you belong to. Then we'll talk, and I'll tell you what really happened to Fernando's wife and child…and why it isn't public knowledge."

Chapter 9
Joy

Emotions tore through me, my skin prickling with heat as my empty pussy clenched and my gaze unwillingly went to Ramón's pants, where I could see the outline of his thick erection testing the limits of the material.

I salivated at the sight, and a little tiny orgasm fluttered across my clit, if that was even possible.

All I knew is that I was so mad at him, and for good reason, but at the same time I wanted to fuck him so bad I was ready to chew these ties off my wrists and jump him.

A low growl escaped me, and I flushed with embarrassment, hoping he'd think I was just clearing my throat as he stripped his shoes, then socks and finally pants off. This left him in only a pair of deep hunter green boxer briefs that more than revealed the thick shaft that I knew would fill me the way I needed.

And boy did I need. My blood seemed to move differently through my body, centering on my pussy which felt uncomfortably swollen. Like I'd been using a vibrator for ages and I was oversensitive. But I hadn't even been touched. All Ramón had to do was look at me and I got wet between the legs.

When he briefly ran his fingertips down my slit, I let out a moan that was downright pitiful.

"Ramón." Embarrassment mixed with my pleasure as I realized how pathetic I sounded.

"I know, *mami*."

The soft laughter lightening his voice irritated me. "It's official, you've given me blue bean with all your cock teasing."

He leaned over me, then hid his face in my neck and laughed while I scowled. "Get off me."

"You're killing me, sweetheart. Just shush and let me take care of you. Be a good little girl."

Suspicion flashed through me and I growled, "I'm not into Daddy play. That's Hannah and Leo's thing."

Above me, Ramón froze. "How do you know this?"

I rolled my eyes. "Do you seriously think that Leo and

Hannah can fuck, with their bedroom wall adjoining mine, and not be freaks? Nope. I have to hear them all damn night, and let me tell you, Hannah can yowl as loud as a cat and it's usually 'Daddy' when she does it, so yeah, I know about their bedroom antics. Every time I hear anyone say the word 'Daddy' in a song, or on TV, or in a video, I shudder. They've traumatized me. I have a 'Daddy' trigger now. So, no, I'm not into that. If you are, well—I guess I can call you my cousin. We could be like fifth cousins four times removed, so it wouldn't be weird, but you can pretend in your head that we're first cousins. But, like, by marriage. You know what? I'm over explaining this. I just…maybe you should gag me because I've evidently lost my mind."

His mouth twitched once, then twice, and the anger broke from his face as he laughed until he'd collapsed on top of my spread body, his face buried in my breasts while he laughed so hard he snorted.

The absurdity of the situation rolled through me, and I wanted to reach out and hold him, but the stupid bastard had me tied up with his freaking neck ties of all things.

And he'd done it while he fought me.

My amusement drained away as heat began to build in my core. I became very conscious of Ramón's weight, his solid male mass pressing me into the mattress.

"Don't worry, *mi amor*, I'm not into any of that shit. I'm into you—however, whenever, and wherever I can get you. I'm gonna live in your pussy." To emphasize this statement, he settled firmly between my legs, spreading me wider than I'm used to in order to accommodate his mass. "I've been holding off because I know, without a doubt, once I've had you, I will never let you leave my side. Do you understand?"

No, I didn't understand shit. The only thing I could think about was how amazingly awesome his pelvis felt against my swollen sex as he pressed his thick, gorgeous cock against me. My body was out of control, begging for this man in a way that dominated my thoughts, stripped away a layer of civility and left me in a raw, exposed state. Instinctively, I fought the loss of control, and fear tried to mix with my arousal, but Ramón wouldn't let it.

Rolling his hips so our bodies, separated by thin pieces of

silky material, ground together in the most delicious way, he whispered my name in a way that gave me chills. I wanted nothing between us, wanted him inside of me, easing this terrible empty feeling that seemed to consume me. I couldn't even think past my body anymore, more than eager to just take the mind-numbing pleasure he offered me.

I loved the feel of his weight on me, his scent filling my nose, the sheer power of his presence blanketing me in an odd mixture of lust and comfort.

He licked along my neck then growled, "You particularly attached to these leggings?"

"I borrowed them from some of the clothes Leo brought here for Hannah."

At the mention of my friend, tears filled my eyes and Ramón made a pained noise. "No, baby, no. Please, no sadness. Not now."

"Everything's so confusing. I don't understand anything anymore. The whole world has gone crazy."

"Look at me," he commanded in such a serious tone that I stopped my sniffling pity party and stared up at him. "You have *me*. I'm your anchor; I'm your rock. I will never let you down, ever. When you're ready to give yourself to me, I want you to know that I will take care of you."

"Ramón," I whispered as his cock stroked me. "We—"

My words choked off in a pinched gargle as he clasped his hand around my throat hard enough that my pulse leapt and my clit twitched. He wasn't hurting me, he was owning me with this gesture. I might have protested, but his other hand was busy ripping open the crotch of my leggings, exposing my dripping wet pussy to the cool air. When Ramón rubbed the tip of his finger on my clit, my back arched, and I would have shouted out if I'd been able to past his grip.

Looking me right in the eye, he rubbed my throbbing clit slowly, up and down. "No more lip from you, brat. Got it?"

I nodded, and when he released his hand, I gasped and tried to grind onto his hand. "Please, more. No more fingers, no more tongue. I need your dick."

His chuckle was downright menacing as he cocked his head and examined me, his gaze heavily lidded with lust. "It's cute you think you get to tell me what to do. While I may not be your

Daddy, I am your man, and you need to understand what I mean when I say that."

"I'm tired of talking. Please, I *need* you."

"I know you do, and I'm going to give it to you, I promise. But there's something you should know, something fucked up, but important."

Dread filled me, but my hips still twitched with the need to be filled. "What?"

He leaned down and to my shock, pulled a knife from beneath the bed. "I am into some kinky shit."

Staring at the big, sharp blade with the dull black grip, I licked my lips, nervous but also curious. "What do you plan on doing with that?"

"Cutting your clothes off with it."

"Why?"

"First, because I don't want to untie you. Seeing you here, smelling your juicy pussy in the air, feeling you…like a dream come true."

"You have some very kinky dreams."

He grinned, then something chilling flashed through his gaze. "You have no idea."

Flipping the knife in the air, he caught it by the hilt without looking, playing with it for a moment before lifting the slightly torn crotch of my pants away from my body.

As he carefully began to slice through the stretchy fabric, he started talking softly, gently, as he stared at my pussy, "I like doing things like this because it shows how much you trust me, and that makes me feel ten fucking feet tall. Being your man, knowing your mine…*owning* you, is what gets me off."

Air drafted over my now entirely exposed sex and Ramón made a sympathetic noise. "Oh, sweetheart, you're so swollen. That poor pussy needs some love. I'm sorry, baby. I didn't know it was that bad."

I let out a little shriek as he casually tossed the knife at the thick wood bedpost, where it stuck perfectly in the middle with a solid thunk.

Before I could look at Ramón, my eyes rolled back in my head as he gave my pussy one long, excruciating lick that ended with a light, thrumming suck on my clit.

I turned my head to the side, cheek pressed to the sheets as my overheated body exploded in a throbbing orgasm that had me jerking in both shock and pleasure. Ramón stroked my body while he nibbled my inner thighs and praised me for coming so hard. I would have laughed if I wasn't floating in a soft, decadent cloud of release, the rush of endorphins so hard I was tingly from my scalp to my toes.

"Joy?"

I scrunched my nose, but didn't bother to reply, too busy enjoying my high.

"If you want my cock, you'll open your eyes."

At the mention of his dick, my eyelids slowly lifted. I was treated to the sight of Ramón, naked, stroking his thick shaft. The pink head of his cock, with its big gold ring piercing, gleamed with his pre-cum. It's crazy, I know, but I swear I could smell that moisture on the swollen head of his shaft, like I could taste his pheromones in the air. A scent that assured me he was a big, healthy male animal capable of taking care of me and giving me healthy babies.

Done with being denied, I looked him dead in the eyes and said, "Ramón, please, make me yours. I want to yours, and I want you to be mine. No more teasing, please, make love to me."

His whole body relaxed, then tightened again. "I've been waiting for you to say that."

He was so hard that when he lowered himself between my thighs, he didn't need to use his hand to tease around the opening of my pussy. "Jesus, *mami*, you're so hot down there. Wet and slippery. Love watching those pretty butterfly lips of your pussy rub my dick."

I jerked at the restraints, wanting to touch his big chest, to run my fingers over the soft hair covering his tattoos. "Ramón, untie me."

He grinned, then freed my right arm. "One hand."

I didn't argue, instead I reached up and curled my hand around the back of his neck, bringing him down so I could kiss him.

The moment our lips met, he began to breech me with his blessedly large dick, the oversized gold ring a different, harder pressure inside my softness. It made me so aware of how deep he was pushing into me, how far he'd penetrated me. My whole body shook as he just kept going, and we panted against each other's mouths as he finally, finally planted himself all the way inside of me.

I whined, the feeling a confusing mixture of pain and pleasure as my body contracted around him.

"Oh my God," Ramón groaned out, pulling his hips back then thrusting forward again in with a grunt. "You are so tight. Gonna have to stretch this pretty cunt out."

All I could do was moan as he thrust in and out, slowly, languid moves that ending with him grinding his pelvis expertly against my clit. I raked my hand down his back and he freed my other, but kept my legs open wide as he fucked me. I wondered why he didn't untie all of me, but could give a shit less as he continued to give me exactly what I needed. With an unusual amount of aggression, I thrust my hips as much as I could against him, my teeth clenched as my orgasm roared over me, my head thrashing until he buried a hand in my curls and fisted it, making me hold still, making me take it.

I tried pushing him away, my body quivering as the waves of the orgasm were triggered again, and I came hard on his cock while he pounded into me, wailing his name.

"That's it," he snarled. "Take it, take me. You want my come in your tight little pussy? I want to feel it splash inside of you. Bet you're so sensitive right now you would be able enjoy every twitch of my cock, bathing you with my cum."

"Yes, yes, yes."

My words came out slurred, but I hoped he understood me as I spasmed around him, so turned on by the thought of him releasing inside of me I was sinking my nails into his ass and holding him to me.

Ramón placed a series of stinging bites along my neck. "That makes you hot, doesn't it? The thought of me giving your sweet pussy my cum. Tell me you want it."

Words were beyond me at this point because he'd began to increase his pace, the relentless drive of his hips making my whole body burst into pleasure.

"Tell me you want it," he repeated.

"Yes!" I screamed as I began to cum again, my cry ragged. "Come with me."

I collapsed against the bed as he did as I begged, finally giving me what he'd promised. With each shuddering pulse of my climax rippling along his length, he filled me up with bursts of his seed, and the desperate way he chanted my name made my heart sing. Clasping him to me, I moaned softly as what felt like a climax aftershock twitched through my thoroughly used sex. Inside of me, Ramón twitched in response, then began to grow hard inside of me…or maybe he never went soft in the first place.

I got lost in that feeling and closed my eyes, savoring the soft roll of his hips as he began to fuck me again.

I don't know how he did it, but suddenly my feet were free, and he flipped us around so I was on top.

The sudden shift in positions drove him deeper into me than before, and I flinched as he went too far.

Instead of pulling back, he held me in place as I squirmed. "Told you, sweetheart, we're going to stretch you out."

"Ramón, it's too much."

"Give your body a chance." He gently rubbed my clit with his thumb as his other hand squeezed my hip. "That's it."

I looked down to where his dark, tattooed, rough and battered hand played between my legs, the contrast of his dark pubic hair against my blonde. My pussy seemed so pink against his skin and the sight of him rubbing my clit sent a rush of hard desire through me. Suddenly the too much inside of me became just right, and I seemed to melt around his cock.

"That's my girl," he encouraged. "Now ride me."

As I did, I looked at Ramón. To my surprise, he gave me this big, beautiful smile. I'd never seen anything like it. My chest ached in an odd, but pleasurable way. Happiness radiated from him, and he cupped my face with his gentle hands as I smiled back at him.

"So, beautiful," he murmured, "never even imagined a girl as pretty as you could exist."

My usual protests had no place in my mind as his piercing hit my g-spot.

"Ramón," I gasped with a shiver.

In one easy move, he flipped us over so I was on my back. "Wasn't kidding when I said your pussy was made for me, just like my cock was made to make you cum."

Throwing my legs over his shoulders, he angled my hips, then began to plunge into me. It only took him a few strokes to find the right position, and once he did, his piercing worked my g-spot like nothing I'd ever felt. I screamed through clenched teeth as my body strained to release, but with Ramón's thick cock stretching me, I didn't get my usual stream of fluid, only a little bit-just enough to give me the sensation of cumming without the full climax. Strange moans were coming from deep in my chest, and I would have been embarrassed if Ramón wasn't obviously loving the fuck out of each one.

"Get me wet," he whispered. "Push out and soak my cock while I fuck you."

I wrapped my arms around his broad shoulders as much as I could, and met him thrust for thrust until I swear I could feel my orgasm starting from the base of my spine and exploding outwards.

This time I did as he asked, straining against his hold. He continued to fuck me while praising me for being such a good, dirty girl.

Gripping my hair, he forced my head back so he could stare at me. "Tell me you're mine."

My words came out thick as my brain continued to send out blissful bursts of pleasure. "I'm yours, Ramón."

His lids came down and his whole face tightened, the muscles on his body all seeming to flex at once as he drove into me. He shivered hard, his cock throbbing, as he released yet another load into my already full pussy.

I was on the pill, so I wasn't worried about a baby, and I knew Ramón would never endanger me. He was the first man I'd ever had sex with bareback, and the intimacy it created between us was like nothing I'd ever experienced. After he was done, he gently pulled out, and I couldn't help but wince. I felt used, wonderfully used, but used nonetheless. My poor sex was so sore.

"Hold on," Ramón murmured, giving me a kiss before going into the bathroom.

When he returned, he cleaned me up with a soft washcloth, then somehow stripped the bedding and remade it without really disturbing me. He just rolled my sleepy body from one side of the bed to the other. I was so zoned out, just a limp bag of unprotesting bones, I couldn't have cared less what he did with me,. Euphoria wasn't a strong enough word for this high. I could only sigh in complete relaxation when he finally turned off the lights, turned on the ocean sound machine, and pulled me next to him.

I cuddled against his big frame like we'd been doing it all our lives. Moving pillows around until I was comfortable, I couldn't resist giving Ramón a little nuzzle and some tender kisses.

His happy sigh made me smile in the dark, and as he covered us up and stroked my body, I drifted off in the safety of his adoring arms.

It was late at night when I stirred again. After bumbling around in the dark then answering the call of nature, I stared at my reflection in equal parts horror and amusement.

I had hickies all over my breasts.

While I'd known he was biting and sucking at my breasts with the reverence of a true tit man, I hadn't realized at the time how rough he'd been.

How absolutely, deliciously rough. I had beard burn on my inner thighs, and my body still bore signs of the beating I'd had mere days ago. For a moment I tensed, waiting for a surge of panic at the brutal memories, but the knowledge that Ramón was in the other room helped me to relax. Even my paranoia couldn't argue with the fact that Ramón was all kinds of badass. He reeked testosterone and his pheromones were strong enough to make any woman putty in his hands.

With a sigh, I took a moment to brush my teeth, and was in the process of drying my mouth when Ramón appeared behind me in the mirror, nude and aroused.

I was reminded of my own naked state when he rubbed his cock against my back, our height difference making me stand on my tiptoes to try and get that dick where I wanted it.

When he moved my hair over to the side and began to kiss my neck, I shivered.

"You look so beautiful right now," he gave my speeding pulse another kiss as tingles spread through me like wildfire. "I'm so fucking lucky you're here."

I manage to gather myself enough to say, "You're darn right you are. I wanted to leave, but your mom wouldn't let me!"

"She wouldn't let you?"

"No." I pushed back at him. "She got me a massage, then

made this lovely dinner and special dessert for me. It would have been rude to leave."

I burst of hot air brushed my neck as Ramón snorted. "Were there handcuffs involved?"

"No! But I wanted to leave after that shit with Fernando. I really did, but somehow after talking to her, I found myself taking a nap, then getting rubbed down by some big woman with the best hands I've ever felt in my life."

To my amusement he got angry. "Were her hands better than mine?"

"You moron." I elbowed him in the stomach and met his stormy gaze in the mirror with a giggle. "She was like your mom's age."

Right away, he mellowed. "That's fine then."

I tried to squirm out of his grasp. "So glad I have your approval."

He took a step back, then grabbed a towel and spread it on the countertop before picking me up like a little doll and seating me on the counter so he could stand between my legs, his cock nestled against my pussy and belly.

"No man gets to touch you."

I wiggled my hips. "No woman gets to touch you."

He rubbed his nose against mine. I inhaled the scent of him, his naked body too tempting to resist. I ran my hands over his hard shoulders, tracing the hollow of his collarbone, then placing a kiss over his heart. I spent a moment there, with my head pressed to his chest, listening to it beat. The sound, the heat of him, soothed me. When he pulled me close into a hug, I let myself absorb some of his endless strength. It had been a long, trying day, after a series of trying days, and I was both physically and mentally exhausted.

"Fernando is suicidal," I whispered, my voice carrying oddly in the large, tiled bathroom.

"I know," Ramón whispered back, grief thick in his voice. "I need to tell you something. It is very, very important that you realize what I'm about to share is something you can never tell anyone, or talk about with anyone outside of my family. I need your word, Joy."

I leaned back enough to look at him, searching his serious face before nodding slowly. "Of course, Ramón. Whatever you tell me will stay strictly between us."

He took in a deep breath, his massive furred chest expanding as his hands came to rest on my hips again. This time it wasn't to grope or squeeze, but rather just to hold on. I wrapped my legs around his trim waist and tried to not notice how sexy he was, and the fact that his fat shaft was splitting my pussy lips.

Taking a strand of my hair between his fingers, he focused on the corkscrew curl as he spoke, "Remember how I told you about people being after my family for money?"

At my nod, he proceeded to tell me a tragic tale about Fernando's evil wife selling her son Jason to a rival cartel, where the five-year-old was tortured and killed, all for money. The depth of her betrayal rocked my soul. I found myself holding back sobs as Ramón broke in my arms, his tears wetting my skin as he clung to me. Great shudders wracked his frame, and I did my best to sooth him, giving him everything he needed. If I wasn't falling in love with him already, this moment in his palatial bathroom, naked as the day I was born, comforting this probably insane man did it.

His trust...humbled me. I couldn't think of a better word for it. Without a doubt Ramón was not a man who opened up easily. I think he might have a split personality, but both sides of him seemed to adore me, so things could be worse. Looking on the bright side of life was a skill my *abuela* had taught me right before she passed away. She said I needed to stop looking for the darkness in life, but for the blessings instead. I'd been seventeen at the time, and miserable, but her words made me think that maybe I needed to take a step back from my drama and really look at the situation.

Even though it had pained him, Ramón opened up to me, and I recognized how important that was. He for sure wasn't the kind of guy who let just anyone into his life. No, I got the impression he had those he considered family, and that was it. The rest of the world wasn't to be trusted. I could see where he'd gotten it from. His mother was the same way. Protecting Fernando at all costs, doing everything she could to keep him safe. A woman like that probably took the betrayal just as hard as her son.

I took in a shuddering breath and continued to gently massage Ramón's back. Bit by bit, he softened under my touch. When our lips met, his were soft and swollen from his tears. Our kiss was unbearably gentle, and I tried to give him everything. To figure out a way to let him know I really understood the value of his trust.

"When I was thirteen," I said in a low, choked voice, "I thought about killing myself."

Ramón instantly stood at full attention, his gaze boring into me. "*Mi carina*. Why? Was it that bitch sister of yours?"

"Her...and my cousin Barb killed herself around that time. Some asshole Barb had dated had videotaped them having sex and posted it for everyone to see. She was destroyed, her life became a living hell. Even her parents were mad at her, and it wasn't her fault. Because she was a girl, she became a whore in the world's eyes while he was seen as some kind of stud."

"Who is he?"

"It doesn't matter. What does matter is, when I found out she'd done it, I was jealous of her. How fucked up is that? See, at the time my sister Brittney was making my life hell at home. My mother and my *abuela* had gotten into a fight over something, something stupid, and as a result my big sister had to watch us after school until my dad got home. Without my *abuela* there to run interference, things got really bad with Brittney." I drew in a deep breath. "She hated me. Her boyfriend had tried to get her to talk me into doing a threesome with them. I was thirteen and had...well, all this. The next day, a boy she had a crush on at school asked her to hook me up with him. From that point on, she detested me, considered me competition in everything."

"Would you be upset if I killed your sister?"

I gave a weak laugh. "No. It's cool. See, when I was sixteen, my mom sent Hannah and me to stay with my *abuela* for the summer. I think she was catching on that my big sister was being a huge bitch and was trying to keep the peace. That summer, Hannah and I soaked up all the love my *abuela* had to offer. She babied us, took care of everything, and made sure we knew how much she cared for us."

"She sounds wonderful."

I reached behind him and grabbed a towel, but Ramón took it from me and began to gently wipe my face as I continued my story. "Totally. Don't get me wrong, we weren't lazy around her house. She felt like she had to cram all the knowledge of how to be a proper woman into our heads in three months. So Hannah and I got a crash course in how to be a Puerto Rican housewife. Some of it was crazy shit that I'll never do, but it was fun to learn. I can my own vegetables, can make any kind of fruit jam you want, and can cook dozens of traditional Latin dishes. I can also kind of sew, know how to do a flower arrangement, and how to treat a husband…in the bedroom. Let me tell you, those lessons were awkward."

"I bet. She give you the birds and the bees speech?"

"No, my conservative 75-year-old grandmother gave us the 'how to make sure your husband is happy' speech." He gave a mock grimace, and I nodded. "Yeah."

"That's just wrong." He rubbed his own face briskly with the towel, then tossed it on the floor.

"Hey, put that in the hamper."

Rolling his eyes, he opened the drawer between my legs and pulled out a tube of ointment with a prescription label on it. "Relax, my mom has an army of maids."

"Spoiled."

He gave me a roguish wink that went right to my sore lady bits, then began to open the tube.

"What's that?" After twisting the cap off and placing it on the counter, he squeezed out a long line of what looked like Vaseline. "Is that lube?"

"No, it's not lube." He swiped the gel between my labia and I hissed as it initially burned, then sighed when it eased into a low heat that felt really good.

Really, really good.

Warm.

Tingly.

With wide eyes I breathed out, "What is that?"

"Experimental healing compound from our lab in El Salvador. It will accelerate the healing of your tender little pussy. I'm afraid I was too rough with you, and I'm sorry I hurt you. Don't worry, I'll fuck that tenderness out of you so you can play with the grownups."

I bit the side of his neck lightly. "Can you not go five minutes without being an asshole?"

His chuckle warmed my already tingling clit further as he massaged my labia, making my eyes roll back in my head.

"Shhhh, *mami*. Let me take care of you."

By take care of me, he meant let him finger fuck me to three hard orgasms before I finally melted into a puddle on the sink.

I was barely aware of him cleaning my body, but I had flashes of almost waking up then drifting off as he hummed while he cared for me, or sang in a low, beautiful voice.

"Should'a been a rock star," I muttered as I leaned into his chest while he carried me.

"Nah, not the life for me."

I surfaced again once he had us arranged for sleeping, with him playing big spoon behind me.

It warmed my heart that he'd take the uncomfortable position, the one where his arm would fall asleep beneath the weight of my head. His sacrifice allowed me the ultimate comfort of pretty much snuggling into his body until every inch of us that could touch, did. For an extra layer of security, I wrapped his arm around me and sighed with happiness.

"You okay, *mi amor*?"

"I'm good. So good I feel like sparkles should be shooting out of my vagina."

His laughter made me giggle and I just basked in the happiness of being in his presence. "I'd pay to see that."

"Perv."

"You brought it up."

He kissed the side of my neck and I softened. "I love you."

I swear he had to feel my heart lurch as I stiffened. "What?"

"Don't worry. You don't have to say it back. Just wanted to let you know, if I wasn't clear, I love you. You're it for me, Joy."

I could only shake my head, then slump when he grabbed my hand and began to massage it. "I—Ramón, this is going too fast."

"I didn't tell you so you'd feel like you had to say it back, sweetheart. I just wanted you to know that I think you're amazing, and I promise you I'm gonna make you see your worth. I'm going to love you until you love yourself."

As usual, I used sarcasm when I felt especially vulnerable. "So, you're going to fuck me until I love myself? That's a rather novel approach. Maybe I could do a thesis on it. We'd have to put a lot of effort into the research. Are you…up to it?"

"Brat." He leaned up and slapped my breast, then pinched the nipple hard. "You do love to mouth off."

I rubbed my ass against his erection, and he rewarded me with a groan. "Maybe you should fuck me and teach me a lesson."

My desire wasn't as fierce as it had been earlier in the night, but a low fire still burned in my belly, embers that could be easily fanned back into a bonfire.

"That hardly sounds like a punishment."

I easily turned in his arms, then pinned him back to the bed. "Put your hands above your head."

"Excuse me?"

Giving him a little pout, I said, "Please, Ramón? I want to explore you. Every time you touch me I end up forgetting everything but your tongue, or your fingers…or your dick. I want a turn. Trust me, I'll make it good for you."

"*Mi amore*, all you have to do is look at me with those big, beautiful, jade green eyes, and it's good for me." Instead of putting his hands up, like I'd asked, he instead laced his hands behind his head and leaned back into the pillows, his biceps bunching up nicely. "But you're right, I've been greedy. Go ahead, touch me wherever and however you want."

He'd left a bedside light on, and I bit my lower lip as I took a moment to admire him, stretched out on the bed like some kind of sultan.

Instead of appearing restrained, he seemed more indulgent than anything, like he was letting me play with him.

Arrogant fuck. He had no idea that not only did I enjoy sex, I'd studied it in college.

I put my skills to good use as I slowly began to seduce and explore him. Starting with the sensitive skin of his inner wrist, I nibbled on the skin there as he tried to capture my breast in his mouth. With a tsking sound I pulled back.

"Uh-uh. Control yourself, Ramón."

He gave me a grin that was more like a snarl. "If you think you're going to wave that big, chocolate nipple in my face and not have me latch on, you're delusional."

I wanted to argue with him, but the way he couldn't resist me made me feel wanted and loved. "Please, baby. Let me do this for you. It's an ancient technique I read about in my sexual history class."

He sank his head back into his pillow and looked up at me with an arched brow. "A what class?"

I stuck my tongue out at him. "It's a real thing! Sex is an essential part of the human experience, and we've been doing it for a long, long time. Most cultures were pretty up front about fucking, unlike the States."

His pretty, full lips twitched as he fought a smile. "I see."

I was tempted to poke him in the chest, but he still hadn't touched me, so I didn't want to provoke him. "Please, Ramón."

His gaze went heavy and he gave me that big smile that never failed to make me happy. "Go ahead. I'll be good."

Unable to stop myself, I rolled my eyes and Ramón laughed, right up to the point where I took his nipple in my mouth, then released it after a little suck. I'd read most of the Kama Sutra and they had a whole section devoted to the male chest and how to stimulate it. His big body bucked, and I grinned to myself and went back to teasing his tight, dark little nipple. Some guys were just meh about it, but other guys loved to have their nipples played with. Ramón was for sure one of those men. My pussy heated as I swirled my tongue up and around the tight little bud, a soft moan of need escaping me as he maneuvered me so he could reach my clit.

I was wet and ready, his fingers sliding along my puffy slit as he teased me just like I was teasing him, little fluttery touches.

"I want to take care of you," I whispered in a breathy moan.

"You want to take care of me?"

He sat up then grabbed me by the waist, hauling us both up the bed until he was sitting upright. Instead of having me wrap my legs around his waist, he had me squat over him, then slowly pushed his cock into me with a smooth glide. My pussy was spread wide open and I gasped as I focused on just the feeling of him inside of me.

"This," he thrust into me with a grunt. "This is how you take care of your man. You let him fuck you whenever and wherever he wants. While I love you worshiping my body, the only time I feel whole is when I'm inside of you. You have no idea how good your sweet, tight little pussy feels."

Once again, his talented fingers started to play with my clit, pinching the bundle of sensitive nerves and making my hips jerk as my walls clenched down hard on him. Ramón began to fuck me with a fluid grace while I placed my hands on his firm, broad chest, giving in completely to this man who seemed determined to fuck me into a coma. I had the inane thought that he'd be an excellent dance partner, the man could move his hips, right before he sent me over the edge into a deep, hot orgasm that nearly swept me under.

Ramón held my limp body tight, fucking himself with my lax form as I drew in shuddering breaths, my brain temporarily cooked by endorphins.

With a shout, he drove himself deep and filled me with his come, my body now conditioned to accept it.

Still holding me tight, he whispered, "This is it, your old life ended in this room tonight. From now on it's you and me against the world."

Running my hands through his dark hair I whispered back, "You and me against the world."

Chapter 10

Joy

One week later

On the big screen against the far wall of Mark's living room, I watched as my dwarf character got demolished during a battle.

From the big easy chair to my left, Mark laughed, his voice echoing just the slightest bit through the big headphones I was wearing.

Hissing softly, I waited to respawn while Mark and his team kicked major ass during a player vs. player battle. We were in some elven city in this big video game virtual world, battling necromancers or some shit. I was a low level dwarf. I accidentally started with the wrong character race and was too lazy to change it. I didn't belong anywhere near the front lines of the battle, where Mark and his team were tearing shit up.

It was fun listening to them yell at each other and call out attack orders. Though it was just a game, they moved with the precision of a military unit, slashing their way through everything in their path.

A woman's husky voice purred through my headphones. "Healing bomb incoming."

That was Layla, or as she was known in the game, Slay'ya. She was the top battlemage of whatever elven city it was we were defending, and one of the few girls on their team. Her voice was pure sex. I mean, I'm straight as they come, but even I got a little tingle when she spoke. The woman could've made a fortune as an erotic romance audio book reader, and she was funny as shit.

She was also the closest thing Mark had to a girlfriend. Though he denied it, he liked her. Like-*liked* her liked her. It gave me no small amount of pleasure to tease Mark about it, but never to the point of tipping Layla off. I think she liked him as well, but neither of them had ever acted on their flirting. Tonight might be different.

Layla was drunk. She'd let it slip that it was her birthday, so she was doing shots. When asked if she was going out to party later, she'd changed the subject and my spidey senses tingled. Mark told me to leave it alone, that Layla didn't have to talk about her real life if she didn't want to, but he was a guy. Guys didn't understand a woman's need to connect. Layla had certainly been nice to me, and I got the feeling she needed a friend. With Hannah still healing, I'd seen her briefly yesterday and confirmed she was indeed a mess, I missed my girl talk.

By the time I made it to the field where they stood triumphant among the enemy corpses, the fight was over, and our side had won.

It was late, but I was still awake, waiting for Ramón to get back. He'd been gone for the past day and a half on business, and I missed him a lot. In fact, I was becoming downright mopey when he wasn't around. I had no desire to do anything but veg in Mark's house. Knowing that Ramón would be returning soon had me edgy. He wasn't due for another hour, but I couldn't wait. Butterflies filled my belly, and I know I was checking my phone ever thirty seconds. Thankfully, Mark hadn't said anything, but I'd caught him rolling his eyes a few times.

I couldn't help it. Tonight, my parents were coming to meet Ramón's for a family dinner at the Cordova's estate. While I knew Judith and Jose would be completely charming with my parents, and that they seemed to love me, it was still a big step. I mean, not only was there the whole 'nice to meet you' awkwardness, there was the fact that the Cordova's lived a crazy lifestyle that I'm not sure my parents had ever been exposed to. I'd had time to get over my awe of them living in absolute luxury, but my mom loved those celebrity home renovation shows, and the Cordova's pad put any mansion to shame.

While I was nervous about my parents meeting Ramón's family, I'm sure all the Cordova's would be welcoming—with the exception of Fernando. Ramón had promised me his brother wouldn't be there, but it didn't sit well with me to exclude him. I planned on talking with Fernando, if he was sober, before my parents arrived to invite him to dinner. My heart hurt for the poor guy, and I wanted him to know that he was always welcome.

Besides, my mom got along great with Ramón, for whatever reason. Well enough that when he extended an invitation to dinner at his parents' place, she happily accepted without asking me first. While I knew in the back of my mind he'd talked to my mother—actually they FaceTimed, so she knew exactly what he looked like—I didn't know they were making plans without including me in the decision-making process.

That was not cool, so I got pissed. Ramón and I argued, then I gave in because make-up sex on the empty construction site of Ramón's new home with my man was *incredible*.

I thought about Ramón's new house, and how close it was to being done, and how much I already loved it. We'd gone shopping one day in the antique and furniture district of Phoenix, and he'd purchased some super comfy stuff for his house. He asked me to pick out his bedroom set, and I'd been happy when he'd instructed me to 'get things that I loved.' I knew it was his way of reminding me that he considered me already moved in with him, but I wasn't quite ready to make that commitment yet. Ramón moved fast, very fast, and I had to make sure I was thinking with both my mind and my heart.

Then again…life was short, so why was I fighting it? If we were meant to be together, forever, why wait? It was crazy talk, the kind of fantasy I made fun of other girls for having about instant-love, but damned if I didn't feel like Ramón was the one. I couldn't imagine a future without him in it. He made my life…better. My sister Brittney would hate how co-dependent that sounded, but my little sister Winter would understand. She was in love with her soul-mate, anyone could see it, even if she was only seventeen.

I loved Winter to bits, even if I did think she lived with her head in the clouds. Part of me wished she could come tonight—she had some cheerleading camp thing with the eight-year-olds she taught after school—but the other part was relieved she'd stay home. I'd have enough trouble handling just my parents, let alone keeping track of my overly honest sibling who considered everyone a friend.

She'd love the idea of Ramón sweeping me off my feet

My throat tightened as I considered that last thought.

I did love him, and the idea should scare me, but all I could feel was happiness and relief that I'd finally found a man who treasured me.

I bit my lower lip and turned my wrist to admire the gorgeous antique emerald bracelet. The stones glinted with a striking inner fire in the flickering light of the TV. I'm not a vain person. I spent the vast majority of my teenage years wishing I was invisible, but seeing what amounted to a fortune in jewelry on my wrist sent a little thrill through me. It showed me that he cared, that he wanted the best for me, that he thought about me. Ramón had given me a matching set of earrings last night, but I hadn't put those on. The bracelet was enough—with the earrings added, I looked like I was going to the Oscars.

I'd picked a subdued, black velvet dress with tiny neon blue flowers, surrounded by lime green leaves embroidered on the fitted bodice. It covered me to my neck, but showed the shape of my figure. Instead of heels, I'd paired it with some cute black and blue leather flip flops that showed off my petal pink pedicure. Ramón had sent me to the spa, and I'd gotten the full package and then some. I was rubbed, buffed, and fluffed to perfection. My phone buzzed and I whipped off my headphones, then answered it with a smile.

"Hi."

Ramón's deep, smooth voice filled me with tingles of anticipation. "Waiting outside for you."

"I'll be right out."

With a skip in my step, I grabbed my purse then gave Mark a one-armed hug, laughing at his total concentration on the screen. "Later, 'gator."

He bobbed and weaved just like his character on the giant screen. "Have fun tonight."

"Oh, yeah, I can't wait. Nothings as relaxing as having your parents meet your boyfriend's parents for the first time."

"Boyfriend? Joy, that man thinks he's already your husband."

I sighed, but didn't say anything. He was right. Ramón acted more like we were married than dating. It was nice, but it was also annoying.

"Tell your girlfriend I said goodnight and happy birthday."

He repeated my words, and whatever Layla said in return made him laugh in loud, happy way he only did for Layla.

Yep, he liked her.

His mirth faded as I practically ran through the house, my eagerness to see Ramón making my skin prickle. I missed him, missed his scent, missed his taste. I'd become addicted to his attention in record time, had reveled in his obsession with me. When we were together, alone, we talked about anything and everything. He seemed fascinated with me, and asked me all about my opinions on the world, and he seemed genuinely interested in my thoughts on life. We discussed current events, and he was starting to ask me my opinion on different experimental ideas the Cordova Group was playing around with.

    I hated sounding like an intellectual snob, but I'd never dated a man as smart as Ramón. He got me and challenged me in a way few people ever did. I was slowly beginning to understand him, his motivations, what made him tick. Without a doubt, the death of his nephew had changed him, but in both a good and bad way. Good, because he seemed to have this…respect for life—no, he *valued* life. He valued his time with me and somehow, I knew I was precious to him. Bad, because I could read him well enough to see the unending pain that filled him whenever he talked about Jason. He trusted me enough to unburden himself and his faith humbled me.

    Gah, I sounded like a lovesick moron, but when I saw him step out of his sleek red Maserati, dressed in a black suit with a white shirt, unbuttoned at the neck, and his hair slicked back, I had to bite my lip. Fuck, he was sexy. My pussy tingled as it began to warm, and I drank him in with a happy sigh. *Mine, all mine.* He strode toward me, his gaze locked on mine. Tino waited for us at the end of Mark's drive, his attention focused on the scenery instead of us. I appreciated his discretion, and used our moment of semi-privacy to wrap my arms around Ramón and kiss the hell out of him.

    Mmmmm. He tasted as good as he smelled.

    When he pulled back, he studied my lips then smiled. "That's it, I'm buying stock in this cosmetic company. Any lipstick that can stand up to our kiss is worth the investment."

    I laughed, then kissed him again. "And it tastes like peaches."

    "That it does," he murmured against my mouth. "You look amazing."

    "Thank you."

    "Can't believe I'm lucky enough to have you."

    "You should be flattered I agree to slum around with you."

    He grabbed my hair lightly in his fist, and tugged my head back. "Don't I know it."

Tino revved his engine, and I sighed. "Come on, don't want to be late."

Ramón helped me into his car. When we were on the road to his parents' place, he reached out and rested his hand on my thigh. "Relax. It'll be okay, I promise."

"You don't know them."

"Yeah, I do. I know all about your family."

"How?"

He turned in the fading sunlight, his brow arched in a sarcastic way that made me want to kiss the smirk off his mouth. "You may have talked about them a time or two."

I groaned, throwing my hands over my face before peeking through my fingers at him. "Then you know they're all crazy. Please, don't let them scare you away."

His laughter filled the car, mingling with the soft R&B station he liked to listen to on long drives. "I don't scare easy."

"You haven't met my sister yet."

"Winter? She doesn't frighten me."

I stuck my tongue out at him as we raced beneath the large palm trees lining the street. "I meant my older sister Brittney."

"She doesn't scare me, either." Before he looked away from me and back to the road, a scary coldness entered his gaze that reminded me of his mother. "If anything, I'm the one she should be scared of."

"Uh, what?"

Abruptly, his mood turned teasing and the tension in the car melted as if it'd never been there. In a mockingly seductive voice, he said, "Come on, what woman can resist my charm?"

When we finally pulled up to his house, he let the car idle just past the gates. "I need to tell you something."

"What?"

"Brittney is coming to dinner at my parents' place with your niece."

With a sick feeling, I hunched forward a little. "Wait, my sister is here? With Memphis?"

"Yeah, she came for a surprise visit with your folks." He rubbed my back. "My well-meaning mother is trying to make you feel welcome in the family by making an effort to meet everyone in yours. It's how she was raised."

"It's okay. I mean, she's my sister." I took a deep breath and let it out. "Everything will be fine."

"You're really freaking out," Ramón muttered. "I hate that your sister does this to you."

"Brittney's been way better since she became a mom, but I'm always afraid she's going to snap back into her bitchy ways."

He gave me a reassuring smile as we pulled into the long drive. "I'm sure you'll have nothing to worry about."

The front door of his parents' house opened. I couldn't help but smile at the sight of my mom, holding my almost two-year-old niece while she stood in the doorway.

I didn't even wait for the car to come to a complete stop before I launched myself out, glad I wore flip flops tonight instead of heels. They allowed me to sprint across the wide cobblestone courtyard and snatch my Memphis from my mother in record time. Everyone laughed, but the moment she saw me, Memphis gave me a toothy little smile and leaned out of my mom's arms so I could catch her.

She giggled while I slowly twirled us around, making loud kissing noises as I covered her chubby baby cheeks, fat little baby neck, and rounded baby arms with love.

"Aunt Joy," Memphis said while she pushed at me with her small hands. "Stop."

"I can't believe how big you are." Leaning back a little bit, I examined her sparkly amethyst purple dress that set off her dark curls. "And so pretty."

"I told you," my mom said off to the side in a low voice. "Right to Memphis. Totally ignored me, like I'm not even here."

Judith gave a soft laugh. "That's as it should be. Every child should be raised with love by their whole family. Makes them healthier, both mentally and physically."

Memphis started playing with my hair when I heard my sister say, "Hi, Joy. She hasn't stopped talking about you the whole trip."

"It's good to see you, Brittney."

To my surprise, she hugged me tight then gave Memphis a kiss on the cheek. "We were both excited to come visit, right, Munchkin?"

"Right, Mommy."

Seeing that my sister seemed to be in a good mood, I hefted Memphis on top my hip while I gave first my mom, then Judith a one-armed hug. They all chatted together, totally at ease while Ramón joined us, his straight white teeth flashing as he gave us his most dashing smile. He placed his hand on my lower back, then grinned down at Memphis, who was hiding in my hair.

"Who is this beautiful princess?" Ramón said in a voice that was sweeter than honey and softer than velvet.

It was a voice I've never heard him use before, and it made my heart flutter. "This is Memphis, my niece. Memphis, this is my boyfriend, Ramón."

She parted my hair enough to cautiously look out, then smiled when Ramón crouched down a little so he was more at her height. "It's nice to meet you. I hope you're hungry."

Memphis slowly nodded her head, watching him closely.

Ramón gave my niece a small smile that once again sent my heart and my ovaries fluttering. "Do you like macaroni and cheese? The kind with the pasta shaped like seashells?"

Memphis gasped, because this was indeed her favorite food. "I hungry now."

We all laughed, and my mom snagged Memphis from me as Jose met us inside. Ramón slipped his hand into mine, and gave me a bemused smile. Brittney laughed at something my mom said, then waited for us to catch up while the mothers went ahead of everyone. Giving me a tight smile, Brittney said, "Joy, can I talk to you for a second?"

Ramón gave her an evil look, but I forced him to release my hand as I faked a smile. "Sure. Um, Ramón, you'll be on the back porch, right?"

"Yeah." He searched my face, his lovely eyes warming slightly before he gave me a brief kiss. "Don't be long. Everyone will be waiting on you."

"We won't."

As he walked away, Brittney fidgeted with her hair, and I noticed she'd dropped some weight—and it didn't look good on her.

Scanning the wide hallway, she said, "Is there somewhere a little more private we can go?"

"Follow me. There's a music room I think you'll like."

"Okay." Her voice was soft, hesitant as she said, "This place sure is something."

I led us into a room a couple of doors down one of the

hallways, a place where Judith kept her piano and violin collection. My sister had played the piano in high school, and I wondered if that was something she'd continued. We'd had to sell our crappy old piano to make ends meet one year when my dad had gotten pneumonia, and I remember Brittney had been devastated.

When we entered the large room with its pale green walls and elegant green and gold Persian carpets, Brittney let out a soft gasp.

"Wow. Okay, this is just insane. Are these…" she turned around the room with wide eyes until she spotted the carved antique mahogany piano. "Oh, that's lovely."

I didn't bother turning the room lights on, instead leaving most of the place in darkness with soft amber lights illuminating various pieces of art and the piano.

She hesitated before touching it, a weary look coming over her face that I wasn't used to seeing. "Does anyone play it?"

"I think Judith does."

Right away, Brittney took a step back. "Never mind."

Laughing, I joined her at the piano and gently ran my fingers up and down the keys. "It's okay. I mean, you know how to play and everything, right? I'm sure she'd love to hear some music."

A look of great longing took over my sister's face, and tears filled her green eyes, so similar to mine. "Maybe later. I don't want to keep Memphis waiting."

"What's going on?"

"I-I'm not just visiting. I left Greg, and I'm staying with Mom and Dad until I can get back on my feet."

"Oh, shit. Brittney, I'm so sorry." I hugged her tight, her chin resting on my shoulder as she made a soft whimper. "What happened?"

"Joy…it's so bad."

Panic filled me as I pulled back and searched her for injuries. "Did he hurt you?"

"Physically? No. But he has eviscerated my heart and trust."

I grabbed her hands in my own and led her over to the red velvet seat of the large piano bench, making her sit next to me. "Brittney, tell me. I promise, I won't judge you, but I might kill him, depending on what he did to you."

"Well…Memphis has a half-sister that's one year younger

than her."

My jaw must have hit my chest. "You are fucking shitting me."

"I wish."

"Holy moly. Did you just find out?"

"Yeah. The other woman—who turns out to be awesome—" Brittney let out a soft, watery laugh, "Anyway, she thought Greg was single, that he traveled a lot for his job, but that he was going to propose to her any day. Then she found out he was married to me, and had me and Memphis at home in California, and she decided to talk to me before she confronted him. She was devastated, like I was, but she never acted like it was anyone's fault but his for being a cheating dick. Karen, Greg's girlfriend, helped me get a lawyer who made sure I had my fair share of our mutual assets and that my personal money was safe before I filed for divorce."

"You're kidding me."

"And he wasn't just cheating on me with Karen. I snagged his laptop and let my lawyer take a look. Greg has profiles on *nine* different dating sites. I'm so glad I insisted on him always wearing a condom. Thankfully, I've tested clean, but I never want to have to go through that fear again. I mean, can you imagine if he'd given me something that had gotten me sick, or made Memphis ill? All because he's some kind of…of relationship addict?"

"This is so crazy."

"And get this—Karen's a lawyer, a really good one. She wanted to make sure Greg paid for what he did to us. She got her child support out of him, and I get my child support and the alimony. Considering I was there the day he founded his company, and considering its current worth is in the billions, Greg will probably buy me out. I don't want crazy money. Just enough to take care of Memphis and stay at home with her in a nice neighborhood, where I can give her the kind of childhood she deserves." Brittney sighed and her shoulders slumped. "I know I haven't been the best sister, but I know you'll be the best Aunt Memphis could ever want. You have so much love to give, and I could use your help once we move down here."

"Anything you need. I mean it." My protective instincts went on high alert. "Do we have to worry about Greg coming after you?"

"Probably not." She chewed her lower lip for a second, her eyes darting away, then back again. "He was really mad when he found half of our checking account missing and one quarter of our savings."

"A quarter? He got off lightly."

She wrinkled her nose at me. "Don't forget, he has to help Karen support her little girl, Opal."

"So does that make Opal my niece?"

"In a way. Karen says we'll always be welcome in Opal's life, and she wants the girls to be able to spend time together. They are sisters, and family is very important to Karen. She's very…loving." An odd expression came over Brittney's face. "She's really nice and kind. I mean, you'd think she'd hate me. I'd hate her because of what Greg did, but she's just an innocent bystander like myself, swept up into his bullshit. I might have lost my husband, but I've gained a…friend who makes me feel happy in a way I haven't experienced in a long time. She's a big believer in good karma, and I sometimes wonder if what happened with Greg was a result of my past sins."

I thought I heard something across the room, but a quick glance didn't reveal much because of the spotlight blinding me. "I don't think it works like that."

"I was a miserable bitch," Brittney said in a rush. "I'm so sorry I took out my bipolar bullshit on you."

"Wait, you're bipolar?"

With tears dripping down her cheeks, Brittney nodded. "I'm finally on medication for it, and I feel worlds better. Clear headed in a way I haven't been in years. Not saying I'm perfect, or that I'm not a bitch, but I'm trying to be a better person for my daughter. I never could have imagined loving someone as much as I love Memphis. I know that if I want to go to heaven with her, I better start stacking up that good karma. The more you have, the easier it will be for you to get into heaven."

I laughed softly and shook my head. "Who are you, and what have you done with my sister?"

"I need you to know I recognize how terrible I was to you and thank you for even giving me the time of day. I don't deserve it, but that's the kind of person you are. I appreciate it."

I couldn't even think of anything to say, so I just sat there and stared at her as she pushed back some of my hair. Movement caught my eye across the room again, and I realized with a start we weren't alone. A vaguely male shape sat in the shadows, still as could be, his attention clearly on us. Anger filled me that someone dared to eavesdrop on such a private moment with my sister, spied on me when I was most vulnerable.

Then that anger turned to worry as Fernando slowly rose from the couch and stepped into the light.

He only smelled like weed now, no alcohol, and his gaze—though bloodshot—was surprisingly clear.

I don't think I'd ever seen him this sober.

Wearing a button down black shirt and khaki shorts, his stride was purposeful as he crossed the room toward us. Behind me, my sister startled hard enough that the bench shook. I reached back, putting my hand on her leg. Fernando must have seen it, because he slowed down, sorrow mixing with his determination.

"I won't hurt you," he rasped. "And I'm sorry that I overheard you, but I'm not sorry for doing it."

"Fernando, Ramón's oldest brother. Recently lost his wife and son," I muttered to my sister before saying in a louder voice, "What the fuck, Fernando?"

He held up his hands, his dark gaze focused on my sister who was now clutching my hand. "Do you really believe that?"

"Believe what?" my sister asked. She released my hand as she stood behind me, placing a protective hand on my shoulder.

"That if you do enough good deeds, you can erase the evil and go to heaven."

I tried to avoid flinching at the grief in his voice, and my sister made a soft sound of sorrow. "I do believe that. Though I don't think evil deeds get erased. I picture it more like scales. At the end of your life, does the good outweigh the evil? If it doesn't, what can you do to change that? Who can you help? Who can you be nice to?"

He blinked rapidly, and my heart broke anew for him when I saw a spark of hope lift some of the darkness from his gaze. "I don't even know where to start."

"Start with your family, those you've loved and wronged."

She gave my shoulder a squeeze, and I placed my hand over hers, shocked by her compassion and understanding. Without a doubt, she was a different person now that she was on medication for her bipolar disorder, and I was so damn proud of her. A knock came from the door. A second later, an unsmiling Ramón appeared. He took one look at the situation, at our teary faces and took off toward Fernando.

I managed to jump between them and had to literally wrap my arms around Ramón. "If you hit him, you'll hurt me!"

Instantly, he stopped, but his chest was heaving against mine as he lifted me up and examined my face. "What the fuck did he do?"

"He didn't do anything." I did my best to soothe him, stroking his face and neck. "I'm okay. These are just emotional tears."

"What happened?" he gritted out.

To my surprise, it was Brittney who literally stood between Fernando and Ramón. "Ramón, it's nothing. We were having a discussion about heaven."

Ramón almost dropped me as he set me on my feet. He frowned over my head at Brittney. "Heaven?"

"Yeah," Fernando said with a harsh, aching laugh. "Brittney here seems to think we can earn our way back into heaven with good deeds. That there's a chance at redemption."

Even I could hear the desperate hope in his voice, that Fernando desperately wanted to believe my sister, and Ramón was no fool. "Of course there is."

"See, I told you," Brittney said in a gentle, teasing voice. "Never doubt one of the Holtz sisters. We're always right."

Fernando didn't say anything, his gaze distant and tortured.

Looping his arm around my waist, Ramón tugged me to his side. "We need to go eat before the parents decide to come look for us."

"Fernando," I gave him what I hoped was a welcoming smile. "Would you like to join us? I'm sure my parents would love to meet you."

Fernando took in a deep breath, then slowly let it out. "Thank you, but no. I need some time alone to think."

Brittney gave him a gentle one-armed hug before joining us as we left Fernando alone with his thoughts in the silence.

Chapter 11
Ramón

Two days later, I prayed to the Blessed Mother for the patience to hold my temper. First, because I was in my parent's home, at my personal office on their estate, and trashing the place in a fit of rage would piss off my mother. Second, because Joy was only a few doors down from us, and I didn't want her to get scared because she could hear me going on a tear. Forcing myself to relax, I took a deep breath and slowly let it out, willing my heart to stop racing as my mind went over all the threats facing my woman.

Tino's normally smiling face was grim after he gave me a detailed report of how hard it would be to keep Joy safe if she went back to school on campus. There were too many civilians, too many bodies, and in the days of cell phones, everyone was a heartbeat away from showing you live on the Internet. No, that was the last place we wanted to have someone try to snatch Joy.

I knew I could get her a diploma within two minutes of making a phone call, but I also knew my girl wouldn't want anything she didn't earn. Joy had pride. While I admired it, I didn't like how her pride ended up hurting her sometimes. She still fought me on the things I bought her, expensive trinkets that I liked to shower her with, but slowly she was letting go of her ridged control. Bit by bit, I was gaining access to her heart, and I knew without a doubt she loved me.

That's why the thought of anything happening to her sent me into a panic. I fought my impulse to yell at Tino, to vent my rage on him like it was his fault.

"Do we have eyes on her family?"

"Of course. Diego already arranged that on Fernando's request. I think he likes Brittney, Joy's sister."

That made me rear back. "What?"

Some of the coldness left Tino's brown eyes as he said, "Relax, not like that. She wouldn't be interested, anyway. Seems she's got a lady love in her life. The mother of Memphis' half-sister."

I shook my head and glanced at the closed doors to my home office at my parents' house. Joy was with Hannah, probably doing homework together, and I wished she was here with me. I was addicted to her, plain and simple, and not having her warm, soft little body within reach made me antsy.

"Her name is Karen," I said absently as I imagined what Joy was doing. "Decent lady, a retired and wealthy criminal defense lawyer who is utterly head over heels for Brittney. I already had her checked out. It's a fucked up situation, to be sure, but other than Brittney's estranged husband, Greg, everyone seems okay with it."

Tino stretched out his neck with a faint pop. "Will you ask Joy to consider staying home?'

"Yeah, I'll ask her. But I can tell you right now, she won't give up her tutoring in Phoenix." Tino's frown drew my attention back fully to the moment. "What? You don't like her tutoring either?"

"No, I think what she's doing is great, but she's forbidden me from coming onto school grounds, and I have to agree."

"Wait, are you fuckin' telling me you aren't with Joy when she's tutoring?"

"With all due respect, I don't belong in that building or in that parking lot."

"You belong wherever the fuck I say you belong," I shouted, incensed that Joy had been left vulnerable.

"Relax, she's covered. I make sure the cops doing overtime by patrolling the school are good guys who look out for her. But I would stick out like a sore thumb, and she doesn't want or need that kind of attention." I started to argue but he held up his hand. "Listen, *mi amigo*, I've been married for many years to a feisty woman like Joy. Let me give you some free advice. There are some arguments you will never win with your wife. This is one of them. Either you respect her boundaries, or you pay the price for breaking her trust in you. And once you lose that trust, it's hard as fuck to win back."

I sagged back into my chair and looked up at the ceiling with a groan, my gaze tracing the patterns cut into ceiling trim. "Fuuuuuuck."

Tino laughed, but he sounded sympathetic. "I know. But it's only for another month or so. Then she'll be done with school and working for Mrs. Cordova. Mark my words, once she gets involved in the Cordova's charities she grab the reins and never look back. That girl has drive, determination, and I look forward to seeing what she'll do with some real assets available to her."

I stood then inwardly groaned as my muscles protested the movement. Last night, I'd spent a couple extra hours training with Leo in the gym. Hannah was still refusing to forgive him, and I could tell it was eating at him. Leo was the kind of guy that liked to take care of things, a fixer, and not being able to mend what he'd broken between him and Hannah was sucking the life out of him. I'd seen it happen before with Fernando, who was finally showing signs of life. The best way to help Leo was to get him into the boxing ring and fight him until we were both left gasping and wrung out on the mat.

My legs ached, and I slowly stretched out my calves.

"I'll talk to her, see what she has to say. Maybe if I let her know how dangerous everything is, how much danger she's really in, she'll understand why this is important."

"Good plan." Tino clapped me on the back. "I wish you luck. Just remember, after every good fight is even better makeup sex. And if she feels guilty, like the fight was her fault, you'll usually get a pretty good blowjob out of it."

Laughing, I exchanged goodbyes then texted Joy.
Where are you?
Watching a movie in your bed.
Our bed.
Whatever.

I found her curled up in my massive down comforter like a mummy, her wide eyes focused on the large screen against the wall at the foot of our bed.

I shrugged out of my shirt, "What are you watching?"

"Shhhh, it's the season finale," Joy waved her hand at me, "I think he's going to finally figure out that Stella's been cheating on him with the dog groomer. Nobody's poodle needs that much trimming."

Laughing, I jerked the blanket way and pulled her squirming body toward mine. She wore cotton pajamas and a ratty old t-shirt, or as she called them, her 'I'm on my period leave me alone', outfit that she'd worn for the last few days. I thought it was cute as hell, but she'd been a little testy so I decided just to hold her for a bit and let her enjoy her show while I watched her instead.

She cuddled right into me, even shared some of her blanket, then started to explain the plot in a whisper, as if the people on the screen could hear us.

Smoothing her hair back, I traced the profile of her features with my eyes. "I thought this is a reality show?"

Darting a glance at me, she snorted. "It's reality TV, not Reality Real Life."

"I don't speak chick; translate for me."

She elbowed me, but her voice held no anger as she said, "It's totally scripted, and everybody knows it, but we all like to pretend it's real."

"Makes sense."

I waited until the end of the show to breech the subject I'd been mulling over. "Joy, I need to talk to you about something."

Right away she turned in my arms then sat up, wrapping her arms around herself in a defensive manner. "Okay…"

With a sigh, I tugged one of her hands free and held it in my own. "I have a huge favor to ask you, and you're not going to like it."

"What?"

"I'm asking—no, I'm begging—you to finish up school online."

"What? No, I'm going back for the last month of classes. We talked about this."

I hesitated, debating on giving her a hint as to how much danger she was really in. "I had a meeting with Tino tonight. He laid out why he really feels that you going back to school is dangerous. Complete with a power point presentation."

The last bit I'd added to try and get her to smile, but instead she grew still. "Why is it dangerous?"

"There have been a few…incidents where we've spotted people watching you. It's to be expected, you're a kidnapping target simply because you're my girlfriend, but Tino is an expert at protection and, if he feels this strongly about it, I have to ask you at least consider it."

"Ramón, I've worked so hard to get to this point. I don't want to feel like I've just been given my diploma without earning it."

My proud, stubborn woman. "Nobody said anything about you not doing your work, or giving you anything. These past few weeks, I've seen how much classwork you do, how much time you devote to getting the best grade you can. You're smart, and driven, and I admire that more than you'll ever know, but I'm asking you to be smart about your personal safety, please. I'm not trying to scare you, but the world is a fucked up place, the kind of place where a mother would sell her own son for money. With people like that out there, people that are willing to do anything, break any rule, to get what they want, I need you to be as safe as possible."

Tears filled her eyes, and I felt like a complete piece of shit. "Okay."

I should have been happy she was agreeing to this, but instead I felt the ugly shadow of remorse in my heart for bringing her into this mess. "I'm so, so sorry, Joy. Things will get better, I promise."

Wiping away her tears with the back of her hand, Joy said, "Can I still tutor?"

"Tino didn't like it, but yeah. With only after school activities going on when you do your tutoring, and the security they have there, I believe you're safe. Besides, even criminals don't want the kind of attention a kidnapping at a school would bring. That's the kind of thing that gets the public up in arms and thirsty for blood."

She abruptly collapsed onto my chest and rubbed her cheek against me. "Sometimes it feels like the whole world is against me, like I'm trapped in some alternate universe where everyone is more apt to be evil than good."

I sighed, her curls moving against my lips as she rose with my breath. "I promise you, as long as I'm around no one will hurt you, ever."

The flickering light of the screen illuminated her face as she leaned up on my torso on one hand. "You must think I'm very naïve, not even considering the dangers of what I do."

"No, I think you have a good heart, and you haven't lived a life where you needed to be afraid. I'm glad you grew up safe, I'm glad you had a normal-ish childhood."

She stroked my chest with a smile. "Normal-ish?"

"Don't forget, I've met your family."

"Good point." She nuzzled her nose against my neck, then licked my skin in a way that had blood rushing to my cock.

"Stop," I groaned. "It's been three days since we've had sex."

Laughing, she tried to push me off her. "Whatever. You've had four pity blowjobs."

I had, and they were damn good. "I'd return the favor if you let me."

She made an icked out face. "You're nasty."

"Yep."

Quieting beneath me, she searched my face while exploring the muscles over my ribs with a soft touch. "Turn off the TV, I'm sleepy."

I got out of bed and did as she asked, returning after I'd brushed my teeth. A soft rush of air scented like my cologne mixed with her perfume washed over me as I lifted covers, then cuddled into my girl. She squirmed against me, but soon settled then whispered, "I tried to get Hannah to talk about what's going on with her and Leo today. She wouldn't tell me anything. I feel bad for the poor guy. He's obviously hurting, and I don't understand why she's so mad at him. Did he do something bad? Did he cheat on her?"

"What? No. Leo *worships* her. Whatever is going on, it's between them, *mami*."

"But she's my best friend."

"Then why haven't you told her about us yet?"

"I don't know..." she was quiet for a few moments and I wondered if she'd fallen asleep before she said, "To be honest, I don't think she's your biggest fan right now. Whatever Leo did to piss her off seems to extend to you and your brothers."

"I have no idea. While we've hung out, we aren't exactly besties like you two."

"Besties," she snorted. "Anyway, I'm worried about her. I mean, she's almost totally healed and should be eager to get back to Leo's place, but it seems like she has no desire to go. Which doesn't make any sense, because Leo's house is all kinds of awesome, and he can't wait for her to come home. He doesn't say it, but I can tell he misses her so much. I wish she'd just talk to me."

If Joy knew how fucked up things were between Hannah and

Leo right now, she'd be making a run for the police with Hannah thrown over her shoulder. "Give her time. I'm sure whatever happened between Hannah and Leo will work itself out."

"I hope so. They're both so miserable apart." She yawned. "Night, honey."

I held her close and felt her finally relax. "Night, sweetheart."

A firm knock on my door awoke me early the next morning, and a still sleeping Joy grumbled in my arms.

Her hair was a wild riot of curls this morning, and so soft it was like touching baby duck down. She was on top of me, draped over my body, her preferred place to lounge. I loved the feeling of her soft warmth pressing into me. Irritation pierced me as the knock came again. I gently moved her off me, her adorable whining protests dying off as I tucked her back in before putting on my boxers then going to my bedroom door.

The place was big enough that, by the time I got to the door, someone was about to get their damn arm ripped off for knocking louder. I wanted to send whoever it was away before they woke up Joy. I wanted to take a rare day off and spend it with her, sleeping and cuddling in bed. I had plans to take her furniture shopping for our home later in the day, and I wanted to have breakfast in bed with her after I fucked her slow and easy.

After unlocking the various bolts on my steel-reinforced door, I swung it open to reveal my father, who looked absolutely furious. Dressed in his usual dark suit and immaculate tie, he appeared every inch the powerful businessman, but a sheen of perspiration dotted his brow, and his fists were clenched at his sides, knuckles torn and his cuffs saturated with blood. My dad runs the legit side of our empire—he has more patience and tact than my mother—so many people assume he's not as violent as her. They'd be wrong.

"Dad," I stepped outside of my room, closing the door behind me.

There were more people outside, a few of my father's top men and a highly distraught Diego, his hair unbraided wearing only pajama pants as he snarled at his phone.

"Ramón," my father said, drawing my attention back to him. "We have a situation. I am so sorry to take you away from Joy, but we need your help. Do you remember Diego's good friend from high school, Tim McCray? His stepdaughter was taken by the Santiago cartel, and we need to get her back before…well, *before*. We have a lead that she's being taken to Mexico City. Get dressed and meet us downstairs. You know Mexico the best, have the most contacts in Mexico City. I hate to take you away from Joy, but we need you."

Our eyes met, and I'm surprised the hallway didn't burst into flames around us as our tempers roared to life. "I understand."

Before I could turn, my father grasped my arm. "Do not tell Joy where you're going, but let her know you'll be gone for a few days. Don't give your mother an excuse to do something rash in our absence."

I flexed his hand off my bicep, torn for the first time in my life between my duties to my family and my woman. "I hate this shit."

"Ramón, you know it's for her own good. Give her some story she'll believe, something about you having to go on a business trip somewhere with no cell phone and spotty satellite. That you'll contact her when you can, but for her not to worry—but do it quick."

Diego joined me as our father moved down the hall to speak with one of his men.

Taking in Diego's distraught state, I said, "We'll get her back."

My father interrupted us, "We have to go."

Years of training kicked in as I went back into my bedroom, regret sinking into my gut that I had to leave Joy's side.

I packed quickly. After I was ready to go, I left Joy a note telling her that I had to make an emergency trip down to South America to visit a sick friend who lived deep in the jungle, and that I would be back as soon as I could.

Before I left, I gave her sleeping lips one last kiss. I slid my knife from my boot and cut off one small curl then put it in my pocket over my heart.

Chapter 12

Joy

Three Weeks Later

The sun beamed down through the windshield of Mark's red SUV, baking my hands as I clutch the wheel. Sweat dripped down my face, even though the air conditioning blasted from the vents and chilled my skin.

I was both freezing and burning, hot and cold, as anxiety sunk its claws into me.

On a clinical level, I know I experienced PTSD from the attack. The level of danger I felt wasn't real, but that knowledge did nothing to curb the anxiety building inside of me.

Scanning my surroundings, I only saw the crowded parking lot of a rough high school in Phoenix. I marveled at how before, I saw no risk here. I'd blithely skipped my way through life like a fool, unaware bad things could happen to me. With my newly opened eyes, I could see the different gangs hanging on their turf, feel the tension between them as a mint green low rider with utterly black windows rolled up. A group of very scantily dressed high school girls approached it, giggling and looking like children playing dress up.

Ever since Ramón mentioned people actively following me, I felt like malevolent forces lurked in every shadow, hidden behind every pair of eyes. Sometimes the hair would lift on the back of my neck, and I'd just know someone dangerous was nearby. Hell, I didn't even feel safe at my parents' house. During a brief visit, I swore I saw someone looking through the tall hedges surrounding our backyard. I hadn't been able to sleep until I'd texted Tino. He set up perimeter guards around my childhood home in the thick of suburbia outside of Tuscan, and I'd only stopped stressing out after he reassured me I was safe.

How fucked up was that?

A car beeped somewhere in the lot, drawing me back to the present.

This was my fourth day back as a tutor. Instead of getting

better, my fear was only getting worse. Every day, the temptation to never leave Leo's compound, to exist only in the bubble of his protection, made me want to become a recluse. The need to flee was strong, but I fought it. I wasn't going to give in to my fears, and I would not let them rule my life. Besides, what did I have to go home to? An empty house? Hannah was busy with Leo, and Mark was always working. If it wasn't for Hannah's dog, Honey, I would be completely alone... other than the guards I never saw, but knew were there.

When I was alone, without fail, my mind went to Ramón while my heart ached.

Three weeks. Three long, long weeks he's been gone, and every day that passed without word, I could feel myself shattering a little more inside. For the first week, he'd texted and called me regularly, but eight days after he left, all communication had stopped. I tried asking the Cordovas what was going on, but they just put me off with vague promises. They said he was okay, and he was in an area with no cell service. In a normal situation, I would have believed them, but I know how the Cordovas work regarding anything they see as a threat to their family. It hurt me that they couldn't trust me with the information about where Ramón really was. Then Hannah let slip that Leo had talked to Ramón. Knowing Ramón took the time to call his friend but not me stung.

After all his promises and sweet words, Ramón was long gone and evidently never contacting me again, but I still had the bodyguards he left me like some odd parting gift.

I hadn't really told Hannah anything about what happened between me and Ramón. She knew *something* went on, but she didn't know the bastard made me fall in love with him. I'd given myself to Ramón, had opened up to him, and let myself believe we really had a future together. He obviously had gotten what he wanted from me, and I wondered if this was a game he played with all women. Maybe he was one of those guys that got off on breaking girl's hearts.

'Cause he'd certainly broken mine.

The loud shouts of teenage boys came from my left, and I jumped in my seat, my breath coming in shallow pants.

I wanted to laugh and cry. For over a year, I had no problem parking in this lot and going into the school, cloaked in my impenetrable layer of ignorant arrogance that nothing bad would ever happen to me. What a fool I'd been, so blind to the dangers around me. This part of the city was rough—and I do mean rough—driven by institutionalized poverty, generations of gangs, and a city more interested in catering to the rich than caring for the poor. The school was surrounded by abandoned or falling down homes that the city needed to condemn, and the neighborhood around us was a constant battle between gangs. Yes, the school had security, but they were stretched thin by budget cuts and stuck mainly to protecting the school, not the parking lot. The only thing that stood between the school and the outside world was a massive chain-link fence with razor wire at the top.

God, the school I worked at resembled a prison.

I wondered if I was being stupid even coming here, or if I should have brought Tino with me. I thought Tino was my friend, that he'd give me some hint about Ramón, but he gave me the same standard answers the Cordovas did. Even though I was irritated with Tino, I really wished he was on campus with me as I tried to get up the courage to leave the safety of Mark's SUV. I noticed a couple of the older, more mature looking teenagers were scoping out the Land Rover, which stuck out like a sore thumb in the parking lot filled with beaten-up older cars. I worried that someone might try to steal it while I was inside tutoring, but if they thought Mark's car was an easy target, they were sadly mistaken.

Mark was a bad ass guy on all levels. Even when he wasn't home, I felt safe in his house. He wasn't around much, worked a lot with Leo. When he was there, he was a major video game player. I'd spent many nights watching him play, glad for the company during my increasingly frequent bouts of insomnia. Mark was quiet, didn't pry, and didn't really answer any personal questions, but he wasn't a bad guy. He was just one of those people that didn't feel the need to fill silence with inane chatter. That's not to say we never talked about ourselves, but he never mentioned his late wife. Still, I could see he carried a massive burden on his soul from her loss.

Part of me wanted to bug him about it, get him to talk about his pain, but I wasn't going to push him. Lord knows, he respected my desire not to talk about my problems, and didn't call me out on my increasingly odd middle of the night hobbies, thanks to my insomnia. See, when you only sleep four to five hours a night you find you have a lot of time to kill. In my case, I used it for canning fruits, vegetables, soups, dry mixes, etc. Thanks to Pintrest, I had a never-ending pool of inspiration for different canning projects. I know it sounds odd, but cooking soothed me.

My *abuela* was an old-school housewife. She'd made the mom in *Leave it to Beaver* look like a crack-addicted hobo, and she did it with grace and style. I'd used the skills she taught me in the past weeks to can enough food for an army. Currently, half my room was taken up with jars of jellies, preserves, and canned veggies to get a family of five through WWIII.

Soon, I'd have to take another trip to the local foodbank where I'd donate the literal fruits of my labor, but the thought of driving down to the rough neighborhood where the foodbank was located made my heart race.

Someone knocked on my window, and I screamed loud enough that I startled myself. When I whipped my head, around I found Devonlin, one of the kids I tutored, staring at me with wide eyes. At seventeen, he was a hulking behemoth of a guy with short dreadlocks who played football and had the massive body of a grown man. He stared at me like I was the scary one. I could only imagine how I must have looked, spacing out in Mark's SUV while staring at the school and shaking. Shame raced through me at how weak I was. One bad thing happens, and I fall into pieces.

No, I was stronger than this, stronger than my irrational fears.

Galvanized into action, I turned my car off and got out. I tried to give Devonlin a reassuring smile as I brushed my hand over my hair, hoping it was under control as I looped my bag over my shoulder. "Hey, Devonlin, sorry about that. I was totally daydreaming."

"It's okay, Ms. Holtz. I just wanted to make sure you were all right." He glanced over at the green low rider idling at the curb near the entrance to the school, the driver's side window now lowered as a guy in in his thirties openly flirted with the high school girls. "You don't need to be hangin' in the parking lot today."

Following his gaze, I took a step closer to Devonlin's side as we crossed the lot, thankful once again that this massive young man had both a heart of gold and a protective streak a mile wide. "Why?"

A loud whistle split the air behind us, and a man with a thick Hispanic accent to his voice yelled out, "Devonlin? That you, boy? Here you got some pro teams lookin' at recrutin' you. We need to talk."

I turned and looked over my shoulder, then froze at the sight of a man in a crisp, black suit stepping out of the passenger side of a black sports car that had just pulled up. He was tall, with pockmarked deep cinnamon brown skin and expertly cut and tousled black hair. Even from this distance, I could feel a bad vibe emanating from the stranger. Devonlin froze then twitched. When I looked up at him, I found him standing there with his eyes shut tight, but his protective stance over me increased until he was crowding my space.

His deep but scared voice reverberated through me as he growled out, "I've got nothin' to say to you."

The other man came closer, and my fear increased as I realized how big he was. The way he carried himself, the way he looked at me, they all reminded me of Manny, and I felt ill. But I noticed all the kids watching us, and my mothering instinct began to kick in—the need to protect those who couldn't protect themselves.

Tilting his head to the side, the stranger smirked. "I think you do, Devonlin. Medication is expensive, isn't it? You already sold everything you own. How you gonna afford her next round of chemo? Gonna have to pick and choose between keeping the lights on or keeping her alive?"

Even though I was freaking out with my heart pounding, Devonlin was my friend, and nobody talked to my friends like that. I'd known him for a while. Even though he was as big as a house, he was still a kid in many ways. A kid being bullied by some scary criminal. No, this wasn't happening. Not here, not at my school. Or kind of my school. Whatever, this was my territory, and he wasn't threatening my students. Schools were supposed to be safe spaces, and this rotten bastard didn't belong there.

"Devonlin," I said in a soft voice, "look at me and keep walking. Whatever he's offering you, it's not worth it."

"My mom…" he whispered.

"Cancer returned?"

"Yeah."

"Boy!" the man shouted. "Stop talking to that *puta* and get over here."

I put some steel in my spine. Even though my voice shook, I said, "Sir, I'm going to have to ask you to leave school property."

He spat at the ground near my feet. Internally, I flinched, fear prickling along my spine, making me want to run. "Stupid bitch. Maybe instead of takin' Devonlin for a ride, I take you for one instead? Teach you some lessons on manners."

Though I was about to barf because I was so afraid, I didn't let it show in my voice, my years of being bullied by my older sister allowing me to remain stone-faced. "You lay one hand on me and I promise you…you will regret it."

He stared at me, his eyes wide before laughing. "You are one ballsy bitch. Just the kind of woman I like to break and put in her place. Have you at my feet like a dog, make you lick the shit off my boots."

I tried to swallow past the fist-sized lump of fear in my throat, and I hated that this predator could sense my fear. Students were all around us now, and I knew it was just a matter of time before someone told the guards. I could only hope it was quick, because I wasn't sure what I would do if he called my bluff.

"Get out." Devonlin suddenly pushed me behind his broad back like a living shield.

Looking around Devonlin's side, I watched as the man lifted his upper lip in a sneer, then the guy tugged at his suit. "You are making a big mistake, Huge. Your mother is gonna die in agony because of you."

A kid yelled from behind us, "Cops!"

The guy in the suit vanished into the sport's car so fast, he moved like a ghost. I stared in disbelief at his retreating taillights.

After a moment of silence, all the kids around us began gossiping. I hurried Devonlin into the building. If security was on the way, I didn't want to be around when they arrived. I know without a doubt Ramón would flip his shit 150 different ways to

Sunday and I did not need that right now. While part of me wanted to raise a stink about that asshole being able to get on campus, I thought it was the wise move to get out of sight.

Keeping his body between mine and parking lot, Devonlin quickly moved me up the front steps. "Ms Holtz, you shouldn't have said anything."

We'd entered the school by this point, and I tried to get more information out of Devonlin as we waited to go through the metal detector. "What?"

Devonlin grunted as he went through the metal detector. "That guy is bad news."

I waited until the guards let us past before saying in a low voice, "Why did that man want to talk to you?"

"He knows I've got some big name teams trying to recruit me, that I'm gonna make money soon. That shithead believes he can buy me now, that he'll own me like a pet dog and use me to throw games. I know all about his bullshit and I'm not interested." His chest puffed up with pride. "He thinks he can own me, thinks he can buy me, but my integrity is not for sale."

My heart panged in sympathy for this proud young man. "Fuck him."

Devonlin started to laugh. Once again, he looked like the kid I watched grow up, instead of a man. "I think that's the first time I've heard you swear."

"Yeah, well, it's been that kind of day. I think I need to go back and talk to the security guards, maybe file a report or something."

"No, you aren't going to do anything." Guiding me deeper into the school, he shook his head adamantly. "That's not how things work around here. Even if someone did call the police, nothing would happen. They're a cartel, and I don't know if you really understand what that is, but it means they have power and money like you couldn't dream of. And they didn't get it by being good people. Those dishonorable bastards would sell their own mother if it earned them a dollar. Only chance I got is hoping I can outlast them until I get drafted, or find another cartel to watch my back."

"Wait, you'd want another cartel to watch your back?"

"Well, yeah. Not all of 'em are like Nova, that guy outside. Some are as close to legit, run by smart people who you can trust."

"But they're criminals, Devonlin."

Shaking his head, he sighed and gave me a look older than his years. "Man, you did grow up sheltered. Don't you know this world is run by criminals?"

"That's not true."

"Yeah, well, true or not, there's people I would trust to have my back. I just can't afford their protection."

"All the more reason to alert the police."

"You aren't getting it. People like Nova have the connections to make any paper trail disappear, to make the police disappear. Meanwhile, you've just painted a big old target on your back 'cause you know the cartel got enough cops in their pocket. Your name and address is only a phone call away. If you don't mind me sayin', you're very pretty, Ms. Holtz, and Nova would love to have an excuse to get his hands on a woman like you. People that go up against Nova and his men don't end up so good."

School had ended an hour ago, so the hallways were mainly empty. I felt like my voice echoed as I whispered, "Seriously?"

Shaking his head, Devonlin looked down and scuffed the floor with his giant foot, his dark skin gleaming. "Know a kid who tried to get his mom to stop working for Nova. My friend beat her pimp up and tried to keep her safe, but he let his guard down. They beat the fuck out of him. Put him in the hospital for months and made an example out of him, 'yah know? No charges were ever brought, no one was ever arrested."

My lips felt numb as I whispered, "That's terrible."

"It is, and you need to stay out of it. You see that guy out there; you turn the other way. He's got a thing for PAWG blondes."

"Um, what?"

He blushed as he stammered out, "Uh, you know. Um..."

"No, I don't know. "

Rubbing the back of his thick neck, Devonlin grinned and said, "I gotta go, see you around, Ms. Holtz."

"Wait," I yelled at his retreating form. "You tell me what PAWG means!"

From further down the hall, a group of teenage boys burst into laughter and one yelled out, "It means Phat Ass White Girl."

With my face no doubt as red as a tomato, I turned and

marched down the hallway, wondering if I'd just been insulted or complimented.

With a low sigh, I rubbed my forehead then tried to find patience as I listened to my younger sister, Winter, complain about my parents on the phone. At seventeen, she had a flair for drama a mile long, but was also as nice as could be. She was a much better kid than I'd been, that was for sure. Instead of sneaking out to go to a party, she'd stay home and happily spend hours hanging out with her small circle of friends. She had a serious boyfriend, and I know they'd had sex. She was open with me about stuff like that, but overall she was a great kid.

Just a little dramatic...then again, what teenager wasn't?

"Mom said I *have* to go on college tours with her!" Winter grumbled as I sat on the back porch of Mark's house, watching the sparkle of the city that stretched into the distance like a field of stars.

"Just a couple local ones. Come on, we all had to go through this with them. Mom loves that shit."

"But you guys were *interested* in college. I'm not."

"I thought your grades were good?"

"They are, but that's not the point. Mom seems to think if I don't go to college I'm doomed to a life of teen pregnancy and working two jobs at minimum wage. She seems to think college is some magic ticket to success, and that's not true. Besides, Paul didn't go to college, and he's got a great career."

Paul was my sister's older boyfriend, nineteen, who worked in heating and cooling for his dad's company. They'd been dating since junior high. I had to admit, Paul was the perfect guy for her. He was sweet, kind, and patient, but strong in a quiet way. You could tell by the way he looked at her that he thought the sun and moon rose and set on Winter.

I sucked in a deep breath of the cool night air, inhaling the slight hint of sage coming from the trees surrounding the backyard. It was a beautiful view. The lit belowground pool shimmered like an aquamarine jewel. While Mark's place wasn't as flat-out pimped as Leo's—that man had some insanely expensive taste—I couldn't deny the luxury surrounding me. As beautiful as his house was, and as welcoming as Mark could be, this place just didn't feel like my home. Weeks of living here, and I still felt like I was a guest in his house.

I needed to get a place of my own, but there was no way I could afford the kind of security I had at Mark's. The house was a luxurious fortress, and I felt safe here, even if I wasn't entirely comfortable. I had a fleeting memory of the last time I felt safe, in Ramón's arms.

Trying to suppress a pang of longing, I rubbed my heels against the soft fabric of the lounge chair I sprawled in, watching my glittering toenail polish sparkle in the low light. "So, just tell her you don't want to go."

"I tried that. Dad's even on my side, but Mom is determined to keep me from 'throwing my life away on some foolish fantasy.' Well, my fantasy isn't foolish; it's my dream. I'm going to make the most beautiful floral hair jewels you've ever seen!"

"Floral hair jewels?"

"Yes," she breathed with a whisper filled with happiness. "Floral hair jewels. It combines everything I've been learning, and gives me the chance to grow some of the most beautiful orchids in the world. I'm going to start small—local weddings, prom, stuff like that—but I'm going to do live tutorials while I put the floral arrangements together. I plan on making the bulk of my income from advertising on my videos."

"Where in the world did you get an idea like that?"

"You know my friend Usha from India? Her mom does it. I've learned from watching her work, and I've been looking into classes that will teach me how to be a florist. I might branch out into corsages in the future, but for now I'm sticking to floral hair jewels. I even got an afterschool job at Millie's Flowers, helping her run her shop." She giggled, and I could help but smile in response to the happiness in her voice. "Paul's work is right across the street, so I get the added bonus of some serious eye-candy when he's in the office."

I played with the hem of my silky, peach pajama pants and smiled. "Sounds like you have it all planned out."

"I do. I know everyone thinks I'm this ditzy blonde airhead, but I know what I'm talking about. I just wish Mom could see that and stop making me try to live the life she wanted, like she did with you and Brittney."

"What?"

"Oh, come on, you know it's true. Mom's pushed all of us to do what she wanted before she got pregnant with Brittney. Go to college, be wild, have a career, then get married. I mean, she's like a stage mom in a weird way, but instead of reliving her youth by making you walk in a pageant, she makes you relive the youth she wished she had by encouraging you to party and date lots of guys."

I sat there, stunned that my little sister had clearly seen what I'd been so blind to. "I never thought about it that way."

"It's not that hard to figure out. I mean, when you lived in the dorms, all she would ever talk about was how much fun you must be having, all the parties you attending. Now that you're in a relationship, she wants to do the same thing with me that she did with you and Brittney. I don't want that. I'm not into drugs, alcohol, or parties. I mean yeah, I smoke weed, but I'm not into doing keg stands or anything."

"What does Dad say?"

"You know how he is, busy working. He did tell me that whatever I wanted to do was my decision. If I wanted to go to a trade school instead of a four-year college, he'd be more than happy to pay for it. He even said I could live at home until I saved up enough money for a place of my own, for however long I needed."

"Dad is awesome."

"He is, but I won't be living with them after graduation." She let out a little squeal, then whispered, "I'm going to move in with Paul."

"Oh my God…Dad is going to lose his shit if you live with a guy before you get married."

"Um, that's kind of the reason I called. I was wondering if you could be there when I break the news to Mom and Dad? You're a calming influence on Mom."

"Me? A calming influence? You do remember the epic fights Mom and I have had, right? You're the one who calms Mom down."

"Fine, I need you there because you make me feel stronger."

"Winter…" I swallowed hard, wishing I was as brave as she thought. "You don't need me, but if you want me for moral support, I'll be there. I can always say something to piss her off and divert her attention, so you can run away."

"Should I have Paul there?"

Chewing on my lip, I shook my head after a moment. "No, you don't want to spring something on them like this with Paul watching. We'll just sit down, and you can tell them that after graduation you're going to take some floral design and art classes, college-level courses, so you can learn your craft. You have the talent, I have no doubt about that, but you still need to learn the basics and the special little tricks that will make your work shine."

"I love you," Winter sighed. "You're always on my side, and you know just what to say. You're my hero."

Laughing, I shook my head and stretched out. "I don't know about that. On a serious note, don't you think you're a little young for this big of a step? Moving in with someone is huge."

"Why can't I meet my soulmate early? Why shouldn't I be with the man I love? Paul is a man. I know he's younger than you, but he's a lot more mature. Besides, it's not like we're running off to get hitched. We just want to live together and see how it goes."

"I think that's a great idea."

"Well, Mom's going to think I'm dumb, like going to a technical college is something only people who can't get into a 'real' college do."

"Don't listen to her. You're smart, and brave, and awesome. Technical colleges are just as good as traditional. Be true to yourself. I'm so proud of you for going after what you want. I wish I'd been brave enough to follow my heart instead of trying to please Mom."

"What are you talking about?"

"I've—" I hesitated, wanting to protect Winter as much as possible from how screwed up my life had become. "I've been thinking a lot about my life, about what I'm doing with it, where it's going, and if I'm really happy. I've thought about it, and I want what Grandma Rosa and Grandpa Felix had. I want to be a stay-at-home mom, to raise my family and be there for them instead of working all the time like Mom did."

"With Ramón?"

Again, I hesitated. I hadn't told my family that we were no longer speaking. First, it was embarrassing to have someone just ghost on you like that. Second, my Mom was really happy with

Sweetest Obsession

my relationship and asked all the time how he was doing. I hated to admit it even to myself, but there was a tiny part of me that still hoped he'd come through the door at any minute. That I'd wake up in bed with him at my side.

A pang of hurt lanced from my heart to my stomach, but I swallowed past the pain. "Maybe with Ramón. We haven't been dating forever like you and Paul."

"Yeah, that makes sense. But you're so…driven about school. I thought you loved being a teacher? You'd give up all you've done, all you've gone to school for, to be a mom?"

I thought of the ideal life I'd imagined with Ramón and said without hesitation, "In a few years, absolutely."

"Wow…I think you'll be an amazing mom, but I also thought you'd be a great teacher. Don't you like teaching anymore?"

Standing, I slowly paced along the wide, long cement back porch, moving in and out of the shadows of dim light coming from hidden spotlights while keeping my eyes open for scorpions or spiders.

"Well, I do and I don't. There are parts of being a teacher that I love, but the more I get into it, the more I realize being a classroom teacher isn't what I want to do."

"Well then, what do you want to do?"

The feeling of being in Ramón's arms flashed through me and my voice came out thick as I said, "I don't know anymore."

"Are you crying?"

"No," I sniffed and wiped my face. "I'm fine."

"What's going on with you? You've been weird over the past few weeks."

"It's nothing," I said in a flat voice.

"Joy," Winter snapped. "What is going on? Is the guy you're staying with creeping on you? Do you need help?"

The thought of my sweet sister trying to rescue me from my situation made me laugh. "No, no creeping going on. I'm okay."

"No, you're not."

"Really, I'm oaky. It's just…boy problems." I decided to give her part of the truth.

"What happened? Did Ramón cheat on you? Need me to nut punch him?"

"No, no. Thank you, but no. It's fine. He went on a business trip and hasn't been in touch in a few weeks. At first he'd text me and call me all the time, telling me he missed me, then radio silence."

"Ugh, that's not good."

"I mean, Ramón's in like some South American jungle or something, so he told me he'd be out of contact, but I didn't think it would be for this long."

"Maybe he really is someplace where they don't have reception. Those places do exist, you know. And, I mean a few weeks isn't that long. Then again, do you think he's really away on business or just avoiding you?"

"No, he's away on business. At least, I think he is." I groaned and rubbed my eyes. "God, I don't know if he was playing me, or if any of it was real, but I miss him, and I really wish he'd contact me and let me know what the fuck is going on."

A sense of relief filled me as I made my way back to my lounge chair and now probably warm iced tea. I hadn't been able to talk to anyone about Ramón, not even Hannah. She'd been so hurt, and her healing had been so rough on her, that when she finally came home to Leo's place, I wanted her to be happy—not worried about me and my totally screwed up love life. I mean, in the grand scheme of things, who gave a fuck about my wounded heart when we had the shit beat out of us?

As far as I knew, no one had ever mentioned that Ramón and I were dating to Hannah. Shit, we'd only been together for a few days, so I knew I was blowing it all out of proportion in my head, but I'd really felt a connection to Ramón. Whenever I was at the Cordovas', they wouldn't talk about him unless I brought it up, then it was just brief and polite. Like I was a stranger asking about his life rather than his girlfriend. The things he said, the way he touched me, the way he looked at me, had all seemed so real. But how real could it be if he didn't let his family know how important I was to him?

Memories assailed me of looking into his eyes, laughing with him, making love and just enjoying life with Ramón at my side.

Everything was just…better when he was around.

I didn't realize how sad and empty my life had been until he was gone.

Winter sighed. "I gotta go. Mom's yelling for me to do the dishes. Email me and let me know when you can come over for 'the talk.'"

I groaned. "That'll be a fun night."

I could hear my mom's voice in the background yelling for Winter to get her butt downstairs, and Winter said quickly, "Gotta go! Love you!"

"Love you too, honey."

Chapter 13

Joy

At 1:30 am, after four hours of broken sleep, I gave up the fight against my insomnia and began what was now my normal routine. First, a shower in the pretty silver, white, and gold bathroom off my bedroom. It was luxurious, especially for a struggling college student, and normally I would have found great pleasure in the decadence that I now called home. Being both mentally and physically exhausted, I found it hard to care about anything. It seemed like, no matter how much sleep I got, or how hard I worked to cheer myself up, I just couldn't shake the fog of depression that drifted in and out of my life.

I wasn't constantly sad, but it seemed to be my default setting these days.

That, and scared.

Memories of that man, Nova, glaring at me back at the high school prickled at my anxiety like little blades. The need to run surged through me, trying to take away my control.

Before I could freak out, I turned the shower on and thrust my hand beneath the ice cold water. It instantly derailed my panic as my body tried to figure out why the fuck I was suddenly freezing. My heart still raced, but for a different reason. As the water warmed my pulse slowed.

Stepping beneath the steaming spray, I tilted my face up as I twisted my wild curls into a bun, letting the water wash the sweat from tonight's nightmares from my body.

When Ramón left, he took my peaceful night's sleep with him.

In tonight's thriller/horror dreams, I'd been back in our old apartment, reliving the moments when I'd been frozen with terror as a massive, nasty old man slapped and hit my best friend, Hannah.

The sound of her screams echoed through the room. Her lip split in a small burst of bright red blood, my dream slowing time down so it felt like everything was distorted. I'd always imagined I'd be brave if any man ever tried to hit me, that I would take advantage of some mistake the bad guys made and save the day. The terrible, gut wrenching truth was that I was a coward. A girl I loved like she was my flesh and blood was being beaten to a pulp, and I couldn't force myself to move. Forget being clever and clear-headed, during my first encounter with true violence, with pure maliciousness, I'd turned into a scared rabbit. I was prey. I wasn't strong, I wasn't level-headed and smart. I flattened myself to the wall, frozen in horror while they hurt her.

Unable to control my dream, I once again experienced the staggering fear caused by one of the bad guys dragging me down the hallway by my hair, a scream choking me as flailed and tried to get away. I lost my mind at that point, fighting like a cornered animal, but he pinned me so fast I didn't stand a chance. That shocked me, honestly—how fast he was able to physically get control of me.

At the time, I had no fighting skills, not real ones. I mean, I'd taken a few women's self-defense classes that one of my mom's feminist friends ran, but when it came down to it, I was a small, out of shape woman who sat on her ass behind a computer way too many hours of the day. The guy on top of me, however, obviously spent time at the gym. I'd been helpless against him as he ground his cock against me. He told me all the vile things he planned on doing with me, his revolting threats mixing with Hannah's distant screams of agony.

Just like all my nightmares, my bedroom morphed to a dingy cell, complete with torture equipment as a group of men stood around. Dirty, disgusting men, all there to rape me while they filmed it.

Pain lanced through me, and I realized I was curving my hands into fists so tight, my tendons ached. If I had any fingernails that I hadn't chewed off left, they would have pierced my palms. For a moment, I welcomed that pain, welcomed how it chased back my guilt and shame. If I were to try to diagnose myself, which we all know is a fool's errand, I'd say I had some fucked up blend of survivor's guilt and PTSD going on. Probably some depression as well, and for sure generalized anxiety.

My love of psychology, of figuring out how the mind worked, and the college classes I'd taken about the topic gave me a vast foundation of knowledge to draw from to realize just how fucked in the head I was.

With a tired sigh, I turned off the shower then stepped out, drying my body before giving my reflection a cursory glance as I brushed my teeth.

Dark circles beneath my eyes were my new norm, and I'd invested quite a bit of money in concealer sticks to try and mask their presence. My eyes were a light green color, so whenever I cried, it was really obvious. The whites of my eyes threaded with bright red and bloodshot. Lately, I'd stopped wearing makeup, not wanting to draw attention to my always-red eyes. The stress was wearing me down, and every day seemed worse than the one before.

I'd discovered a few weeks ago that sleeping pills made me feel even more depressed, so those weren't an option for me. I had an appointment to see a psychiatrist, but it wasn't for another three weeks. Only a few places took my shit insurance, and I was on a waiting list at each with instructions to see my primary caregiver right away if I felt like harming myself. I had no urges to hurt myself. I wasn't suicidal like I'd been as a teenager, but I was becoming agoraphobic. The thought of going someplace crowded, like a mall or a concert, made me break out into a cold sweat.

Going into the small walk-in closet, I dug through the built-in drawer containing my sweatpants and leggings. Because of my promise to Ramón, at Tino's insistence, and the power of the Cordova name, I was finishing my last semester of school from home. This meant I could basically live in my scrubby clothes, so I did.

As I tugged on a pair of leggings printed with an Alice in Wonderland theme, I tried to remember the last time I'd made an effort to look nice. It had to be a week ago, when I'd gone to dinner at the Cordova house with Hannah and Leo. The Cordovas had been different with me…distant, almost. Like I was a welcome guest, but a guest nonetheless. It hurt my feelings, and I'd pleaded a stomach ache, so I could get out of having to sit through dinner with people who no longer liked me.

Tying my hair up with a pink scrunchie, I slid my feet into a pair of fawn brown leather slippers and shuffled my way out the door.

I wondered, once again, as I moved through the really nice house, why Mark was single. He had money, good looks, and sure he was older, but he was still hot. We had no chemistry together—I mean none, to the point it was almost like we had negative chemistry—which was nice. It allowed me to relax around him, instead of wondering if I'd have to fight off his advances at some point. From the time I hit puberty onward, men seem to mistake my friendship for flirting. I've, unfortunately, gotten very good at turning men down without insulting them. I'd learned early on that men got super defensive if you shot them down and didn't soothe their ego about it, so I'd become a master at deescalating potentially embarrassing situations.

Memories of all the unwanted advances I've dealt with over the years left me feeling slightly ill, so I didn't notice at first when I entered the kitchen that I wasn't alone. I wasn't expecting anyone—Mark was usually off working his odd hours or sleeping at this time of night—so when I caught movement out of the corner of my eye, I screamed and dropped to the ground.

"Jesus Christ," Hannah's familiar voice, rough with sleep, came closer a moment before she emerged from the shadows leading to the living room. "Are you okay?"

I tried to speak, but all that came out was a pathetic whimper that made me feel unbearably weak and ashamed.

Dressed in a pair of pajama pants with kittens on them and a white tank top, Hannah tossed her long black hair over her shoulder before she hugged me, "Joy, it's just me, sweetheart. I'm sorry, I didn't mean to startle you."

I tried to laugh it off, but what came out was a watery, hiccupping sob. "It's okay, you didn't scare me."

"Riiiggghhht," Hannah said as she helped me up and brought me into the living room. "We'll pretend you pee'd yourself with 'Happy to see you' pee instead of 'I almost crapped my pants' pee."

I gave her a weak smile. "You're weird."

"I know."

The wide, well-lit sitting area was done in shades of cinnamon and gold, perfectly complimenting the wonderful desert landscape views that were visible during the day. Right now, the backyard was illuminated by tasteful lighting around the different types of cactus and native trees decorating the space. Down in the valley below, and on the mountains in the distance, golden lights twinkled. I spied a pillow and blanket on the massive rust red leather sofa that faced the gigantic TV across the room.

"Why are you sleeping in the living room instead of at your place?" I asked my best friend as she tugged me down onto the couch next to her. "Did you and Leo have a fight?"

"No, no. Nothing like that." Hannah's long black hair was down. It fell forward to partially obscure her delicate face before she pushed it back then looked at me. "I had a talk with Mark yesterday."

"What?"

"He asked me to keep an eye on you while he was gone. He's worried about you."

"What? I don't—"

"Cut the shit, Joy. Ever since the attack at our apartment, you've been different. I knew something was up, but I was hoping it was just the stress of the whole thing. That, with time, you'd get better, but you're getting worse." I tried to defend myself again, the stupid need to not appear weak making me want to argue my false strength, but Hannah didn't let me get a word in. "You're not sleeping. You're compulsive cleaning—which I know is something you do while you're stressed. You barely leave the house, and you jump at every and any noise. I'm worried about you."

Even now, drowning on my own, I had too much pride to reach out to her. "I'm…I'm fine."

"No, you're not fine, and that's okay." Hannah held my cold hands in her warm ones, empathy filling her big eyes. "I want to help you be fine again. Whatever you're going through, whatever's eating you alive, you have to let it out. I promise, you can trust me. We've been through so much, Joy. Honestly, your behavior is scaring me. If you don't knock it off, I'm going to kick your ass. You've been taking self-defense lessons with me from Leo, you know I can neutralize any threat. Like, I can kill a guy with a pencil four different ways."

"A pencil?"

"Or a pen. You just have to jam it through your attacker's

eye, really hard, to pop it and get to the brain. If you can, try to wiggle it around so you destroy as much of the brain as possible." I stared at her, and Hannah said defensively, "What? It's true. If you want them dead, you have to scramble the brain. Like a zombie."

"You've been watching way to much *Walking Dead*."

It was weird hearing Hannah, my usually timid and sweet friend, talk casually about killing someone. So weird that I couldn't help but snicker, then giggle, and finally outright laugh. The offended look on her face only set me off in more laughter until I was holding my sides and crying.

"If we're ever at an office supply store, I'll be sure to stay well away from you."

"You *should* be afraid," Hannah grumbled, though she was trying to hold back her own giggles. "I could kill you with this throw pillow."

"I am," I protested between snorts, standing and going over to a mission-style cupboard on the other side of the room to get some tissue to wipe my face.

"But seriously, what's going on? Talk to me. If you're having problems processing what those motherfuckers did to us, I can help, I promise." She gave me puppy dog eyes that I was powerless to withstand. "Please, Joy, you're my best friend, and it kills to see you so…not you."

With a long, long sigh that seemed to come from the pit of my soul, I gave up trying to pretend everything in my life was perfect with a feeling of profound relief. Though Hannah might come off as fragile and delicate, she had a core of steel built up from withstanding years of neglectful abuse by her parents. It was probably one of the reasons she bounced back from the attack while my mind seemed determined to make me relive every moment of it on a nightly basis.

With hitching sobs—I was tired of crying all the time—I told her about my lack of sleep, my growing paranoia when I was out in public, and the panic attack I'd had in the parking lot of the high school. I left out the part about Nova threatening me. I went on about how I doubted myself about everything, how I wished I'd been strong enough to go after what I really wanted in life—a home and family—and how much I missed my *abuela*. The list of things wrong with my life continued on and on, jumping from topic to topic in a frantic way that probably made me sound like a crazy person. During my meltdown Hannah merely held my hand and rubbed it, her touch slow and soothing as she listened to me with tear filled eyes. I realized then how much I missed being touched with affection, and how fucking miserable I was without Ramón, so I told her about him as well.

When I let that last part spill out, Hannah froze and said slowly, "Excuse me? Ramón? As in Ramón Cordova?"

I pulled my hand away from hers to nod and uselessly wipe at my damp face. Shit, I must look as big of a hot mess as I felt.

"Joy," Hannah snapped, "what in the ever-loving fuck is going on?"

"I dated Ramón," I said in a rush. "While you were still recovering. He was…he was so nice to me, so sweet, and he said he loved me. He made it sound like we were going to be together forever and then he just took off. Now I'm alone, and I miss him, and I'm worried about him, even if he is an asshole. None of what happened between us makes any sense. I feel like I'm losing my mind, doubting it even happened."

Frowning, Hannah held up her hand. "Wait, Ramón said he *loved* you?"

I nodded, big fat tears spilling down my cheeks. "I'm such a moron. Who believes guys when they say things like that? I knew he was too good at eating pussy to be true."

Making a sour face, Hannah said, "Yuck, stop right there. Don't need to know that part. Moving on…why didn't you tell me this before?"

"Because it all happened so fast! It was while you were still healing after the attack, and you were still in so much pain. I was going to tell you when you got better, but then Ramón took off, and I never heard from him again. If he loved me, why hasn't he tried to contact me in some way?" Wiping at my cheeks with more tissue, I tried to smile. "Sorry, I didn't mean get all hysterical on you."

"You have every right to be hysterical," Hannah muttered, a distant look in her eyes. "That would explain why Judith is so into you."

"What?"

"She's almost as worried about you as I am. Always asking how you're doing, if you're coming over with me." Hannah gave me an apprehensive look. "I didn't know it was because Ramón wants to marry you. Now that I think about it, we did end up talking about you a lot. Son of a bitch, he liked you. I didn't see it at the time, but now it's totally obvious."

The stupid, insecure part of myself made me whisper, "You believe me?"

"What? That Ramón loves you? Of course, you're a total catch. Besides, I should have known something was up when he started work on his house. I thought it was just because he wanted a place close to Leo, but now that I think about it…" Hannah suddenly gave me a searching look. "Did he show you his new place? Did you like it?"

"Yeah, he did, and it's totally beautiful." My heart gave a weak thump as both pleasure and pain broke through me at the memories of our picnic. "He has a backyard to die for, and his house is totally fabulous. It's brand new, but they managed to make it look lived in, like a home. I don't know how to explain it, but while it doesn't have a sitting area with a fire pit in the middle of a pool, like your place, it's the kind of home I'd build if I was a grown up with a billion dollars to spare."

To my surprise, Hannah closed her eyes and a tear rolled down her cheek.

"Hannah? What is it?"

When she looked up at me, the sadness in her expression took me aback.

"I…I—" she tried again to clear her throat, but no words came out as she struggled to speak.

"Relax," I urged her, pulling Hannah in for a hug. "Don't try to force the words. They'll come."

She gave a frustrated growl then pulled out of my arms. "Sorry, sorry. Okay, let's try this. I'm happy because if you and Ramón do end up together, that means we'll always be in each other's lives because our men are like brothers. I'm worried, because being in a relationship with Ramón…" She cleared her throat with a determined expression and continued, "Dating Ramón, because of who he is, is dangerous. He's a very rich man, from a very wealthy family, and there are people out there who will do whatever, and hurt whoever, they need to in order to try and get that money."

"I know, he's told me all about it."

"What has he told you?"

For the first time in my life, I hesitated telling Hannah the truth. Ramón had trusted me with the info about Fernando's son, and I didn't want to betray that trust, even though I wanted to talk with Hannah about it. I assumed Leo told Hannah, but it really wasn't my story to share. I looked up at the sound of nails clicking on the floor, then smiled when Hannah's tan and white pit bull, Honey, jumped up on the couch between us where she was promptly kissed and cuddled by both of us.

"Just about how being as high profile and rich as the family is, they have more than their fair share of people that are willing to do anything to get that money."

Something close to disappointment shimmered in Hannah's brown eyes, but she turned away before I could figure it out. "There are lots of really bad people gunning for the Cordova's, but they aren't easy prey. Trust me on this one."

"Well, considering your boyfriend is the chief of their security, I'll take your word on it. Speaking of Leo, he never mentioned anything about me and Ramón?"

Her lips tightened into a thin, white line and I worried that I'd just put Leo in the doghouse somehow. "No, he didn't say a word."

"Weird, but don't be mad at Leo," I added quickly as her dark look grew. "He was probably just trying to stay out of it. Besides, whatever was or wasn't happening between myself and Ramón is a moot point anyways. Ramón's not here and…and I'm done waiting around for him to come back."

Hannah's focus remained on Honey as she scratched the dog's big square head. "What if Ramón really is unable to call you right now? What if he comes back and expects you to be waiting for him?"

I shrugged, pretending to be way more cavalier about the situation than I was. "I can't live my life on what ifs."

"True," Hannah chewed on her thumb, a physical tell she had for when she was holding something back.

Giving her my best intimidating stare, the one I used on my students, I asked, "Hannah, do you know something about Ramón? Did Leo say something?"

She opened her mouth to say something, but closed it again then cleared her throat with a frustrated look. No, Leo hasn't said anything. Look, you need to get out of the house. Let's go out tomorrow, just the two of us. We'll have a girl's day, it'll be fun. Are you doing anything tomorrow?"

Truth be told, I didn't really want to go anywhere, but I also didn't want to end up a shut-in. he paranoid part of my mind insisted that was a bad idea, but I was starting to get desperate to feel some kind of normal again. I couldn't go through life like this anymore. A year ago, I would have been giddy with the idea of going to a spa, but now the thought made me break out in a cold sweat.

"No. I have some online tutoring to do in the afternoon, but nothing in person."

"Awesome." She glanced down at her gold and diamond wrist watch. "Let me call Leo, he's at some event at Obsession with Diego tonight doing security, and let him know I'm spending the night, then we'll get some good snacks and watch some crappy TV."

Guilt prickled at me, knowing that Hannah was rearranging her already busy schedule to spend time with me. She'd started working part-time with Judith at the Cordova Group in the event planning division. Yes, my formerly shy and meek friend now enjoyed helping put together big shindigs with million dollar budgets. I always knew she had it in her, but to be honest, I'd given up on ever getting her out of her shell. No matter how jealous I'd initially been of Leo and Hannah's relationship, I had to say he was a miracle worker in turning my introverted and timid friend into a confident social butterfly.

I smiled at her, my chest warm with love as I linked my hand with hers and gave it a squeeze. "You don't have to do that."

"I know, but we haven't hung out in forever and I miss you. I mean, you're more family than my own. I've really, really missed you."

I gave her a big, squishy hug, my tension easing as Hannah relaxed against me. "I've missed you, too."

Hannah drew back with a laugh when Honey tried to shove her way between us to get in on the love. "Then it's settled. You get some snacks together, make it something good, and I'll be right back. I just need to call Leo and tell him goodnight. He gets pissy if I don't."

Before she could leave, I grabbed her arm gently. "Hey,

thanks. I really needed to talk to someone about all of this."

Her lower lip wobbled, and she lowered her head to mine until our foreheads touched. "I will always be here for you, do you hear me? Always. No matter what."

Chapter 14
Ramón

The doctor finished examining the healing injuries on my face then muttered something, her expression intense as she concentrated on her work. They'd stitched me up as best they could, but even the most outlawed, cutting edge science in the world couldn't disguise the deep lacerations that stretched from the back of my head to my jaw. When the helicopter I was in was shot down over the jungle, the thick canopy of trees had cushioned our fall enough that some of us survived, but a branch had broken through the window near me as we went down and tore my right side up. I was lucky—of the seven men who'd accompanied me on the rescue mission, only three, including myself, had returned.

My other men, guys I've known for years, had given their lives so we could rescue the girl from the hands of a group of South American slave traders.

Dr. Stein leaned back, her aged face set in her usual no bullshit expression. "Looks good, Ramón. How does it feel?"

I opened and closed my jaw, the stitches stretching from my lower lip and up to my temple pulling tight. They'd dissolve soon, but the scars would remain. Not for the first time. I wondered how Joy would react when she saw my battered face, shaved head, and weight loss. With no food, we'd had to scavenge whatever we could from the jungle. While we didn't starve, my body had used up pretty much all my fat reserves to give me enough energy to get to safety. There had been points I was ready to give up, ready to put a bullet in my head so I'd at least have a quick death, but my love for Joy kept me going. I kept a lock of her hair with me like a talisman, and used it to give me focus.

When we'd finally reached civilization, I'd been in bad shape, incoherent, unable to speak due to my injuries. I'd slept pretty much a week straight. I'd only been deemed strong enough to travel back to the States on a private plane two days ago. Even though I was dying to see Joy again, I needed more time to heal first.

Remembering her overblown reaction to a few bruises, I didn't want her to have a complete meltdown when she saw me really hurt. I could still barely stay awake, and I wasn't strong enough to be there for her like she would need. No, as much as I wanted to see her, to touch her, and feel the life warming her body, I couldn't be selfish and drag her to my bedside to watch me sleep and heal.

Tracing the scar, I flexed my jaw again and looked up at my doctor from my bed. "Good, a lot better than it should. Is this the new healing compound?"

"Yes," she gave me a rare semi-smile. "Considering the right side of your jaw was attached by heavily damaged ligaments and muscles, and you're now able to talk, I'd say the accelerated stem-cell healing is a success."

With a sigh I slowly stretched out, a low ache breaking through the painkillers. "How long until I'm well enough to function?"

"Function how?"

"Let me rephrase that. How long until I can stand up for more than five minutes without passing out?"

"Four days, minimum. But I'd say that in a week, you should be able to do more…energetic activities."

The thought of waiting that long to see Joy was unacceptable. "That's too long. Isn't there something you can do to cut the time?"

"Look, we're already pushing your body to the limits, healing you as much as we can. While I understand that you did what you had to do in order to get out, you *destroyed* your already damaged body in the process. Do you have any idea what a miracle it is that you survived? That you aren't maimed or in constant agony? There is a price for accelerated healing, Mr. Cordova, and if you don't pay that price, the healing will stop and you will never be able to have a normal life again." Her lips thinned and she lowered her head slightly to look me in the eyes. "When you stumbled out of that jungle, your heart was maybe a dozen beats away from giving up. If it hadn't been for your men dragging you the last five miles, you would have never made it.

You're lucky you're even alive."

I looked away, my chest aching at the thought of my men, the ones who would never make it home. "How long will my jaw be numb like this?"

"For the next few days," Dr. Stein returned as she stripped off her gloves and tossed them in a basket next to the sink in her exam room. "As long as you take it easy. You must rest, Ramón. If I'm not being clear enough, let me put it into terms that you can understand. If you don't rest, if you reinjure yourself, you will lose your jaw. How pretty do you think sweet Joy will find you then? Not to mention the fact you're as weak as a kitten. You know how dangerous that is in our line of work."

Before I could respond, a knock came from the door of the room. A second later, Leo and Mark came in, the tension rolling off Leo in waves. "Ramón, I need to speak with you for a moment."

I waved him into my bedroom on the top floor of the Cordovas' headquarters. "Of course."

Dr. Stein, after grabbing her laptop, left without a word, used to the way our world worked. She should be, her office was located on the medical floor of our headquarters, and she'd been in the cartel's employ for longer than I'd been alive. Luckily, I had a penthouse suite in the building, so it made the perfect place for me to recover in secrecy and safety. My enemies would be pissing themselves with happiness at the anticipation of my death if they learned of my weakened state.

Sitting up, I rolled my stiff shoulders as I took Leo in, the healing wounds on my back itching. "What's wrong?"

With a sigh Leo said, "It's Joy. She's not doing very well."

Fear flowed through me, and I clenched my hands into tight fists as I fought to remain calm. "What do you mean, not well? Everyone told me she's fine. I thought you were keeping an eye on her? What's wrong with her?"

"She's not sleeping, not taking care of herself, chewing her nails, no longer laughing, not well," Mark snapped. "Because of your stupid order that we leave her alone in your absence and not tell her where you are, I've been unable to help her like she needs. She thinks you abandoned her."

"Abandoned her? Why the fuck would she think that?"

Mark glared at me. "Because you haven't contacted her in

weeks, and the excuses we give her about your absence are fucking flimsy as hell. Joy's too smart to fall for our bullshit, and because you're a selfish fuck who forbid anyone from giving her any kind of real answers, or truth about where you really are, she just assumes that you were playing some kind of game with her, you stupid asshole."

"Watch your mouth," Leo said with a low growl.

"No," I closed my eyes as his words hit me in the gut and my chest felt too tight. "No, he's right. I shouldn't have forbidden everyone from talking to her. In my defense, I never thought I'd be ambushed and have to fight my way back to civilization."

Mark shook his head, his lips tight. "You have to start putting her first."

"I fucking *do* put her first."

I fiercely wished I was strong enough to get in a fight, because I wanted to kick Mark's smirking ass.

"No, you don't. If you'd been thinking about Joy you would have done everything to cover all your bases before you left. You would have really thought about how she would react to seeing you gone, and realized when you gave that asinine order that everyone was to leave her alone and keep her in the dark, you were hurting more than helping Joy. She has a support system around her unique in its ability to help her through the transition from her world and into ours. You took that away from her because you didn't want to share."

"Bullshit," I seethed while pointing a shaking hand at Mark and a silent Leo. "I was trying to protect her. My mother was ready to brainwash Joy the first night she was beneath our roof, but I held her off as long as I could."

Mark's hard gaze softened, and his shoulders lowered a touch. "I didn't know that."

Leo stepped away from his second-in-command. "It's true. I've been helping Ramón put Judith off, but you know how she is. When she learned about Ramón's obsession with Joy, she was beside herself with happiness and had all kinds of fantasies about Ramón having a big happy family."

I snorted in contempt, my healing jaw itching something fierce. "That doesn't give my mother the right to play with people's lives at will. Joy is hands off to her, in every way. I'm still fucking pissed she gave my girl D128 without my permission."

"I'm afraid," Leo said in a dark voice, "that your mother's patience has just about run out. Seeing you injured has her more determined than ever to bring Joy into the family. You know Judith will do anything to protect you, Ramón. For Joy's sake, you need do her programming, and soon, or I fear your mother will step in. Not out of malice, but in a screwed-up effort to make you happy."

Pressure built in my head as I tried to sit upright on the bed, but my arms shook like I'd just done a hundred bench presses. I'd delayed Joy's programming as long as I could, but if my mom was ready to step in and break her promise to me, Joy was in trouble and she needed me. Fuck, I might have to be brought to her side in a wheelchair, but I had to move, *now*. The thought of my crazy mother fucking around with Joy's sweet, beautiful mind and soul made me ill.

"Where is she? Get Dr. Stein back in here. I need her to give me something to keep me awake."

Leo held up his hands as I struggled to move, the pain around my ribs almost to a manageable level now. "At Mark's house, but hold on. We need to go over how the truth serum works, how the programming works, and what you plan on saying."

Exhaustion tugged at me, my head throbbing with every beat of my heart, but I tried to remain awake and focused. "We don't have time. I have to help her."

"Yes, we do," Mark muttered as he did something on his phone. "I'll call Diego and Jose and get them to buy some time with Judith. You and I both know that while you're on the accelerated healing drugs, you're basically narcoleptic. Can't have you falling asleep during the programming or fucking it up in some way. If we give Joy more than one heavy dose of the truth serum, you run the risk of messing with large chunks of her memory. She could lose months, even years, if we dose her twice, so you have one shot to do it right. Don't rush it now and do something you'll spend the rest of your life regretting."

Closing my eyes, I tried to think past the pounding in my head. I'd been up for more than two hours now. While that doesn't sound like a lot, when your body is basically speed healing exhaustion is always nipping at your heels. All the adrenaline coursing through my system began to ebb, and I had to force myself to focus on Leo.

He returned my gaze and said, "You need to remember to work with her personality, making suggestions that she's naturally open to works far better than commands that her subconscious doesn't like. You *can't* order her to love you. Emotions just don't work that way."

I sneered at him. "I'd never do that anyway. And I know I can't turn her into a sex robot or any crazy shit like that. I don't want to do any of that. I love her, and I want to make her happy. I want to heal her, to make her laugh again. If programming can do that, I need you to tell me how."

Mark gave me an approving look, and Leo tilted his head in thought, then nodded. "I think we can do that. I'll go home and talk to Hannah, get her input, and we can meet again tomorrow evening."

"No, tonight."

"No," Leo said in a way that I knew he was going to be a pain in the fucking ass about it. "You need to sleep."

I gritted my teeth, but didn't argue. I couldn't, he was right and there was no way in hell I wanted Joy to forget a moment we'd had together. All those sweet fucking memories of being in her presence soothed me. My racing thoughts slowed, like the very thought of her was a balm to my soul. I centered myself with the memory of her peaches and strawberry perfume, the sweet tang of her cunt, the way her body felt draped over mine.

"You're right. Fuck, I hate it, but you're right." I leaned back into the pillows and fought to stay awake.

Leo exchanged a glance with Mark then said, "We have a plan. Our best chance to do this is going to be tomorrow evening. Hannah's going to take Joy to the spa, and we can drug her before her massage so she's nice and relaxed. As soon as she's under, you come in and everyone leaves. You'll only have roughly fifteen minutes to say what you need to say, and you must repeat your instructions more than once. I have a file made on Joy with my observations and suggestions for how to word some of the commands."

"Understood."

Mark added from behind me, "We think touch is an important part of the process, as is taste and smell. You'll need to hold her, kiss her, and cuddle her tight while you give her instructions.

The physical reassurance seems to be key to getting her mind to accept the commands."

"We'll be there to help you," Leo added.

Despite my best efforts, sleep was pulling me under and my words came out slurred, "No, I do it alone."

"But—"

"Alone," I said with all the strength I had left. "She's mine, mine to love, mine to protect, mine."

I didn't catch whatever their response was, the drugs stronger than my will as they pulled me under, but it didn't matter. No one was going to be in the room with us because I didn't plan on following whatever script Leo and my mother had come up with. I was going to do what was best for Joy, no matter what, and no one was going to stop me.

Chapter 15

Ramón

The next day, my mother glared down at me in my wheelchair. "Ramón, you're being ridiculous."

I returned her glare as Dr. Stein gave me a shot that would help keep me awake and aware long enough to take care of Joy. "No, no one is going to be in there with me. Not you, not Leo, not dad. No one."

"At least keep the cameras on," she pleaded as her dark eyes filled with tears. "What if something happens to you? It could hurt Joy."

My mom was the master of manipulation, but I wasn't giving into her this time. "No."

Anger tightened her face before she managed to once again control her features. "But, Ramón—"

"Enough, I don't have time to argue with you mother. I know you're trying to do what you think is best, but whatever happens in that room is none of your business. Stay out of it."

Diego made a soft hissing noise as my mother dropped the sweet old lady act. "It is entirely my business. Everything to do with this family is my business."

"No."

"Ramón—"

My father, dressed in a grey suit that went well with my mother's plum silk dress, put his weathered hand on her shoulder. "Judith, let it go."

"I—"

"Judith," my father said again, this time in a stern voice. "We don't have time for this. Let Ramón do what he has to do and stop fighting him."

She sagged against my dad, but her expression wasn't happy. "Fine. But if her programming doesn't work, don't blame me."

Anger roared through me, but I didn't have time to get into it with my mom. Already the serum was working its way through Joy's body, and I had work to do. Looking up at Leo and ignoring my parents, I said, "Take me to her."

We both disregarded my mother as she tried a last ditch effort to be part of Joy's programming. When the door closed behind us, she was still trying to plead her case.

We were in a small dressing room. I knew Joy waited for me through the door to the left. In this room, Leo was going to monitor me. I was allowing one live camera in the room to record the event. It was also set up so if I lost track at any point during the programming due to exhaustion, or some other unforeseen event, Leo could step in and complete the programming so Joy wasn't harmed. I felt good for the moment, but I knew how quickly the exhaustion could hit me. Never in my life have I been as tired as I've been these past few days, and my body was weak from lack of exercise.

Still, I would do whatever I needed to in order to make sure Joy was taken care of.

As Leo set up his laptop, a call came on his phone.

Frowning, he answered it, "What's wrong?"

A second later, a knock came from the door, and a pissed off Leo stormed over to answer it.

I leaned against a sturdy leather chair, getting some of the weight off my legs as Leo opened the door, revealing a determined looking Hannah.

Before Leo could argue with her, I sighed. "Let her in. I was expecting this."

Hannah, her face covered in some kind of green clay looking stuff, glared at me as Leo closed the door behind her. She was wearing one of the spa robes, and still wore those foam things women wear between their toes when getting a pedicure. Leo tried to hold her back, but she shrugged him off and marched over to me while he gave me an apologetic look.

"You're damn right, I want to talk to you. I know what you're up to, Ramón, and you're not going to do it without my input."

I had been waiting for her to argue with me, to plead with me not to program Joy, so I might have appeared a bit shocked as I stared at her. "You're not upset I'm doing this?"

She took another step forward, once again shoving Leo away when he tried to pull her to his side. "I know Judith, Ramón. I know your mother, and I know she's chomping at the bit to bring

Joy officially into the family. Am I right?"

I cut a glare at him for telling his woman my business, but the bastard merely rolled his eyes at me behind Hannah's back. "You're right."

"Leo wouldn't tell me what happened to you, but I'm guessing by your injuries, you were hurt too badly to respond to Joy. I know you would have if you could have, but it hurt her to have you vanish like that. You can't make this a habit, Ramón. If you're going to marry my friend, you have to promise me you'll be a good father and husband."

While Hannah could be annoying as hell, I was glad Joy had her in her life. "Don't worry, *mi amiga*, I had a…what does Joy call them? A *come to Jesus moment* in the jungle when I was sure I was a walking dead man. When I thought the end was near, all I could concentrate on was the life I wish I'd had the chance to live with Joy. My mind was filled with thoughts of the kids we'd never have, the places I'd never take her, the things I'd never get a chance to experience with her. Trust me, Hannah, I will be a good husband and father to your friend."

She bit her lip, then nodded. "Okay, but I want to stay and watch with Leo."

"No," Leo and I both said at once.

Shrugging, she toyed with the belt of her robe. "Fine, then I'll be forced to tell Joy what you did."

Leo gritted his teeth. "You won't tell her anything, Hannah."

"You're right," she smiled at me and I recognized it as the smile my mother used right before she nailed someone to the wall. "Because if you let me stay, I will never tell her. I can't make the same promise if you make me leave."

"This is a dangerous game you're playing." I checked my watch. "I don't have time to argue with you right now, so you can stay. But, be sure, we will discuss this in the future."

Hannah paled, then lifted her trembling chin. "Okay."

Rolling my eyes, I stood and waited for my knees to have the strength to hold me up. "Relax, I'm not going to beat you or anything. There may be some yelling involved. I'll trust your Daddy to carry out any…corporal punishments on my behalf."

Leo gave Hannah a smile that even I found off-putting, and I jerked my head. "Let's go."

Adrenaline fueled my movements as I quickly crossed the

room and opened the door, my body shaking the slightest bit as I finally got to see my woman again.

There, in the center of the tan and gold room with its low lighting and soft music, lay my beautiful Joy. Dressed only in a pair of plain pink cotton panties, her were eyes closed as she lay on her stomach on the massage table. Her golden blonde curls were pulled up into a bun on top of her head, and the smooth skin of her back gleamed with oil. Even from here, I could see the dark circles beneath her closed eyes and the fact that she'd lost weight. Lines of tension bracketed her mouth. I felt a pang of guilt that I was at least partially responsible for her depression.

But I was going to fix it, fix her. If I had my way, she'd never be unhappy again.

Leo helped me onto the long cream leather couch on the side of the room and arranged pillows on either side. I was still pitifully weak, too weak to stand up, let alone carry Joy from the table, but that didn't mean I was happy that Leo got to see her partially naked body as he lifted her and carried her to my waiting arms. Rationally, I knew he could give a shit less about Joy being naked, that he was utterly and completely devoted to Hannah in every way, but that still didn't stop the burn of jealousy.

Joy stirred as he lowered her into my arms, her head resting on the pillow as she snuggled into me with a happy sigh.

Leaning down, he whispered into my ear, "The camera is recording. I'd estimate you have about thirteen minutes until the serum wears off. Use it wisely."

After partially covering her with a clean white sheet, he left us without saying another word.

As the door closed behind him I tried to calm my nerves, to remember everything I wanted to say to her, but at this moment all I could do was rejoice on a soul deep level that after everything I'd been through I finally had my reward.

My Joy.

"Sweetheart, can you hear me?" I asked in a soft voice as I used my free hand to stroke her body, trying to ignore the faint tremor shaking my fingers.

"Ramón," Joy sighed and snuggled further into me. "I missed you."

While I would love nothing better than to sit here and cuddle her, the minutes on my watch were ticking down faster than I expected. "I missed you too, my strong, beautiful girl."

"I was so scared without you."

"You'll never be scared again, I promise. Now listen very carefully to everything I say…"

Chapter 16
Joy

I piled my hair up and turned my head in the mirror considering if I should bother to try and tame it, or just let it do its thing. Whatever special conditioner they'd put in it at the spa last week had worked miracles, making my normally frizzy curls behave and fall in perfect ringlets. My whole body was still as smooth as a baby's butt, thanks to the waxing I'd had done. It was easy to forget just how rich Leo was until he treated us to the kind of spa day reserved for Hollywood stars and royalty.

"Are you okay?" Hannah asked me for the like the millionth time as we got ready to go to Obsession, a super-hot club that the Cordovas' owned.

We were hanging out at the house she shared with Leo in the master closet, which was more like an apartment than any closet I'd ever been in.

It had three rooms—one entirely dedicated to shoes, and a seating area complete with couches, a table, and a TV. There was a faux fireplace, and the cream walls were tastefully lit by recessed lighting. Thick, soft copper carpet warmed the room and music came from speakers hidden in the ceiling and among the racks of clothes. And I do mean racks. Say what you will about Leo, but he spoiled the shit out of my best friend. Walking into her closet was like walking into an exclusive designer boutique. I was happy my friend had finally found a man worthy of her.

Messing with my hair, I said, "I'm fine, in fact, I feel better than I have in a while. That spa day must have been just what I needed. I'm finally sleeping through the night, and I haven't had any panic attacks."

And I wasn't lying. This morning, when I'd woken up, it wasn't a struggle to get out of bed and face the day. I felt a new sense of…peace for lack of a better term, and hope. Like maybe the world wasn't as scary and dangerous as I thought, that maybe it wouldn't try to destroy me the second I left the safety of

Mark's home. My thoughts seemed clearer, like all the doubts and bullshit that had been weighing me down were no longer there. I'd even gone out and started to explore the surrounding area on my own—well, kind of my own. Tino was still my constant companion, and I was glad for his company.

Hannah got a weird look on her face before she turned away to peer into the mirror of her big vanity and put some mascara on. "Well, I'm glad you're feeling better. You look great, by the way. I love that dress on you."

I smiled and checked the cool black, white, and red abstract print dress that I was wearing to make sure I hadn't gotten any makeup on it. "Thanks, and thank you again for getting me out of the house, and for talking with me. I feel a thousand percent better."

Hannah turned to me and took my hands in hers, an unexpected sadness on her face. "You know I love you, right?"

"Uh, yeah." I frowned at her. "Why do I feel like you're about to throw a 'but' in there?"

Closing her eyes, grey shadow sparkling on her lids, she shook her head. "No, no buts. I just want you to know that no matter what happens, I love you and I'd do anything to keep you safe. You're my sister from another mister."

I pulled my hands from hers and waved at my face. "Bitch, you're going to make me cry and I'm wearing waaayyyy too much makeup for that."

Hannah's phone chimed, and she tensed while she looked at the screen. "Leo says it's time to go."

When we arrived at Obsession, the three-story club was packed as usual on a Saturday night, but we didn't have to wait in line to get in.

No, we got to stroll past the masses and head right up to the front door, where the big bouncers were practically falling all over themselves in difference to Leo.

Purple neon lights lined the doorway and as we walked in the pulse of the music hit me almost like a physical blow.

While the club was well air conditioned, there was still a heaviness to the atmosphere that came from hundreds of people dancing and sweating at once, an almost undetectable smell of humanity. It wasn't bad, like BO or anything, just a combination of musk, perfume, and cologne mixed with alcohol. My heart began to beat faster, and I tapped my high heel clad foot in time with the music, my hips wiggling a little bit to one of my favorite songs.

Hannah grabbed my hand as we were led to the second level VIP floor of the club, the walk up the steps giving us a great view of the dancefloor below.

Normally, I'd be scanning for a hot guy to dance with, but I really had no desire to have some stranger pawing at me.

I only wanted one man's hands on me, and he seemed to have vanished into thin air.

Determined to not let thoughts of Ramón ruin my night, I chugged down my first glass of complimentary champagne, the bubbles tickling my tongue and throat.

"Take it easy," Hannah said as she fidgeted and watched me from across the table.

The white leather couches in the VIP section were set up in U shapes, with sheer white drapes separating the seating sections. A smaller dance floor took up one half of the area, with a long glass and stainless steel bar on the other side. Beautiful women and men ground against each other, and I tapped my toe along to the music. Part of me wanted to get up and dance, but Leo was already refilling my glass with champagne, so I decided to sit back for a minute and scope things out.

Leo and Hannah began to whisper to each other, and I sipped my champagne as she got increasingly pissed. Feeling like I was intruding, I angled my body away from them and gave them as much privacy as possible. Thankfully, the music was loud enough that I couldn't hear what they were saying, but it was still awkward as hell, especially when Leo decided to shut her up by grabbing her face with both of his hands and kissing the hell out of her. I couldn't help but feel sad that I had no one to kiss me like that. I finished off my second drink in record time, considering going for my third until I saw someone familiar.

Diego, dressed in a sharp black suit, made his way through the crowd to us, a broad smiling lighting his sculpted face. "Fancy seeing you here, little sister."

I scooted over so he could have a seat, eager to have someone to talk to who wasn't either fighting or sucking face. "Hey, Diego."

Leo, instead of greeting his friend, dragged a protesting

Hannah out of the booth and onto the dance floor, arguing in whispers the whole way.

Arching his dark brows in a questioning look, Diego said, "What's up with them?"

I shrugged. "I have no idea."

"Well, while they're busy, you want a tour of the club?"

I smiled, glad I wasn't going to have to sit here by myself like a loser. "Sure, that would be great."

Diego led me through the VIP area, pointing out different details about the building and staff, clearly proud of the place.

"So is Obsession like your baby?"

He nodded. "I spend most of my time here. My office is up on the third floor, want to see it?"

I glanced back over at our table, but Hannah and Leo were still dancing. "Yeah, I'd love to see behind the scenes."

We passed a set of big bouncers guarding a hallway off to the side of the VIP area, then passed yet another pair of bouncers before we took some stairs to the third level. The music was more muted up here, a distant background thump of bass muffled by the thick gold carpeting. We went down a long hallway with various closed doors until we came to the end.

Diego placed his palm on the digital pad next to the door, and there was a small beep before he opened the door and ushered me in.

My first impression of the room was a big office done in shades of black, plum, and silver, elegant yet masculine. The lighting was low, and my attention was caught by a large bank of screens that showed camera feeds from different parts of the club. It was cool to watch what everyone was doing, from the kitchens to the bouncers out front, and I wandered over to get a closer look. All the champagne I'd downed was starting to get to me, and I had to lean against the edge of Diego's large black lacquered desk as I wobbled in my heels.

It was only after the door shut that I realized Diego hadn't followed me into the room, but I wasn't alone.

"Joy."

That one word tore through me, and my heart thrummed so hard in my chest I thought I might be having a heart attack.

Spinning around, I put my hand to my mouth in shock as I tried to understand what I was seeing.

It was Ramón...but not the Ramón I remembered. Gone was his shoulder length dark hair, his head now buzzed so short that at one point I know he'd been bald, revealing thick, pink healing scars that raked down the right side of his once perfect face. He stood across the room from me, dressed in a tight maroon button-down men's shirt and black slacks, his fists clenched at his side.

My stomach lurched and I managed to stammer out, "Ramón? What...what happened?"

He crossed the room to me. Just as my knees started to give out, he managed to sweep me into his arms before I hit the floor.

His body shook as he held me, and I struggled to make sense of what was going on.

"Joy," he whispered as he sank to the ground, sitting on the floor with me curled in his lap. "I missed you."

Sudden anger filled me, and I tried to push my way out of his arms before he made a pained grunt that stopped my thrashing even as I yelled at him, "What the fuck is going on?"

"Shhh," he soothed me even as the lines around his eyes tightened with pain. "I'll explain, just please, calm down."

Tears burned my nose, and I was torn between kissing the hell out of him, demanding that he show me his injuries, and killing him. "I am calm!"

The darkness in his gaze lifted, the green in his eyes standing out as his lips twitched in a smile. "So I see."

Unable to help myself, I ghosted my fingertips over the healing scars on his cheeks. "Ramón, what the hell happened? Where have you been? Why didn't you call me?"

He took a deep breath and held me close, his body shaking beneath mine. "Because my helicopter was shot down over the jungle in El Salvador during a rescue mission."

"What?"

He proceeded to tell me this crazy story about this girl being kidnapped and how she was sold into slavery, her virginity to be auctioned off to the highest bidder. It sounded like something out of a movie, but the scars covering his face were all too real, and I knew from my own brush with Manny and his goons what terrible fate awaited the girl. Even with her virginity intact, there were ways that they could have...defiled her. The thought of someone doing that created a fire inside of me, a burning need for justice. I internally cheered when I learned Ramón and his men had slaughtered the bastards holding that girl. When Ramón got to the part about his helicopter crash and subsequent flight through the jungle to safety, I started sobbing, my heart hurting for all that he'd endured.

"But…but why didn't anyone tell me where you were? I asked and asked, but they just brushed it off like you were visiting friends in the jungle. Don't they know how much you mean to me?"

He gave me a sad, slightly lopsided smile, the scars pulling at the left side of his mouth. "I'm sorry, sweetheart, but it was a matter of security. The less people that knew, the better."

Clinging to him, I buried my face in his strong chest, inhaling his cologne and struggling to contain my sobs. "I'm so sorry. I was so mad at you. I thought you'd played me."

"Why the hell would you think that?"

Feeling dumb and petty, considering what Ramón had been through these past few weeks, I looked away. "You disappeared. And I…I needed you."

Holding me tighter, he buried his face against my neck. "I'm so sorry, *mi amore*. I promise I'll never leave you like that again. I love you, Joy. You're the only reason I made it out of there alive. When the pain was so bad that all I wanted to do was end it any way I could, it was the memory of holding you, the promise of having you in my life, that gave me the strength to get out."

This confession brought on another round of crying. Ramón tried to sooth me as I basically had a hysterical breakdown. Through it all, he held me, rocking me and letting me soak his shirt with my tears. All the crap I'd been through in his absence, all the nights I'd woken up alone in bed, rushed through my mind in a blur of aching loneliness. By the time I'd calmed down, my breath was coming out in those ugly hitches I hated. I felt as worn out as if I'd just run a thousand-mile race, but I felt better. Good enough to realize I probably looked like a hot fucking mess.

"Oh God," I moaned as I tried to push away. "I'm so sorry. I didn't mean to freak out like this. You must think I'm a lunatic."

"I think you're amazing." He used his thumb to wipe under my eyes. "And I'm so sorry you were hurting while I was gone."

I wrapped my arms around him and rested my head on his shoulder, my thoughts spinning out of control even as exhaustion seemed to sap all the strength from me. "I'm so glad you're okay."

"Me too, sweetheart." He sighed and gently moved me off his lap. "Come on, let's go home."

With Tino driving us in Ramón's SUV, we made it to his house in what seemed like record time. I spent the drive in the backseat with Ramón, my tired mind and body luxuriating in the feeling of being in his arms again. For his part, he simply held me close, constantly stroking me and whispering how much he loved me. The more I relaxed, the more my libido woke up and soon I was eager for more than comfort. I worried about Ramón's injuries and inadvertently hurting him, so I managed to control my wandering hands.

Kind of.

I couldn't resist the urge to touch him back, but I kept my hands above his waist, instead caressing every inch of him I could reach, reassuring myself that he was really here with me.

By the time we pulled up to his house, it was still pitch black outside. I had no idea what time it was. He led me out of the car, nodding to Tino, who gave us a jaunty salute and a small smile. I waved goodbye to him and cuddled into Ramón's side as he led us into his home.

A small gasp escaped me as we entered the lit foyer. Instead of the construction site I'd seen last time were here, I found a fully furnished and finished home.

An enormous spray of red roses and ivy sat on the dark wood table in the middle of the circular foyer, and double staircases led to the second floor. I had an odd sense of seeing into the future as I imagined what my daughters and sons would look like, coming down that staircase for prom. It was a beautiful space, but not pretentious. There were coat hooks for both kids and adults on one wall. And they were really cool, shaped like different fantastical animal heads and made of gleaming silver. The more I looked around, the more I took in the little details of the house, the attention that had been paid to every part of its construction.

"Do you like it?" Ramón whispered against the top of my

head as I turned in his arms to get a look at everything.

"It's perfect," I breathed. "Ramón, it's absolutely wonderful. After talking about it with you, and that meeting we had with your interior decorator…I never imagined it would be this perfect."

"Think you could be happy living here?"

Laughing, I smiled up at him. "Well, there aren't any water stains on the ceiling, and it doesn't smell like mold and Indian food like my old apartment, but yeah, I think I could deal with it."

"Good, because you're moving in."

"Are you asking me or telling me?"

He grinned, the expression now slightly lopsided on his face because of his scarring. "Asking?"

"Well, I might consider it," I teased, not wanting to jump up and down with excitement. "Will you do the dishes?"

"I have no problem doing that, but you know we'll have maids."

"Maids?"

"Yes. Simone and Raquel have been working for me for ten years. They're sisters, twins."

Right away, images of hot, twin naughty French maids with big old boobs and mile long legs filled my head. "Really."

Laughter filled his eyes as he stroked my cheek. "Relax, sweetheart. They're in their fifties and happily married."

Trying to pretend I hadn't turned into a crazy, jealous girlfriend, I rubbed my face into his palm, delighting in the feeling of his touch. "Why don't you show me the master bedroom and we'll see if you can convince me to move in with you."

The mood changed from playful and happy to hot and erotic in a heartbeat. "It would be my pleasure."

He led me into the master suite I'd help design and decorate, and I let out a happy little gasp and this time I did do a small hop or two. "Oh, Ramón, it turned out great."

He paused and gave me a second to drink the room in with an indulgent smile. "It reminds me of you."

"How so?"

He winked. "Bright and joyful."

His compliment sent little tickles of pleasure, but something sparkling caught my attention. I looked away from Ramón, wandering over to inspect a very pretty and modern looking chandelier lamp that cast a mellow, golden glow over the heavy walnut dresser it sat on.

The scent of vanilla drew my attention next, and I found a big candle burning on a small table next to a comfy beige loveseat beneath the window, perfect for reading and snuggling. I admired how the pale cream walls shimmered slightly in the candlelight, how the paint had a pearlescent sheen. I turned off the light, leaving the candle still burning, and a little tingle went through my core as Ramón groaned softly, but I pretended not to hear him. He made me wait to know that he was all right, and that still pissed me off. So he could wait for my attention.

Not that I was going to last much longer. I needed his big, pierced dick in a way that was growing more intense by the moment. My nipples stiffened into hard points as I imagined the feeling of his hands on me, something I thought I'd never have again outside of my memories. After too many nights without Ramón, I was having a hard time processing his sudden appearance, and used the distraction of the room to try and let some of my anxiety go.

The main feature of the space was the bed, and I'm not ashamed to say I went all balls out crazy on it. With eleven foot ceilings, this eight hundred square foot monstrosity of a room could house the kind of bed I'd always dreamed of. A big, four poster, dark walnut canopy bed with navy blue velvet drapes held back by thick gold tassels. I thought Ramón might twitch at having to sleep in a bed that was big enough to fit six people, and had to have an expensive custom order mattress made to fit, but he'd merely smiled and said he had some ideas for those four posts. I was curious if he'd done as he'd threatened, if there was a restraint system hidden behind those velvet coverings, but I was almost afraid to ask.

Already, I was losing myself in him, in his scent, in his strength. He'd lost a great deal of weight, and his scars still jarred me every time I looked at him, but I was so damn happy to have him home. I had these weird urges to cook for him and fatten him back up, to take care of him, of to heal him. Our gazes met. While the lust in his hazel eyes burned me, I could see the exhaustion adding lines to his face that hadn't been there before.

There was no way on earth I'd be able to handle not fucking him, but I needed to do it in a way that wouldn't hurt him.

"Ramón?"

He allowed me to pull him toward the bed. "Yes, my love?"

"Can I tie you up?"

His eyebrows flew up, but he nodded, "If that's what you wish."

"It is." I gently pushed him back onto the bed. He complied with my wordless request, laying back on his elbows and studying me in the dim light.

"Why?"

"Because I want to ride you, slow and easy, and you're going to try to rush me, to fuck as many orgasms out of me as you can."

"And that's a bad thing?"

"I need slow right now, honey. I need to feel you."

He studied me, then nodded slowly. "I'm here, sweetheart. Do whatever you want."

"Really?"

His now lopsided grin both broke and healed my heart. "Absolutely. But I have one condition."

My whole body throbbed with need, and I couldn't wait to gorge myself on Ramón. I was going to ride him raw, drain him, fuck him until he passed out. The thought of his cum filling me up, over and over, had me practically climaxing on the spot. The hard beat of my heart seemed to push all the blood in my body to my erogenous zones. My clothing felt constricting and I had to keep my hands on my fists so I didn't just grab Ramón and maul him.

"What's that?"

"Let me undress you first, let me worship you just a little bit before you tie me up."

My voice came out breathy with the desire now roaring through me and I smiled. "Deal. Now show me where the ropes are."

Chapter 17
Ramón

When Joy said she wanted to tie me up, I wondered if I'd misread her and she had more of a Dominant personality in bed than I'd initially thought. But then I realized it was just her way of trying to take care of me. Lord knows why she'd equate tying me up with safety, but if she needed it, I'd give it to her. Besides, it would be interesting to be on the other side of the ropes for once.

The more I thought about it, the harder I got. If I was tied up, Joy would be able to really let loose, to do whatever she wanted with me. I'll admit, usually if she's touching me, I'm touching her because I can't keep my hands off her gorgeous ass. A full, round, perfect ass that was just waiting for my attention. Joy's body practically vibrated with lust, and my cock was so fucking hard, it hurt as I took her in. I'd already stripped off her dress, and the little black bra and panty combo she wore beneath set my body on fire.

By giving myself an extra day after the doctor deemed me fit to leave the house, I'd regained enough strength to keep up with Joy. At least, I hoped I had enough. If my body failed me, I had a drawer full of toys waiting on either side of the bed, toys that I planned on using on Joy. There were so many things I wanted to do to her body, I didn't know where to start.

"Come here," I whispered as I sat on the edge of the bed.

She still wore her heels, and they added a sexy sway to her ample hips that had me desperate to get my cock inside of her.

Once she was close enough to touch, I drew her forward until my face brushed her cleavage, inhaling the warmth of her body, the slight hint of strawberries and peaches that lingered on her skin. She was so, so soft, and I took in the delicious sight of her dark nipple pressing against the sheer black lace. Unable to resist such a sweet treat, I grasped her nipple through the fabric of her bra with my teeth, then began to lave the hard tip with my tongue. Her reaction was intense, her hips lifting forward, asking for my cock while her hands clutched at my shoulders.

The D128 should be coursing through her system by now, and I knew her need for an orgasm would build quickly. Her eagerness showed when she was the one who removed her bra and stepped out of her panties, but left her heels on. She knew I liked that, and my cock twitched in agreement. To my surprise, I found her slit completely bare of hair, and so wet with her juices that her inner thighs were slick.

"Nice," I groaned before rubbing my thumb over her clit, now peeking out from its soft little hood. "So soft and pretty."

"Ramón," she said in a tormented whine.

"Hold your pussy lips open for me."

"What?"

"Do it."

She licked her lips, then nodded, widening her stance so I could see every detail of her swollen flesh. *Dios*, she was so wet, it threatened to drip from her. I couldn't wait to get my mouth on her. But first, I needed to see how she liked a little pain with her pleasure.

I gave her pussy a little sharp slap, and to my surprise, she almost fell to the floor before I could catch her, gasping and moaning as her body shook with a hard orgasm.

I couldn't help but laugh as I hauled her onto the bed with me. "I would ask if you liked it, but I think I have my answer."

"Holy fuck," Joy gasped, her eyes still closed. "It hurt, but oh my god, I can still feel it."

"Let me kiss it and make it better."

She didn't resist as I lowered myself between her full thighs, my fingers sinking into their softness as I kissed her puffed up labia before focusing on the entrance to her body. Darting my tongue into her sheath, I loved the way she tried to clench down on me, the restless shift of her hips seeking my touch. I rubbed my nose against her clit as I tongued her, my jaw aching slightly. That physical reminder of how close I'd come to losing her had me pausing for a moment, closing my eyes as I moved up to lightly suckle her clit. Her reaction was instant and I drank down her orgasm, living in the moment, feeling her shake with pleasure as I continued to toy with her.

By the time Joy was able to move, I was already naked and waiting for her at the head of the bed with one wrist strapped into the velvet lined cuffs attached to a restraint system beneath the mattress.

Joy pushed up on her arms and prowled across the bed toward me with the grace of a lioness. Her big breasts swayed with each movement, and I was mesmerized by her curves as she wrapped a restraint around my other wrist, pausing to kiss all the healing scars on my forearm and hand. With each little kiss she whispered how much she loved me, how much she missed me, and I swear my love for Joy grew with every passing second. Then Joy made a soft, sad sound and I looked up from her breasts to find her eyes filled with tears.

I was thinking about taking off the restraints before she said, "You were hurt so bad."

Glancing down, I took in my almost healed injuries, glad I'd waited until I didn't resemble a corpse dragged behind a car for twenty miles. "I'm fine, really. Maybe not as pretty as I was, but I'll live a long, long life."

She sniffled, but leaned down and gave me a kiss on the cheek, her tears falling onto my skin like warm raindrops. "You better."

"I will. Promise."

Her lips were incredibly soft as she began to kiss her way across my body, showering every ache and pain with attention and love. I'd never felt anything like it from any woman I've ever been with, and I basked in her attentions. The world around me melted away. All I could think about was how good her mouth felt on my hipbone as it got closer, and closer to where my cock lay against my abs, thrusting up and pulsing softly with each beat of my heart. Her curls tickled the side of my shaft and I groaned.

"Suck me."

Her pleased, soft murmur had me smiling. "Ask nicely."

"Put my cock down your throat, please."

It was odd to have a woman take my dick into her mouth while she was giggling, but the sensation wasn't unpleasant, especially when she flicked the swollen head with her soft little tongue. The warmth of her mouth and her throaty hums of pleasure as she coaxed the pre-cum from the tip of my dick only made me harder. When she toyed with the ring going through the head of my erection, I jerked beneath her.

"Enough. I want to come in your pussy."

I know she wanted the same thing, because she released my dick with a wet slurp that drew my balls up tight. "Yes, sir."

"Climb on top of me, grab my cock, and sit down on it very, very slowly. Do it now."

In a daze, she stared at me as she straddled my hips. "How do you manage to be bossy even when you're tied up?"

"It's a gift. Now grab my dick and get it wet."

"You're such a…" Her words faded off as she rubbed the engorged head of my erection and pressed it against her clit.

"I'm a what?" I teased, arching my hips so I could grind into her wet heat.

Whatever she was going to say became an incoherent moan as she fit me against her entrance, then began to press down. She was wet, so wet and soft, parting around me then hugging my cock tight as she moaned long and loud. I jerked at my bonds, wishing I could touch her. She grabbed her breasts, pulling at her nipples as she sank further. When I was almost all the way in, she abruptly climaxed, slamming down the rest of the way and making me see stars. Her inner muscles gripped and rippled all over my dick, trying to pull the cum from me.

I fought the need to release, fought to keep fucking her through her own orgasm with sharp snaps of my hips that nearly unseated her.

She braced herself on my chest then collapsed forward, her hips rolling into mine as she panted, "I love you. Oh Ramón, I love you so much."

Her words sent me into a frenzy, and I pulled the quick release on each of the restraints, freeing myself to hold her.

Flipping Joy over onto her back, I wrenched one leg up and held it tight as I pounded into her. "Take it, take all of me. I'm fuckin' yours, sweetheart. My heart, my soul, everything I have belongs to you."

She tried to arch and buck as I fucked another orgasm out of her, the skin of her chest all the way up to her hairline flushed red as her eyes rolled back in her head.

"Fuck yeah, soak my cock, Joy." I pulled out and she squirted long and hard on my dick while I stroked myself, both of us getting messy and wet, dirty in the best of ways.

With a grunt, I thrust back into her, changing my angle so I could work her just right.

"Whose pussy is this?"

Joy gurgled something out, so I put my hand around her throat, choking her lightly to get her attention. "Whose pussy is this?"

"Yours," she moaned. "Harder."

I tightened my grip and she smiled for a moment, then her eyes closed and her pussy snapped tight around me. Holding her neck, controlling her pleasure, controlling her life, I fucked Joy so hard the massive bed shook and my orgasm was roaring like a freight train. She wrapped her legs around me, grunting while she ground herself into every thrust, fucking me as hard as I was fucking her.

The sight of my hand around her throat, of the way she wasn't fighting me, her sweet submission, set me off, and everything went black in that one intense second before I began to come.

My cock swelled inside of her. I went as deep as I could, my balls flat against her ass as I began to spurt inside of her, filling her up like I promised as I released my hold on her neck.

She held me tight, sobbing as her body twitched with aftershocks beneath me, her heart racing and her legs entwined tight around me.

"I love you so much," I gasped. "So fucking much. Marry me. Be my wife."

She let out an exhausted giggle. "You're proposing...now?"

"Yeah." I dragged her onto my chest, running my hands over her sweat slick body. "Romantic, isn't it?"

"Yes."

"Yes, it's romantic, or yes, you'll marry me?"

Pushing up on her elbows, careful of my still healing injuries, she grew serious. "Yes, I'll marry you, Ramón Cordova. I never want to lose you again."

"You never will, Mrs. Joy Cordova. Your life will be nothing but happiness, I swear it."

Overcome with love for this woman, I grabbed her small hand in my own, then dug around in the drawer of the table next to the bed for the ring box.

Joy leaned over my shoulder, then laughed as she saw all the sex toys I had ready to use on her inside the drawer. "Holy crap,

Ramón, what is all that stuff?"

"Hold on," I muttered before pulling out the black velvet ring box. "I need to make this official."

She let out a soft gasp of surprise as I pulled out her engagement ring, a three carat pigeon blood ruby surrounded by diamonds. I'd bought it before I unexpectedly left, planning on an elaborate proposal for Joy. While things hadn't worked out quite how I thought they would, I still somehow managed to win Joy's heart.

After I slipped the ring on her finger, Joy let out a squeal then launched herself at me and I found myself being covered in kisses. "Ramón! I love it! But how did you know I always wanted a ruby engagement ring?"

"I have my ways," I said with a chuckle.

Laughing, she gave me a kiss that had my toes curling and my dick twitching before pulling back. "I love it, I love you, and I'm so, so happy."

Tears gleamed in her eyes and I leaned back against the head of the bed, arranging her on my side so she wasn't pressing on my injuries. "Sweetheart, you have no idea how glad I am to hear that."

She was quiet for a moment, then began to giggle. "Did you really have my ring stored next to a giant dildo?"

I chuckled. "It's not that big, smaller than mine."

With a wicked smile she slipped her hand between us and gave my rapidly hardening cock a stroke. "Mmmm, that's true, you are blessed. Are you tired?"

I glanced down at my thick erection while she stroked me. "Exhausted."

"Oh, I'm so sorry."

She started to pull away with a guilty look and I hauled her back to my side. "Get over here. I'm fine and 'up' for whatever you need."

Leaning down, Joy began to kiss her way over my chest, pausing to lick and suck at one of my nipples. "Mmm, good. Let me go get cleaned up and we can play."

I pushed her over onto her back, skimming my hands over her curves while I drank her in. "You feeling dirty?"

Her breasts shook as she giggled. "Very."

"Well then, let me clean you up."

Before she could protest I was between her legs, spreading her wide with my shoulders.

"Wait, Ramón, you came inside of me. I messy."

"Fuck yeah you are," I breathed as I took in the sight of my seed dripping out of her body.

Diving in, I licked her swollen pussy lips, sucking on the velvety skin and reveling in the taste of our combined pleasure. Joy tried to push me away at first, babbling something about my eating her creampie being wrong, but I ignored her. I loved the way she blushed as I gave her pleasure, loved how quickly I worked her up to the point where she was writhing on our bed, breathing out my name as I sucked her clit into my mouth. That hard little bundle of nerves grew even bigger under my attentions and soon Joy was mindless with passion, just the way I liked her.

Right before she climaxed I moved away.

"Ramón!" She whined as she reached for me, "Don't stop."

I pulled open the drawer and found I was looking for then grabbed it and a small tube of lube.

When I sat back up Joy's eyes went wide, and the flush on her cheeks darkened. "Is that a butt plug?"

"Yep." I leaned over and rubbed my nose against hers. "Gonna plug you, then fuck you."

"Oh, yes please."

As I smiled down at her I marveled at how…happy our lovemaking was. I've never smiled or laughed this much during sex before, but it was nice. Hell, it was more than nice, it was amazing. The pure bliss I felt being with this woman chased all the shadows from my life, leaving light and love where there was once only darkness.

I gave her rounded hip a smack. "Roll over."

The bed shifted as Joy went on all fours, then looked over her shoulder and widened her stance. "Like this?"

I gazed at her wet, sweet brown and pink pussy as I growled out, "Yeah, like that."

She gave her ass a little wiggle and I couldn't resist the need to bite it, making her squeal. "Ow!"

"Such a pretty ass," I said reverently as I gave one of the round globes a good smack, watching it jiggle. "Love it. Now go down on your elbows and give your man what he wants."

Doing as I ordered, she closed her eyes with a smile, "Yes, sir."

I slapped her ass again, not hard enough to hurt, but enough to leave my handprint. "Fuck yeah."

I set the silver butt plug over to the side, then leaned forward and grasped handfuls of her round cheeks, spreading them open and showing me the little star of her anus. She was beautiful all over, even here, and I began to kiss my way across the smooth expanse of her ass before dipping my tongue between her cheeks. At first she was stiff, uncertain, and I didn't have to ask if a man had ever done this for her before. The idea of being the first to show her this naughty pleasure had my dick leaking pre-cum and my balls drawn up tight.

Her soft moans filled the air while I darted my tongue in and out of her puckered star, that little opening slowly relaxing beneath the onslaught of my tongue. With one hand I stroked her clit, drawing louder noises from her until she was rocking her body against my face and whimpering. With a low growl I pulled away from her temping ass, giving her clit a firm pinch before releasing it and picking up the butt plug. It wasn't huge, but it was big enough to start the process of stretching her to comfortably take my cock one day.

"Hold your ass open for me, *mi amore*," I whispered as I watched her reveal her body to me.

With a whimper she did, arching her back and showing me without words how eager she was for me to take and own all of her body. I rubbed the blunt metal tip first over the entrance to her pussy, teasing her until she was begging me to take her, begging me to fill her anywhere I wanted. I loved it, loved the power I had over her, the way I could make her mindless for my cock. She gave without hesitation, her trust in me a dizzying thing.

I squirted a generous amount of lube onto my fingers, then began to slip them in and out of her tight ass, making sure she was ready.

With the plug I ever so slowly, I breached the tight ring of muscles of her anus, working her clit with my free hand as I slowly pushed it in. "Relax, sweetheart, let it in."

She made a little pained sound as the fat part of the butt plug widened her body, then a moan as it sank in all the way. The flared base had a big garnet jewel that sparkled as I let go of the plug, her hips twitching and wiggling as she adjusted to the sensation. I stroked my cock as I watched her, still holding her butt cheeks open for me like a good girl.

"Ramón," she whimpered, "Fuck me."

I gave my cock a hard squeeze, the need to fill her up with my cum already tugging on my balls. "Say please."

She lifted her head and looked over her shoulder, then growled, "Please."

"That wasn't very convincing."

Instead of begging like I thought she would, she backed her ass up against me until her hot, wet pussy rubbed against my stiff dick. "Ramón, *fuck me*."

The sensation of her slick labia rubbing against my piercing had me seeing stars, so I stopped tormenting her and gave her what we both wanted. With a low groan I placed the head of my shaft against her tight opening and began to push in. Right away I could feel the butt plug rubbing against my cock as I forced my way into her, the toy making her tighter than usual. Considering she was already tight enough to strangle my dick, the feeling was somewhere between bliss and torture as I tried to hold back the need to rut.

Her body shook as she pushed back against me, helping me fill her up. Tingles raced from my scalp, down my back, and into my sac as I finally filled her up like I wanted, the hot clasp of her cunt around me better than anything I'd ever felt. It seemed like no matter how many times I had sex with Joy it just got better and better. A low groan burst from me as I began to move, her sheath sucking at me, growing even hotter as she rocked her hips into my every thrust. Her first orgasm almost triggered mine, but I managed to hold on, to shake and moan behind her like I was the one climaxing. Her body grew looser after that, allowing me to move in her despite the thick bulge of the butt plug.

Grabbing her hips, I fucked her with abandon, grunting with each thrust as she chanted my name. The need for release was tearing at my control and when Joy screamed out her second orgasm I followed her, my back arching, my head thrown back as I roared and emptied myself inside of her. The pulsing clasp of her pussy milked me dry, and when I collapsed on top of her, I was close to blacking out. The combination of two hard orgasms, a long night, and my still healing body had me limp as Joy wiggled out from under me.

"Ramón?"

I grunted, unable to force my mouth to shape words as I panted.

"Did I…did I break you?"

I grunted again, but managed to lift one hand to flip her off.

Laughing, she cuddled into me, stroking my sweaty back. "Poor baby. Think you can make it to the bathroom?"

I tried to open my eyes, but my heavy lids refused to raise.

More giggles. "Okay, you stay here and I'll be right back."

Sleep was already tugging at me as I felt a warm, wet cloth being dragged over my back. Joy hummed as she slowly cleaned the drying sweat off of me, her soft touch unbelievably soothing. She paid extra attention to my healing injuries, and I was only vaguely aware that she'd turned me over to clean my front. It was a testament to how wiped out I was when she cleaned my dick and it only became semi-hard.

After a small struggle, she managed to get both of us beneath the sheets and turned off the light. In the darkness, she cuddled into my side and I drifted off to sleep, happier and more content than I'd ever been in my life now that I finally had my fiancé back in my arms.

Chapter 18
Joy

As I pulled into the parking lot of the high school, I sang along with the radio, unable to wipe the smile off my face. It had been a week since Ramón returned, and I'd spent every day with him since. He'd taken time off work to heal and recover, and we spent every moment together in what had to be a disgusting display of love. We'd had Hannah and Leo over for dinner to celebrate their engagement—Leo popped the question the same day as Ramón, and Hannah had teased us about our PDA more than once. Like she had room to talk. I think Leo would have had her sewn to his side, if he could.

Not that Ramón and I had been any different. When we went to see his parents, to let them know we were getting married, he'd practically had me sitting on his lap the whole time, refusing to have me even a room away from him. I'd protested, but secretly loved his open affection. His parents had apologized profusely about keeping me in the dark about his helicopter crash, and I'd forgiven them. Even if I didn't like it, I understood why they'd kept his condition a secret, even from me.

My ruby and diamond engagement ring sparkled in the bright light beaming through the windshield of my new baby blue Land Rover, a gift from Ramón. Without a doubt, he spoiled the hell out of me, but I've never had anyone spoil me before, so I didn't mind it one bit. If giving me things made him happy, why would I take that away from him? Besides, he didn't just buy me expensive gifts.

A horn beeped, and I narrowly avoided another car as I circled the lot, looking for a spot big enough to squeeze the Land Rover into without taking out the cars on either side. There must have been some kind of after school event going on, because the parking lot was almost full. I found an empty space way at the back of the fenced-in lot. Turning the radio down, I grabbed my new Gucci purse and matching giant satchel from the floorboards, smiling as I remembered being fucked up against a wall after I'd given Ramón a big thank you kiss for the present.

A low heat simmered in my sex, but I forced myself to get a grip. I'd had fun this past week with Ramón in our new home, fucking our days away without a care in the world, but it was time to return from our self-imposed isolation.

Ramón was doing some kind of stockholders meeting with his dad, a big deal because rumors had started about his absence. He wanted everyone to see him healthy and whole, if a little damaged. The scars on his face continued to heal, now a pale pinkish white instead of angry red, but his face would never be the same. Not that I minded. Those scars were a constant reminder of how close I'd come to losing him. They made me value our time together, made me aware of how easily everything could change. His hair had grown a bit as well, and I loved the soft, yet stubbly feeling of his almost shaved head. While I missed his long hair, there was something to be said for a scarred, sexy bald man.

Thinking about Ramón wasn't helping me calm down, so I opened the door and got out, letting the blast of heated desert air clear my mind. It was hot out, super-hot, the kind of heat where everyone goes indoors as soon as possible. My black pantsuit seemed like a poor choice as the sun instantly roasted me. The fabric was light and airy, the pants blousy at the ankles, so it almost looked like I was wearing a skirt. The jacket was made of the same breathable fabric, but I instantly started to sweat as I tried to shove everything I needed for my students into my satchel.

Grabbing a pair of silver chopsticks from my purse, I twisted my hair up into a bun and shoved them in. It was too fucking hot having it down, even though Ramón loved to play with my curls. Memories of laying on his chest, blissed out from orgasms, while he slowly wound and unwound my curls from his fingers filled me. When we were alone, Ramón was incredibly gentle and loving with me, and he allowed me to be the same. We were always touching each other and the pit of my stomach gave a happy little tingle as I reveled in the feeling of being in love and happy.

I waved to the security guard driving by, then hustled into the school and smiled at the guards as they searched my bags.

The first person I was going to see today was Devonlin, and I had some great news for him.

When I came into the empty English classroom I called my own while I was here, I found Devonlin already waiting by my desk.

Standing, he came over and gave me a quick hug. "Thank you."

Pulling out of his arms, I smiled up at him as he bashfully rubbed the back of his thick neck, his green t-shirt straining around his biceps. "For what?"

"For the protection for me and my family."

I must have looked like a confused dog as I cocked my head at him. "While I'd love to take credit, I have no idea what you're talking about."

He frowned down at me as voices echoed down the hall outside the classroom. "He said you sent him."

Getting worried, I led him over to the desk so I could dump my stuff off and sit down. "Who said? I don't understand what you're talking about."

"The guy form the Cordova cartel, Mark."

I blinked at him, unable to believe what I was hearing. "The Cordova cartel? You mean the Cordova Group?"

He studied me, then frowned. "Yeah, they've got a legit business, but everyone knows they're one of the biggest cartels in the US."

"You're trying to tell me Judith and Jose Cordova are leaders of a cartel."

Looking worried, Devonlin shook his head quickly. "Uh, no, I must be wrong. Was thinkin' of someone else."

"Don't lie to me," I snapped as my head began to pound. "You said cartel, and you meant it."

He took a step toward me, his hand outstretched. "Ms. Holtz, you okay?"

My lungs refused to expand enough for me to take a deep breath, and my voice came out weak as I said, "You said someone came to visit you, who?"

"I've got the guy's card right here in my wallet. Guy named Mark Lake. You know him?"

"He's...he was my roommate. Oh my God, my roommate is a criminal."

"Don't freak out, Ms. Holtz. The Cordova cartel isn't bad. They ain't exactly good, but they take care of their people, and they're gonna keep me safe from the Santiago cartel. Gonna keep them off my back, so I can focus on football. And they didn't want anything in return, just for me to have a chance at a better life." His eyes lit up and he smiled, big. "And they're helpin' my mom, getting her the kind of medicine she needs. You should see her now, Ms. Holtz. She's got hope of livin' long enough to see me play in the pros. All thanks to you. Mark said you told him about my situation, and he thought it was a damn shame that life had dealt me such a shit hand. He's a really cool guy. He even brought tons of groceries with him."

While all of that was wonderful, I was still having a meltdown as I faced all the truths I'd tried to hide from myself, all the things I'd tried to explain away. Yeah, I'd told Mark about Devonlin, but I was hoping he'd have some kind of security suggestions, or would know someone who could help the kid. Somewhere, down deep, I knew something wasn't right about the Cordova family, but I never imagined that they were a cartel. I watched the news, and I wasn't naïve. I knew our country was run as much by criminals as it was by the government, but I never imagined I'd fall in love with a crime lord.

Shit, that was the reason why Manny and his goons had freaked out when they realized who Hannah was dating. Leo must be high ranking in the cartel, he was the reason those men beat us. As soon as that thought crossed my mind, I dismissed it. Kayla brought those men into the house. I had a feeling our fate was sealed the moment they crossed the threshold, regardless of any connection Hannah had to the Cordova cartel.

Shit, what kind of bad stuff was Ramón into? Did he deal drugs? Did he addict little kids to crack? Did he sell guns? Worse yet…did the Cordova cartel *traffic women*?

My skin prickled with stinging sweat, and I suddenly felt cold as I hunched over, my stomach cramping.

Devonlin caught me easily and sat me on the desk, propping me up as my mind short circuited. "Whoa, Ms. Holtz, are you okay?"

No, I wasn't okay.

So, so far from okay.

I tried to take a deep breath, but my anxiety made it feel like I was drowning. "I-I…I have to go."

"I don't think you should go anywhere. You don't look so good. Stay here, we'll get you some water, okay?"

I stumbled out of his arms, glad for once I'd worn sensible ballet flats instead of sky high heels. "I have to go."

He kept protesting as I grabbed my stuff and practically ran out of the room, wanting to get to at least the safety of my car before I lost it. I could feel the panic attack creeping up on me, working to convince me I was dying, wanting to rob me of my strength. A few people wandering the halls started at me as I sprinted past, my satchel and purse thumping against my body, but I ignored their whispers and stares.

I hit the doors with a bang and flat out sprinted across the lot. I didn't feel anything, the hot pavement beneath my feet, the burning sun overhead, my breath tearing from my body in pained sobs. My mind was a whirling mess of guilt, anger, betrayal, and sadness. I wasn't paying attention to anything at all when, out of nowhere, someone grabbed me then shoved me into a waiting car, my scream cutting off as the door slammed behind us.

The car sped out of the parking lot, and I slammed into the door before long, cruel fingers gripped my arm hard enough to bruise.

I screamed, but it was cut off by Nova Santiago slapping me hard across the face.

"Shut up, you stupid cunt, before I cut your throat."

Shaking so hard my teeth chattered, I darted a panicked glance around the interior of a large town car. There was a big guy with light brown hair driving up front, but he wasn't looking back at us, intent on driving. Pain splintered through me as Nova hit me again, drawing my attention back to him as I tried to shield myself from his blows.

"Stupid," *punch* "Fucking," *punch* "Bitch. You had to go stick your fucking nose where it didn't belong, had to get the Cordova Cartel involved. How the fuck do you know them?"

A strange roaring sound filled my ears, and an odd sense of calm fell over me. It was like I'd been standing in the middle of a heavy metal concert, my head being blasted by noise, then suddenly found myself in a soundproof room. My thoughts became organized, focused, and even the pain he'd inflicted on me fell away.

"I asked you a fucking question, bitch!" He slapped me again and the tang of blood hit my tongue. "You better answer me, or I swear to fuck I'll sell you to the most twisted fucker I know, and he'll slowly rape you to death."

My gaze zeroed on in Nova. I knew, without a doubt, he meant every word he said. I had to save myself, had to do whatever I needed to stay safe. Over and over, the words whispered through my head, *save yourself save yourself, save yourself...at any cost.*

Moving almost in a daze, I slipped the solid silver chopsticks from my hair, then shoved both of them through Nova's eyes with perfect accuracy, right into his brain.

His shrill, harsh scream barely registered as I turned my attention to the driver. He was trying to keep control of the car, while turning around to look at why his boss was suddenly screaming his death throes. I was already moving, untangling myself from Nova's flailing arms and reaching for the front seat. Once again, I felt as if I was watching someone else as I reached forward and hooked my fingers into claws, sinking them deep into his face and scratching so deep, blood covered my fingertips.

He let go of the wheel and tried to pry me off as I shredded his face. The last thing I saw before everything went black was the oncoming cement divider between the lanes of traffic.

Chapter 19
Ramón

I looked out over the long stainless steel and glass table that dominated the conference room, making brief eye contact with every one of the seated people.

"Lastly, we're proud to announce our newest drug, a promising treatment for Parkinson's disease, has had spectacular results in the small clinical trials we've done so far. We're happy to announce we will soon be able to open those trials to a larger audience."

This declaration was met with pleased murmurs by the board members. They all knew our power as a cartel and a company would skyrocket. People would be willing to pay or do anything to get a shot at a cure, a chance at a longer life. While we always made sure to include worthy candidates who couldn't afford it, the rest were the beloved of the movers and shakers of this world, because it never hurt to gain their loyalty.

The doors at the back of the room opened and Mark came in, his face tense and his eyes meeting mine. Right away, I could tell something was very wrong, and I cut my speech short. "Thank you for your time. I'll now turn you over to my father."

My dad, being the professional that he was, picked up the meeting where I'd left off as I made my way over to Leo and Mark. Instead of heading toward me, they started to leave the room. I hurried to catch up, not giving a shit that everyone was openly watching me. A terrible fear had begun to creep over me, tearing at my chest and sinking my stomach.

As soon as we were outside, Leo grabbed me by my shoulders and looked me dead in the eye. "Joy is missing. We have reason to believe Nova Santiago has her."

"What!"

Mark grabbed me by one arm, Leo the other, and they practically dragged me down the hallway as they lowered their voices. "Listen, we'll find her. She has multiple tracking devices all over, including your engagement ring. It's only a matter of time until we get her back."

"She could already be dead!"

We'd made it to the stairway, and my voice echoed all around us.

Leo shook his head. "No, don't even think it. We're going to find her."

I couldn't answer him, my mind too full of the horrors Joy could be enduring right at this moment. Nova Santiago was a thug through and through, an acting lieutenant for the Santiago cartel for a long time. I'd had a run in with him in the past, which hadn't ended well for him, and I knew Joy was as good as dead if he knew who she was to me. The only consolation I had was he'd need to get permission from his higher ups before taking her out. Killing the fiancée of a Cordova would bring death raining down on them and they knew it, but those crazy fuckers would do it anyway.

My mother was waiting for us in the main control room of security floor, her back stiff as she stared at a map of Phoenix on the wall with a series of blinking red dots. Despite being perfectly dressed in a no doubt designer gown, there was a feeling of unraveling coming from her that plucked at my nerves.

She didn't even notice we'd arrived until Leo said, "Judith, have we learned anything?"

When my mom turned around and looked at me, her eyes were red and swollen from crying. "Nothing. Tino found Joy's satchel in the parking lot. Her purse was tossed on the side of the road about two blocks away. It looks like they were trying to get rid of any electronics that we could use to track her, but they haven't taken away the ones in her rings or earrings yet."

I'd initially felt guilt knowing practically everything I gave Joy had a minute tracker in it somewhere, but now I was glad. "Where is Joy?"

"I think here." She pointed to a dot heading west, out of the city. "We have men on their way to intercept, but they're about ten minutes away."

I shrugged Mark and Leo off. "What the fuck happened?"

Leo spoke up, his deep voice gruff. "One of Joy's students called Mark. It seems he had Mark's number because Joy asked him to watch out for the kid, Devonlin. He said she freaked out about something and ran out of the school. Devonlin was following her into the parking lot where he saw Nova Santiago grab her and stuff her in a car then take off."

I crouched down, nausea filling me, making my mouth water and my stomach cramp. "They're going to kill her."

"She's a strong, smart girl. She'll be okay until we can get to her."

"She has fucking panic attacks! They're going to kill her and all she can do is suffer! My woman could be dying out there right fucking now, and I can't do anything to help her!"

My mother moved over to me then grabbed my face between her hands, forcing me to look at her. "We will find her, Ramón, I promise. She will be okay."

I closed my eyes, fighting back the tears of grief, rage, and frustration as I whispered, "Somewhere, out there, right now Joy is terrified, praying for me to rescue her, and I can't do a thing to help her."

"Listen to me, Ramón. She will be okay. Joy is very smart, and she's been training with Leo on how to defend herself."

"Defend herself?" I barked out. "How the fuck is she going to defend herself against someone like Nova Santiago?"

My mother released my face and looked away, fiddling with her ring. "Have faith, Ramón. Joy will do whatever is necessary to save her own life, I'm certain of it."

Something about what my mother said caught my attention. Before I could question her further, Mark interrupted us. "Come on, we're going to take the helicopter. They've found Joy."

"Thank the Sweet Blessed Mother. Is she okay?"

"She's been in a car accident. I don't have the details, but I know they're flying her to the hospital right now."

Five hours later, I sat at Joy's bedside, waiting for her to open her eyes. She had a broken leg, sprained wrist, and a mild concussion, along with cuts, scrapes, and bruises. Laying in the middle of her big hospital bed in her private suite, she looked so tiny and frail, but from what we learned at the scene of the accident Joy was anything but. We aren't totally sure what happened. Joy is the only one that survived the crash, but we're pretty sure Joy somehow managed to stab Nova in both of his eye sockets with some sticks from her hair, then she literally tore the driver's eyes out.

I had no fucking clue what to make of that.

Looking down at her, I was proud as hell that she'd fought them off, that she'd managed to basically rescue herself, but I was also really worried about the aftermath. Joy was so kindhearted, so sweet, that I wondered if she'd feel guilt for killing those bastards. Holding her limp but warm hand in my own, I continued my constant vigil at her side while people filtered in and out of the room.

The doctors said to allow her wake up on her own, but I was having a hard time letting her sleep. I wanted to see her open those beautiful green eyes, to know that she was okay. We'd learned that the reason Joy had run was because she'd finally figured out the dark side of my family's empire, and I couldn't help but wonder if she would still love me. The thought of losing her forever threatened my sanity, so I focused on watching her sleep and counting her breaths.

Voices hummed behind me, Hannah and my mother talking softly while Leo spoke with my father near the door. We had guards stationed outside, and the floor was secure as could be, but I still felt better knowing Leo was there. So far, we'd managed to keep the media at bay, but eventually someone would find out that my fiancée had been involved in a car crash and kidnapping. Thankfully, our lawyers would make sure Joy was protected, but I still hated her being exposed like this.

Joy's hand twitched in mine, and I instantly sat up straight, leaning over her bed to study her face. Her eyes moved behind her closed eyelids, and her breathing picked up. I waited, not wanting to startle her.

"Joy?"

Instantly, the room got quiet and everyone moved closer to the bed.

Her eyelids fluttered open, and she squinted.

"Joy?" I tried again, needing to hear her voice. "Sweetheart, can you hear me?"

She nodded slowly, then turned her head to look at me. She whispered in a ragged voice, "Where am I?"

"You're in the hospital. Can you remember how you got here?"

Her brows drew down, and she tried to lift her broken leg,

then winced. "No. Why am I here?"

My mother joined me, her hand resting on Joy's blanket-covered leg. "You're okay, darling. You were in a car accident. What's the last thing you remember?"

"Need water," she rasped. I helped her sit up while Hannah poured her a cup then handed it to her friend

"Thanks," Joy said in a stronger voice then groaned. "My head hurts."

"You have a mild concussion, in addition to your other injuries."

Looking down at her arm encased in a cast, she frowned. "I remember driving to my tutoring job…but that's it. What happened?"

I hesitated, torn between telling the truth and upsetting her or distracting her.

My mother took the choice out of my hands by saying, "A man by the name of Nova Santiago tried to abduct you from the school."

"What?" Her grip on my hand tightened. "I don't remember."

"It's okay," I soothed after giving my mom a disapproving glare. "Don't worry about that now. You're safe."

Joy shook her head, then groaned. "Everything hurts."

"Take it easy," Hannah said in a soft voice while she crouched down by Joy's bedside. "The only thing you have to worry about is getting better, okay?"

Looking up at me, Joy whispered, "I'm so confused."

My mother spoke up again, "Everything is going to be okay. You saved yourself."

"Save myself…" Joy's gaze went distant. "I remember that. *Save myself.* It kept repeating over and over in my head…but I don't know why. I can't remember."

"Ms Holtz," came a woman's voice from the doorway. "So good to see you awake. I'm Dr. Francis. How are you feeling?"

The older doctor with her white hair in a bun made her way into the crowded room, trailed by other physicians and a few nurses.

"Fine," Joy said, then winced. "Okay, maybe not fine."

The doctor checked her tablet then looked over at me where I still sat, holding Joy's hand protectively. "Mr. Cordova, if you could give us some room, I'd like to take a look at Ms. Holtz."

I waited until they were done, hovering over them while they asked Joy questions until my mother dragged me over to the corner of the room. "Ramón, let them work."

By the time they were done, exhaustion lined Joy's face. I knew the accelerated healing drugs we had Dr. Francis give her were kicking in. I knew all too well how drained she would be feeling, so when I resumed my station by the side of her bed, I stroked her hair and whispered for her to go to sleep. She did, holding my hand and looking into my eyes while I whispered to her how much I loved her before she lost the fight and slept.

I had no idea what time it was when I woke up later that night, but it was dark and the usually busy hospital was quiet. Everyone had gone home except for me and my guards, though Leo had to practically drag Hannah out. I stirred in my chair that pulled out into a bed next to Joy, wondering what had woken me up.

Then I heard Joy crying.

I tossed the blanket off and moved to her side, sitting on the edge of the bed and looking down at my woman as she sobbed. "Hey, hey, Joy, it's okay."

"It's not okay," she cried in a raw voice. "You're a criminal."

That was one of the last things I expected her to say. "What?"

"I remember. Devonlin said the Cordova *cartel*." The rest came out garbled as she turned her face into her pillow.

"Joy, I don't understand what you're saying."

"I'm in love with a monster!"

That hurt, but I'd been preparing for this moment since I decided to make Joy my own. Too bad all my pretty speeches and explanations seemed weak as shit. Still, I had to try, because losing Joy was unacceptable.

"I'm not a monster."

She peeked at me through swollen eyes. "Is it true? Is there a Cordova cartel?"

I met her gaze, even though it pained me. "Yes."

Her lower lip trembled. "And you...you do bad things?"

"I guess that depends on who you ask."

"Do you...do you hurt people?"

"We don't hurt innocent people."

I took her uninjured hand in my own, grateful when she

didn't jerk away. "But you're criminals."

"We are. The things we do aren't always legal, but we don't just randomly go out destroying people."

"Wh-what do you do?" Tears filled her eyes again. "Are you like the Santiagos? Do you sell women?"

"No!" I lowered my voice, hating that I made her jump. "No, sweetheart, we're nothing like those sick fucks."

"So, you don't sell women?"

We had a thriving prostitution business, but I don't think that's what she meant. "No, we don't kidnap and sell women. We don't do human trafficking of any kind. We specialize in drugs." She tried to pull her hand away, but I wouldn't let her. "Yeah, we sell recreational drugs, but that's not where our money comes from. We also sell cutting edge cures, things the FDA hasn't approved, medicines that are desperately needed, but people can't get their hands on for various reasons. Cancer drugs, infertility drugs, experimental treatments and therapies that save people's lives."

For a long moment she stared at me, searching my face. "But you also sell recreational drugs."

"I'm not going to lie to you Joy, we do, but I swear to you, we don't hurt innocents."

"Your mom...your dad. They're the head of the cartel?"

"They are."

I waited, my muscles tense with the need to keep her, to make her love me, to never let me go, but at this moment I was powerless.

"Were you ever going to tell me?"

"Yes. I had planned on telling you after we got married."

Her gaze flicked to mine. "After?"

"I didn't want to give you a chance to run. I love you, Joy, with everything I have. I'd walk away from it all. Today, if that's what it took to keep you."

She frowned. "You would?"

"I would, but I'm afraid it would put us in grave danger to be without the protection of my family, so I beg you not to ask that of me."

"Hannah...does she know?"

"Yes."

"But she didn't tell me?"

"She couldn't. Leo made her promise not to until I had a chance to talk to you first. She didn't like it, but she understood the need to keep you unaware, to protect you as much as we could from the truth."

Joy closed her eyes and turned her head away from me, but didn't let go of my hand. "I don't know what to do. I should hate you, be disgusted by all of this...but I can't. I love you. Does that make me a terrible person?"

"No, sweetheart, not at all. You're the best person I know, the absolute best. You are everything good in this world, everything we're trying to protect. If it wasn't for the Cordova cartel, people like the Santiago's would have free rein to spread the evil. We keep them in check, we fight where the government can't, do what the police won't. They come to us when they have a problem they can't handle."

"The police come to you?"

"Yeah. Cops, politicians, lawyers, priests. They all know they can come to us for help they can't get anywhere else."

"For a price."

"For a price," I agreed, waiting to see how Joy would react.

Letting out a big sigh, she whispered, "Can you please hold me? I'm so tired, and the only time I feel safe is in your arms. How fucked up is that?"

Moving as quickly as I could, I slid into the bed next to her, careful of her IV and broken leg. Once I was lying on my side looking down at her, she burrowed into my chest and got as close to me as she physically could. I held her against me, thanking God, the blessed Mother, and all the saints, that Joy hadn't rejected me, at least not yet.

"I'm so sorry you got hurt today," I whispered against the top of her head. "When I found out you'd been taken...when I thought I'd never get to see you again, I thought my heart was going to stop."

"I know how you feel." She tilted her head up from my chest so her words weren't muffled. "When you were missing, I felt the same way. I was so lost without you, Ramón."

"Never again, sweetheart. I swear, I'll do a better job protecting you."

She shivered against me. "I killed those men, didn't I?"

"Can you remember anything about what happened?"

She went through her abduction, but her voice turned odd, cold as she talked about killing Nova. Almost clinical in her detachment, like she was talking about someone else. I listened carefully, grateful beyond words that she'd managed save herself, even as I mourned the loss of her innocence.

"You did what you had to do, never doubt that."

She rubbed her face against my shirt, getting it damp with her tears. "I know. Trust me, I know. And this may sound messed up, but I'm kinda proud of myself. Proud that I didn't sit there and cry like a victim. Proud that, even when I was so scared I was about to puke, I pulled it together enough to eliminate the threat."

Once again, her voice went odd, cold, and I hugged her closer. "You're amazing, Joy. I love you."

"God help me, Ramón, but I love you to. More than I've ever loved anyone or anything."

"Do you forgive me for not telling you the truth sooner?"

I held my breath, hoping against hope.

"This...this is a lot to deal with."

"It is." The bed creaked beneath us as I shifted into a more comfortable position, my gaze on the closed door, my men visible through the window flanking it. "But I'm here to help you. So is Hannah, and my family."

"It all makes sense now," she said in a low voice while petting my chest with her free hand. "There were so many things that didn't seem right...but I ignored them, or tried to pretend I didn't notice, but I did. I think I've known for a while, I just...was in denial or something."

"I'm sorry," I said again, unable to find anything better to say to try and convey just how much I meant it. "Please forgive me. Please tell me you're not leaving me."

"No, no I'm not leaving you." She took a deep breath, then let it out, the warmth seeping through my shirt. "My mom would shoot me for saying this, but I felt so lost without you. You make me happy, really and truly happy. Even knowing you're a criminal doesn't make me love you any less."

"That's because what we've got, me and you, it's stronger than anything on this earth. I will do anything, absolutely anything, for you."

Her body softened against mine, her breath evening out. "I'm so tired."

"Accelerated healing medicines. They'll wipe you out, but you'll heal in half the time." I pressed my face into the soft mass of her curls. "One of the perks of being the fiancée of a cartel lord."

Her giggle was soft, but my heart rejoiced. "Well, that is a nice bonus."

"Go to sleep, *mi amor*. I won't let anything harm you."

"I know."

Epilogue

Ramón

Seven Years Later

Even through the thick glass windows looking out into the backyard, I can hear the squeals of dozens of little girls filling the air as they whack at a giant piñata hanging from the old cedar tree. Lillian, my oldest daughter, is turning six today and Joy, with Hannah's help, organized the kind of birthday party all kids dream of. There was a bounce house, magicians, face painters, and even a cotton candy machine, though I think that was as much for my pregnant wife as anyone else. Right now, Joy was eating a huge blue mound of cotton candy. Our three-year-old middle daughter, Grace, clung to her long skirt with a big blue ring around her mouth from melted candy.

Inwardly, I groaned, knowing Grace was going to be pinging off the walls, even after the guests left. While Lillian was a girly girl, quiet and sweet, Grace was a handful even at three. She had no fear, none, and her curiosity about the world led her to wandering off more than once. At her preschool, the teachers had her wear a special wristband that would activate an alarm anytime she managed to sneak out of the building—which happened more than you'd think. She was just so small and quick. Hell, I'd lost her more than once, though I'd never admit it to my darling wife. Especially when she was pregnant. Because of the hormones, she became easily irritated, and I knew I couldn't soothe her with an orgasm in the middle of a party.

Rubbing the back of my neck, I wondered how much longer I could hide out in my study before anyone noticed I was missing.

"Ramón," my mother said from behind me. "There you are."

Moving slower than she had in the past, my mother joined me at my study window, watching the crowd in the backyard with me. The sunlight glinted off her hair, almost entirely silver now, and deepened the heavy lines beginning to fill her face. Though she was getting older, she was still as active as ever, and I gave her a one-armed hug.

"Hey, Mom."

"Why are you hiding in here?"

I wanted to say I wasn't hiding, but that wasn't quite the truth. Lillian was trying to guilt me into getting my face painted, and she was a master at getting me to do what she wanted. I was hoping that the piñata would distract her from her burning desire to see her daddy made up like her favorite cartoon teddy bear.

A low chuckle escaped me as I caught sight of Leo, looking very uncomfortable as he stood watching his and Hannah's daughter clap and squeal as a little boy swung at the piñata with all his might. Leo had been trapped earlier by our little darlings and now sported face paint that made him look like a lion. A very grumpy, pissed off lion.

Mom must have followed my line of sight, because she laughed as well. "Poor Leo. He can't just can't say no to his girls."

"I know the feeling."

We watched everyone for a few more minutes before my mother said in a thin voice, "Ramón, there's something I need to tell you."

Distracted by the sight of Grace making a run for it, with my waddling wife following after her, I said, "What's up, Mom?"

"I...let's sit down."

Looking over at her, I easily read the worry she was trying to hide. "Okay."

As we sat down together on the navy leather sofa facing my desk, I stretched my arm over the back, waiting for her to continue.

Taking a deep breath, my mother laced her fingers together. She looked up at me with an expression so worried, so sorrowful, I immediately leaned forward and clasped her hands in mine. "Are you okay? Is it Dad? What's going on?"

"No, no. We're fine. Old, but fine. This is something...else. Something that I've been waiting years to tell you, until you were a father yourself, until you understood a parent's endless love for their child."

"Mom," I said gently, letting go of her hands so I could grab some tissue out of the box on the coffee table. I kept some in every room while Joy was pregnant, because she tended to cry over any and everything. "You're scaring me."

Her thin lower lip trembled, but she said, "You never programmed Joy. I did."

At first, her words didn't make sense. I stared at her. "What are you talking about?"

"You never programmed her. That day at the spa all those years ago? The serum you used was fake."

Stunned, I collapsed against the back of the couch, trying to make sense of what she said. "But...why?"

"I didn't want you to harm Joy by double dosing her with it."

I shook my head rapidly. "That doesn't make any sense. You *wanted* me to program her."

Fiddling with her ring, her hands shaking, she sighed. "It was a ruse so no one would figure out that I'd already programmed her on my own."

"When?"

"The day you had the big fight with Joy, and she came to our house. I couldn't let her leave without binding her to us. She'd heard too much, and I knew you weren't ready, so I did what had to be done."

A sudden rage filled me. I picked up the nearest object, a large brass statue of a horse, then hurled it at the wall. "How dare you! What the fuck is wrong with you?"

"I did it because I love you," my mother yelled back. "And I love Joy. I never wanted to see her go through what Hannah did. I kept my instructions very simple. That she wouldn't betray our family, that she would know that she was safe when she was with you, and that if she was ever threatened, she wouldn't hesitate to save herself."

I staggered to the wall then slumped down, ignoring my mother when she slowly crouched next to me. "All these years...you let me believe a lie all these years? Did you tell her to love me? Did you program her to love me? Tell me!"

"Of course not!" She stood and began to pace. "I told you, I kept it very simple. I never did anything that would have falsely bound her to you. That's why I waited so long to tell you, so that you could see for yourself that Joy loves you for who you are, that I did the right thing."

"Get out."

"Ramón, listen to me. You're a parent, you know you would

do anything—anything at all—to keep your children safe, to make them happy. I was trying to protect you, trying to protect Joy. I love her like my own. Please forgive me."

"GET. OUT."

My mother began to cry, but I tuned her out, my mind swirling as I thought back to everything that had happened with Joy. The odd way she talked about killing Nova, how she didn't sound like herself when she spoke about it.

We didn't talk about it often, but when we did, Joy would always say it was like an out-of-body experience. From what she remembered, she had no qualms about saving herself. She found some hidden strength to do what needed to be done. Fuck, it had been my mother's programming that saved her that day, my mother's evil genius at work. My rage surfaced again, churning through my guilt and sorrow, making me wish my mom was still here so I could make her see how fucked up her actions were. I knew that, even now, she probably felt like she'd done the right thing for the family.

My chest hurt, and I stumbled over to the bar in my office, pouring myself a stiff drink with shaking hands.

Fuck, what did I do? I looked out the window at my beautiful, glowing with happiness, pregnant wife as she laughed at something Hannah said. I'd never told her about the programming, promising myself that someday I would, but that day had never come around. Now that I knew the truth, I'm glad I never said anything. Did that make me as big of a hypocrite as my mom?

I was tempted to pour another glass of alcohol, but a text came through on my phone from Joy, wondering where I was.

After a long moment, I texted her back that I was dealing with some business, would be out in a moment, and that I loved her. Through the window, I watched her smile down at her phone. Her text back a moment later sent her love in return. Even now, almost three kids later, my entire body lit up with happiness when she said she loved me.

I couldn't give that up.

I wouldn't.

Setting my glass down on the table, I took a deep breath and tried to let go of my anger, of my sense of betrayal. My love, my family, was real, no matter how my relationship with Joy started.

She was still the same woman I'd spent practically every day with over the last seven years, still the mother of my children, still the love of my life. I knew, deep down in my heart, that our bond was real. It was strong, and no amount of brainwashing in the world could force it to happen.

As I made my way out of the house to rejoin the party, I was reminded again how easily it could all be taken from me in an instant. I decided I didn't give a fuck what my mom had done. I was pissed, plenty pissed, that she'd hidden it from me all these years, but I'd hidden my actions from Joy, so that made me a hypocrite. The alcohol burned warm in my stomach, but it held nothing to the heat that filled my body when I finally had my wife in my arms.

As soon as I reached her side, I swept her into my arms—four-month pregnant belly and all—then kissed the hell out of her in front of God and everyone, not giving one shit.

Giggles broke out around us, along with adult laughter. When I pulled back, Joy's beautiful eyes, now bracketed with smile lines, glowed up at me. "Well, hello there."

"Hey, sweetheart."

As I slid her down to her feet, she reached up and cupped my scarred cheek with her soft hand. "Baby, what's wrong?"

"Nothing, just work stuff."

"Is everything okay?"

I gave her a kiss on the forehead. "It is now."

Grace sprinted over, holding her arms out and jumping at me as she shrieked, "Daddy!"

I easily caught her small body, swinging her over my head, making her dark curly hair fly about as I tossed her up then caught her again. My little daredevil loved it, and she threw her arms around my neck, laughing as she kissed my cheek. "Again!"

"Maybe later, honey." I set her down on her feet, and she was off again, this time heading toward Mark and his four-year-old daughter Willow.

Joy slipped her arm around my waist and let out a deep sigh. "Thank you for all of this, Ramón. You're the best husband and father ever."

A pang of guilt went through me at the secrets I was keeping from Joy, but I let it go. "Anything, for you, my love."

Holding my wife, surrounded by my friends and family, I knew my life wasn't conventional. Most people considered me a scary man, but I would do everything all over again, endure every bit of pain, just for the privilege of living this moment of perfect happiness with the woman I was born to love.

Nine months later

"Ramón," Joy cajoled, "I know you're mad at your mom about something, but can you at least act civilized toward her? Alexa's baptism is today, and I don't want our family pictures to be of you scowling at your mom."

I watched her as she put our youngest daughter Alexa into her christening gown, the same one her older sisters had worn. Alexa was smaller than her sisters, taking more after her mom, and she had the same blonde curls as Joy, though Alexa's hair was so pale it was almost white. She was a good baby, quiet and watchful, and she gurgled as Joy held her and fussed with her hat. I watched them from the rocking chair in the nursery, drinking in the sight of my lovely wife and child, thinking what a lucky bastard I was.

"Ramón," Joy said with exasperation heavy in her voice. "Are you even listening to me?"

"I am."

"Are you going to be nice to your mom?"

Ever since my mom's revelation, things had been tense between us. While I wasn't a big enough of a bastard to try to cut her out of my family's life—the girls and Joy adored her—that didn't mean I had to be welcoming. While I was civil to her, Joy had picked up on the underlying hostility, but she didn't press me on why I was upset with my mom. She was used to there being things I couldn't talk about with her. While she didn't like it, she accepted it. At least, she used to accept it.

"I am nice to her."

Joy rolled her eyes, then handed me Alexa so she could pack up the diaper bag, her pale pink dress swishing attractively around her full hips. "Seriously? You wouldn't even speak to her at Christmas other than hello and goodbye."

I focused on the baby in my arms, not wanting to meet my wife's overly astute gaze. "I wished her a merry Christmas."

Joy snorted. "And at Easter, she tried to hug you and you dodged her like a quarterback evading the opposing team's lineman."

"Did not." I sounded petulant even to myself, so I sighed and shook my head. "Sorry, you're right."

"So, what happened? Why are you so mad at her?"

In my arms, Alexa began to wiggle, so I started rocking. She settled right down, her gentle weight in my arms easing the bitterness in my heart. "She did something that pissed me off."

"Will you tell me what she did that made you so mad you'd give her the silent treatment for almost a whole year?"

"It happened a long time ago…something she did without my permission. Something that could have hurt you."

She went quiet as she grabbed a stack of diapers from the changing table. "Did she finally tell you about the programming?"

I stared at Joy while she continued to straighten the room like she didn't have a care in the world. "What?"

"Ramón, I know all about it. She told me years ago, after I had Lillian."

Stunned, I began to rock so fast Alexa grumbled a complaint, so I slowed down while soothing her. "You knew? She told you?"

When Joy looked at me, the expression on her face wasn't one of anger or betrayal, but compassion. "Yes, and while I was plenty mad, I understood why she did it."

"What did she tell you she did?"

Joy crouched down in front of me, placing one hand on my knee, and the other over my arm holding a now sleeping Alexa. "She didn't tell me, she showed me the recording she made while programming me…and she showed me the recording of when you programmed me, as well."

Making a little unhappy sound, Alexa shifted in my arms as I tensed, waiting for Joy's well-earned wrath. "I…I'm so sorry."

"Don't be. I heard what you said, what you tried to do. You never cared about my loyalty, you only mentioned it once. Instead you tried to heal me, to make me believe that I was brave, strong, wonderful, that I could do anything. You weren't trying to make me into a robot or rob me of my freewill, you were trying to build me up the best way you knew how.

Everything you said to me that day, you said out of love and a desire to protect me and make me happy." She gave my knee a reassuring squeeze. "That doesn't mean I'm not pissed that you hid it from me all this time, that you didn't trust me with the truth. You should have told me."

"Why didn't you say anything?"

"I wanted to give you a chance to tell me yourself."

I groaned and reached out with my free hand, cupping her cheek and stroking her skin with my thumb. "I was going to."

"When?"

"Um, after the girls got married?"

Laughing softly, Joy rolled her eyes. "Ramón."

"I didn't want to lose you. I thought if I waited that long, you'd know in your heart that we were meant to be, that our family was meant to be. That I didn't brainwash you into loving me."

"I already know that, silly. And you can't brainwash someone into loving you. Hannah said that's not how it works. Considering Leo is the one who came up with the whole crazy idea, she would know."

"You've talked to Hannah about this?"

"Of course, but she's the only one. I haven't mentioned it to the other wives." She cocked her head to the side. "Were they programmed, as well?"

I nodded. "They were."

She stroked her finger along my leg, my cock twitching at the touch. "The same way Hannah and I were?"

"I don't know. I wasn't part of their programming."

She sucked in her lips and began to fidget. "I have something I need to tell you, as well."

My already racing heart picked up speed. "What is it?"

"Your mom just thinks she programmed me, but she didn't. You did."

"I don't understand."

"After your mom informed me about her actions, I went to Hannah and Leo was there. He took me aside and told me that, all those years ago, he'd give Judith a version of the serum that had been watered down with saline solution to the point of being basically purified water. She may have messed with me a little bit, but nothing major or lasting."

"Holy shit...why didn't he tell me?"

She gave me a half smile. "You know Leo; he's loyal to a fault. He knew if you found out your mom had tried to program me without your permission, you would have flipped out. At the time, he was barely holding his shit together. He admitted he wasn't doing it as much to protect me, as to keep you from going crazy on Judith. Plus, he gave you the full-strength serum when you programmed me, so he figured there was no need to rock the boat. Only he hadn't counted on Judith telling me the truth, so she forced his hand."

"Jesus, I can't believe he did that."

"Well, I'm happy he did. And I'm glad you programmed me, Ramón. If you hadn't, I'd be dead. During the tape, you kept telling me to protect myself, that I was strong and brave, that I was smart, that I had nothing to be afraid of because I was an amazing woman. You told me not to feel any guilt about defending myself or my loved ones, told me over and over again that I could protect myself, that I had no reason to be scared." She closed her eyes and let out a long breath. "You gave me the tools I needed to fight off our enemies, Ramón. Not just Nova, but all the bastards since who've tried to hurt me and my family. You gave me the strength to protect everyone I love, and I'm endlessly grateful to you for that."

Shaking my head, I took a deep breath as a weight I didn't know I was carrying around lifted from my shoulders. "You're amazing. I love you so much."

"And I love you, even if your family is insane."

"They're your family now, too."

She gave me that bright, dimpled smile that never failed to make my heart beat a little faster. "Yes, they are, and I couldn't choose a better family. Crazy and all."

My phone beeped, letting me know it was time to leave for the church. "Shit, we're going to be late if we don't get moving. Ready to go?"

"Will you be nice to your mom? Please, for me?"

I sighed then stood, shifting Alexa onto my shoulder as I grabbed the diaper bag. "Yes."

Leaning up on her tiptoes, Joy kissed me then Alexa. "Thank you."

"Anything for you, my love. I mean it."

"I know." She winked. "Now let's go baptize this baby and hope you don't burst into flames as you walk through the church doors."

"Ha, ha." I smacked her round ass lightly. "Funny girl."

"You love me."

"More than anything."

Dear Reader,

Thank you for giving me the chance to entertain you. I really hope you enjoyed Joy and Ramón's story. Please consider leaving a review and let me know what you thought of it. 😉 Up next...Mark! He never thought he'd fall in love again, but fate has different plans. A broken and battered woman desperately needs him in her life, but can Mark let go of his past enough to give her hope for the future?

Ann

Love bad boys? Keep reading for a sneak peek at the dangerous and steamy world of the Iron Horse MC!

Sweetest Obsession

Chapter 1

Miguel 'Smoke' Santos

From my vantage point in the empty shithole house I'd bought on the outskirts of Houston, I watched the most beautiful woman in the world get into her reliable old car with a flash of her mile long legs that made my cock twitch. Fuck, everything about that fine piece of ass made my cock twitch, but the fantasy of her legs wrapped around my head while I made her scream my name was one of my favorites. As she started her car up, I idly wondered if the hair on her little pussy matched the blond on her head, or if she shaved her sweet cunt bald.

It was just after five o'clock, and the street was getting busy with all the blue-collar workers coming home from a hard day on the job. The woman whose life I was in charge of protecting pulled out of her driveway and I smiled at the sight of her moving in her seat to the music. I focused my binoculars on her full, naturally pink lips, but she was driving down the street before I could get a good look and figure out what song made her happy like that. As soon as her car was out of my sight, I picked up my phone and called Vance, my right-hand man and the vice president of the security company I own. He's also a brother—not a brother by blood, but a brother by choice. We go back, way back, to Marine basic training; even though he can be a real asshole, I trust him.

He answered right away. "I've got her."

"Any sign of trouble?"

Vance sighed, and I wanted to reach through the phone and punch him. "No. In the fifteen seconds she's been out of your sight there's been no sign of trouble."

"Fuck you."

Vance's laughter filled the large room I was in, and I stood up to stretch my back and groaned. The only pieces of furniture in the whole house were an air mattress, two lamps, the chair, and a small breakfast table with a computer. That's it. But it was all we needed. This wasn't a home; this was a stakeout house.

"Anything happens to her and it's your ass I'm coming for."

"Sensitive." Mirth still filled Vance's voice. "You gonna go sniff her panties before work? Bet her pussy smells like baby powder and tastes like sugar."

That pissed me off. "Don't you ever fucking talk about her like that. Got me, brother?"

"Easy, Smoke. I got you." He was silent for a moment and a horn beeped in the background. "You talk to Beach yet?"

"Yeah."

"And?"

"He wants me to bring Swan in."

"Are you going to?"

In yet another sign that I'd totally lost my mind over this bitch, I bit out, "I'm not going to disrupt her life just because of some fucked-up shit her mom did."

"This isn't just about her mom, Smoke. If it was just about that old bitch I'd say fuck it, but if we don't find Sarah soon, Beach is going to lose his fucking mind. And we all know bad shit happens when Beach loses it. Think about how many people would like to get back at Beach by fucking up or killing his old lady...or her identical twin sister. If anyone, anyone at all, touches Swan...there's gonna be hell to pay."

I rubbed the space between my eyes, then paced to the back door and opened it to a blast of hot Texas summer air. Even having lived in Austin for the past eight years, I was still momentarily stunned by the humidity that seemed to blanket Houston. I took a deep breath before I shut the door behind me and crossed the short distance between my house and Swan's little hovel. Okay, so maybe her home wasn't that bad, but I had a deep and abiding need to get her the fuck out of there, take her away from that working class ghetto, and give her the kind of life she deserved. I wanted to spoil her, to love her, and I wished with all my fucking rotten heart that this shitty situation she was currently, and unknowingly, in was different.

"Look"—I glanced out the window to make sure no unexpected guests had shown up at Swan's—"I gotta go. I'll be at the titty bar in a couple hours."

"Roger that," Vance said, and we hung up as I fit my key into the rear door of the house where the most innocent woman in the world lived.

As soon as I was inside, I shoved my phone into my pocket with one hand and disabled her security system with the other. While I approved of the ornate wrought iron bars covering all of her windows and doors, I didn't like her security system. It was cheap and easy to hack into, but I understood that it was all she could afford. As soon as the beeping stopped, I took a deep breath of the air saturated with her delicate scent and began my daily stalking routine. Even on my days off I came and visited her home to check for any contact from her relatives. It wasn't that I didn't trust the men and women who worked for me to check her home in a professional manner, but I didn't want anyone breathing Swan's scent but me.

A quick glance around showed the usual cheap-ass plywood furniture mixed with secondhand items she used to decorate her place. She made decent money as a server, but most of it went toward paying for school. I knew that little fact because I hacked into her computer and looked through her bills and bank account. It pissed me off that she lived like this because her dad was loaded, but for whatever reason, she didn't want anything to do with his money. Maybe she knew it wasn't legally earned. I had found ripped up checks for tens of thousands of dollars from him. Just thinking about Swan's dad pissed me off, and I shoved him from my mind.

Motherfucker was one of the biggest arms dealers in the country, and from what I'd learned from Sarah, he was a complete psycho who loved his daughters more than anything in the world, but was just as ruthless with them in his own way.

Then again, some might consider me a bit fucked in the head, because I spent every day trying to learn as much about Swan as I could by going through her home while she was at work or out running errands.

A year ago if you'd told me that I'd be going through the house of some bitch I'd never met, inch by inch, reconstructing her day because I was *that* fucking obsessed with her, I would've

Sweetest Obsession

told you that you were full of shit, and to go fuck yourself. I might've even punched you in the throat for it if I was in a real shitty mood. But now? Now, I treasured every small glimpse I got into the life of Sue Wanda Anderson, known to her friends and family as Swan. The name fit her. She had the body of a goddess and unique elegance, a delicacy around her that drove me crazy. It was the difference between a woman who was a lady and a woman who was one of the sweet butts at my clubhouse who used her pussy like currency. I didn't want to think about that shit right then and I paused, as usual, and stared at pictures on the walls of her with her family.

When I was awake all I seemed to do was think about her, and when I slept I dreamed of her—every damn night.

She was an intensely private woman, almost a recluse, but she had a few friends who came over to hang out. In the last year that I'd been watching Swan, all of the friends she had over were female, thank fuck. I would've had to kill any asshole who touched her. Sarah, Swan's sister, had clued me in to a few things about Swan that explained her lack of a dating life, and as always, I wondered how the stunning blonde would react to my touch. Would she shrink from me like I was covered with filth as I stroked the perfectly tanned skin on her freckled shoulders? Or would she purr?

Once again, I got an uncomfortable hard-on and adjusted myself with a grimace.

I looked through her trash to figure out what she had for dinner. Unhealthy crap, as usual. Even though she ate like a frat boy, she had the hottest damn body I'd ever seen. Long legs, high ass, and big, real breasts topped off by natural pale blond hair and big, sky-blue eyes. Just a hint of baby fat remained in her cheeks and gave her an innocent look that killed me and every other heterosexual male who saw her. She was a total knockout, but it wasn't her looks that had me sniffing after her like a stag in heat. No, it was Swan herself. Not only was she beautiful, she was brilliant, kind, and heartbreakingly naïve.

Made me all the more fucking pissed at her complete waste of a mother for exposing Swan to the danger she was in now, even if Swan didn't know it.

I took a quick glance at the book she was currently reading and frowned in displeasure. It was some chick romance with a ripped guy on the cover smiling at the camera. I had a better body. I was irritated that it wasn't one of the BDSM romances she seemed to love. Whenever she was reading those books I always took a few minutes to see where she'd left off in the story and what kind of fantasies she was learning about. The first time I saw one of those erotic romance books on her coffee table, I knew this beautiful creature had been made for me. I just wished like fuck circumstances were different so I could make her fall in love with me. Fucking hell, I was already more than half in love with her.

Shit, I sounded like a bitch about to have her period.

I went to the small foyer where she kept her mail and sorted through it. Nothing but bills, crap, and more bills. I wanted to take care of all her finances for her and had more than enough money to support her in comfort for the rest of her life. She sure as fuck wouldn't have to work at any more titty bars.

The thought of the titty bar reminded me the clock was ticking, and I went down the hallway to her bedroom.

The cool, dark room was drenched with her tempting scent. I paused in the doorway, then closed my eyes and imagined her here, waiting for me with her legs spread wide and her hands gripping the rails of her brass headboard, anticipating me tying her up then fucking her until she passed out with a dreamy smile on her face.

My fantasy was so vivid that, for a moment, when I opened my eyes I saw her there, but a heartbeat later, I was just looking at rumpled bed sheets again. I picked up the phone next to her bed and checked her voice mail, hoping that either Sarah or their mom, Billie, had tried to contact Swan, but there was nothing other than a missed call from one of her friends. After I set the phone down, I completed my daily routine by picking up her pillow and taking deep inhalations of her scent. I didn't know what it was about her, but her fucking smell went straight to my brain like high-grade coke. Her scent amped me up and made my dick go into overdrive; I couldn't contain the growl of need that escaped me.

I was so fucking addicted to her natural aroma that I couldn't stand the stink of other bitches now. They smelled spoiled to me, like rotten meat left out in the sun for too long. Yeah, I still had a few of the club sweet butts that I let suck my cock, but I hadn't fucked a woman since a month ago when I started spending most of my days sitting in that shitty-ass house nearby and watching over Swan. This whole celibacy thing was new to me, but that little girl had me so wrapped around her finger, all I wanted was her sweet pussy wrapped around my dick.

The sight of the oversized T-shirt on the floor she wore to bed made me really want to pick it up, but I didn't touch any of her clothing. I had already invaded her privacy like a motherfucker, but even I had standards. So I never touched her drawers or did anything more than take a quick look through her closet.

I glanced over at her computer and wondered if I had enough time to check what kind of porn she watched last night. Despite having no man of any kind in her life, Swan watched an amazing number of dirty movies. First time I went through her browser history, I had to go into her bathroom and jack off like a hormonal thirteen-year-old. Fucking embarrassing, but knowing her sexual tastes only fueled my daydreams about her. She watched all kinds of kinky shit, and while I would never share her with another man, I was determined to be the only man who actually did most of that kinky shit with her. Thoughts of all the ways I would sexually corrupt her made my dick hard as fuck, and my breath caught as I thought about Swan's graceful throat wearing my collar and her killer body wearing my patch.

My phone rang and snapped me out of my trance. I answered it and tried to ignore the guilty heat that burned my face as I stared at a pair of her pink lace panties hanging half out of her hamper and how badly I wanted to wrap them around my cock while I jerked off.

"What's up?"

"Smoke?" The deep, slightly raspy voice on the other end of the call was Beach, President of the Iron Horse MC and one of my best friends. "Anything?"

Part of me wanted to snap that if I'd fucking found anything I would have fucking contacted him, but even as the Master at Arms of the Iron Horse MC I knew better than to lip off to the

Prez, especially now. "Nope, nothing new."

A long stream of swearing came from Beach before he finally said, "Keep an eye on her tonight. One of our informants said there's a rumor going around the bounty on her mom from those fucking Russians in Las Vegas has been upped. Who knows what dumb fucks might come after Swan now in an effort to find her mom. And don't forget how much the Russians would love to pimp out a beautiful girl like Swan to pay off her mama's debt."

Now it was my turn to curse. "Is that why you want me to bring her in?"

"Yeah. I was hoping Sarah would go to Swan for help, but it's been two weeks and things are only getting more dangerous for Swan. Swan needs to go off the grid, and soon."

As I stared at Swan's bed, I fought a battle with myself. The small, good guy part of me that my mom and dad had tried so hard to nurture insisted that I should just fucking walk away, that I should give Swan's protection over to Vance, but I couldn't. The selfish, tainted part of my soul urged me to tell Beach that I was bringing Swan home with me, for her own protection, of course, right the fuck now. Yeah, having her in my home, in my bed, was totally for her safety.

Even I didn't believe that bullshit.

"So what do you want me to do?"
"Let's give it a couple more days before we bring her in." He sighed. "I know Swan and

Sarah don't always get along, but my old lady loves her. If anythin' happened to Swan while

Sarah's…gone…and I could have prevented it, she'd never forgive me."

I strode over to the window and took a quick glimpse of the slowly darkening sky before letting the frilly lace curtain fall back into place. "I'm gonna head out to her club."

"You talked to her yet?"

"No, not yet. She's skittish. I don't want to freak her out and scare her off."

I didn't add that I was unusually nervous around her as well. For the past two nights I sat in her section of the titty bar where she worked, sporting my cut and waiting for her to say something to me. I know Sarah said her sister had no idea about the MC life, that Swan was about as sheltered as you could get, but I kept hoping she'd ask me about it, but she barely spoke to me. I'd seen her gaze roving over the patches of my vest, but there was no recognition. Not like the sluts who worked at her club. Those bitches saw who I am, and they were all over me like flies on shit. Even though Iron Horse is based in Austin, we've got a branch in Houston as well and we're tight with most of the local motorcycle clubs that run different portions of Houston.

"Well, keep an eye on her, man. She's one of the only links we have to that fucking bitch-asscrack-whore-skank mother of hers."

"Got it."

Beach hung up on me—he wasn't big on goodbyes—and I strode through Swan's house, reset her security system, then let myself out the back door. While I was inside, night had started to fall, cooling things down a little bit. There was still enough light to see by as I opened the garage at the stakeout place I'd bought, wheeled my bike out, and shut it again. The air was still thick with humidity and I found myself wishing I could go swimming in the spring-fed river behind my house.

Beach's info about the bounty on Swan made my gut clench and I had to resist the urge to call Vance again. My boys were the best of the best at security, all either former military or, ironically enough, law enforcement, and all of 'em were members of Iron Horse MC. We didn't exactly operate on the right side of the law—our protection had been used for some less than honorable purposes—but it had made us all rich, so I couldn't fucking complain.

As I rode down the street, my mind was once again focused totally on Swan, and the anticipation heating my blood had me roaring onto the freeway, eager to get close enough to her to see the flecks of silver in her bluer-than-blue eyes.

Yeah, I was fucking whipped, and even more pathetic, I was whipped by a girl who didn't even know I existed.

I made my way through traffic and ignored the stares of the civilians as I let my mind fill with dreams of a woman who could really use a fucking hero to save her right now, but instead, she got stuck with me. I'm more of the villain in the story, the one you fear is hovering behind you in a dark alley, certainly not the guy who should be the one rescuing the beautiful princess. But she didn't need a prince. Right now, she needed a warrior. And while I might not ever write her poetry, I would kill for her.

Of that, there was no doubt.

About the Author

With over forty published books, Ann is Queen of the Castle to her wonderful husband and three sons in the mountains of West Virginia. In her past lives she's been an Import Broker, a Communications Specialist, a US Navy Civilian Contractor, a Bartender/Waitress, and an actor at the Michigan Renaissance Festival. She also spent a summer touring with the Grateful Dead-though she will deny to her children that it ever happened.

From a young age Ann has been fascinated by myths and fairytales, and the romance that was often the center of the story. As Ann grew older and her hormones kicked in, she discovered trashy romance novels. Great at first, but she soon grew tired of the endless stories with a big wonderful emotional buildup to really short and crappy sex. Never a big fan of purple prose, throbbing spears of fleshy pleasure and wet honey pots make her giggle, she sought out books that gave the sex scenes in the story just as much detail and plot as everything else-without using cringe worthy euphemisms. This led her to the wonderful world of Erotic Romance, and she's never looked back.

Now Ann spends her days trying to tune out cartoons playing in the background to get into her 'sexy space' and has accepted that her Muse has a severe case of ADD.

Ann loves to talk with her fans, as long as they realize she's weird and that sarcasm doesn't translate well via text.

Website
http://www.annmayburn.com/

Facebook
https://www.facebook.com/ann.mayburn.5

Pintrest
http://pinterest.com/annmayburn/

Twitter
https://twitter.com/AnnMayburn

Made in the USA
San Bernardino, CA
13 June 2017